Mistress of Mellyn
AND
Kirkland Revels

VICTORIA HOLT

Mistress of Mellyn

AND

Kirkland Revels

DOUBLEDAY & COMPANY, Inc.
Garden City, New York

Mistress of Mellyn

1

"There are two courses open to a gentlewoman when she finds herself in penurious circumstances," my Aunt Adelaide had said. "One is to marry, and the other to find a post in keeping with her gentility."

As the train carried me through wooded hills and past green meadows, I was taking this second course; partly, I suppose, because I had never had an opportunity of trying the former.

I pictured myself as I must appear to my fellow travelers if they bothered to glance my way, which was not very likely: a young woman of medium height, already past her first youth, being twenty-four years old, in a brown merino dress with cream lace collar and little tufts of lace at the cuffs. (Cream being so much more serviceable than white, as Aunt Adelaide told me.) My black cape was unbuttoned at the throat because it was hot in the carriage, and my brown velvet bonnet, tied with brown velvet ribbons under my chin, was of the sort which was so becoming to feminine people like my sister Phillida but, I always felt, sat a little incongruously on heads like mine. My hair was thick with a coppery tinge, parted in the center, brought down at the sides of my too-long face, and made into a cumbersome knot to project behind the bonnet. My eyes were large, in some lights the color of amber, and were my best feature; but they were too bold—so said Aunt Adelaide; which meant that they had learned none of the feminine graces which were so becoming to a woman. My nose was too short, my mouth too wide. In fact, I thought, nothing seemed to fit; and I must resign myself to journeys such as this when I travel to and from the various posts which I shall occupy for the rest of my life, since it is necessary for me to earn a living, and I shall never achieve the first of those alternatives: a husband.

We had passed through the green meadows of Somerset and were now deep in the moorland and wooded hills of Devon. I had been told to take good note of that masterpiece of bridgebuilding, Mr. Brunel's bridge, which spanned the Tamar at Saltash and, after crossing which, I should have left England behind me and have passed into the Duchy of Cornwall.

I was becoming rather ridiculously excited about crossing the bridge. I was not a fanciful woman at this time—perhaps I changed later, but then a stay in a house like Mount Mellyn was enough to make the most practical of people fanciful—so I could not understand why I should feel this extraordinary excitement.

It was absurd, I told myself. Mount Mellyn may be a magnificent mansion; Connan TreMellyn may be as romantic as his name sounds; but that will be no concern of yours. You will be confined to below stairs, or perhaps to the attics above stairs, concerned only with the care of little Alvean.

What strange names these people had! I thought, staring out of the window. There was sun on the moorland but the gray tors in the distance looked oddly menacing. They were like petrified people.

This family to which I was going was Cornish, and the Cornish had a language of their own. Perhaps my own name, Martha Leigh, would sound odd to them. Martha! It always gave me a shock when I heard it. Aunt Adelaide always used it, but at home when my father had been alive he and Phillida never thought of calling me Martha. I was always Marty. I could not help feeling that Marty was a more lovable person than Martha could ever be, and I was sad and a little frightened because I felt that the river Tamar would cut me off completely from Marty for a long time. In my new post I should be Miss Leigh, I supposed; perhaps miss, or more undignified still—Leigh.

One of Aunt Adelaide's numerous friends had heard of "Connan TreMellyn's predicament." He needed the right person to help him out of his difficulties. She must be patient enough to care for his daughter, sufficiently educated to teach her, and genteel enough for the child not to suffer through the proximity of someone who was not quite of her own class. Obviously what Connan TreMellyn needed was an impoverished gentlewoman. Aunt Adelaide decided that I fitted the bill.

When our father, who had been vicar of a country parsonage, had died, Aunt Adelaide had swooped on us and taken us to London.

There should be a season, she told us, for twenty-year-old Martha and eighteen-year-old Phillida. Phillida had married at the end of that season; but after four years of living with Aunt Adelaide, I had not. So there came a day when she pointed out the two courses to me.

I glanced out of the window. We were drawing into Plymouth. My fellow passengers had alighted and I sat back in my seat watching the activities on the platform.

As the guard was blowing his whistle and we were about to move on, the door of the carriage opened and a man came in. He looked at me with an apologetic smile as though he were hinting that he hoped I did not mind sharing the compartment with him, but I averted my eyes.

When we had left Plymouth and were approaching the bridge, he said: "You like our bridge, eh?"

I turned and looked at him.

I saw a man, a little under thirty, well dressed, but in the manner of the country gentleman. His tail coat was dark blue, his trousers gray; and his hat was what in London we called a "pot hat" because of its resemblance to that vessel. This hat he had laid on the seat beside him. I thought him somewhat dissipated, with brown eyes that twinkled ironically as though he were fully aware of the warnings I must have received about the inadvisability of entering into conversation with strange men.

I answered: "Yes, indeed. I think it is a very fine piece of workmanship."

He smiled. We had crossed the bridge and entered Cornwall.

◈

His brown eyes surveyed me and I was immediately conscious of my somewhat drab appearance. I thought: He is only interested in me because there is no one else to claim his attention. I remembered then that Phillida had once said I put people off by presuming, when they showed interest, that it was because no one else was available. "See yourself as a makeshift," was Phillida's maxim, "and you'll be one."

"Traveling far?" he asked.

"I believe I have now only a short distance to go. I leave the train at Liskeard."

"Ah, Liskeard." He stretched his legs and turned his gaze from me to the tips of his boots. "You have come from London?" he went on.

"Yes," I answered.

"You'll miss the gaiety of the big city."

"I once lived in the country, so I know what to expect."

"Are you staying in Liskeard?"

I was not sure that I liked this catechism, but I remembered Phillida again: "You're far too gruff, Marty, with the opposite sex. You scare them off."

I decided I could at least be civil, so I answered: "No, not in Liskeard. I'm going to a little village on the coast called Mellyn."

"I see." He was silent for a few moments and once more turned his attention to the tips of his boots.

His next words startled me. "I suppose a sensible young lady like you would not believe in second sight . . . and that sort of thing?"

"Why . . ." I stammered. "What an extraordinary question!"

"May I look at your palm?"

I hesitated and regarded him suspiciously. Could I offer my hand to a stranger in this way? Aunt Adelaide would suspect that some nefarious advances were about to be made. I thought in this case she might be right. After all, I was a woman, and the only available one.

He smiled. "I assure you that my only desire is to look into the future."

"But I don't believe in such things."

"Let me look anyway." He leaned forward and with a swift movement secured my hand.

He held it lightly, scarcely touching it, contemplating it with his head on one side.

"I see," he said, "that you have come to a turning point in your life. You are moving into a strange new world which is entirely different from anything you have known before. You will have to exercise caution . . . the utmost caution."

I smiled cynically. "You see me taking a journey. What would you say if I told you I was visiting relatives and could not possibly be moving into your strange new world?"

"I should say you were not a very truthful young lady." His smile was puckish. I could not help feeling a little liking for him. I thought he was a somewhat irresponsible person, but he was very light-hearted and, being in his company, to some extent made me share that lightheartedness. "No," he went on, "you are traveling to a new life, a new post. There's no mistake about that. Before, you lived a secluded life in the country; then you went to the town."

"I believe I implied that."

"You did not need to imply it. But it is not the past which concerns us on occasions like this, is it? It is the future."

"Well, what of the future?"

"You are going to a strange house, a house full of shadows. You will have to walk warily in that house, Miss . . . er . . ."

He waited, but I did not supply what he was asking for, and he went on: "You have to earn your living. I see a child there and a man . . . Perhaps it is the child's father. They are wrapped in shadows. There is someone else there . . . but perhaps she is already dead."

It was the deep sepulchral note in his voice rather than the words he said which momentarily unnerved me.

I snatched my hand away. "What nonsense!" I said.

He ignored me and half closed his eyes. Then he went on: "You will need to watch little Alice, and your duties will extend beyond the care of her. You must most certainly beware of Alice."

I felt a faint tingling which began at the base of my spine and seemed to creep up to my neck. This, I supposed, was what is known as making one's flesh creep.

Little Alice! But her name was not Alice. It was Alvean. It had unnerved me for the moment because it had sounded similar.

Then I felt irritated and a little angry. Did I look the part then? Was it possible that I already carried the mark of the penurious gentlewoman forced to take the only course open to her? A governess!

Was he laughing at me? He lay back against the upholstery of the carriage, his eyes still closed. I looked out of the window as though he and his ridiculous fortunetelling were not of the slightest interest to me.

He opened his eyes then and took out his watch. He studied it gravely, for all the world as though this extraordinary conversation had not taken place between us.

"In four minutes' time," he said briskly, "we shall pull into Liskeard. Allow me to assist you with your bags."

He took them down from the rack. "Miss Martha Leigh," was clearly written on the labels, "Mount Mellyn, Mellyn, Cornwall."

He did not appear to glance at these labels and I felt that he had lost interest in me.

When we came into the station, he alighted and set my bags on the platform. Then he took off the hat which he had set upon his head when he picked up the bags, and with a deep bow he left me.

While I was murmuring my thanks I saw an elderly man coming

toward me, calling: "Miss Leigh! Miss Leigh! Be you Miss Leigh
then?" And for the moment I forgot about my traveling companion.

I was facing a merry little man with a brown, wrinkled skin and
eyes of reddish brown; he wore a corduroy jacket and a sugar-loaf
hat which he had pushed to the back of his head and seemed to
have forgotten. Ginger hair sprouted from under this, and his brows
and mustaches were of the same gingery color.

"Well, miss," he said, "so I picked you out then. Be these your
bags? Give them to me. You and me and old Cherry Pie 'ull soon
be home."

He took my bags and I walked behind him, but he soon fell into
step beside me.

"Is the house far from here?" I asked.

"Old Cherry Pie'll carry us there all in good time," he answered,
as he loaded my bags into the trap and I climbed in beside him.

He seemed to be a garrulous man and I could not resist the
temptation of trying to discover, before I arrived, something about
the people among whom I was going to live.

I said: "This house, Mount Mellyn, sounds as though it's on a
hill."

"Well, 'tis built on a cliff top, facing the sea, and the gardens run
down to the sea. Mount Mellyn and Mount Widden are like twins.
Two houses, standing defiant-like, daring the sea to come and take
'em. But they'm built on firm rock."

"So there are two houses," I said. "We have near neighbors."

"In a manner of speaking. Nansellocks, they who are at Mount
Widden, have been there these last two hundred years. They be
separated from us by more than a mile, and there's Mellyn Cove in
between. The families have always been good neighbors until——"

He stopped and I prompted: "Until . . . ?"

"You'll hear fast enough," he answered.

I thought it was beneath my dignity to probe into such matters,
so I changed the subject. "Do they keep many servants?" I asked.

"There be me and Mrs. Tapperty and my girls, Daisy and Kitty.
We live in the rooms over the stables. In the house there's Mrs. Polgrey and Tom Polgrey and young Gilly. Not that you'd call her a servant. But they have her there and she passes for such."

"Gilly!" I said. "That's an unusual name."

"Gillyflower. Reckon Jennifer Polgrey was a bit daft to give her
a name like that. No wonder the child's what she is."

"Jennifer? Is that Mrs. Polgrey?"

"Nay! Jennifer was Mrs. Polgrey's girl. Great dark eyes and the littlest waist you ever saw. Kept herself to herself until one day she goes lying in the hay—or maybe the gillyflowers—with someone. Then, before we know where we are, little Gilly's arrived; as for Jennifer—her just walked into the sea one morning. We reckoned there wasn't much doubt who Gilly's father was."

I said nothing and, disappointed by my lack of interest, he went on: "She wasn't the first. We knowed her wouldn't be the last. Geoffry Nansellock left a trail of bastards wherever he went." He laughed and looked sideways at me. "No need for you to look so prim, miss. He can't hurt you. Ghosts can't hurt a young lady, and that's all Master Geoffry Nansellock is now . . . nothing more than a ghost."

"So he's dead too. He didn't . . . walk into the sea after Jennifer?"

That made Tapperty chuckle. "Not him. He was killed in a train accident. You must have heard of that accident. It was just as the train was running out of Plymouth. It ran off the lines and over a bank. The slaughter was terrible. Mr. Geoff, he were on that train, and up to no good on it either. But that was the end of him."

"Well, I shall not meet him, but I shall meet Gillyflower, I suppose. And is that all the servants?"

"There be odd boys and girls—some for the gardens, some for the stables, some in the house. But it ain't what it was. Things have changed since the mistress died."

"Mr. TreMellyn is a very sad man, I suppose."

Tapperty lifted his shoulders.

"How long is it since she died?" I asked.

"It would be little more than a year, I reckon."

"And he has only just decided that he needs a governess for little Miss Alvean?"

"There have been three governesses so far. You be the fourth. They don't stay, none of them. Miss Bray and Miss Garrett, they said the place was too quiet for them. There was Miss Jansen—a real pretty creature. But she was sent away. She took what didn't belong to her. 'Twas a pity. We all liked her. She seemed to look on it as a privilege to live in Mount Mellyn. Old houses were her hobby, she used to tell us. Well, it seemed she had other hobbies besides, so out she went."

I turned my attention to the countryside. It was late August and, as we passed through lanes with banks on either side, I caught occasional glimpses of fields of corn among which poppies and pimpernels grew; now and then we passed a cottage of gray Cornish stone which looked grim, I thought, and lonely.

I had my first glimpse of the sea through a fold in the hills, and I felt my spirits lifted. It seemed that the nature of the landscape changed. Flowers seemed to grow more plentifully on the banks; I could smell the scent of pine trees; and fuchsias grew by the roadside, their blossoms bigger than any we had ever been able to cultivate in our vicarage garden.

We turned off the road from a steep hill and went down and down nearer the sea. I saw that we were on a cliff road. Before us stretched a scene of breath-taking beauty. The cliff rose steep and straight from the sea on that indented coast; grasses and flowers grew there, and I saw sea pinks and red and white valerian mingling with the heather—rich, deep, purple heather.

At length we came to the house. It was like a castle, I thought, standing there on the cliff plateau—built of granite like many houses I had seen in these parts, but grand and noble—a house which had stood for several hundred years, and would stand for several hundred more.

"All this land belongs to the master," said Tapperty with pride. "And if you look across the cove, you'll see Mount Widden."

I did look, and saw the house. Like Mount Mellyn it was built of gray stone. It was smaller in every way and of a later period. I did not give it much attention because now we were approaching Mount Mellyn, and that was obviously the house which was more interesting to me.

We had climbed to the plateau and a pair of intricately wrought-iron gates confronted us.

"Open up there!" shouted Tapperty.

There was a small lodge beside the gates and at the door sat a woman knitting.

"Now, Gilly girl," she said, "you go and open the gates and save me poor old legs."

Then I saw the child who had been sitting at the old woman's feet. She rose obediently and came to the gate. She was an extraordinary-looking girl with long straight hair almost white in color and wide blue eyes.

"Thanks, Gilly girl," said Tapperty as Cherry Pie went happily through the gates. "This be miss, who's come to live here and take care of Miss Alvean."

I looked into a pair of blank blue eyes which stared at me with an expression impossible to fathom. The old woman came up to the gate and Tapperty said: "This be Mrs. Soady."

"Good day to you," said Mrs. Soady. "I hope you'll be happy here along of us."

"Thank you," I answered, forcing my gaze away from the child to the woman. "I hope so."

"Well, I do hope so," added Mrs. Soady. Then she shook her head as though she feared her hopes were somewhat futile.

I turned to look at the child but she had disappeared. I wondered where she had gone, and the only place I could imagine was behind the bushes of hydrangeas which were bigger than any hydrangeas I had ever seen, and of deep blue, almost the color of the sea on this day.

"The child didn't speak," I observed as we went on up the drive.

"No. Her don't talk much. Sing, her do. Wander about on her own. But talk . . . not much."

The drive was about half a mile in length and on either side of it the hydrangeas bloomed. Fuchsias mingled with them, and I caught glimpses of the sea between the pine trees. Then I saw the house. Before it was a wide lawn where two peacocks strutted before a pea-hen, their almost incredibly lovely tails fanned out behind them. Another sat perched on a stone wall; and there were two palm trees, tall and straight, one on either side of the porch.

The house was larger than I had thought when I had seen it from the cliff path. It was of three stories, but long and built in an L-shape. The sun caught the glass of the mullioned windows and I immediately had the impression that I was being watched.

Tapperty took the gravel approach to the front porch and when we reached it, the door opened and I saw a woman standing there. She wore a white cap on her gray hair; she was tall, with a hooked nose and, as she had an obviously dominating manner, I did not need to be told that she was Mrs. Polgrey.

"I trust you've had a good journey, Miss Leigh," she said.

"Very good, thank you," I told her.

"And worn out and needing a rest, I'll be bound. Come along in. You shall have a nice cup of tea in my room. Leave your bags. I'll have them taken up."

I felt relieved. This woman dispelled the eerie feeling which had begun, I realized, when I encountered the man in the train. Joe Tapperty had done little to disperse it, with his tales of death and suicide. But Mrs. Polgrey was a woman who would stand no nonsense, I was sure of that. She seemed to emit common sense, and perhaps because I was fatigued by the long journey I was pleased about this.

I thanked her and said I would greatly enjoy the tea, and she led the way into the house.

We were in an enormous hall which in the past must have been used as a banqueting room. The floor was of flagstone, and the timbered roof was so lofty that I felt it must extend to the top of the house. The beams were beautifully carved and the effect decorative. At one end of the hall was a dais and back of it a great open fireplace. On the dais stood a refectory table on which were vessels and plates of pewter.

"It's magnificent," I said involuntarily; and Mrs. Polgrey was pleased.

"I superintend all the polishing of the furniture myself," she told me. "You have to watch girls nowadays. Those Tapperty wenches are a pair of flibbertigibbets, I can tell 'ee. You'd need eyes that could see from here to Land's End to see all they'm up to. Beeswax and turpentine, that's the mixture, and nothing like it. All made by myself."

"It certainly does you credit," I complimented her.

I followed her to the door at the end of the hall. She opened it and a short flight of some half-dozen steps confronted us. To the left was a door which she indicated and after a moment's hesitation, opened.

"The chapel," she said, and I caught a glimpse of blue slate flagstones, an altar, and a few pews. There was a smell of dampness about the place.

She shut the door quickly.

"We don't use it nowadays," she said. "We go to the Mellyn church. It's down in the village, the other side of the cove . . . just beyond Mount Widden."

We went up the stairs and into a room which I saw was a dining room. It was vast and the walls were hung with tapestry. The table was highly polished, and in several cabinets I saw beautiful glass and china. The floor was covered with blue carpet and through the enormous windows I saw a walled courtyard.

"This is not *your* part of the house," Mrs. Polgrey told me, "but I thought I would take you round the front of the house to my room. It's as well you know the lay of the land, as they say."

I thanked her, understanding that this was a tactful way of telling me that as a governess I would not be expected to mingle with the family.

We passed through the dining room to yet another flight of stairs and mounting these we came to what seemed like a more intimate sitting room. The walls were covered with exquisite tapestry and the chair backs and seats were beautifully wrought in the same manner. I could see that the furniture was mostly antique and that it all gleamed with beeswax and turpentine and Mrs. Polgrey's loving care.

"This is the punch room," she said. "It has always been called so because it is here that the family retires to take punch. We still follow the old customs in this house."

At the end of this room was another flight of stairs; there was no door leading to them, merely a heavy brocade curtain which Mrs. Polgrey drew aside, and when we had mounted these stairs we were in a gallery, the walls of which were lined with portraits. I gave each of them a quick glance, wondering if Connan TreMellyn were among them; but I could see no one depicted in modern dress, so I presumed his portrait had not yet taken its place among those of his ancestors.

There were several doors leading from the gallery, but we went quickly along it to one at the far end. As we passed through it I saw that we were in a different wing of the house, the servants' quarters I imagined, because the spaciousness was missing.

"This," said Mrs. Polgrey, "will be *your* part of the house. You will find a staircase at the end of this corridor which leads to the nurseries. Your room is up there. But first come to my sitting room and we'll have that tea. I told Daisy to see to it as soon as I heard Joe Tapperty was here. So there shouldn't be long to wait."

"I fear it will take some time to learn my way about the house," I said.

"You'll know it in next to no time. But when you go out you won't go the way I brought you up. You'll use one of the other doors; when you've unpacked and rested awhile, I'll show you."

"You're very kind."

"Well, I do want to make you happy here with us. Miss Alvean needs discipline, I always say. And what can I do about giving it to her, with all I have to do! A nice mess this place would be in if I let Miss Alvean take up *my* time. No, what she wants is a sensible governess, and 'twould seem they'm not all that easy to come by. Why, miss, if you show us that you can look after the child, you'll be more than welcome here."

"I gather I have had several predecessors." She looked a trifle blank and I went on quickly: "There have been other governesses."

"Oh yes. Not much good, any of them. Miss Jansen was the best, but it seemed she had habits. You could have knocked me down with a feather. She quite took *me* in!" Mrs. Polgrey looked as though she thought that anyone who could do that must be smart. "Well, I suppose appearances are deceptive, as they say. Miss Celestine was real upset when it came out."

"Miss Celestine?"

"The young lady at Widden. Miss Celestine Nansellock. She's often here. A quiet young lady and she loves the place. If I as much as move a piece of furniture she knows it. That's why she and Miss Jansen seemed to get on. Both interested in old houses, you see. It was such a pity and such a shock. You'll meet her sometime. As I say, scarcely a day passes when she's not here. There's some of us that think . . . Oh, my dear life! 'twould seem as though I'm letting my tongue run away with me, and you longing for that cup of tea."

She threw open the door of the room and it was like stepping into another world. Gone was the atmosphere of brooding antiquity. This was a room which could not have fitted into any other time than the present, and I realized that it confirmed my impression of Mrs. Polgrey. There were antimacassars on the chairs; there was a whatnot in the corner of the room filled with china ornaments including a glass slipper, a gold pig, and a cup with "A present from Weston" inscribed on it. It seemed almost impossible to move in a room so crammed with furniture. Even on the mantelpiece Dresden shepherdesses seemed to jostle with marble angels for a place. There was an ormolu clock which ticked sedately; there were chairs and little tables everywhere, it seemed. It showed Mrs. Polgrey to me as a woman of strong conventions, a woman who would have a great respect for the right thing—which would, of course, be the thing she believed in.

Still, I felt something comfortingly normal about this room as I did about the woman.

She looked at the main table and tutted in exasperation; then she went to the bell rope and pulled it. It was only a few minutes later that a black-haired girl with saucy eyes appeared carrying a tray on which was a silver teapot, a spirit lamp, cups and saucers, milk and sugar.

"And about time too," said Mrs. Polgrey. "Put it here, Daisy."

Daisy gave me a look which almost amounted to a wink. I did not wish to offend Mrs. Polgrey, so I pretended not to notice.

Then Mrs. Polgrey said: "This is Daisy, miss. You can tell her if you find anything is not to your liking."

"Thank you, Mrs. Polgrey, and thank you, Daisy."

They both looked somewhat startled and Daisy dropped a little curtsy, of which she seemed half-ashamed, and went out.

"Nowadays . . ." murmured Mrs. Polgrey, and lighted the spirit lamp.

I watched her unlock the cabinet and take out the tea canister which she set on the tray.

"Dinner," she went on, "is served at eight. Yours will be brought to your room. But I thought you would be needing a little reviver. So when you've had this and seen your room, I'll introduce you to Miss Alvean."

"What would she be doing at this time of day?"

Mrs. Polgrey frowned. "She'll be off somewhere by herself. She goes off by herself. Master don't like it. That's why 'e be anxious for her to have a governess, you see."

I began to see. I was sure now that Alvean was going to be a difficult child.

Mrs. Polgrey measured the tea into the pot as though it were gold dust, and poured the hot water on it.

"So much depends on whether she takes a fancy to you or not," went on Mrs. Polgrey. "She's unaccountable. There's some she'll take to and some she won't. Her was very fond of Miss Jansen." Mrs. Polgrey shook her head sadly. "A pity she had habits."

She stirred the tea in the pot, put on the tea cosy, and asked me: "Milk? Sugar?"

"Yes, please," I said.

"I always do say," she remarked, as though she thought I needed some consolation, "there ain't nothing like a good cup of tea."

❦

We ate tea biscuits with the tea, and these Mrs. Polgrey took from a tin which she kept in her cabinet. I gathered, as we sat together, that Connan TreMellyn, the master, was away.

"He has an estate farther west," Mrs. Polgrey told me. "Penzance way." Her dialect was more noticeable when she was relaxed as she was now. "He do go to it now and then to see to it like. Left him by his wife, it were. Now *she* was one of the Pendletons. They'm from Penzance way."

"When does he return?" I asked.

She looked faintly shocked, and I knew that I had offended because she said in a somewhat haughty way: "He will come back in his own time."

I saw that if I was going to keep in her good books, I must be strictly conventional; and presumably it was not good form for a governess to ask questions about the master of the house. It was all very well for Mrs. Polgrey to speak of him; she was a privileged person. I could see that I must hastily adjust myself to my new position.

Very soon after that she took me up to my room. It was large with big windows, and from the window seats there was a good view of the front lawn, the palm trees, and the approach. My bed was a four-poster and seemed in keeping with the rest of the furniture; but though it was a big bed it looked dwarfed in a room of this size. There were rugs on the floor, the boards of which were so highly polished that the rugs looked somewhat dangerous. I could see that I might have little cause to bless Mrs. Polgrey's love of polishing everything within sight. There was a tallboy and a chest of drawers; and I noticed that there was a door in addition to the one by which I had entered.

Mrs. Polgrey followed my gaze. "The schoolroom," she said. "And beyond that is Miss Alvean's room."

"I see. So the schoolroom separates us."

Mrs. Polgrey nodded.

Looking round the room I saw a screen in one corner and as I approached it I noticed that it shielded a hip bath.

"If you want hot water at any time," she said, "ring the bell and Daisy or Kitty will bring it to you."

"Thank you." I looked at the open fireplace and pictured a roaring fire there on winter days. "I can see I'm going to be very comfortable here."

"It's a pleasant room. You'll be the first governess to have it. The other governesses used to sleep in a room on the other side of Miss Alvean's room. It was Miss Celestine who thought this would be better. It's a more pleasant room, I must say."

"Then I owe thanks to Miss Celestine."

"A very pleasant lady. She thinks the world of Miss Alvean." Mrs. Polgrey shook her head significantly and I wondered whether she was thinking that it was only a year since the master's wife had died, and that perhaps one day he would marry again. Who more suitable to be his wife than this neighbor who was so fond of Miss Alvean? Perhaps they were only waiting for a reasonable lapse of time.

"Would you like to wash your hands and unpack? Dinner will be in two hours' time. But perhaps first you would like to take a look at the schoolroom."

"Thank you, Mrs. Polgrey," I said, "but I think I'll wash and unpack first."

"Very well. And perhaps you'd like a little rest. Traveling is so fatiguing, I do know. I'll send Daisy up with hot water. Meals could be taken in the schoolroom. Perhaps you'd prefer that?"

"With Miss Alvean?"

"She takes her meals nowadays with her father, except her milk and biscuits last thing. All the children have taken meals with the family from the time they were eight years old. Miss Alvean's birthday was in May."

"There are other children?"

"Oh, my dear life, no! I was talking of the children of the past. It's one of the family rules, you see."

"I see."

"Well, I'll be leaving you. If you cared for a stroll in the grounds before dinner, you could take it. Ring for Daisy or Kitty and whoever is free will show you the stairs you will use in future. It will take you down to the kitchen garden, but you can easily get from there to wherever you want to go. Don't 'ee forget though—dinner at eight."

"In the schoolroom."

"Or in your own room if you prefer it."

"But," I added, "in the governess's quarters."

She did not know what to make of this remark, and when Mrs. Polgrey did not understand, she ignored. In a few minutes I was alone.

As soon as she had gone the strangeness of the house seemed to envelop me. I was aware of silence—the eerie silence of an ancient house.

I went to the window and looked out. It seemed a long time ago that I had driven up to the house with Tapperty. I heard the August notes of a bird which might have been a linnet.

I looked at the watch pinned to my blouse and saw that it was just past six o'clock. Two hours to dinner. I wondered whether to ring for Daisy or Kitty and ask for hot water; but I found my eyes turning to the other door in my room, the one which led to the schoolroom.

The schoolroom was, after all, my domain, and I had a right to inspect it, so I opened the door. The room was larger than my bedroom but it had the same type of windows and they were all fitted with window seats on which were red plush fitted cushions. There was a table in the center of the room. I went over to it and saw that there were scratches on it and splashes of ink, so I guessed that this was the table where generations of TreMellyns had learned their lessons. I tried to imagine Connan TreMellyn as a little boy, sitting at this table. I imagined him a studious boy, quite different from his erring daughter, the difficult child who was going to be my problem.

A few books lay on the table. I examined them. They were children's readers, containing the sort of stories and articles which looked as if they were of an uplifting nature. There was an exercise book on which was scrawled "Alvean TreMellyn. Arithmetic." I opened it and saw several sums, to most of which had been given the wrong answers. Idly turning the pages I came to a sketch of a girl, and immediately I recognized Gilly, the child whom I had seen at the lodge gates.

"Not bad," I muttered. "So our Alvean is an artist. That's something."

I closed the book. I had the strange feeling, which I had had as soon as I entered the house, that I was being watched.

"Alvean!" I called on impulse. "Are you there, Alvean? Alvean, where are you hiding?"

There was no answer and I flushed with embarrassment, feeling rather absurd in the silence.

Abruptly I turned and went back to my room. I rang the bell and when Daisy appeared I asked her for hot water.

By the time I had unpacked my bags and hung up my things it was nearly eight o'clock, and precisely as the stable clock was striking eight Kitty appeared with my tray. On it was a leg of roast chicken with vegetables and, under a pewter cover, an egg custard.

Daisy said: "Are you having it in here, Miss, or in the schoolroom?"

I decided against sitting in that room where I felt I was overlooked.

"Here, please, Daisy," I answered. Then, because Daisy looked the sort of person who wanted to talk, I added: "Where is Miss Alvean? It seems strange that I have not seen her yet."

"She's a bad 'un," cried Daisy. "Do 'ee know what would have happened to Kit and me if we'd got up to such tricks? A good tanning

—that's what we'd have had—and in a place where 'tweren't comfortable to sit down on after. Her heard new miss was coming, and so off her goes. Master be away and we don't know where her be until the houseboy comes over from Mount Widden to tell we that she be over there—calling on Miss Celestine and Master Peter, if you do please."

"I see. A sort of protest at having a new governess."

Daisy came near and nudged me. "Miss Celestine do spoil the child. Dotes on her so's you'd think she was her own daughter. Listen! That do sound like the carriage." Daisy was at the window beckoning me. I felt I ought not to stand at the window with a servant, spying on what was happening below, but the temptation to do so was too strong for me.

So I stood beside Daisy and saw them getting out of the carriage . . . a young woman, whom I judged to be of my own age or perhaps a year or so older, and a child. I scarcely looked at the woman; my attention was all on the child. This was Alvean on whom my success depended, so naturally enough in those first seconds I had eyes for no one but her.

From what I could see she looked ordinary enough. She was somewhat tall for her eight years; her light brown hair had been plaited, and I presumed it was very long, for it was wound round her head; this gave her an appearance of maturity and I imagined her to be terrifyingly precocious. She was wearing a dress of brown gingham with white stockings and black shoes with ankle straps. She looked like a miniature woman and, for some vague reason, my spirits fell.

Oddly enough she seemed to be conscious that she was being watched, and glanced upward. Involuntarily I stepped back, but I was sure she had seen the movement. I felt at a disadvantage before we had met.

"Up to tricks," murmured Daisy at my side.

"Perhaps," I said as I walked into the center of the room, "she is a little alarmed at the prospect of having a new governess."

Daisy let out a burst of explosive laughter. "What, her! Sorry, miss, but that do make me laugh, that do."

I went to the table and, sitting down, began to eat my dinner. Daisy was about to go when there was a knock on the door and Kitty entered.

She grimaced at her sister and grinned rather familiarly at me. "Oh, miss," she said, "Mrs. Polgrey says that when you'm finished, will you go down to the punch room. Miss Nansellock be there and her would

like to see you. Miss Alvean have come home. They'd like 'ee to come
down as soon as you can. 'Tis time Miss Alvean were in her own
room."

"I will come when I have finished my dinner," I said.

"Then would you pull the bell when you'm ready, miss, and me or
Daisy'll show you the way."

"Thank you." I sat down and, in a leisurely fashion, ate my meal.

🙞

I rose and went to the mirror which stood on my dressing table. I
saw that I was unusually flushed and that this suited me; it made my
eyes look decidedly the color of amber. It was fifteen minutes since
Daisy and Kitty had left me and I imagined that Mrs. Polgrey, Alvean,
and Miss Nansellock would be impatiently awaiting my coming. But
I had no intention of becoming the poor little drudge that so many
governesses were. If Alvean were what I believed her to be, she
needed to be shown, right at the start, that I was in charge and must be
treated with respect.

I rang the bell and Daisy appeared.

"They'm waiting for you in the punch room," she said. "It's well
past Miss Alvean's supper time."

"Then it is a pity that she did not return before," I replied serenely.

When Daisy giggled, her plump breasts, which seemed to be bursting out of her cotton bodice, shook. Daisy enjoyed laughing, I could
see. I judged her to be as lighthearted as her sister.

She led the way to the punch room through which I had passed
with Mrs. Polgrey on my way to my own quarters. She drew aside the
curtains and with a dramatic gesture cried: "Here be miss!"

Mrs. Polgrey was seated in one of the tapestry-backed chairs, and
Celestine Nansellock was in another. Alvean was standing, her hands
clasped behind her back. She looked, I thought, dangerously demure.

"Ah," said Mrs. Polgrey, rising, "here is Miss Leigh. Miss Nansellock have been waiting to see you." There was a faint reproach in her
voice. I knew what it meant. I, a mere governess, had kept a *lady*
waiting while I finished my dinner.

"How do you do?" I asked.

They looked surprised. I suppose I should have curtsied or made
some gesture to show that I was conscious of my menial position. I
was aware of the blue eyes of the child fixed upon me; indeed I was
aware of little but Alvean in those first few moments. Her eyes were
startlingly blue. I thought: She will be a beauty when she grows up.
And I wondered whether she was like her father or mother.

Celestine Nansellock was standing by Alvean, and she laid a hand on her shoulder.

"Miss Alvean came over to see us," she said. "We're great friends. I'm Miss Nansellock of Mount Widden. You may have seen the house."

"I did so on my journey from the station."

"I trust you will not be cross with Alvean."

Alvean bristled and her eyes glinted.

I answered, looking straight into those defiant blue eyes: "I could hardly scold for what happened before my arrival, could I?"

"She looks on me . . . on us . . . as part of her own family," went on Celestine Nansellock. "We've always lived so close to each other."

"I am sure it is a great comfort to her," I replied; and for the first time I gave my attention solely to Celestine Nansellock.

She was taller than I, but by no standards a beauty. Her hair was of a nondescript brown and her eyes were hazel. There was little color in her face and an air of intense quietness about her. I decided she had little personality, but perhaps she was overshadowed by the defiance of Alvean and the conventional dignity of Mrs. Polgrey.

"I do hope," she said, "that if you need my advice about anything, Miss Leigh, you won't hesitate to call on me. You see, I am quite a near neighbor, and I think I am looked on here as one of the family."

"You are very kind."

Her mild eyes looked into mine. "We want you to be happy here, Miss Leigh. We all want that."

"Thank you. I suppose," I went on, "the first thing to do is to get Alvean to bed. It must be past her bedtime."

Celestine smiled. "You are right. Indeed it is. She usually has her milk and biscuits in the schoolroom at half past seven. It is now well past eight. But tonight I will look after her. I suggest that you return to your room, Miss Leigh. You must be weary after your journey."

Before I could speak Alvean cried out: "No, Celestine. I want *her* to. She's my governess. She should, shouldn't she?"

A hurt look immediately appeared in Celestine's face, and Alvean could not repress the triumph in hers. I felt I understood. The child wanted to feel her own power; she wanted to prevent Celestine from superintending her retirement simply because Celestine wished so much to do it.

"Oh, very well," said Celestine. "Then there's no further need for me to stay."

She was looking at Alvean as though she wanted her to beg her to stay, but Alvean's curious gaze was all for me.

"Good night," she said flippantly. And to me: "Come on. I'm hungry."

"You've forgotten to thank Miss Nansellock for bringing you back," I told her.

"I didn't forget," she retorted. "I never forget anything."

"Then your memory is a great deal better than your manners," I said.

They were astonished—all of them. Perhaps I was a little astonished myself. But I knew that if I were going to assume control of this child I should have to be firm.

Her face flushed and her eyes grew hard. She was about to retort, but not knowing how to do so, she ran out of the room.

"There!" said Mrs. Polgrey. "Why, Miss Nansellock, it was good of you . . ."

"Nonsense, Mrs. Polgrey," said Celestine. "Of course I brought her back."

"She will thank you later," I assured her.

"Miss Leigh," said Celestine earnestly, "it will be necessary for you to go carefully with that child. She has lost her mother . . . quite recently." Celestine's lips trembled. She smiled at me. "It is such a short time ago and the tragedy seems near. She was a dear friend of mine."

"I understand," I replied. "I shall not be harsh with the child, but I can see she needs discipline."

"Be careful, Miss Leigh." Celestine had taken a step closer and laid a hand on my arm. "Children are delicate creatures."

"I shall do my best for Alvean," I answered.

"I wish you good luck." She smiled and then turned to Mrs. Polgrey. "I'll be going now. I want to get back before dark."

Mrs. Polgrey rang the bell and Daisy appeared.

"Take miss to her room, Daisy," she commanded. "And has Miss Alvean got her milk and biscuits?"

"Yes, m'am," was the answer.

I said good night to Celestine Nansellock, who inclined her head. Then I left with Daisy.

⚜

I went into the schoolroom where Alvean sat at a table drinking milk and eating biscuits. She deliberately ignored me as I went to the table and sat beside her.

"Alvean," I said, "if we're going to get along together, we'd better come to an understanding. Don't you think that would be advisable?"

"Why should I care?" she replied curtly.

"But of course you'll care. We shall all be happier if we do."

Alvean shrugged her shoulders. "If we don't," she told me brusquely, "you'll have to go. I'll have another governess. It's of no account to me."

She looked at me triumphantly and I knew that she was telling me I was merely a paid servant and that it was for her to call the tune. I felt myself shiver involuntarily. For the first time I understood the feelings of those who depended on the good will of others for their bread and butter.

Her eyes were malicious and I wanted to slap her.

"It should be of the greatest account," I answered, "because it is far more pleasant to live in harmony than in discord with those about us."

"What does it matter, if they're *not* about us . . . if we can have them sent away?"

"Kindness matters more than anything in the world."

She smiled into her milk and finished it.

"Now," I said, "to bed."

I rose with her and she said: "I go to bed by myself. I am not a baby, you know."

"Perhaps I thought you were younger than you are because you have so much to learn."

She considered that. Then she gave that shrug of her shoulders which I was to discover was characteristic.

"Good night," she said, dismissing me.

"I'll come and say good night when you are in bed."

"There's no need."

"Nevertheless, I'll come."

She opened the door which led to her room from the schoolroom. I turned and went into mine.

I felt very depressed because I was realizing the size of the problem before me. I had had no experience in handling children, and in the past when I thought of them I had visualized docile and affectionate little creatures whom it would be a joy to care for. Here I was with a difficult child on my hands. And what would happen to me if it were decided that I was unfit to undertake her care? What did happen to penurious gentlewomen who failed to please their employers?

I could go to Phillida. I could be one of those old aunts who were at the beck and call of all and lived out their miserable lives dependent on others. I was not the sort of person to take dependence lightly. I should have to find other posts.

I accepted the fact that I was a little frightened. Not until I had come face to face with Alvean had I realized that I might not succeed with this job. I tried not to look down the years ahead when I might slip from one post to another, never giving satisfaction. What happened to women like myself, women who, without those attractions which were so important, were forced to battle against the world for a chance to live?

I felt that I could have thrown myself on my bed and wept, wept with anger against the cruelty of life, which had robbed me of two loving parents and sent me out ill-equipped into the world.

I imagined myself appearing at Alvean's bedside, my face stained with tears. What triumph for her! That was no way to begin the battle which I was sure must rage between us.

I walked up and down my room, trying to control my emotions. I went to the window and looked out across the lawns to the hilly country beyond. I had no view of the sea because the house was so built that the back looked out on the coast and I was at the front. Instead, I looked beyond the plateau on which the house stood, to the hills.

Such beauty! Such peace without, I thought. Such conflict within. When I leaned out of the window I could see Mount Widden across the cove. Two houses standing there over many years: generations of Nansellocks, generations of TreMellyns had lived here and their lives had intermingled so that it could well be that the story of one house was the story of the other.

I turned from the window and went through the schoolroom to Alvean's room.

"Alvean," I whispered. There was no answer. But she lay there in the bed, her eyes tightly shut, too tightly.

I bent over her.

"Good night, Alvean. We're going to be friends, you know," I murmured.

There was no answer. She was pretending to be asleep.

❧

Exhausted as I was, my rest was broken that night. I would fall into sleep and then awake startled. I repeated this several times until I was fully awake.

I lay in bed and looked about my room in which the furniture appeared in intermittent moonlight like dim figures. I had a feeling that I was not alone; that there were whispering voices about me. I had an impression that there had been tragedy in this house which still hung over it.

I wondered if it was due to the death of Alvean's mother. She had been dead only a year; I wondered in what circumstances she had died.

I thought of Alvean who showed a somewhat aggressive face to the world. There must be some reason for this. I was sure that no child would be eager to proclaim herself the enemy of strangers without some cause.

I determined to discover the reason for Alvean's demeanor. I determined to make her a happy, normal child.

It was light before sleep came; the coming of day comforted me because I was afraid of the darkness in this house. It was childish, but it was true.

I had breakfast in the schoolroom with Alvean, who told me, with pride, that when her father was at home she had breakfast with him.

Later we settled to work, and I discovered that she was an intelligent child; she had read more than most children of her age and her eyes would light up with interest in her lessons almost in spite of her determination to preserve a lack of harmony between us. My spirits began to rise and I felt that I would in time make a success of this job.

Luncheon consisted of boiled fish and rice pudding, and afterward when Alvean volunteered to take me for a walk, I felt I was getting on better with her.

There were woods on the estate, and she said she wished to show them to me. I was delighted that she should do so and gladly followed her through the trees.

"Look," she cried, picking a crimson flower and holding it out to me. "Do you know what this is?"

"It's betony, I believe."

She nodded. "You should pick some and keep it in your room, miss. It keeps evil away."

I laughed. "That's an old superstition. Why should I want to keep evil away?"

"Everybody should. They grow this in graveyards. It's because people are buried there. It's grown there because people are afraid of the dead."

"It's foolish to be afraid. Dead people can hurt no one."

She was placing the flower in the buttonhole of my coat. I was rather touched. Her face looked gentle as she fixed it and I had a notion that she felt a sudden protective feeling toward me.

"Thank you, Alvean," I said gently.

She looked at me and all the softness vanished from her face. It was defiant and full of mischief.

"You can't catch me," she cried; and off she ran.

I did not attempt to do so. I called: "Alvean, come here." But she disappeared through the trees and I heard her mocking laughter in the distance.

I decided to return to the house, but the woods were thick, and I was not sure of my direction. I walked back a little way but it seemed to me that it was not the direction from which we had come. Panic seized me, but I told myself this was absurd. It was a sunny afternoon and I could not be half an hour's walk from the house. Moreover, I did not believe that the woods could be very extensive.

I was not going to give Alvean the satisfaction of having brought me to the woods to lose me. So I walked purposefully through the trees; but as I walked they grew thicker and I knew that we had not come this way. My anger against Alvean was rising when I heard the crackle of leaves as though I were being followed. I was sure the child was somewhere near, mocking me.

Then I heard singing; it was a strange voice, slightly off key, and the fact that the song was one of those which were being sung in drawing rooms all over the country did nothing to reassure me.

"Alice, where art thou?
One year back this even
And thou wert by my side,
Vowing to love me,
Alice, what e'er may betide . . ."

"Who is there?" I called.

There was no answer, but in the distance I caught a glimpse of a child with lint-white hair, and I knew that it was only little Gilly who had stared at me from the hydrangea bushes by the lodge gates.

I walked swiftly on and after a while the trees grew less dense and through them I saw the road; then I realized that I was on the slope which led up to the plateau and the lodge gates.

Mrs. Soady was sitting at the door of the lodge as she had been when I arrived, her knitting in her hands.

"Why, miss," she called. "So you've been out walking then?"

"I went for a walk with Miss Alvean. We lost each other in the woods."

"Ah yes. So her run away, did her." Mrs. Soady shook her head as she came to the gate trailing her ball of wool behind her.

"I expect she'll find her way home," I said.

"My dear life, yes. There ain't an inch of them woods Miss Alvean don't know. Oh, I see you've got yourself a piece of betony. Like as not 'tis as well."

"Miss Alvean picked it and insisted on putting it in my buttonhole."

"There now! You be friends already."

"I heard the little girl Gilly, singing in the woods," I said.

"I don't doubt 'ee. Her's always singing in the woods."

"I called to her but she didn't come."

"Timid as a doe, she be."

"Well, I think I'll be getting along. Good-by, Mrs. Soady."

"Good day to 'ee, miss."

I went up the drive, past the hydrangeas and the fuchsias. I realized I was straining my ears for the sound of singing, but there was no sound except that of an occasional small animal in the undergrowth.

I was hot and tired when I reached the house. I went straight up to my room and rang for water and, when I had washed and brushed my hair, went into the schoolroom where tea was waiting for me.

Alvean sat at the table; she looked demure and made no reference to our afternoon's adventure, nor did I.

After tea I said to her: "I don't know what rules your other governesses made, but I propose we do our lessons in the morning, have a break between luncheon and tea, and then start again from five o'clock until six, when we will read together."

Alvean did not answer; she was studying me intently.

Then suddenly she said: "Miss, do you like my name? Have you ever known anyone else called Alvean?"

I said I liked the name and had never heard it before.

"It's Cornish. Do you know what it means?"

"I have no idea."

"Then I will tell you. My father can speak and write Cornish." She looked wistful when she spoke of her father, and I thought: He at least is one person she admires and for whose approval she is eager. She went on: "In Cornish, Alvean means Little Alice."

"Oh!" I said, and my voice shook a little.

She came to me and placed her hands on my knees; she looked up into my face and said solemnly: "You see, miss, my mother was Alice.

She isn't here any more. But I was called after her. That's why I am little Alice."

I stood up because I could no longer bear the scrutiny of the child. I went to the window.

"Look," I said, "two of the peacocks are on the lawn."

She was standing at my elbow. "They've come to be fed. Greedy things! Daisy will soon be coming with their peas. They know it."

I was not seeing the peacocks on the lawn. I was remembering the mocking eyes of the man on the train, the man who had warned me that I should have to beware of Alice.

2

Three days after my arrival at Mount Mellyn, the master of the house returned.

I had slipped into a routine as far as my duties were concerned. Alvean and I did lessons each morning after breakfast, and apart from an ever present desire to disconcert me by asking questions which, I knew, she hoped I should not be able to answer, I found her a good pupil. It was not that she meant to please me; it was merely that her desire for knowledge was so acute that she could not deny it. I believe there was some plot in her head that if she could learn all I knew, she could then confront her father with the question: Since there is no more miss can teach me, is there any point in her remaining here?

I often thought of tales I had heard of governesses whose declining years were made happy by those whom they had taught as children. No such happy fate would be mine—at least as far as Alvean was concerned.

I had been shocked when I first heard the name of Alice mentioned, and after the daylight had passed I would consequently feel that the house was full of eerie shadows. That was pure fancy of course. It had been a bad beginning, meeting that man in the train with his talk of second sight.

I did wonder, when I was alone in my room and the house was quiet, of what Alice had died. She must have been quite a young woman. It was, I told myself, because she was so recently dead—for after all a year was not a very long time—that her presence seemed to haunt the place.

I would wake in the night to hear what I thought were voices, and they seemed to be moaning: "Alice. Alice. Where is Alice?"

I went to my window and listened, and the whispering voices seemed to be carried on the air.

Daisy, who like her sister, was by no means a fanciful person, explained away my fancies the very next morning when she brought my hot water.

"Did 'ee hear the sea last night, miss, in old Mellyn Cove? Sis . . . sis . . . sis . . . woa . . . woa . . . woa . . . all night long. Just like two old biddies having a good gossip down there."

"Why yes, I heard it."

" 'Tis like that on certain nights when the sea be high and the wind in a certain direction."

I laughed at myself. There was an explanation to everything.

I had grown to know the people of the household. Mrs. Tapperty called me in one day for a glass of her parsnip wine. She hoped I was comfortable at the house; then she told me of the trial Tapperty was to her because he couldn't keep his eyes nor his hands from the maidens —and the younger the better. She feared Kitty and Daisy took after their father. It was a pity, for their mother was, according to herself, a God-fearing body who would be seen in Mellyn Church every Sunday, night and morning. Now the girls were grown up she had to wonder not only whether Joe Tapperty was after Mrs. Tully from the cottages, but what Daisy was doing in the stables with Billy Trehay or Kitty with that houseboy from Mount Widden. It was a hard life for a God-fearing woman who only wanted to do right and see right done.

I went to see Mrs. Soady at the lodge gates and heard about her three sons and their children. "Never did I see such people for putting their toes through their stockings. It's one body's work to keep them in stockings."

I was very eager to learn about the house in which I lived, and the intricacies of heel-turning did not greatly excite me; therefore I did not often call on Mrs. Soady.

I tried on occasions to catch Gilly and talk to her; but although I saw her now and then, I did not succeed. I called her, but that only made her run away more swiftly. I could never hear her soft crooning voice without being deeply disturbed.

I felt that something should be done for her. I was angry with these country folk who, because she was unlike them, believed her to be mad. I wanted to talk to Gilly if that were possible. I wanted to find out what went on behind that blank blue stare.

I knew she was interested in me, and I believed that in some way she had sensed my interest in her. But she was afraid of me. Something must have happened to frighten her at some time because she was so unnaturally timid. If I could only discover what, if I could teach her that in me at least she had nothing to fear, I believed I could help her to become a normal child.

During those days I believe I thought more—or at least as much—of Gilly than I did of Alvean. The latter seemed to me to be merely a naughty spoiled child; there were thousands such. I felt that the gentle creature called Gillyflower was unique.

It was impossible to talk to Mrs. Polgrey about her granddaughter, for she was such a conventional woman. In her mind a person was either mad or sane, and the degree of sanity depended on the conformity with Mrs. Polgrey's own character. Since Gilly was as different from her grandmother as anyone could be, Gilly was therefore irremediably crazy.

So although I did broach the subject with Mrs. Polgrey, she was grimly uncommunicative and told me by her looks alone to remember that I was here to take charge of Miss Alvean, and that Gilly was no concern of mine.

This was the state of affairs when Connan TreMellyn returned to Mount Mellyn.

❧

As soon as I set eyes on Connan TreMellyn he aroused deep feelings within me. I was aware of his presence, indeed, before I saw him.

It was afternoon when he arrived. Alvean had gone off by herself and I had sent for hot water to wash before I went for a stroll. Kitty brought it and I noticed the difference in her from the moment she entered the room. Her black eyes gleamed and her mouth seemed a little slack.

"Master be home," she said.

I tried not to show that I was faintly disturbed; and at that moment Daisy put her head round the door. The sisters looked very much alike just then. There was about them both a certain expectancy which sickened me. I thought I understood the expression in the faces of these lusty girls. I suspected that neither of them was virgin. There was suggestion in their very gestures and I had seen them in scuffling intimacy with Billy Trehay in the stables and with the boys who came in from the village to work about the place. They changed subtly when they were in the presence of the opposite sex and I understood what that meant. Their excitement over the return of the master, of whom I gathered everyone was in awe, led me to one conclusion, and I felt faintly disgusted, not only with them but with myself for entertaining such thoughts.

Is he *that* sort of man then? I was asking myself.

"He came in half an hour ago," said Kitty.

They were studying me speculatively and once more I thought I read their thoughts. They were telling themselves that there would be little competition from me.

My disgust increased and I turned away.

I said coolly: "Well, I'll wash my hands and you can take the water away. I am going for a walk."

I put on my hat and, even as I went out quickly by way of the back stairs, I sensed the change. Mr. Polgrey was busy in the gardens, and the two boys who came in from the village were working as though their lives depended on it. Tapperty was cleaning out the stables; he was so intent on his work that he did not notice me.

There was no doubt that the whole household was in awe of the master.

As I wandered through the woods I told myself that if he did not like me I could leave at any time. I supposed I could stay with Phillida while I looked round. At least I had some relations to whom I could go. I was not entirely alone in the world.

I called to Alvean, but my voice was lost in the thickness of the trees and there was no response. Then I called: "Gilly! Are you there, Gillyflower? Do come and talk to me if you are. I won't hurt you."

There was no answer.

At half past three I went back to the house and, as I was mounting the back stairs to my quarters, Daisy came running after me.

"Master have been asking for you, miss. He do wish to see you. He be waiting in the punch room."

I inclined my head and said: "I will take off my things and then go to the punch room."

"He have seen you come in, miss, and have said for you to go right away."

"I will take off my hat first," I answered. My heart was beating fast and my color was heightened. I did not know why I felt antagonistic. I believed that I should soon be packing my bags and going back to Phillida; and I decided that if it had to be done it should be done with the utmost dignity.

In my room I took off my hat and smoothed my hair. My eyes were certainly amber today. They were resentful, which seemed ridiculous before I had met the man. I told myself as I went down to the punch room that I had built up a picture of him because of certain looks I had seen in the faces of those two flighty girls. I had already assured myself that poor Alice had died of a broken heart because she had found herself married to a philanderer.

I knocked at the door.

"Come in." His voice was strong—arrogant, I called it even before I set eyes on him.

He was standing with his back to the fireplace and I was immediately conscious of his great height; he was well over six feet tall, and the fact that he was so thin—one could almost say gaunt—accentuated this. His hair was black but his eyes were light. His hands were thrust into the pockets of his riding breeches and he wore a dark blue coat with a white cravat. There was an air of careless elegance about him as though he cared nothing for his clothes but could not help looking well in them.

He gave an impression of both strength and cruelty. There was sensuality in that face, I decided—that came through; but there was much else that was hidden. Even in that moment when I first saw him I knew that there were two men in that body—two distinct personalities—the Connan TreMellyn who faced the world, and the one who remained hidden.

"So, Miss Leigh, at last we meet."

He did not advance to greet me, and his manner seemed insolent as though he were reminding me that I was only a governess.

"It does not seem a long time," I answered, "for I have only been in your house a few days."

"Well, let us not dwell on the time it has taken us to get together. Now you are here, let that suffice."

His light eyes surveyed me mockingly, so that I felt awkward and unattractive, and was aware that I stood before a connoisseur of women when even to the uninitiated I was not a very desirable specimen.

"Mrs. Polgrey gives me good reports of you."

"That is kind of her."

"Why should it be kind of her to tell me the truth? I expect that from my employees."

"I meant that she has been kind to me and that has helped to make this good report possible."

"I see that you are a woman who does not use the ordinary clichés of conversation but means what she says."

"I hope so."

"Good. I have a feeling that we shall get on well together."

His eyes were taking in each detail of my appearance, I knew. He probably was aware that I had been given a London season and what Aunt Adelaide would call "every opportunity," and had failed to acquire a husband. As a connoisseur of women he would know why.

I thought: At least *I* shall be safe from the attentions which I feel sure he tries to bestow on all attractive women with whom he comes into contact.

"Tell me," he said, "how do you find my daughter? Backward for her age?"

"By no means. She is extremely intelligent, but I find her in need of discipline."

"I am sure you will be able to supply that lack."

"I intend to try."

"Of course. That is why you are here."

"Please tell me how far I may carry that discipline."

"You are thinking of corporal punishment?"

"Nothing was farther from my thoughts. I mean, have I your permission to apply my own code? To restrict her liberty, shall we say, if I feel she needs such punishment."

"Short of murder, Miss Leigh, you have my permission to do what you will. If your methods do not meet with my approval, you will hear."

"Very well, I understand."

"If you wish to make any alterations in the—curriculum, I think is the word—you must do so."

"Thank you."

"I believe in experiments. If your methods have not made an improvement in, say, six months . . . well, then we could review the situation, could we not?"

His eyes were insolent. I thought: He intends to get rid of me soon. He was hoping I was a silly, pretty creature not averse to carrying on an intrigue with him while pretending to look after his daughter. Very well, the best thing I can do is to get out of this house.

"I suppose," he went on, "we should make excuses for Alvean's lack of good manners. She lost her mother a year ago."

I looked into his face for a trace of sorrow. I could find none.

"I had heard that," I answered.

"Of course you had heard. I'll swear there were many ready to tell you. It was doubtless a great shock to the child."

"It must have been a great shock," I agreed.

"It was sudden." He was silent for a few seconds and then he continued: "Poor child, she has no mother. And her father . . . ?" He lifted his shoulders and did not complete his sentence.

"Even so," I said, "there are many more unfortunate than she is. All she needs is a firm hand."

He leaned forward suddenly and surveyed me ironically.

"I am sure," he said, "that you possess that necessary firm hand."

I was conscious in that brief moment of the magnetism of the man. The clear-cut features, the cool, light eyes, the mockery behind them —all these I felt were but a mask hiding something which he was determined to keep hidden.

At that moment there was a knock on the door and Celestine Nansellock came in.

"I heard you were here, Connan," she said, and I thought she seemed nervous. So he had that effect even on those of his own station.

"How news travels!" he murmured. "My dear Celestine, it was good of you to come over. I was just making the acquaintance of our new governess. She tells me that Alvean is intelligent and needs discipline."

"Of course she is intelligent!" Celestine spoke indignantly. "I hope Miss Leigh is not planning to be too harsh with her. Alvean is a *good* child."

Connan TreMellyn threw an amused glance in my direction. "I don't think Miss Leigh entirely agrees with that," he said. "You see our little goose as a beautiful swan, Celeste my dear."

"Perhaps I am overfond . . ."

"Would you like me to leave now?" I suggested, for I had a great desire to get away from them.

"But I am interrupting," cried Celestine.

"No," I assured her. "We had finished our talk, I believe."

Connan TreMellyn looked in some amusement from her to me. It occurred to me that he probably found us equally unattractive. I was sure that neither of us was the least like the woman he would admire.

"Let us say it is to be continued," he said lightly. "I fancy, Miss Leigh, that you and I will have a great deal more to discuss, regarding my daughter."

I bowed my head and left them together.

In the schoolroom tea was laid, ready for me. I felt too excited to eat, and when Alvean did not appear I guessed she was with her father.

At five o'clock she still had not put in an appearance, so I summoned Daisy and sent her to find the child and to remind her that from five to six we had work to do.

I waited. I was not surprised because I had expected Alvean to rebel. Her father had arrived and she preferred to be with him rather than come to me for the hour of our reading.

I wondered what would happen when the child refused to come to the schoolroom. Could I go down to the punch room or the drawing room or wherever they were and demand that she return with me? Celestine was with them and she would take her stand on Alvean's side against me.

I heard footsteps on the stairs. The door of Alvean's room which led into the schoolroom was opened, and there stood Connan TreMellyn holding Alvean by the arm.

Alvean's expression astonished me. She looked so unhappy that I found myself feeling sorry for her. Her father was smiling and I thought he looked like a satyr, as though the situation which caused pain to Alvean and embarrassment to me amused him—and perhaps for these reasons. In the background was Celestine.

"Here she is," announced Connan TreMellyn. "Duty is duty, my daughter," he said to Alvean. "And when your governess summons you to your lessons, you must obey."

Alvean muttered and I could see that she was hard put to restrain her sobs: "But it is your first day, Papa."

"But Miss Leigh says there are lessons to be done, and she is in command."

"Thank you, Mr. TreMellyn," I said. "Come and sit down, Alvean."

Alvean's expression changed as she looked at me. All the wistfulness was replaced by anger and a fierce hatred.

"Connan," Celestine said quietly, "it is your first day back, you know, and Alvean so looked forward to your coming."

He smiled but I thought how grim his mouth was.

"Discipline," he murmured. "That, Celeste, is of the utmost importance. Come, we will leave Alvean with her governess."

He inclined his head in my direction, while Alvean threw a pleading glance at him which he quite obviously ignored.

The door shut leaving me alone with my pupil.

That incident had taught me a great deal. Alvean adored her father and he was indifferent to her. My anger against him increased as my pity for the child grew. Small wonder that she was a difficult child. What could one expect when she was such an unhappy one? I saw her

. . . ignored by the father whom she loved, spoiled by Celestine Nansellock. Between them they were doing their best to ruin the girl.

I would have liked Connan TreMellyn better, I told myself, if he had decided to forget discipline on his first day back, and devote a little time to his daughter's company.

❦

Alvean was rebellious all that evening, but I insisted on her going to bed at her usual time. She told me she hated me, though there was no need for her to have mentioned a fact which was apparent.

I felt so disturbed when she was in her bed that I slipped out of the house and went into the woods, where I sat on a fallen tree trunk, brooding.

It had been a hot day and there was a deep stillness in the woods.

I wondered whether I was going to keep this job. It was not easy to say at this stage, and I was not sure whether I wanted to go or stay.

There were so many things to keep me. There was, for one thing, my interest in Gillyflower; there was my desire to wipe the rebellion from Alvean's heart. But I felt less eagerness for these tasks now that I had seen the master.

I was a little afraid of the man although I could not say why. I was certain that he would leave *me* alone, but there was something magnetic about him, some quality which made it difficult for me to put him out of my mind. I thought more of dead Alice than I had before, because I could not stop myself wondering what sort of person she could have been.

I amused him in some way. Perhaps because I was so unattractive in his eyes; perhaps because he knew that I belonged to that army of women who are obliged to earn their living and so are dependent on the whim of people like himself. Was there a streak of sadism in his nature? I believed so. Perhaps poor Alice had found it intolerable. Perhaps she, like poor Gillyflower's mother, had walked into the sea.

As I sat there I heard the sound of footsteps coming through the wood and I hesitated, wondering whether to wait there or go back to the house.

A man was coming toward me, and there was something familiar about him which made my heart beat faster.

He started when he saw me; then he began to smile and I recognized him as the man I had met on the train.

"So we meet," he said. "I knew our reunion would not be long delayed. Why, you look as though you have seen a ghost. Has your stay at Mount Mellyn made you look for ghosts? I've heard some say that there *is* a ghostly atmosphere about the place."

"Who are you?" I asked.

"My name is Peter Nansellock. I have to confess to a little deception."

"You're Miss Celestine's brother?"

He nodded. "I knew who you were when we met in the train. I deliberately bearded you in your carriage. I saw you sitting there, looking the part, and I guessed. Your name on the labels of your baggage confirmed my guess, for I knew that they were expecting Miss Martha Leigh at Mount Mellyn."

"I am comforted to learn that my looks conform with the part I have been called upon to play in life."

"You really are a most untruthful young lady. I remember I had reason to reprimand you for the same sort of thing at our first meeting. You are in fact quite discomfited to learn that you were taken for a governess."

I felt myself grow pink with indignation. "Because I am a governess, that is no reason why I should be forced to accept insults from strangers."

I rose from the tree trunk, but he laid a hand on my arm and said pleadingly: "Please let us talk awhile. There is much I have to say to you. There are things you should know."

My curiosity overcame my dignity and I sat down.

"That's better, Miss Leigh. You see I remember your name."

"Most courteous of you! And how extraordinary that you should first notice a mere governess's name and then keep it in your memory."

"You are like a hedgehog," he retorted. "One only has to mention the word 'governess' and up come your spines. You will have to learn resignation. Aren't we taught that we must be content in that station of life to which we have been called?"

"Since I resemble a hedgehog, at least I am not spineless."

He laughed and then was immediately sober. "I do not possess second sight, Miss Leigh," he said quietly. "I know nothing of palmistry. I deceived you, Miss Leigh."

"Do you think I was deceived for a moment?"

"For many moments. Until this one, in fact, you have thought of me with wonder."

"Indeed, I have not thought of you at all."

"More untruths! I wonder if a young lady with such little regard for veracity is worthy to teach our little Alvean."

"Since you are a friend of the family your best policy would be to warn them at once."

"But if Connan dismissed his daughter's governess, how sad that would be! I should wander through these woods without hope of meeting her."

"I see you are a frivolous person."

"It's true." He looked grave. "My brother was frivolous. My sister is the only commendable member of the family."

"I have already met her."

"Naturally. She is a constant visitor to Mount Mellyn. She dotes on Alvean."

"Well, she is a very near neighbor."

"And we, Miss Leigh, shall in future be very near neighbors. How does that strike you?"

"Without any great force."

"Miss Leigh, you are cruel as well as untruthful. I hoped you would be grateful for my interest. I was going to say, if ever things should become intolerable at Mount Mellyn you need only walk over to Mount Widden. There you would find me most willing to help. I feel sure that among my wide circle of acquaintances I could find someone who is in urgent need of a governess."

"Why should I find life intolerable at Mount Mellyn?"

"It's a tomb of a place, Connan is overbearing, Alvean is a menace to anyone's peace, and the atmosphere since Alice's death is not congenial."

I turned to him abruptly and said: "You told me to beware of Alice. What did you mean by that?"

"So you did remember?"

"It seemed such a strange thing to say."

"Alice is dead," he said, "but somehow she remains. That's what I always feel at Mount Mellyn. Nothing was the same after the day she . . . went."

"How did she die?"

"You have not heard the story yet?"

"No."

"I should have thought Mrs. Polgrey or one of those girls would have told you. But they haven't, eh? They're probably somewhat in awe of the governess."

"I should like to hear the story."

"It's a very simple one. The sort of thing which must happen in many a home. A wife finds life with her husband intolerable. She walks out . . . with another man. It's ordinary enough, you see. Only Alice's story had a different ending."

He looked at the tips of his boots as he had when we were traveling in the train to Liskeard together. "The man in the case was my brother," he went on.

"Geoffry Nansellock!" I cried.

"So you have heard of him!"

I thought of Gillyflower, whose birth had so distressed her mother that she had walked into the sea.

"Yes," I said, "I've heard of Geoffry Nansellock. He was evidently a philanderer."

"It sounds a harsh word to apply to poor old Geoff. He had charm . . . all the charm of the family, some say." He smiled at me. "Others may think he did not get it all. He was not a bad sort. I was fond of old Geoff. His great weakness was women. He loved women; he found them irresistible. And women love men who love them. How can they help it? I mean, it is such a compliment, is it not? One by one they fell victim to his charm."

"He did not hesitate to include other men's wives among his victims."

"Spoken like a true governess! Alas, my dear Miss Leigh, it appeared he did not . . . since Alice was among them. It is true that all was not well at Mount Mellyn. Do you think Connan would be an easy man to live with?"

"It is surely not becoming for a governess to discuss her employer in such a manner."

"What a contrary young lady you are, Miss Leigh. You make the most of your situation. You use the governess when you wish to, and then expect others to ignore her when you do not wish her to be recognized. I believe that anyone who is obliged to live in a house should know something of its secrets."

"What secrets?"

He bent a little closer to me. "Alice was afraid of Connan. Before she married him she had known my brother. She and Geoffry were on the train . . . running away together."

"I see." I drew myself away from him because I felt it was undignified to be talking of past scandals in this way, particularly as these scandals had nothing whatever to do with me.

"They identified Geoffry although he was badly smashed up. There was a woman close to him. She was so badly burned that it was impossible to recognize her as Alice. But a locket she was wearing was recognized as one she was known to possess. That was how she was identified . . . and of course there was the fact that Alice had disappeared."

"How dreadful to die in such a way!"

"The prim governess is shocked because poor Alice died in the act of forming a guilty partnership with my charming but erring brother."

"Was she so unhappy at Mount Mellyn?"

"You have met Connan. Remember, he knew that she had once been in love with Geoffry, and Geoffry was still in the offing. I can imagine life was hell for Alice."

"Well, it was very tragic," I said briskly. "But it is over. Why did you say, 'Beware of Alice,' as though she were still there?"

"Are you fey, Miss Leigh? No, of course you are not. You are a governess with more than your fair share of common sense. You would not be influenced by fantastic tales."

"What fantastic tales?"

He grinned at me, coming even closer, and I realized that in a very short time it would be dark. I was anxious to get back to the house, and my expression became a little impatient.

"They recognized her locket, not her. There are some who think that it was not Alice who was killed on the train with Geoffry."

"Then if it was not, where is she?"

"That is what some people ask themselves. That is why there are long shadows at Mount Mellyn."

I stood up. "I must get back. It will soon be dark."

He was standing beside me—a little taller than I—and our eyes met.

"I thought you should know these things," he said almost gently. "It seems only fair that you should know."

I began walking back in the direction from which I had come.

"My duties are with the child," I answered somewhat brusquely. "I am not here for any other purpose."

"But how can even a governess, overburdened with common sense though she may be, know to what purposes fate will put her?"

"I think I know what is expected of me." I was alarmed because he walked beside me; I wanted to escape from him that I might be alone with my thoughts. I felt this man impaired my precious dignity to which I was clinging with that determination only possible to those who are in constant fear of losing what little they possess. He had mocked me in the train. I felt he was waiting for an opportunity to do so again.

"I am sure you do."

"There is no need for you to escort me back to the house."

"I am forced to contradict you. There is every reason."

"Do you think I am incapable of looking after myself?"

"I think none more capable of doing that than yourself. But as it happens I was on my way to call, and this is the most direct way to the house."

I was silent until we came to Mount Mellyn.

Connan TreMellyn was coming from the stables.

"Hello there, Con!" cried Peter Nansellock.

Connan TreMellyn looked at us in mild surprise, which I supposed was due to the fact that we were together.

I hurried round to the back of the house.

✦✦✦✦✦

It was not easy to sleep that night. The events of the day crowded into my mind and I saw pictures of myself and Connan TreMellyn, pictures of Alvean, of Celestine, and of myself in the woods with Peter Nansellock.

The wind was in a certain direction that night, and I could hear the waves thundering into Mellyn Cove.

In my present mood it certainly seemed that there were whispering voices down there, and that the words they said to each other were: "Alice! Alice! Where is Alice? Alice, where are you?"

3

In the morning the fancies of the previous night seemed foolish. I asked myself why so many people—including myself—wanted to make a mystery of what had happened in this house. It was an ordinary enough story.

I know what it is, I told myself. When people consider an ancient house like this, they make themselves believe it could tell some fantastic stories if it could only speak. They think of the generations who have lived and suffered within these walls, and they grow fanciful. So that when the mistress of the house is tragically killed they imagine her ghost still walks and that, although she is dead, she is still here. Well, I am a sensible woman, I hope. Alice was killed on a train, and that was the end of Alice.

I laughed at my folly in allowing myself to be caught up in such notions. Had not Daisy or Kitty explained that the whispering voices, which I thought I heard in the night, were merely the sound of waves thundering in the cove below?

From now on I was entertaining no more such fantastic thoughts.

My room was filled with sunshine and I felt different from the way I had felt on any other morning. I was exhilarated. I knew why. It was due to that man, Connan TreMellyn. Not that I liked him—quite the reverse; but it was as though he had issued a challenge. I was going to make a success of this job. I was going to make of Alvean not only a model pupil but a charming, unaffected uninhibited little girl.

I felt so pleased that I began to hum softly under my breath.

"Come into the garden, Maud" . . . That was a song Father used to like to play while Phillida sang, for in addition to her other qualities Phillida possessed a charming voice. Then I passed to "Sweet and Low," and for a moment I forgot the house I was in and saw Father at the piano, his glasses slipping down his nose, his slippered feet making the most of the pedals.

I was almost astonished to find that I had unconsciously slipped into the song I had heard Gilly singing in the woods. "Alice, where art thou . . ."

Oh no, not that, I said sharply to myself.

I heard the sound of horses' hoofs and I went to the window to look out. No one was visible. The lawns looked fresh and lovely with the early morning dew on them. What a beautiful sight, I thought; the palm trees gave the scene a tropical look and it was one of those mornings when there was every promise of a beautiful day.

"One of the last we can expect this summer, I daresay," I said aloud; and I threw open my window and leaned out, my thick coppery plaits, the ends tied with pieces of blue ribbon for bedtime, swinging out with me.

I went back to "Sweet and Low" and was humming this when Connan TreMellyn emerged from the stables. He saw me before I was able to draw back, and I felt myself grow scarlet with embarrassment to be seen with my hair down and in my nightgown thus.

He called jauntily: "Good morning, Miss Leigh."

In that moment I said to myself: So it was his horse I heard. And has he been riding in the early morning, or out all night? I imagined his visiting one of the gay ladies of the neighborhood, if such existed. That was my opinion of him. I was angry that he should be the one to show no embarrassment whatsoever while I was blushing—certainly in every part that was visible.

"Good morning," I said, and my voice sounded curt.

He was coming swiftly across the lawn, hoping, I was sure, to embarrass me further by a closer look at me in my night attire.

"A beautiful morning," he cried.

"Extremely so," I answered.

I withdrew into my room as I heard him shout: "Hello, Alvean! So you're up too."

I was standing well back from the window now and I heard Alvean cry: "Hello, Papa!" and her voice was soft and gentle with that wistful note which I had detected when she spoke of him on the previous day. I knew that she was delighted to have seen him, that she had been awake in her room when she had heard his voice, and had dashed to her window, and that it would make her extremely happy if he stopped awhile and chatted with her.

He did no such thing. He went into the house. Standing before my mirror, I looked at myself. Most unbecoming, I thought. And quite undignified. Myself in a pink flannelette nightdress buttoned high at the throat, with my hair down and my face even now the color of the flannelette!

I put on my dressing gown and on impulse crossed the schoolroom to Alvean's room. I opened the door and went in. She was sitting astride a chair and talking to herself.

"There's nothing to be afraid of really. All you have to do is hold tight and not be afraid . . . and you won't fall off."

She was so intent on what she was doing that she had not heard the door open, and I stood for a few seconds watching her, for she had her back to the schoolroom door.

I learned a great deal in that moment. He was a great horseman, this father of hers; he wanted his daughter to be a good horsewoman, but Alvean, who desperately wanted to win his approval, was afraid of horses.

I started forward, my first impulse to talk to her, to tell her that I would teach her to ride. It was one thing I could do really well because we had always had horses in the country, and at five Phillida and I were competing in local shows.

But I hesitated because I was beginning to understand Alvean. She was an unhappy child. Tragedy had hit her in more ways than one. She had lost her mother, and that was the biggest tragedy which could befall any child; but when her father did not seem anything but indifferent to her, and she adored him, that was a double tragedy.

I quietly shut the door and went back to my room. I looked at the sunshine on the carpet and my elation returned. I *was* going to make a success of this job. I was going to fight Connan TreMellyn, if he wanted it that way. I was going to make him proud of his daughter; I was going to force him to give her that attention which was her right and which none but a brute would deny her.

⊷⧉⊷

Lessons were trying that morning. Alvean was late for them, having breakfasted with her father in accordance with the custom of the family. I pictured them at the big table in the room which I had discovered was used as a dining room when there were no guests. They called it the small dining room, but it was only small by Mount Mellyn standards.

He would be reading the paper, or looking through his letters, I imagined; Alvean would be at the other end of the table hoping for a word, which of course he would be too selfish to bestow.

I had to send for her to come to lessons; and that she deeply resented.

I tried to make lessons as interesting as I could, and I must have succeeded, for in spite of her resentment toward me she could not hide her interest in the history and geography lessons which I set for that morning.

She took luncheon with her father while I ate alone in the schoolroom, and after that I decided to approach Connan TreMellyn.

While I was wondering where I could find him I saw him leave the house and go across to the stables. I immediately followed him and, when I arrived at the stables, I heard him giving orders to Billy Trehay to saddle Royal Russet for him.

He looked surprised to see me; and then he smiled and I was sure that he was remembering the last time he had seen me—in dishabille.

"Why," he said, "it is Miss Leigh."

"I had hoped to have a few words with you," I said primly. "Perhaps this is an inconvenient time."

"That depends," he said, "on how many words you wish us to exchange." He took out his watch and looked at it. "I can give you five minutes, Miss Leigh."

I was aware of Billy Trehay, and if Connan TreMellyn was going to snub me I was eager that no servant should overhear.

Connan TreMellyn said: "Let us walk across the lawn. Ready in five minutes, Billy?"

"Very good, master," answered Billy.

With that, Connan TreMellyn began to walk away from the stables, and I fell into step beside him.

"In my youth," I said, "I was constantly in the saddle. I believe Alvean wishes to learn to ride. I am asking your permission to teach her."

"You have my permission to try, Miss Leigh," he said.

"You sound as though you doubt my ability to succeed."

"I fear I do."

"I don't understand why you should doubt my ability to teach when you have not tested my skill."

"Oh, Miss Leigh," he said almost mockingly, "you wrong me. It is not your ability to teach that I doubt; it is Alvean's to learn."

"You mean others have failed to teach her?"

"I have failed."

"But surely . . ."

He lifted a hand. "It is strange," he said, "to find such fear in a child. Most children take to it like breathing."

His tone was clipped, his expression hard. I wanted to shout at him: What sort of father are you! I pictured the lessons, the lack of understanding, the expectation of miracles. No wonder the child had been scared.

He went on: "There are some people who can never learn to ride."

Before I could stop myself I had burst out: "There are some people who cannot teach."

He stopped to stare at me in astonishment, and I knew that nobody in this house had ever dared to talk to him in such a way.

I thought: This is it. I shall now be told that my services are no longer required, and at the end of the month I may pack my bags and depart.

There was a violent temper there, and I could see that he was fighting to control it. He still looked at me but I could not read the expression in those light eyes. I believed it was contemptuous. Then he glanced back at the stables.

"You must excuse me, Miss Leigh," he said; and he left me.

❧

I went straight to Alvean. I found her in the schoolroom. There was the sullen, defiant look in her eyes, and I believed she had seen me talking to her father.

I came straight to the point. "Your father has said I may give you riding lessons, Alvean. Would you like that?"

I saw the muscles of her face tighten, and my heart sank. Would it be possible to teach a child who was as scared as that?

I went on quickly, before she had time to answer: "When we were your age my sister and I were keen riders. She was two years younger than I and we used to compete together in the local shows. The exciting days in our lives were those when there was a horse show in our village."

"They have them here," she said.

"It's great fun. And once you've really mastered the trick, you feel quite at home in the saddle."

She was silent for a moment, then she said: "I can't do it. I don't like horses."

"You don't like horses!" My voice was shocked. "Why, they're
the gentlest creatures in the world."

"They're not. They don't like me. I rode Gray Mare and she ran
fast and wouldn't stop, and if Tapperty hadn't caught her rein she
would have killed me."

"Gray Mare wasn't the mount for you. You should have a pony
to start with."

"Then I had Buttercup. She was as bad in a different way. She
wouldn't go when I tried to make her. She took a mouthful of the
bushes on the bank and I tugged and tugged and she wouldn't move
for me. When Billy Trehay said 'Come on, Buttercup,' she just let
go and started walking away as though it were all my fault."

I laughed and she threw me a look of hatred. I hastened to assure
her that was the way horses behaved until they understood you. When
they did understand you they loved you as though you were their
very dear friend.

I saw the wistful look in her eyes then and I exulted because I
knew that the reason for aggressiveness was to be found in her intense loneliness and desire for affection.

I said: "Look here, Alvean, come out with me now. Let's see what
we can do together."

She shook her head and looked at me suspiciously. I knew she felt
that I might be trying to punish her for her ungraciousness toward me
by making her look foolish. I wanted to put my arm about her, but I
knew that was no way to approach Alvean.

"There's one thing to learn before you can begin to ride," I said
as though I had not noticed her gesture, "and that is to love your
horse. Then you won't be afraid. As soon as you're not afraid, your
horse will begin to love you. He'll know you're his master, and he
wants a master; but it must be a tender, loving master."

She was giving me her attention now.

"When a horse runs away as Gray Mare did, that means that she is
frightened. She's as frightened as you are, and her way of showing it
is to run. Now when you're frightened you should never let her
know it. You just whisper to her, 'It's all right, Gray Mare . . . I'm
here.' As for Buttercup—she's a mischievous old nag. She's lazy and
and she knows that you can't handle her, so she won't do as she's told.
But once you let her know you're the master, she'll obey. Look how
she did with Billy Trehay!"

"I didn't know Gray Mare was frightened of me," she said.

"Your father wants you to ride," I told her.

It was the wrong thing to have said; it reminded her of past fears, past humiliations; I saw the stubborn fear return to her eyes, and felt a new burst of resentment toward that arrogant man who could be so careless of the feelings of a child.

"Wouldn't it be fun," I said, "to surprise him? I mean . . . suppose you learned and you could jump and gallop, and he didn't know about it . . . until he saw you do it."

It hurt me to see the joy in her face and I wondered how any man could be so callous as to deny a child the affection she asked.

"Alvean," I said, "let's try."

"Yes," she said, "let's try. I'll go and change into my things."

I gave a little cry of disappointment, remembering that I had no riding habit with me. During my years with Aunt Adelaide I had had little opportunity for wearing it. Aunt Adelaide was no horsewoman herself and consequently was never invited to the country to hunt. Thus I had had no opportunities for riding. To ride in Rotten Row would have been far beyond my means. When I had last looked at my riding clothes I had seen that the moths had got at them. I had felt resigned. I believed that I should never need them again.

Alvean was looking at me and I told her: "I have no riding clothes."

Her face fell and then lit up. "Come with me," she said. She was almost conspiratorial, and I enjoyed this new relationship between us which I felt to be a great advance toward friendship.

We went along the gallery until we were in that part of the house which Mrs. Polgrey had told me was not for me. Alvean paused before a door and I had the impression that she was steeling herself to go in. She at length threw open the door and stood aside for me to enter, and I could not help feeling that she wanted me to go in first.

It was a small room which I judged to be a dressing room. In it was a long mirror, a tallboy, a chest of drawers, and an oak chest. Like most of the rooms in the house this room had two doors. These rooms in the gallery appeared to lead from one to another, and this other door was slightly opened and, as Alvean went to it and looked round the room beyond, I followed her.

It was a bedroom, a large room beautifully furnished, the floor carpeted in blue, the curtains of blue velvet; the bed was a four-poster and, although I knew it to be large, it was dwarfed by the size of the room.

Alvean seemed distressed to see my interest in the bedroom. She went to the communicating door and shut it.

"There are lots of clothes here," she said. "In the chests and the tallboy. There's bound to be riding clothes. There'll be something you can have."

She had thrown up the lid of the chest and it was something new for me to see her so excited. I was so delighted to have discovered a way to her affections that I allowed myself to be carried along.

In the chest were dresses, petticoats, hats, and boots.

Alvean said quickly: "There are a lot of clothes in the attics. Great trunks of them. They were Grandmamma's and Great-grandmamma's. When there were parties they used to dress up in them and play charades. . . ."

I held up a lady's black beaver hat—obviously meant to be worn for riding. I put it on my head and Alvean laughed with a little catch in her voice. That laughter moved me more than anything had since I had entered this house. It was the laughter of a child who is unaccustomed to laughter and laughs in a manner which is almost guilty. I determined to have her laughing often and without the slightest feeling of guilt.

She suddenly controlled herself as though she remembered where she was.

"You look so funny in it, miss," she said.

I got up and stood before the long mirror. I certainly looked unlike myself. My eyes were brilliant, my hair looked quite copper against the black. I decided that I looked slightly less unattractive than usual, and that was what Alvean meant by "funny."

"Not the least like a governess," she explained. She was pulling out a dress, and I saw that it was a riding habit made of black woollen cloth and trimmed with braid and ball fringe. It had a blue collar and blue cuffs and was elegantly cut.

I held it up against myself. "I think," I said, "that this would fit."

"Try it on," said Alvean. Then . . . "No, not here. You take it to your room and put it on." She suddenly seemed obsessed by the desire to get out of this room. She picked up the hat and ran to the door. I thought that she was eager for us to get started on our lesson, and there was not a great deal of time if we were to be back for tea at four.

I picked up the dress, took the hat from her, and went back to my room. She hurried through to hers, and I immediately put on the riding habit.

It was not a perfect fit, but I had never been used to expensive clothes and was prepared to forget that it was a little tight at the waist and that the sleeves were on the short side, for a new woman looked back at me from my mirror, and when I set the beaver hat on my head I was delighted with myself.

I ran along to Alvean's room; she was in her habit, and when she saw me her eyes lit up and she seemed to look at me with greater interest than ever before.

We went down to the stables and I told Billy Trehay to saddle Buttercup for Alvean and another horse for myself, as we were going to have a riding lesson.

He looked at me with some astonishment, but I told him that we had little time and were impatient to begin.

When we were ready I put Buttercup on a leading rein and, with Alvean on her, took her back into the paddock.

For nearly an hour we were there and when we left I knew that Alvean and I had entered into a new relationship. She had not accepted me completely—that would have been asking too much—but I did believe that from that afternoon she knew I was not an enemy.

I concentrated on giving her confidence. I made her grow accustomed to sitting her horse, to talking to her horse. I made her lean back full length on Buttercup's back and look up at the sky; then I made her shut her eyes. I gave her lessons in mounting and dismounting. Buttercup did no more than walk round that field, but I do believe that at the end of the hour I had done a great deal toward making Alvean lose her fear; and that was what I had determined should be the first lesson.

I was astonished to find that it was half past three, and I think Alvean was too.

"We must return to the house at once," I said, "if we are to change in time for tea."

As we came out of the field a figure rose from the grass and I saw to my surprise that it was Peter Nansellock.

He clapped his hands as we came along.

"Here endeth the first lesson," he cried, "and an excellent one. I did not know," he went on, turning to me, "that equestrian skill was included in your many accomplishments."

"Were you watching us, Uncle Peter?" demanded Alvean.

"For the last half hour. My admiration for you both is beyond expression."

Alvean smiled slowly. "Did you really admire us?"

"Much as I could be tempted to compliment two beautiful ladies," he said placing his hand on his heart and bowing elegantly, "I could never tell a lie."

"Until this moment," I said tartly.

Alvean's face fell and I added: "There is nothing very admirable in learning to ride. Thousands are doing it every day."

"But the art was never so gracefully taught, never so patiently learned."

"Your uncle is a joker, Alvean," I put in.

"Yes," said Alvean almost sadly, "I know."

"And," I added, "it is time that we returned for tea."

"I wonder if I might be invited to schoolroom tea?"

"You are calling to see Mr. TreMellyn?" I asked.

"I am calling to take tea with you two ladies."

Alvean laughed suddenly; I could see that she was not unaffected by what I supposed was the charm of this man.

"Mr. TreMellyn left Mount Mellyn early this afternoon," I said. "I have no idea whether or not he has returned."

"And while the cat's away . . ." he murmured, and his eyes swept over my costume in a manner which I could only describe as insolent.

I said coolly: "Come along, Alvean; we must go at once if we are to be in time for tea."

I let the horse break into a trot, and holding Buttercup's leading rein, started toward the house.

Peter Nansellock walked behind us, and when we reached the stables I saw him making for the house.

Alvean and I dismounted, handed our horses to two of the stable boys, and hurried up to our rooms.

I got out of the riding habit and into my dress and, glancing at myself, I thought how drab I looked in my gray cotton. I made a gesture of impatience at my folly and picked up the riding habit to hang in my cupboard, deciding that I would take the first opportunity of asking Mrs. Polgrey if it was in order for me to use it. I was afraid I had acted on impulse by doing so this afternoon, but I had been stung into prompt action, I realized, by the attitude of Connan TreMellyn.

As I lifted the habit I saw the name on the waistband. It gave me a little start, as I suppose everything in that connection would do for sometime. "Alice TreMellyn" was embossed in neat and tiny letters on the black satin facings.

Then I understood. That room had been her dressing room; the bedroom I had glimpsed, her bedroom. I wondered that Alvean had taken me there and given me her mother's clothes.

My heart felt as though it were leaping into my throat. This, I said to myself, is absurd. Where else could we have found a modern riding habit? Not in those chests in the attics she had spoken of; the clothes in those were used for charades.

I was being ridiculous. Why should I not wear Alice's riding habit? She had no need of it now. And was I not accustomed to wearing cast-off clothes?

Boldly I picked up the riding dress and hung it in my cupboard.

I was impelled to go to my window and looked along the line of windows, trying to place the one which would have been that of her bedroom. I thought I placed it.

In spite of myself I shivered. Then I shook myself. She would be glad I had used her habit, I told myself. Of course she would be glad. Am I not trying to help her daughter?

I realized that I was reassuring myself—which was ridiculous.

What had happened to my common sense? Whatever I told myself I could not hide the fact that I wished the dress had belonged to anyone but Alice.

⋘⧕⧕⧕⧕⋙

When I had changed there was a knock on my door and I was relieved to see Mrs. Polgrey standing there.

"Do come in," I said. "You are just the lady I wished to see."

She came sailing into my room, and I felt very fond of her in that moment. There was an air of normality about her such as must inevitably put fancy to flight.

"I have been giving Miss Alvean a riding lesson," I said quickly, for I was anxious to have this matter of the dress settled before she could tell me why she had come. "And as I had no riding habit with me she found one for me. I believe it to have been her mother's." I went to my wardrobe and produced it.

Mrs. Polgrey nodded.

"I wore it this once. Perhaps it was wrong of me."

"Did you have the master's permission to give her this riding lesson?"

"Oh yes, indeed. I made sure of that."

"Then there is nothing to worry about. He would have no objection to your wearing the dress. I can see no reason why you should not keep it in your room, providing of course you only wear it when giving Miss Alvean her riding lesson."

"Thank you," I said. "You have set my mind at rest."

Mrs. Polgrey bowed her head in approval. I could see that she was rather pleased that I had brought my little problem to her.

"Mr. Peter Nansellock is downstairs," she said.

"Yes, we saw him as we came in."

"The master is not at home. And Mr. Peter has asked that you entertain him for tea—you and Miss Alvean."

"Oh, but should we . . . I mean should I?"

"Well yes, miss, I think it would be in order. I think that is what the master would wish, particularly as Mr. Peter suggests it. Miss Jansen, during the time she was here, often helped to entertain. Why, there was an occasion I remember, when she was invited to the dinner table."

"Oh!" I said, hoping I sounded duly impressed.

"You see, miss, having no mistress in the house makes it a little difficult at times; and when a gentleman expressly asks for your company—well, I really don't see what harm there could be in it. I have told Mr. Nansellock that tea will be served in the punch room and that I am sure you will be ready to join him and Miss Alvean. You have no objection?"

"No, no. I have no objection."

Mrs. Polgrey smiled graciously. "Then will you come down?"

"Yes, I will."

She sailed out as majestically as she had arrived; and I found myself smiling not without a little complacence. It was turning out to be a most enjoyable day.

≈§§≈

When I reached the punch room, Alvean was not there, but Peter Nansellock was sprawling in one of the tapestry-covered chairs.

He leaped to his feet on my entrance.

"But this is delightful."

"Mrs. Polgrey has told me that I am to do the honors in the absence of Mr. TreMellyn."

"How like you, to remind me that you are merely the governess!"

"I felt," I replied, "that it was necessary to do so, since you may have forgotten."

"You are such a charming hostess! And indeed I never saw you look less like a governess than when you were giving Alvean her lesson."

"It was my riding habit. Borrowed plumes. A pheasant would look like a peacock if it could acquire the tail."

"My dear Miss Pheasant, I do not agree. 'Manners makyth the man'—or woman—not fine feathers. But let me ask you this before our dear little Alvean appears. What do you think of this place? You are going to stay with us?"

"It is really more a question of how this place likes me, and whether the powers that be decide to keep me."

"Ah—the powers that be in this case are a little unaccountable, are they not? What do you think of old Connan?"

"The adjective you use is inaccurate, and it is not my place to give an opinion."

He laughed aloud showing white and perfect teeth. "Dear governess," he said, "you'll be the death of me."

"I'm sorry to hear it."

"Though," he went on, "I have often thought that to die of laughing must be a very pleasant way to do so."

This banter was interrupted by the appearance of Alvean.

"Ah, the little lady herself!" cried Peter. "Dear Alvean, how good it is of you and Miss Leigh to allow me to take tea with you."

"I wonder why you want to," replied Alvean. "You never have before . . . except when Miss Jansen was here."

"Hush, hush! You betray me," he murmured.

Mrs. Polgrey came in with Kitty. The latter set the tray on a table, while Mrs. Polgrey lighted the spirit lamp. I saw that a canister of tea was on the tray. Kitty laid a cloth on a small table and brought in cakes and cucumber sandwiches.

"Miss, would you care to make the tea yourself?" asked Mrs. Polgrey.

I said I would do so with pleasure, and Mrs. Polgrey signed to Kitty, who was staring at Peter Nansellock with an expression close to idolatry.

Kitty seemed reluctant to leave the room and I felt it was unkind to have dismissed her. I believed that Mrs. Polgrey was also to some extent under the spell of the man. It must be, I told myself, because he is such a contrast to the master. Peter managed to flatter with a look, and I had noticed that he was ready to lavish this flattery on all females: Kitty, Mrs. Polgrey, and Alvean, no less than on me.

So much for its worth! I told myself and I felt a little piqued, for the man had that comforting quality of making any woman in his company feel that she was an attractive one.

I made tea and Alvean handed him bread and butter.

"What luxury!" he cried. "I feel like a sultan with two beautiful ladies to wait on me."

"You're telling lies again," cried Alvean. "We're neither of us ladies, because I'm not grown up and miss is a governess."

"What sacrilege!" he murmured, and his warm eyes were on me, almost caressingly. I felt uncomfortably embarrassed under his scrutiny.

I changed the conversation briskly. "I think Alvean will make a good horsewoman in time," I said. "What was your opinion?"

I saw how eagerly the girl waited on his words.

"She'll be the champion of Cornwall; you see!"

She could not hide her pleasure.

"And," he lifted a finger and wagged it at her—"don't you forget whom you have to thank for it."

The glance Alvean threw at me was almost shy, and I felt suddenly happy, and glad that I was here. My resentment against life had never been so far away; I had ceased to envy my charming sister. At that moment there was only one person I wanted to be: that person was Martha Leigh, sitting in the punch room taking tea with Peter Nansellock and Alvean TreMellyn.

Alvean said: "It's to be a secret for a while."

"Yes, we're going to surprise her father."

"I'll be silent as the grave."

"Why do people say 'silent as the grave'?" asked Alvean.

"Because," put in Peter, "dead men don't talk."

"Sometimes they have ghosts perhaps," said Alvean looking over her shoulder.

"What Mr. Nansellock meant," I said quickly, "was that he will keep our little secret. Alvean, I believe Mr. Nansellock would like some more cucumber sandwiches."

She leaped up to offer them to him; it was very pleasant to have her so docile and friendly.

"You have not paid a visit to Mount Widden yet, Miss Leigh," he said.

"It had not occurred to me to do so."

"That is a little unneighborly. Oh, I know what you're going to say. You did not come here to pay calls; you came to be a governess."

"It is true," I retorted.

"The house is not so ancient nor so large as this one. It has no history, but it's a pleasant place and I'm sure my sister would be de-

lighted if you and Alvean paid us a visit one day. Why not come over
and take tea with us?"

"I am not sure . . ." I began.

"That it lies within your duties? I'll tell you how we'll arrange it.
You shall bring Miss Alvean to take tea at Mount Widden. Bringing
her to us and taking her home again, I am sure, would come well
within the duties of the most meticulous governess."

"When shall we come?" asked Alvean.

"This is an open invitation."

I smiled. I knew what that meant. He was again talking for the
sake of talking; he had no intention of asking me to tea. I pictured
him, coming over to the house, attempting a flirtation with Miss Jansen who, by all accounts, was an attractive young woman. I knew his
sort, I told myself.

The door opened suddenly and to my embarrassment—which I
hoped I managed to hide—Connan TreMellyn came in.

I felt as though I had been caught playing the part of mistress of
the house in his absence.

I rose to my feet, and he gave me a quick smile. "Miss Leigh,"
he said, "is there a cup of tea for me?"

"Alvean," I said, "ring for another cup, please."

She got up to do so immediately but she had changed. Now she
was alert, eager to do the right thing and please her father. It made
her somewhat clumsy, and as she rose from her chair she knocked
over her cup of tea. She flushed scarlet with mortification.

I said: "Never mind. Ring the bell. Kitty will clear it up when she
comes."

I knew that Connan TreMellyn was watching with some amusement. If I had known he would return I should have been very reluctant to entertain Peter Nansellock at tea in the punch room, which
I was sure my employer felt was definitely not my part of the house.

Peter said: "It was most kind of Miss Leigh to act as hostess. I
begged her to do so, and she graciously consented."

"It was certainly kind," said Connan TreMellyn lightly.

Kitty came and I indicated the mess of tea and broken china on
the carpet. "And please bring another cup for Mr. TreMellyn," I
added.

Kitty was smirking a little as she went out. The situation evidently
amused her. As for myself, I felt it ill became me. I was not the type
to make charming play with the teacups and, now that the master

of the house had appeared, I felt awkward, even as I knew Alvean had. *I* must be careful to avoid disaster.

"Had a busy day, Connan?" asked Peter.

Connan TreMellyn then began to talk of complicated estate business, which I felt might have been to remind me that my duties consisted of dispensing tea and nothing else. I was not to imagine that I was in truth a hostess. I was there as an upper servant, nothing more.

I felt angry with him for coming in and spoiling my little triumph. I wondered how he would react when I presented him with the good little horsewoman I was determined Alvean was to become. He would probably make some slighting remark and show us such indifference that we should feel our trouble was wasted.

You poor child, I thought, you are trying to win the affections of a man who doesn't know the meaning of affection. Poor Alvean! Poor Alice!

Then it seemed to me that Alice had intruded into the punch room. In that moment I pictured her more clearly than I had ever done before. She was a woman of about my height, a little more slender at the waist—but then I had never gone in wholeheartedly for tight lacing—a trifle shorter. I could fit this figure into a black riding habit with blue collar and cuffs and black beaver hat. All that was vague and shadowy was the face.

The cup and saucer was brought to me and I poured out his tea. He was watching me, expecting me to rise and take it to him.

"Alvean," I said, "please pass this to your father."

And she was very eager to do so.

He said a brief "Thanks," and Peter took advantage of the pause to draw me into the conversation.

"Miss Leigh and I met on the train on the day she arrived."

"Really?"

"Indeed yes. Although of course she was not aware of my identity. How could she be? She had never heard then of the famous Nansellocks. She did not even know of the existence of Mount Widden. I knew her of course. By some strange irony of chance I shared her compartment."

"That," said Connan, "is very interesting." And he looked as though nothing could be less so.

"So," went on Peter, "it was a great surprise to her when she found that we were near neighbors."

"I trust," said Connan, "that it was not an unpleasant one."

"By no means," I said.

"Thank you, Miss Leigh, for those kind words," said Peter.

I looked at my watch, and said: "I am going to ask you to excuse Alvean and me. It is nearly five o'clock and we have our studies between five and six."

"And we must," said Connan, "on no account interfere with those."

"But surely," cried Peter, "on such an occasion there could be a little relaxation of the rules."

Alvean was looking eager. She was unhappy in her father's presence but she could not bear to leave him.

"I think it would be most unwise," I said, rising. "Come along, Alvean."

She threw me a look of dislike and I believed that I had forfeited the advance I had made that afternoon.

"Please, Papa . . ." she began.

He looked at her sternly. "My dear child, you heard what your governess said."

Alvean blushed and looked uncomfortable, but I was already saying "Good afternoon" to Peter Nansellock and making my way to the door.

In the schoolroom Alvean glared at me.

"Why do you have to spoil everything?" she demanded.

"Spoil?" I repeated. "Everything?"

"We could have done our reading any time . . . any time . . ."

"But we do our reading between five and six, not any time," I retorted, and my voice sounded the colder because I was afraid of the emotion which was rising in me. I wanted to explain to her: You love your father. You long for his approval. But, my dear child, you do not know the way to make it yours. Let me help you. But of course I said no such thing. I had never been demonstrative and could not begin to be so now.

"Come," I went on, "we have only an hour, so let us not waste a minute of that time."

She sat at the table sullenly glaring at the book which we were reading. It was Mr. Dickens's *Pickwick Papers* which I had thought would bring light relief into my pupil's rather serious existence.

She had lost her habitual enthusiasm; she was not even attending, for she looked up suddenly and said: "I believe you hate him. I believe you cannot bear to be in his company."

I replied: "I do not know to whom you refer, Alvean."

"You do," she accused. "You know I mean my father."

"What nonsense," I murmured; but I was afraid my color would deepen. "Come," I said, "we are wasting time."

And I concentrated on the book and told myself that we could not read together the nightly adventure concerning the elderly lady in curlpapers. That would be most unsuitable for a child of Alvean's age.

❦

That night when Alvean had retired to her room I went for a stroll in the woods. I was beginning to look upon these woods as a place of refuge, a place in which to be quiet and think about my life while I wondered what shape it would take.

The day had been eventful, a pleasant day until Connan Tre-Mellyn had come into it and disturbed the peace. I wondered if his business ever took him away for long periods—really long periods, not merely a matter of a few days. If this were so, I thought, I might have a chance of making Alvean into a happier little girl.

Forget the man, I admonished myself. Avoid him when possible. You can do no more than that.

It was all very well but, even when he was not present, he intruded into my thoughts.

I stayed in the woods until it was almost dusk. Then I made for the house, and I had not been in my room more than a few minutes when Kitty knocked.

"I thought I 'eard 'ee come in, miss," she said. "Master be asking for 'ee. He be in his library."

"Then you had better take me there," I said, "for it is a room I have never visited."

I should have liked to comb my hair and tidy myself a little, but I had a notion that Kitty was constantly looking for one aspect of the relationship between any man or woman and I was not going to have her thinking that I was preening myself before appearing before the master.

She led me to a wing of the house which I had as yet not visited, and the vastness of Mount Mellyn was brought home to me afresh. These, I gathered, were the apartments which were set aside for his special use, for they seemed more luxurious than any other part of the house which I had so far seen.

Kitty opened a door, and with that vacuous smile on her face announced: "Miss be here, master."

"Thank you, Kitty," he said. And then, "Oh, come along in, Miss Leigh."

He was sitting at a table on which were leatherbound books and papers. The only light came from a rose quartz lamp on the table.

He said: "Do sit down, Miss Leigh."

I thought: He has discovered that I wore Alice's riding habit. He is shocked. He is going to tell me that my services are no longer required.

I held my head high, even haughtily, waiting.

"I was interested to learn this afternoon," he began, "that you had already made the acquaintance of Mr. Nansellock."

"Really?" The surprise in my voice was not assumed.

"Of course," he went on, "it was inevitable that you would meet him sooner or later. He and his sister are constant visitors at the house, but . . ."

"But you feel that it is unnecessary that he should make the acquaintance of your daughter's governess," I said quickly.

"That necessity, Miss Leigh," he replied reprovingly, "is surely for you or him to decide."

I felt embarrassed and I stumbled on: "I imagine you feel that, as a governess, it is unbecoming of me to be . . . on terms of apparently equal footing with a friend of your family."

"I beg you, Miss Leigh, do not put words into my mouth which I had no intention of uttering. What friends you make, I do assure you, must be entirely your own concern. But your aunt, in a manner of speaking, put you under my care when she put you under my roof, and I have asked you to come here that I may offer you a word of advice on a subject which, I fear, you may think a little indelicate."

I was flushing scarlet and my embarrassment was not helped by the fact that this, I was sure, secretly amused him.

"Mr. Nansellock has a reputation for being . . . how shall I put it . . . susceptible to young ladies."

"Oh!" I cried, unable to suppress the exclamation, so great was my discomfort.

"Miss Leigh." He smiled, and for a moment his face looked almost tender. "This is in the nature of a warning."

"Mr. TreMellyn," I cried, recovering myself with an effort, "I do not think I am in need of such a warning."

"He is very handsome," he went on, and the mocking note had come back to his voice. "He has a reputation for being a charming fellow. There was a young lady here before you, a Miss Jansen.

He often called to see her. Miss Leigh, I do beg of you not to mis-understand me. And there is another thing I would also ask: Please do not take all that Mr. Nansellock says too seriously."

I heard myself say in a high-pitched voice unlike my habitual tone: "It is extremely kind of you, Mr. TreMellyn, to concern yourself with my welfare."

"But of course I concern myself with your welfare. You are here to look after my daughter. Therefore it is of the utmost importance to me."

He rose and I did the same. I saw that this was dismissal.

He came swiftly to my side and placed his hand on my shoulder.

"Forgive me," he said. "I'm a blunt man, lacking in those graces which are so evident in Mr. Nansellock. I merely wish to offer you a friendly warning."

For a few seconds I looked into those cool light eyes and I thought I had a fleeting glimpse of the man behind the mask. I was sobered suddenly and, in a moment of bewildering emotion, I was deeply conscious of my loneliness, of the tragedy of those who are alone in the world with no one who really cares for them. Perhaps it was self-pity. I do not know. My feelings in that moment were so mixed that I cannot even at this day define them.

"Thank you," I said; and I escaped from the library back to my room.

❧

Each day Alvean and I went to the field and had an hour's riding. As I watched the little girl on Buttercup I knew that her father must have been extremely impatient with her, for the child, though not a born rider perhaps, would soon be giving a good account of herself.

I had discovered that every November a horse show was held in Mellyn village, and I had told Alvean that she should certainly enter for one of the events.

It was enjoyable planning this, because Connan TreMellyn would be one of the judges and we both imagined his astonishment when a certain rider, who came romping home with first prize, was his daughter who he had sworn would never learn to ride.

The triumph in that dream was something Alvean and I could both share. Hers was of course the more admirable emotion. She wanted to succeed for the sake of the love she bore her father; for myself I wanted to imply: See, you arrogant man, I have succeeded where you failed!

So every afternoon, I would put on Alice's riding habit (I had ceased to care to whom it had previously belonged, for it had become mine now) and we would go to the field and there I would put Alvean through her paces.

On the day we tried her first gallop we were elated.

Afterward we returned to the house together and because I was with her I went in by way of the front entrance, as I had when I had first arrived at the house.

No sooner were we in the hall than Alvean ran from me and left by that door through which Mrs. Polgrey had taken me. I followed her and as I passed out of the hall I noticed a damp, musty smell and saw that the door leading to the chapel was slightly ajar. Thinking that Alvean had gone in there, I went in. It was cold in the place, and I shivered as I stood on the blue flagstones and gazed at the altar and the pews.

I had taken a few steps inside the room and was standing with my back to the door when I heard a gasp behind me and a quick intake of breath.

"No!" said a voice, so horrified that I did not recognize it.

For some unaccountable reason my whole body seemed to freeze. I turned sharply, but it was only Celestine Nansellock who stood looking at me.

She was so white that I thought she was going to faint—or perhaps it was the dimness of the chapel which made her appear so. I thought I understood. She had seen me in Alice's riding habit and she had believed in that second that I *was* Alice.

"Miss Nansellock," I said quickly to reassure her, "Alvean and I have been having a riding lesson."

She swayed a little; her face was now a grayish color.

"I'm sorry I startled you," I went on.

"I wondered who was here," she said almost sharply. "Whatever made you come into the chapel?"

"I came in this way with Alvean. She ran off and I thought she might be in here."

"Alvean! Oh no . . . no one ever comes in here. It's a gloomy place, don't you think? Let's go."

"You look . . . unwell, Miss Nansellock. Would you like me to ring for some brandy?"

"Oh, no . . . no. I'm perfectly well."

I said boldly: "You're looking at my clothes. They're . . . borrowed. I have to give Alvean riding lessons and I lacked the suitable clothes. These were . . . her mother's."

"I see."

"I did explain to Mrs. Polgrey, who thought it was quite in order for me to use them."

"Of course. Why not?"

"I'm afraid I startled you."

"Oh no, you mustn't say that. I'm quite all right. It's the light in the chapel. It makes us all look so ghastly. You yourself look a little pale, Miss Leigh. It's those windows . . . that particular type of stained glass. It plays havoc with our complexions." She laughed. "Let's get out of here."

We went down the few steps and back to the hall, and then out of the house. I noticed that she had regained her normal color.

She had been shocked to see me. I told myself I knew why. She had seen the back of me in Alice's riding clothes and she had thought for the moment that it was Alice standing there.

"Does Alvean enjoy her riding lessons?" she asked. "Tell me, are you getting along with her better now? I fancied when you arrived there was a little antagonism on her part."

"She is the kind of child who would automatically be antagonistic to authority. Yes, I think we are becoming friends. These riding lessons have helped considerably. By the way, they are a secret from her father."

Celestine Nansellock looked a little shocked, and I hurried on: "Oh, it is only her good progress which is a secret. He knows about the lessons. Naturally I asked his permission first. But he does not realize how well she is coming along. It is to be a surprise."

"I see. Miss Leigh, I do hope she is not overstrained by these lessons."

"Overstrained? But why? She is a normal, healthy child."

"She is highly strung. I wonder whether she is of the temperament to make a rider."

"She is so young that we have a chance of forming her character which will have its effect on her temperament. She is enjoying her lessons and is very eager to surprise her father."

"So she is becoming your friend, Miss Leigh. I am glad of that. Now I must go. I was just on my way out when I passed the chapel and saw the door open."

I said good-by to her and went up to my room by the usual way. I went to a mirror and looked at myself. I'm afraid this was becoming a habit since I had come here. I murmured: "That might be Alice . . . apart from the face." Then I half-closed my eyes and let the face become blurred while I imagined a different face there.

Oh yes, it must have been a shock for Celestine.

I wondered then what Connan TreMellyn would say if he knew that I was going about in his wife's clothes and had frightened practical people like Celestine Nansellock when they saw me in dim places.

I felt he would not wish me to continue to look like Alice.

But since I needed Alice's clothes for my riding lessons with Alvean, and since I was determined that those lessons should continue—that I might have the pleasure of saying: "I told you so!" to Alvean's father—I was as anxious, as I was sure Celestine Nansellock was, that nothing should be said about our encounter in the chapel.

◈

A week passed and I felt I was slipping into a routine. Lessons in the schoolroom and the riding field progressed favorably. Peter Nansellock came over to the house on two occasions, but I managed to elude him. I was deeply conscious of Connan TreMellyn's warning and I knew it to be reasonable. I faced the fact that I was stimulated by Peter Nansellock and that I could very easily find myself in a state of mind when I was looking forward to his visits. I had no intention of placing myself in that position, for I did not need Connan TreMellyn to tell me that Peter Nansellock was a philanderer.

I thought now and then of his brother Geoffry, and I concluded that Peter must be very like him; and when I thought of Geoffry I thought also of Mrs. Polgrey's daughter of whom she had never spoken: Jennifer with "the littlest waist you ever saw," and a way of keeping herself to herself until she had lain in the hay or the gillyflowers with the fascinating Geoffry—the outcome of which had been that one day she walked into the sea.

I shivered to contemplate the terrible pitfalls which lay in wait for unwary women. There were unattractive ones like myself who depended on the whims of others for a living; but there were those even more unfortunate creatures who attracted the roving eyes of philanderers and found one day that the only bearable prospect life had to offer was its end.

My interest in Alvean's riding lessons and her father's personality had made me forget little Gillyflower temporarily. The child was so quiet that she was easily forgotten. Occasionally I heard her thin reedy voice, in that peculiar off key, singing out of doors or in the house. The Polgreys' room was immediately below my own, and Gillyflower's was next to theirs, so that when she sang in her own room her voice would float up to me.

I used to say to myself when I heard it: If she can learn songs she can learn other things.

I must have been given to daydreams, for side by side with that picture of Connan TreMellyn, handing his daughter the first prize for horse-jumping at the November horse show and giving me an apologetic and immensely admiring and appreciative glance at the same time, there was another picture. This was of Gilly sitting at the schoolroom table side by side with Alvean, while I listened to whispering in the background: "This could never have happened but for Miss Martha Leigh. You see she is a wonder with the children. Look what she has done for Alvean . . . and now for Gilly."

But at this time Alvean was still a stubborn child and Gillyflower, elusive and, as the Tapperty girls said: "With a tile loose in the upper story."

Then into those more or less peaceful days came two events to disturb me.

The first was of small moment, but it haunted me and I could not get it out of my mind.

I was going through one of Alvean's exercise books, marking her sums, while she was sitting at the table writing an essay; and as I turned the pages of the exercise book a piece of paper fell out.

It was covered with drawings. I had already discovered that Alvean had a distinct talent for drawing, and one day, when the opportunity offered itself, I intended to approach Connan TreMellyn about this, for I felt she should be encouraged. I myself could teach her only the rudiments of the art, but I believed she was worth a qualified drawing teacher.

The drawings were of faces. I recognized one of myself. It was not bad. Did I really look as prim as that? Not always, I hoped. But perhaps that was how she saw me. There was her father . . . several of him. He was quite recognizable too. I turned the page and this was covered with girls' faces. I was not sure who they were meant to be. Herself? No . . . that was Gilly, surely. And yet it had a look of herself.

I stared at the page. I was so intent that I did not realize she had leaned across the table until she snatched it away.

"That's mine," she said.

"And that," I retaliated, "is extremely bad manners."

"You have no right to pry."

"My dear child, that paper was in your arithmetic book."

"Then it had no right to be there."

"You must take your revenge on the paper," I said lightly. And then more seriously: "I do beg of you not to snatch things in that ill-mannered way."

"I'm sorry," she murmured still defiantly.

I turned back to the sums, to most of which she had given inaccurate answers. Arithmetic was not one of her best subjects. Perhaps that was why she spent so much of her time drawing faces instead of getting on with her work. Why had she been so annoyed? Why had she drawn those faces which were part Gilly's, part her own?

I said: "Alvean, you will have to work harder at your sums."

She grunted sullenly.

"You don't seem to have mastered the rules of practice nor even simple multiplication. Now if your arithmetic were half as good as your drawing I should be very pleased."

Still she did not answer.

"Why did you not wish me to see the faces you had drawn? I thought some of them quite good."

Still no answer.

"Particularly," I went on, "that one of your father."

Even at such a time the mention of his name could bring that tender, wistful curve to her lips.

"And those girls' faces. Do tell me who they were supposed to be —you or Gilly?"

The smile froze on her lips. Then she said almost breathlessly: "Who did you take them for, miss?"

"Whom," I corrected gently.

"*Whom* did you take them for then?"

"Well, let me look at them again."

She hesitated, then she brought out the paper, and handed it to me; her eyes were eager.

I studied the faces. I said: "This one could be either you or Gilly."

"You think we're alike then?"

"No-no. I hadn't thought so until this moment."

"And now you do," she said.

"You are of an age, and there often seems to be a resemblance between young people."

"I'm not like her!" she cried passionately. "I'm not like that . . . idiot."

"Alvean, you must not use such a word. Don't you realize that it is extremely unkind?"

"It's true. But I'm not like her. I won't have you say it. If you say it again I'll ask my father to send you away. He will . . . if I ask him. I only have to ask and you'll go."

She was shouting, trying to convince herself of two things, I realized. One that there was not the slightest resemblance between herself and Gilly, and the other that she only had to ask her father for something and her wishes would be granted.

Why? I asked myself. What was the reason for this vehemence?

There was a shut-in expression on her face.

I said, calmly looking at the watch pinned to my gray cotton bodice: "You have exactly ten minutes in which to finish your essay."

I drew the arithmetic book toward me and pretended to give it my attention.

~~~~~

The second incident was even more upsetting.

It had been a moderately peaceful day, which meant that lessons had gone well. I had taken my late evening stroll in the woods and when I returned I saw two carriages drawn up in front of the house. One I recognized as from Mount Widden, so I guessed that either Peter or Celestine was visiting. The other carriage I did not know, but I noticed the crest on it, and it was a very fine carriage. I wondered to whom it belonged before I told myself that it was no concern of mine.

I went swiftly up the back stairs and to my apartment.

It was a warm night and as I sat at my window I heard music coming from another of the open windows. I realized that Connan TreMellyn was entertaining guests.

I pictured them in one of the rooms which I had not even seen. Why should you? I asked myself. You are only a governess. Connan TreMellyn, his gaunt body clothed elegantly, would be presiding at the card table or perhaps sitting with his guests listening to music.

I recognized the music as from Mendelssohn's "Midsummer Night's Dream" and I felt a sudden longing to be down there among them; but I was astonished that this desire should be greater than any I had ever had to be present at Aunt Adelaide's *soirées* or the dinner parties Phillida gave. I was overcome with curiosity and could not resist the temptation to ring the bell and summon Kitty or Daisy who always knew what was going on and were only too happy to impart that knowledge to anyone who was interested to hear it.

It was Daisy who came. She looked excited.

I said: "I want some hot water, Daisy. Could you please bring it for me?"

"Why yes, miss," she said.

"There are guests here tonight, I understand."

"Oh yes, miss. Though it's nothing to the parties we used to have. I reckon now the year's up, the master will be entertaining more. That's what Mrs. Polgrey says."

"It must have been very quiet during the last year."

"But only right and proper . . . after a death in the family."

"Of course. Who are the guests tonight?"

"Oh, there's Miss Celestine and Mr. Peter of course."

"I saw their carriage." My voice sounded eager and I was ashamed. I was no better than any gossiping servant.

"Yes, and I'll tell you who else is here."

"Who?"

"Sir Thomas and Lady Treslyn."

She looked conspiratorial as though there was something very important about these two.

"Oh?" I said encouragingly.

"Though," went on Daisy, "Mrs. Polgrey says that Sir Thomas bain't fit to go gallivanting at parties, and should be abed."

"Why, is he ill?"

"Well, he'll never see seventy again and he's got one of those bad hearts. Mrs. Polgrey says you can go off sudden with a heart like that, and don't need no pushing neither. Not that——"

She stopped and twinkled at me. I longed to ask her to continue, but felt it was beneath my dignity to do so. Disappointingly she seemed to pull herself up sharply.

"*She's* another kettle of fish."

"Who?"

"Why, Lady Treslyn of course. You ought to see her. She's got a gown cut right down to here and the loveliest flowers on her shoulder. She's a real beauty, and you can see she's only waiting . . ."

"I gather she is not of the same age as her husband."

Daisy giggled. "They say there's nearly forty years' difference in their ages, and she'd like to pretend it was fifty."

"You don't seem to like her."

"Me? Well, if I don't, some do!" That sent Daisy into hysterical
laughter again, and as I looked at her ungainly form in her tight
clothes and listened to her wheezy laughter, I was ashamed of myself for sharing the gossip of a servant, so I said: "I *would* like that
hot water, Daisy."

Daisy subsided and went off to get it, leaving me with a clearer
picture of what was happening in that drawing room.

I was still thinking of them when I had washed my hands and un-
pinned my hair preparatory to retiring for the night.

The musicians had been playing a Chopin waltz and it had seemed
to spirit me away from my governess's bedroom and tantalize me
with pleasures outside my reach—a dainty beauty, a place in salons
such as that somewhere in this house, wit, charm, the power to make
the chosen man love me.

I was startled at such thoughts. What had they to do with a governess such as I?

I went to the window. The weather had been fine and warm for so
long that I did not believe it could continue. The autumn mists
would soon be with us and I had heard that they and the gales which
blew from the southwest were, as Tapperty would say, "something
special in these parts."

I could smell the sea and hear the gentle rhythm of the waves.
The "voices" were starting up in Mellyn Cove.

And then suddenly I saw a light in a dark part of the house and
I felt the goose pimples rise on my flesh. I knew that window belonged to the room to which Alvean had taken me to choose my
riding habit. It was Alice's dressing room.

The blind had been down. I had not noticed that before. Indeed
I was sure it had not been like that earlier in the evening because,
since I had known that that was Alice's room, I had made a habit—
which I regretted and of which I had tried to cure myself—of glancing at the window whenever I looked out of my own.

The blind was of thin material, for behind it I distinctly saw the
light. It was a faint light but there was no mistaking it. It moved before
my astonished eyes.

I stood at my window staring out and, as I did so, I saw a shadow
on the blind. It was that of a women.

I heard a voice close to me saying: "It is Alice!" and I realized
that I had spoken aloud.

I'm dreaming, I told myself. I'm imagining this.

Then again I saw the figure silhouetted against the blind.

My hands which gripped the window sill were trembling as I watched that flickering light. I had an impulse to summon Daisy or Kitty, or go to Mrs. Polgrey.

I restrained myself, imagining how foolish I should look. So I remained staring at the window.

And after a while all was darkness.

I stood at my window for a long time watching, but I saw nothing more.

They were playing another Chopin waltz in the drawing room, and I stood until I was cold even on that warm September night.

Then I went to bed but I could not sleep for a long time.

And at last, when I did sleep, I dreamed that a woman came into my room; she was wearing a riding habit with blue collar and cuffs, trimmed with braid and ball fringe. She said to me: "I was not on that train, Miss Leigh. You wonder where I was. It is for you to find me."

Through my dreams I heard the whispering of the waves in the caves below; and the first thing I did on rising next morning—which I did as soon as the dawn appeared in the sky—was to go to my window and look across at the room which—little more than a year ago—had belonged to Alice.

The blinds were drawn up. I could clearly see the rich blue velvet curtains.

4

It was about a week later that I first saw Linda Treslyn.

It was a few minutes past six o'clock. Alvean and I had put away our books and had gone down to the stables to look at Buttercup, who we thought had strained a tendon that afternoon.

The farrier had seen her and given her a poultice. Alvean was really upset, and this pleased me because I was always delighted to discover her softer feelings.

"Don't 'ee fret, Miss Alvean," Joe Tapperty told her. "Buttercup'll be as right as two dogs on a bright and frosty morning afore the week's out; you see! Jim Bond, he be the best horse doctor between here and Land's End, I do tell 'ee."

She was cheered and I told her that she should take Black Prince in Buttercup's place tomorrow.

She was excited about this, for she knew Black Prince would test her mettle, and I was glad to see that her pleasure was only faintly tinged with apprehension.

As we came out of the stables I looked at my watch.

"Would you care for half an hour's stroll through the gardens?" I asked. "We have half an hour to spare."

To my surprise she said she would, and we set off.

The plateau on which Mount Mellyn stood was a piece of land a mile or so wide. The slope to the sea was steep but there were several zigzag paths which made the going easier. The gardeners spent a great deal of time on this garden, which was indeed beautiful with the flowering shrubs which grew so profusely in this part. At various points arbors had been set up, constructed of trellis work around which roses climbed. They were beautiful even as late as this and their perfume hung on the air.

One could sit in these arbors and gaze out to sea; and from these gardens the south side of the house was a vision of grandeur, rising nobly, a pile of gray granite there on the top of the cliff like a mighty fortress. It was inevitable that the house should have a defiant air, as though it represented a challenge, not only to the sea but to the world.

We made our way down those sweet-smelling paths and were level with the arbor before we noticed that two people were there.

Alvean gave a little gasp and, following her gaze, I saw them. They were sitting side by side and close. She was very dark and one of the most beautiful women I had ever seen; her features were strongly marked and she wore a gauzy scarf over her hair, and in this gauze sequins glistened. I thought that she looked like someone out of *A Midsummer Night's Dream*—Titania perhaps, although I had always imagined her fair. She had that quality of beauty which attracts the eyes as a needle is attracted by a magnet. You have to look whether you want to or not; you have to admire. Her dress was pale mauve of some clinging material such as chiffon and it was caught at the throat with a big diamond brooch.

Connan spoke first. "Why," he said, "it is my daughter with her governess. So, Miss Leigh, you and Alvean are taking the air."

"It is such a pleasant evening," I said, and I made to take Alvean's hand, but she eluded me in her most ungracious manner.

"May I sit with you and Lady Treslyn, Papa?" she asked.

"You are taking a walk with Miss Leigh," he said. "Do you not think that you should continue to do so?"

"Yes," I answered for her. "Come along, Alvean."

Connan had turned to his companion: "We are very fortunate to have found Miss Leigh. She is . . . admirable!"

"The perfect governess this time, I hope for your sake, Connan," said Lady Treslyn.

I felt awkward, as though I were in the position of a horse standing there while they discussed my points. I was sure he was aware of my discomfiture and rather amused by it. There were times when I believed he was a very unpleasant person.

I said, and my voice sounded very chilly: "I think it is time we turned back. We were merely taking an airing before Alvean retires for the night. Come, Alvean," I added. And I seized her arm so firmly that I drew her away.

"But," protested Alvean, "I want to stay. I want to talk to you, Papa."

"But you can see I am engaged. Some other time, my child."

"No," she said, "it is important . . . now."

"It cannot be all that important. Let us discuss it tomorrow."

"No . . . no . . . Now!" Alvean's voice had a hysterical note in it; I had never before known her defy him so utterly.

Lady Treslyn murmured: "I see Alvean is a very determined person."

Connan TreMellyn said coolly: "Miss Leigh will deal with this matter."

"Of course. The perfect governess . . ." There was a note of mockery in Lady Treslyn's voice, and it goaded me to such an extent that I seized Alvean's arm roughly and almost dragged her back the way we had come.

She was half-sobbing, but she did not speak until we were in the house.

Then she said: "I hate her. You know, don't you, Miss Leigh, that she wants to be my new mamma."

I said nothing then. I thought it dangerous to do so because I always felt that it was so easy to be overheard. It was only when we reached her room and I had followed her in and shut the door that I said: "That was an extraordinary remark to make. How could she wish to be your mamma when she has a husband of her own?"

"He will soon die."

"How can you know that?"

"Everybody says they are only waiting."

I was shocked that she should have heard such gossip and I thought: I will speak to Mrs. Polgrey about this. They must be careful what they say in front of Alvean. Is it those girls, Daisy and Kitty . . . or perhaps Joe Tapperty or his wife?

"She's always here," went on Alvean. "I won't let her take my mother's place. I won't let anybody."

"You are becoming quite hysterical about improbabilities, and I must insist that you never allow me to hear you say such things again. It is degrading to your papa."

That made her thoughtful. How she loves him! I thought. Poor little Alvean, poor lonely child!

A little while before, I had been sorry for myself as I stood in that beautiful garden and was forced to be quizzed by the beautiful woman in the arbor. I had said to myself: "It is not fair. Why should one person have so much, and others nothing? Should I be beautiful in chiffon and diamonds? Perhaps not as Lady Treslyn was, but I am sure they would be more becoming than cotton and merino and a turquoise brooch which had belonged to my grandmother."

Now I forgot to be sorry for myself, and my pity was all for Alvean.

❦

I had seen Alvean to bed and had returned to my room, conscious of a certain depression. I kept thinking of Connan TreMellyn out there in the arbor with Lady Treslyn, asking myself if he were still there and what they talked about. Each other! I supposed. Of course Alvean and I had interrupted a flirtation. I felt shocked that he should indulge in such an undignified intrigue, for it seemed wholly undignified to me, since the lady had a husband to whom she owed her allegiance.

I went to the window and I was glad that it did not give me a view of the south gardens and the sea. I leaned my elbows on the sill and looked out at the scented evening. It was not quite dark yet, but the sun had disappeared and the twilight was on us. My eyes turned to the window where I had seen the shadow on the blind.

The blinds were drawn up and I could see the blue curtains clearly. I stared at them, fixedly. I don't know what I expected. Was it to see a face appear at the window, a beckoning hand? There were times when I could laugh at myself for my fancies, but the twilight hour was not one of them.

Then I saw the curtains move, and I knew that someone was in that room.

I was in an extraordinary mood that evening. It had something to do with meeting Connan TreMellyn and Lady Treslyn together in the arbor, but I had not sufficiently analyzed my feelings at this date to understand it. I felt our recent encounter to have been humiliating, but I was ready to risk another which might be more so. Alice's room was not in my part of the house but I was completely at liberty to walk in the gardens if I wished to. If I were caught I should look rather foolish. But I was reckless. I did not care. Thoughts of Alice obsessed me. There were times when I felt such a burning desire to discover what mystery lay behind her death that I was prepared to go to any lengths.

So I slipped out of my room. I left my wing of the house and went along the gallery to Alice's dressing room. I knocked lightly on the door and, with my heart beating like a sledge hammer, I swiftly opened it.

For a second I saw no one. Then I detected a movement by the curtains. Someone was hiding behind them.

"Who is it?" I asked, and my voice successfully hid the trepidation I was feeling.

There was no answer, but whoever was behind those curtains was very eager not to be discovered.

I strode across the room, drew aside the curtains, and saw Gilly cowering there.

The lids of her blank blue eyes fluttered in a terrified way. I put out a hand to seize her and she shrank from me toward the window.

"It's all right, Gilly," I said gently. "I won't hurt you."

She continued to stare at me, and I went on: "Tell me, what are you doing here?"

Still she said nothing. She had begun to stare about the room as though she were asking someone for help, and for a moment I had the uncanny feeling that she *saw* something—or someone—I could not see.

"Gilly," I said, "you know you should not be in this room, do you not?" She drew farther away from me, and I repeated what I had said.

Then she nodded and immediately afterward shook her head.

"I am going to take you back to my room, Gilly. Then we'll have a little talk."

I put my arm about her; she was trembling. I drew her to the door but she came very reluctantly, and at the threshold of the room she looked back over her shoulder; then she cried out suddenly: "Madam . . . come back, madam. Come . . . *now!*"

I led her firmly from the room and shut the door behind us, then almost had to drag her along to my bedroom.

Once there I firmly shut my door and stood with my back against it. Her lips were trembling.

"Gilly," I said, "I do want you to understand that I won't hurt you. I want to be your friend." The blank look persisted and taking a shot in the dark I went on: "I want to be your friend as Mrs. TreMellyn was."

That startled her and the blank look disappeared for a moment. I had stumbled on another discovery. Alice had been kind to this poor child.

"You went there to look for Mrs. TreMellyn, did you not?"

She nodded.

She looked so pathetic that I was moved to a demonstration of feeling unusual with me. I knelt down and put my arms about her; now our faces were level.

"You can't find her, Gilly. She is dead. It is no use looking for her in this house."

Gilly nodded and I was not sure what she implied—whether she agreed with me that it was no use, or whether she believed that she could find Mrs. TreMellyn in the house.

"So," I went on, "we must try to forget her, mustn't we, Gilly?"

The pale lids fell over the eyes to hide them from me.

"We'll be friends," I said. "I want us to be. If we were friends, you wouldn't be lonely, would you?"

She shook her head, and I fancied that the eyes which surveyed me had lost something of their blankness; she was not trembling now, and I was sure that she was no longer afraid of me.

Then suddenly she slipped out of my grasp and ran to the door. I did not pursue her and, as she opened the door and turned to look back at me, there was a faint smile on her lips. Then she was gone.

I believed that I had established a little friendliness between us. I believed that she had lost her fear of me.

Then I thought of Alice, who had been kind to this child. I was beginning to build up the picture of Alice more clearly in my mind.

I went to the window and looked across the L-shaped building to the window of the room, and I thought of that night when I had seen the shadow on the blind.

My discovery of Gilly did not explain that. It was no child I had seen silhouetted there. It had been a woman.

Gilly might hide herself in Alice's room, but the shadow I had seen on the blind that night did not belong to her.

◈

It was the next day when I went to Mrs. Polgrey's room for a cup of tea. She was delighted to invite me. "Mrs. Polgrey," I had said, "I have a matter which I feel to be of some importance, and I should very much like to discuss this with you."

She bridled with pride. I could see that the governess who sought her advice must be, in her eyes, the ideal governess.

"I shall be delighted to give you an hour of my company and a cup of my best Earl Grey," she told me.

Over the tea cups she surveyed me with an expression bordering on the affectionate.

"Now, Miss Leigh, pray tell me what it is you would ask of me."

"I am a little disturbed," I told her, stirring my tea thoughtfully. "It is due to a remark of Alvean's. I am sure that she listens to gossip, and I think it most undesirable in a child of her age."

"Or in any of us, as I am sure a young lady of your good sense would feel," replied Mrs. Polgrey with what I could not help feeling was a certain amount of hypocrisy.

I told her how we had walked in the cliff gardens and met the master with Lady Treslyn. "And then," I went on, "Alvean made this offensive remark. She said that Lady Treslyn hoped to become her mamma."

Mrs. Polgrey shook her head. She said: "What about a spoonful of whisky in your tea, miss? There's nothing like it for keeping up the spirits."

I had no desire for the whisky but I could see that Mrs. Polgrey had, and she would have been disappointed if I had refused to join her in her tea tippling, so I said: "A small teaspoonful, please, Mrs. Polgrey."

She unlocked the cupboard, took out the bottle and measured out the whisky even more meticulously than she measured her tea. I found myself wondering what other stores she kept in that cupboard of hers.

Now we were like a pair of conspirators and Mrs. Polgrey was clearly enjoying herself.

"I fear you will find it somewhat shocking, miss," she began.

"I am prepared," I assured her.

"Well, Sir Thomas Treslyn is a very old man and only a few years ago he married this young lady, a play-actress, some say, from London. Sir Thomas went there on a visit and returned with her. Her set the neighborhood agog, I can tell you, miss."

"I can well believe that."

"There's some that say she's one of the handsomest women in the country."

"I can believe that too."

"Handsome is as handsome does."

"But it remains handsome outwardly," I added.

"And men can be foolish. The master has his weakness," admitted Mrs. Polgrey.

"If there is gossip I am most anxious that it shall not reach Alvean's ears."

"Of course you are, miss. But gossip there is, and that child's got ears like a hare's."

"Do you think Daisy and Kitty chatter?"

Mrs. Polgrey came closer and I smelled the whisky on her breath. I was startled, wondering whether she could smell it on mine. "Everybody chatters, miss."

"I see."

"There's some as say that they'm not the sort to wait for blessing of clergy."

"Well, perhaps they are not."

I felt wretched. I hate this, I told myself. It's so sordid. So horrible for a sensitive girl like Alvean.

"The master is impulsive by nature and in his way he is fond of the women."

"So you think . . ."

She nodded gravely. "When Sir Thomas dies there'll be a new mistress in this house. All they have to wait for now is for him to go. Mrs. TreMellyn, her . . . her's already gone."

I did not want to ask the question which came to my lips but it seemed as though there were some force within me which would not let me avoid it. "And was it so . . . when Mrs. TreMellyn was alive?"

Mrs. Polgrey nodded slowly. "He visited her often. It started almost as soon as she came. Sometimes he rides out at night and we don't see him till morning. Well, he'm master and 'tis for him to make his own rules. 'Tis for us to cook and dust and housekeep, or teach the child . . . whatsoever we'm here for. And there's an end of it."

"So you think that Alvean is only repeating what everyone knows? When Sir Thomas dies Lady Treslyn *will* be her new mamma."

"There's some of us that thinks it's more than likely, and some that wouldn't be sorry to see it. Her ladyship's not the kind to interfere much with our side of the house; and 'tis better to have these things regularized, so I do say." She went on piously: "I'd sooner see the master of the house I serve living in wedlock than in sin, I do assure you. And so would we all."

"Could we warn the girls not to chatter, before Alvean, of these matters?"

"As well try to keep a cuckoo from singing in the spring. I could wallop them two till I dropped with exhaustion and still they'd gossip. They can't help it. It be in their blood. And there's nothing much to choose between one girl and the other. Nowadays . . ."

I nodded sympathetically. I was thinking of Alice, who had watched the relationship between her husband and Lady Treslyn. No wonder she had been prepared to run away with Geoffry Nansellock.

Poor Alice! I thought. What you must have suffered, married to such a man.

Mrs. Polgrey was in such an expansive mood that I felt I might extend the conversation to other matters in which I happened to be very interested.

I said: "Have you ever thought of teaching Gilly her letters?"

"Gilly! Why, that would be a senseless thing to do. You must know, miss, that Gilly is not quite as she should be." Mrs. Polgrey tapped her forehead.

"She sings a great deal. She must have learned the songs. If she could learn songs, could she not learn other things?"

"She's a queer little thing. Reckon it was the way she come. I don't often talk of such things, but I'll swear you've been hearing about my Jennifer." Mrs. Polgrey's voice changed a little, became touched with sentiment. I wondered if it had anything to do with the whisky and how many spoonfuls she had taken that day. "Sometimes I think that Gillyflower be a cursed child. Us didn't want her; why, she was only a little thing in a cradle . . . two months old . . . when Jennifer went. The tide brought her body in two days after. 'Twas found there in Mellyn Cove."

"I'm sorry," I said gently.

Mrs. Polgrey shook herself free of sentiment. "Her'd gone, but there was still Gilly. And right from the first her didn't seem quite like other children."

"Perhaps she sensed the tragedy," I ventured.

Mrs. Polgrey looked at me with hauteur. "We did all we could for her—me and Mr. Polgrey. He thought the world of her."

"When did you notice that she was not like other children?"

"Come to think of it, it would be when she was about four years old."

"That would be how many years ago?"

"About four."

"She must be the same age as Alvean. She looks so much younger."

"Born a few months after Miss Alvean. They'd play together now and then . . . being in the house, you do see, and being of an age. There was an accident when she was, let me see . . . she'd be approaching her fourth birthday."

"What sort of accident?"

"She were playing in the drive there, not far from the lodge gates. The mistress were riding along the drive to the house. She was a great horsewoman, the mistress. Gilly, her darted out from the bushes and caught a blow from the horse. She fell on her head. It was a mercy she weren't killed."

"Poor Gilly," I said.

"The mistress were distressed. Blamed herself although 'twas no blame to her. Gilly should have known better. She'd been told to watch the roads often enough. Darted out after a butterfly, like as not. Gilly has always been taken with birds and flowers and insects and such like. The mistress made much of her after that. Gilly used to follow her about and fret when she was away."

"I see," I said.

Mrs. Polgrey poured herself another cup of tea and asked me if I would have another. I declined. I saw her tilt the teaspoonful of whisky into the cup. "Gilly," she went on, "were born in sin. Her had no right to come into the world. It looks like God be taking vengeance on her, for it do say that the sins of the fathers be visited on the children."

I felt a sudden wave of anger sweep over me. I was in revolt against such distortions. I felt I wanted to slap the face of the woman who could sit there calmly drinking her whisky and accepting the plight of her little granddaughter as God's will.

I marveled too at the ignorance of these people, who did not connect Gilly's strangeness with the accident she had had but believed it was due punishment for her parents' sins meted out to her by a vengeful God.

But I said nothing, because I believed that I was battling against strange forces in this house and if I were going to succeed, I needed all the allies I could command.

I wanted to understand Gilly. I wanted to soothe Alvean. I was discovering a fondness for children in myself which I had not known I possessed before I came into this house. Indeed, since I had come here I had begun to discover quite a lot about myself.

There was one other reason why I wanted to concentrate on the affairs of these two children; doing so prevented my thinking of Connan TreMellyn and Lady Treslyn. Thoughts of them made me feel quite angry; at this time I called my anger "disgust."

So I sat in Mrs. Polgrey's room, listening to her talk, and I did not tell her what was in my mind.

❧

There was excitement throughout the house because there was to be a ball—the first since Alice's death—and for a week there was little talk of anything else. I found it difficult to keep Alvean's attention on her lessons; Kitty and Daisy were almost hysterical with delight, and I was constantly coming upon them clasped in each other's arms in an attempt to waltz.

The gardeners were busy. They were going to bring in flowers from the greenhouses to decorate the ballroom and were eager that the blooms should do them credit; and invitations were being sent out all over the countryside.

"I fail to see," I said to Alvean, "why you should feel this excitement. Neither you nor I will take part in the ball."

Alvean said dreamily: "When my mother was alive there were lots of balls. She loved them. She danced beautifully. She used to come in and show me how she looked. She was beautiful. Then she would take me into the solarium and I would sit in a recess behind the curtains and look down on the hall through the peep."

"The peep?" I asked.

"Ah, you don't know." She regarded me triumphantly. I suppose it was rather pleasing to her to discover that her governess, who was constantly shocked by her ignorance, should herself be discovered in that state.

"There is a great deal about this house that I do not know," I said sharply. "I have not seen a third of it."

"You haven't seen the solarium," she agreed. "There are several peeps in this house. Oh, miss, you don't know what peeps are, but a lot of big houses have them. There's even one in Mount Widden. My mother told me that it is where the ladies used to sit when the men were feasting and it was considered no place for them among the men. They could look down and watch, but they must not *be* there. There's one in the chapel . . . a sort of one. We call it the lepers' squint there. They couldn't come in because they were lepers, so they could only look through the squint. But I shall go to the solarium and look down on the hall through the peep up there. Why, miss, you ought to come with me. Please do."

"We'll see," I said.

⊷⊰⊱⊸

On the day of the ball Alvean and I took our riding lesson as usual, only instead of riding Buttercup, Alvean was mounted on Black Prince.

When I had first seen the child on that horse I had felt a faint twinge of uneasiness, but I stifled this, for I told myself that if she were going to become a rider she must get beyond the Buttercup stage. Once she had ridden Prince she would gain more confidence, and very likely never wish to go back to Buttercup.

We had done rather well for the first few lessons. Prince behaved admirably and Alvean's confidence was growing. We had no doubt, either of us, that she would be able to enter for at least one of the events at the November horse show.

But this day we were not so fortunate. I suspect that Alvean's thoughts were on the ball rather than on her riding. She was still diffident with me, except perhaps during our riding lessons, when oddly enough we were the best of friends; but as soon as we had divested ourselves of our riding kit we seemed automatically to slip back to the old relationship. I had tried to change this, without success.

We were about halfway through the lesson when Prince broke into a gallop. I had not allowed her to gallop unless she was on the leading rein; in any case there was little room for that sort of thing in the field; and I wanted to be absolutely sure of Alvean's confidence before I allowed her more license.

All would have been well if Alvean had kept her head and remembered what I had taught her, but as Prince started to gallop she gave a little cry of fear and her terror seemed immediately to communicate itself to the frightened animal.

Prince was off; the thud of his hoofs on the turf struck terror into me. I saw Alvean, forgetting what I had taught her, swaying to one side.

It was all over in a flash because as soon as it happened I was on the spot. I was after her immediately. I had to grasp Prince's bridle before he reached the hedge, for I believed that he might attempt to jump and that would mean a nasty fall for my pupil. Fear gave me new strength and I had his rein in my hands and had pulled him up just as he was coming up to the hedge. I brought him to a standstill while a white-faced, trembling Alvean slid unharmed to the ground.

"It's all right," I said. "Your mind was wandering. You haven't reached that stage when you can afford to forget for a moment what you're doing."

I knew that was the only way to deal with her. Shaken as she was, I made her remount Prince; I knew that she had become terrified of horses through some such incident as this. I had overcome that fear and I was not going to allow it to return.

She obeyed me, although reluctantly. But by the time our lesson was finished she was well over her fright, and I knew that she would want to ride next day. So I was more satisfied that day that I would eventually make a rider of Alvean than I had been before.

It was when we were leaving the field that she suddenly burst out laughing.

"What is it?" I asked, turning my head, for I was riding ahead of her.

"Oh, miss," she cried. "You've split!"

"What *do* you mean?"

"Your dress has split under the armhole. Oh . . . it's getting worse and worse."

I put my hand behind my back and realized what had happened. The riding habit had always been a little too tight for me, and during my efforts to save Alvean from a nasty fall, the sleeve seam had been unable to stand the extra strain.

I must have shown my dismay, for Alvean said: "Never mind, miss. I'll find you another. There *are* more, I know."

Alvean was secretly amused as we went back to the house. Odd that I had never seen her in such good spirits. It was however somewhat disconcerting to discover that the sight of my discomfiture could give her so much pleasure that she could forget the danger through which she had so recently passed.

❧

The guests had begun to arrive. I had been unable to resist taking peeps at them from my window. The approach was filled with carriages, and the dresses I had glimpsed made me gasp with envy.

The ball was being held in the great hall which I had seen earlier that day. Before that I had not been in it since my arrival, for I always used the back staircase. It was Kitty who had urged me to take a peep. "It looks so lovely, miss. Mr. Polgrey's going round like a dog with two tails. He'll murder one of us if anything happens to his plants."

I thought I had rarely seen a setting so beautiful. The beams had been decorated with leaves. "An old Cornish custom," Kitty told me, "specially at Maytime. But what's it matter, miss, if this be September. Reckon there'll be other balls now the period of mourning be up. Well, so it should be. Can't go on mourning forever, can 'ee. You might say this is a sort of Maytime, don't 'ee see? 'Tis the end of one old year and the beginning of another like."

I said, as I looked at the pots of hothouse blooms which had been brought in from the greenhouses and the great wax candles in their sconces, that the hall did Mr. Polgrey and his gardeners great credit. I pictured how it would look when those candles were lighted and the guests danced in their colorful gowns, their pearls and their diamonds.

I wanted to be one of those guests. How I wanted it! Kitty had begun to dance in the hall, smiling and bowing to an imaginary partner. I smiled. She looked so abandoned, so full of joy.

Then I thought that I ought not to be here like this. It was quite unbecoming. I was as bad as Kitty.

I turned away and there was a foolish lump in my throat.

Alvean and I had supper together that evening. She obviously could not dine with her father in the small dining room, as he would be busy with his guests.

"Miss," she said, "I've put a new riding habit for you in your cupboard."

"Thank you," I said; "that was thoughtful of you."

"Well, you couldn't go riding in that!" cried Alvean, pointing derisively at my lavender gown.

So it was only that I might not miss a riding lesson for want of the clothes that she had taken such trouble on my behalf! I should have known that.

I asked myself in that moment whether I was not being rather foolish. Did I expect more than people were prepared to give? I was nothing to Alvean except when I could help her to attain what she wanted. It was as well to remember that.

I looked down distastefully at my lavender cotton gown. It was the favorite of the two which had been specially made for me by Aunt Adelaide's dressmaker when I had obtained this post. One was of gray—a most unbecoming color to me—but I fancied I looked a little less prim, a little less of a governess in the lavender. But how unbecoming it seemed, with its bodice buttoned high at the neck and the cream lace collar and the cream lace cuffs to match. I realized I was comparing it with the dresses of Connan TreMellyn's guests.

Alvean said: "Hurry and finish, miss. Don't forget we're going to the solarium."

"I suppose you have your father's permission . . ." I began.

"Miss, I always peep from the solarium. Everybody knows I do. My mother used to look up and wave to me." Her face puckered a little. "Tonight," she went on, as though she were speaking to herself, "I'm going to imagine that she's down there, after all . . . dancing there. Miss, do you think people come back after they're dead?"

"What an extraordinary question! Of course not."

"You don't believe in ghosts then. Some people do. They say they've seen them. Do you think they lie when they say they see ghosts, miss?"

"I think that people who say such things are the victims of their own imaginations."

"Still," she went on dreamily, "I shall imagine she is there . . . dancing there. Perhaps if I imagine hard enough I shall see her. Perhaps I shall be the victim of my imagination."

I said nothing because I felt uneasy.

"If she *were* coming back," she mused, "she would come to the ball, because dancing was one of the things she liked doing best." She seemed to remember me suddenly. "Miss," she went on, "if you'd rather not come to the solarium with me, I don't mind going alone."

"I'll come," I said.

"Let's go now."

"We will first finish our meal," I told her.

❧

The vastness of the house continued to astonish me, as I followed Alvean along the gallery, up stone staircases through several bedrooms, to what she told me was the solarium. The roof was partly of glass and I understood why it had received its name. I thought it must be unbearably warm in the heat of the summer.

The walls were covered with exquisite tapestries depicting the story of the Great Rebellion and the Restoration. There was the execution of the first Charles, and the second shown in the oak tree, his dark face peering down at the Roundhead soldiers; there were pictures of his arrival in England, of his coronation, and a visit to his shipyards.

"Never mind those now," said Alvean. "My mother used to love being here. She said you could see what was going on. There are two peeps up here. Oh, miss, don't you want to see them?"

I was looking at the escritoire, at the sofa and the gilt-backed chairs; and I saw her sitting here, talking to her daughter here—dead Alice who seemed to become more and more alive as the days passed.

There were windows at each end of this long room, high windows curtained with heavy brocade. The same brocade curtains hung before what I presumed to be doors of which there appeared to be four in this room—the one by which we had entered, another at the extreme end of the room, and one on either side. But I was wrong about the last two.

Alvean had disappeared behind one of these curtains and called to me in a muffled voice, and when I went to her I found we were in an alcove. In the wall was a star-shaped opening, quite large but decorated so that one would not have noticed it unless one had been looking for it.

I gazed through it and saw that I was looking down into the chapel. I could see clearly all but one side—the small altar with the triptych and the pews.

"They used to sit up here and watch the service if they were too ill to go down, my mother told me. They had a priest in the house in the old days. My mother didn't tell me that. She didn't know about the history of the house. Miss Jansen told me. She knew a lot about the house. She loved to come up here and look through the peep. She used to like the chapel too."

"You were sorry when she went, Alvean, I believe."

"Yes, I was. The other peep's on the other side. Through that you can see into the hall."

She went to the other side of the room and drew back the hangings there. In the wall was a similar star-shaped opening.

I looked down on the hall and caught my breath, for it was a magnificent sight. Musicians were on the dais and the guests who had not yet begun to dance, stood about talking.

There were a great many people down there and the sound of the chatter rose clearly up to us. Alvean was breathless beside me, her eyes searching . . . in a manner which made me shiver slightly. Did she really believe that Alice would come from the tomb because she loved to dance?

I felt an impulse to put my arms about her and draw her to me. Poor motherless child, I thought. Poor bewildered little creature!

But of course I overcame that impulse. Alvean had no desire for my sympathy, I well knew.

I saw Connan TreMellyn in conversation with Celestine Nansellock, and Peter was there too. If Peter was one of the most handsome men I had ever seen, Connan, I told myself, was the most elegant. There were few in that brilliant assembly whose faces were known to me, but I did see Lady Treslyn there. Even among that magnificently brilliant gathering she stood out. She was wearing a gown which seemed to be composed of yards and yards of chiffon, which was the color of flame, and I guessed that she was one of the few who would have dared to wear such a color. Yet had she wanted to attract attention to herself she could not have chosen anything more calculated to bring about this result. Her dark hair looked almost black against the flame; her magnificent bust and shoulders were the whitest I had ever seen. She wore a band of diamonds in her hair, which was like a tiara, and diamonds sparkled about her person.

Alvean's attention was caught by her even as mine was and her brows were drawn together in a frown.

"*She* is there then," she murmured.

I said: "Is her husband present?"

"Yes, the little old man over there, talking to Colonel Penlands."

"And which is Colonel Penlands?" She pointed the colonel out to me, and I saw with him a bent old man, white-haired and wrinkled. It seemed incredible that he should be the husband of that flamboyant creature.

"Look!" whispered Alvean. "My father is going to open the ball. He used to do it with Aunt Celestine, and at the same time my mother used to do it with Uncle Geoffry. I wonder who he will do it with this time."

"With whom he will do it," I murmured absent-mindedly, but my attention, like Alvean's was entirely on the scene below.

"The musicians are going to start now," she said. "They always start with the same tune. Do you know what it is? It's the "Furry Dance." Some of our ancestors came from Helston way and it was played then and it always has been since. You watch! Papa and Mamma used to dance the first bar or so with their partners, and all the others fell in behind."

The musicians had begun, and I saw Connan take Celestine by the hand and lead her into the center of the hall; Peter Nansellock followed, and he had chosen Lady Treslyn to be his partner.

I watched the four of them dance the first steps of the traditional dance, and I thought: Poor Celestine! Even gowned as she was in blue satin she looked ill at ease in that quartet. She lacked the elegance and nonchalance of Connan, the beauty of Lady Treslyn, and the dash of her brother.

I thought it was a pity that he had to choose Celestine to open the ball. But that was tradition. This house was filled with tradition. Such and such was done because it always had been done, and often for no other reason. Well, that was the way in great houses.

Neither Alvean nor I seemed to tire of watching the dancers. An hour passed and we were still there. I fancied that Connan glanced up once or twice. Did he know of his daughter's habit of watching? I thought that it must be Alvean's bedtime, but that perhaps on such an occasion a little leniency would be permissible.

I was fascinated by the way she watched the dancers tirelessly, fervently, as though she were certain that if she looked long enough she would see that face there which she longed to see.

It was now dark, but the moon had risen. I turned my eyes from the dance floor to look through the glass roof at that great gibbous moon which seemed to be smiling down on us. No candles for you, it seemed to say; you are banished from the gaiety and the glitter, but I will give you my soft and tender light instead.

The room, touched by moonlight, had a supernatural character all its own. I felt in such a room anything might happen.

I turned my attention back to the dancers. They were waltzing down there and I felt myself swaying to the rhythm. No one had been more astonished than I when I had proved to be a good dancer. It had brought me partners at the dances to which Aunt Adelaide had taken me in those days when she had thought it possible to find a husband for me; alas for Aunt Adelaide, those invitations to the dances had not been extended to other pursuits.

And as I listened entranced I felt a hand touch mine and I was so startled that I gave an audible gasp.

I looked down. Standing beside me was a small figure, and I was relieved to see that it was only Gillyflower.

"You have come to see the dancers?" I said.

She nodded.

She was not quite so tall as Alvean and could not reach the star-shaped peep, so I lifted her in my arms and held her up. I could not see very clearly in the moonlight but I was sure the blankness had left her eyes.

I said to Alvean: "Bring a stool and Gillyflower can stand on it; then she will be able to see quite easily."

Alvean said: "Let her get it herself."

Gilly nodded and I put her on the floor; she ran to the stool and brought it with her. I thought, since she understands, why can she not talk with the rest of us?

Alvean did not seem to want to look now that Gilly had come. She moved away from the peep and as the musicians below began the opening bars of that waltz which always enchanted me—I refer to Mr. Strauss's "Blue Danube" waltz—Alvean began to dance across the floor of the solarium.

The music seemed to have affected my feet. I don't know what came over me that night. It was as though some spirit of daring had entered into my body, but I could not resist the strains of "The Blue Danube". I danced toward Alvean. I waltzed as I used to in those ballrooms to which I went accompanied by Aunt Adelaide, but I was sure that I never danced as I did that night in the solarium.

Alvean cried out with pleasure; I heard Gilly laugh too.

Alvean cried: "Go on, miss. Don't stop, miss. You do it well."

So I went on dancing with an imaginary partner, dancing down the moonlit solarium with the lopsided moon smiling in at me. And when I reached the end of the room a figure moved toward me and I was no longer dancing alone.

"You're exquisite," said a voice, and there was Peter Nansellock in his elegant evening dress, and he was holding me as it was the custom to hold a partner in the waltz.

My feet faltered. He said: "No . . . no. Listen, the children are protesting. You must dance with me, Miss Leigh, as you were meant to dance with me."

We went on dancing. It was as though my feet, having begun, would not stop.

But I said: "This is most unorthodox."

"It is most delightful," he answered.

"You should be with the guests."

"It is more fun to be with you."

"You forget . . ."

"That you are a governess? I could, if you would allow me to."

"There is no earthly reason why you should forget."

"Only that I think you would be happier if we could all forget it. How exquisitely you dance!"

"It is my only drawing-room accomplishment."

"I am sure it is one of many that you are forced to squander on this empty room."

"Mr. Nansellock, do you not think this little jest has been played out?"

"It is no jest."

"I shall now rejoin the children." We had come close to them and I saw little Gilly's face enrapt, and I saw the admiration in Alvean's. If I stopped dancing I should revert to my old position; while I went on dancing I was an exalted being.

I thought how ridiculous were the thoughts I was entertaining; but tonight I wanted to be ridiculous, I wanted to be frivolous.

"So here he is."

To my horror I saw that several people had come into the solarium, and my apprehension did not lessen when I saw the flame-colored gown of Lady Treslyn among them, for I was sure that wherever that flame-colored dress was, there Connan TreMellyn would be.

Somebody started to clap; others took it up. Then "The Blue Danube" ended.

I put my hand up to my hair in my acute embarrassment. I knew that dancing had loosened the pins.

I thought: I shall be dismissed tomorrow for my irresponsibility, and perhaps I deserve it.

"What an excellent idea," said someone. "Dancing in moonlight. What could be more agreeable? And one can hear the music up here almost as well as down there."

Someone else said: "This is a beautiful ballroom, Connan."

"Then let us use it for that purpose," he answered.

He went to the peep and shouted through it! "Once more—'The Blue Danube'."

Then the music started.

I turned to Alvean and I gripped Gilly by the hand. People were already beginning to dance. They were talking together and they did not bother to lower their voices. Why should they? I was only the governess.

I heard a voice: "The governess. Alvean's, you know."

"Forward creature! I suppose another of Peter's light ladies."

"I'm sorry for the poor things. Life must be dull for them."

"But in broad moonlight! What could be more depraved?"

"The last one had to be dismissed, I believe."

"This one's turn will come."

I was blushing hotly. I wanted to face them all, to tell them that my conduct was very likely less depraved than that of some of them.

I was furiously angry and a little frightened. I was aware of Connan's face in moonlight for he was standing near me, looking at me, I feared, in a manner signifying the utmost disapproval, which I was sure he was feeling.

"Alvean," he said, "go to your room and take Gillyflower with you."

She dared not disobey when he spoke in those tones.

I said as coolly as I could: "Yes, let us go."

But as I was about to follow the children I found my arm gripped and Connan had come a little closer to me.

He said: "You dance extremely well, Miss Leigh. I could never resist a good dancer. Perhaps it is because I scarcely excel in the art myself."

"Thank you," I said. But he still held my arm.

"I am sure," he went on, "that 'The Blue Danube' is a favorite of yours. You looked . . . enraptured." And with that he swung me into his arms and I found that I was dancing with him among his guests. . . . I in my lavender cotton and my turquoise brooch, they in their chiffons and velvets, their emeralds and diamonds.

I was glad of the moonlight. I was so overcome with shame, for I believed that he was angry and that his intention was to shame me even further.

My feet caught the rhythm and I thought to myself: Always in future "The Blue Danube" will mean to me a fantastic dance in the solarium with Connan TreMellyn as my partner.

"I apologize, Miss Leigh," he said, "for my guests' bad manners."

"It is what I must expect and no doubt what I deserve."

"What nonsense," he said, and I told myself that I was dreaming, for his voice which was close to my ear sounded tender.

We had come to the end of the room and, to my complete astonishment, he had whirled me through the curtains and out of the door. We were on a small landing between two flights of stone stairs in a part of the house which I had not seen before.

We stopped dancing, but he still kept his arms about me. On the wall a paraffin lamp of green jade burned; its light was only enough to show me his face. It looked a little brutal I thought.

"Miss Leigh," he said, "you are very charming when you abandon your severity."

I caught my breath with dismay, for he was forcing me against the wall and kissing me.

I was horrified as much by my own emotions as by what was happening. I knew what that kiss meant: You are not averse to a mild flirtation with Peter Nansellock; therefore why not with me?

My anger was so great that it was beyond my control. With all my might I pushed him from me and he was so taken by surprise that he reeled backward. I lifted my skirts and began to run as fast as I could down the stairs.

I did not know where I was but I went on running blindly and eventually found the gallery and so made my way back to my own room.

There I threw myself onto my bed and lay there until I recovered my breath.

There is only one thing I can do, I told myself, and that is get away from this house with all speed. He has now made his intentions clear to me. I have no doubt at all that Miss Jansen was dismissed because she refused to accept his attentions. The man is a monster. He appeared to think that anyone whom he employed belonged to him completely. Did he imagine he was an eastern pasha? How dared he treat me in such a way!

There was a constricted feeling in my throat which made me feel as though I were going to choke. I was more desperately unhappy than I had ever been in my life. It was due to him. I would not face the truth, but I really cared more deeply than I had about anything else that he should regard me with such contempt.

These were the danger signals.

I had need now of my common sense.

I rose from my bed and locked my door. I must make sure that my door was locked during the last night I would spend in this house. The only other way to my room would be through Alvean's room and the schoolroom, and I knew he would not attempt to come that way.

Nevertheless I felt unsafe.

Nonsense, I said to myself, you can protect yourself. If he should dare enter your room you could pull the bell rope immediately.

The first thing I would do would be to write to Phillida. I sat down and tried to do this but my hands were trembling and my handwriting was so shaky that the note looked ridiculous.

I could start packing.

I did this.

I went to the cupboard and pulled open the door. For a moment I thought someone was standing there, and I cried out in alarm; this showed the nervous state to which I had been reduced. I saw what it was almost immediately: the riding habit which Alvean had procured for me. She must have hung it in my wardrobe herself. I had forgotten all about this afternoon's little adventure, for what had happened in the solarium and after had temporarily obliterated everything else.

I packed my trunk in a very short time, for my possessions were not many. Then, as I was more composed, I sat down and wrote the letter to Phillida.

When I had finished writing I heard the sound of voices below and I went to my window. Some of the guests had come out onto the lawn, and I saw them dancing down there. More came out.

I heard someone say: "It's such a heavenly night. That moon is too good to miss."

I stood back in the shadows watching, and eventually I saw what I had been waiting for. There was Connan. He was dancing with Lady Treslyn; his head was close to hers. I imagined the sort of things he was saying to her.

Then I turned angrily from the window and tried to tell myself that the pain I felt within me was disgust.

I undressed and went to bed. I lay sleepless for a long time and when I did sleep I had jumbled dreams that were of Connan, myself, and Lady Treslyn. And always in the background of these dreams was that shadowy figure who had haunted my thoughts since the day I had come here.

I awoke with a start. The moon was still visible and in the room in my half-awakened state I seemed to see the dark shape of a woman.

I knew it was Alice. She did not speak, yet she was telling me something. "You must not go from here. You must stay. I cannot rest. You can help me. You can help us all."

I was trembling all over. I sat up in bed. Now I saw what had startled me. When I had packed I had left the door of the cupboard open, and what appeared to be the ghost of Alice was only her riding habit.

᭝ঌ৹ৎ᭝

I was up late next morning because when I had slept, I had done so deeply, and it was Kitty banging on the door with my hot water who awakened me. She could not get in and clearly she wondered what was wrong.

I leaped out of bed and unlocked the door.

"Anything wrong, miss?" she asked.

"No," I answered sharply, and she waited a few seconds for my explanation of the locked door.

I was certainly not going to give it to her, and she was so full of last night's ball that she was not so interested as she would have been had there been nothing else to absorb her.

"Wasn't it lovely, miss? I watched from my room. They danced on the lawn in the moonlight. My dear life, I never saw such a sight. It was like it used to be when the mistress was here. You look tired, miss. Did they keep you awake?"

"Yes," I said, "they did."

"Oh well, it's all over now. Mr. Polgrey's already having the plants taken back. Fussing over them like a hen with her chicks, he be. The hall do look a sorry mess this morning, I can tell 'ee. It's going to take Daisy and me all day to get it cleared up, you see."

I yawned and she put my hot water by the hip bath and went out. In five minutes' time she was back again.

I was half clothed, and wrapped a towel about me to shield myself from her too inquisitive eyes.

"It's master," she said. "He's asking for you. Wants to see you right away. In the punch room. He said, 'Tell Miss Leigh it is most urgent.'"

"Oh," I said.

"Most urgent, miss," Kitty repeated, and I nodded.

I finished washing and dressed quickly. I guessed what this meant. Very likely there would be some complaint. I would be given my notice because I was inefficient in some way. I began to think of Miss Jansen, and I wondered whether something of this nature had happened in her case. "Here one day and gone the next." Some trumped-up case against her. What if he should trump up a case against me?

That man is quite unscrupulous! I thought.

Well, I would be first. I would tell of my decision to leave before he had a chance to dismiss me.

I went down to the punch room prepared for battle.

He was wearing a blue riding jacket and he did not look as though he had been up half the night.

"Good morning, Miss Leigh," he said, and to my astonishment he smiled.

I did not return the smile. "Good morning," I said. "I have already packed my bags and should like to leave as soon as possible."

"Miss Leigh!" His voice was reproachful, and I felt an absurd joy rising within me. I was saying to myself: He doesn't want you to go. He's not asking you to go. He's actually going to apologize.

I heard myself say in a high, prim voice, which I should have hated in anyone else as self-righteous and priggish: "I consider it the only course open to me after——"

He cut in: "After my outrageous conduct of last night. Miss Leigh, I am going to ask you to forget that. I fear the excitement of the moment overcame me. I forgot with whom I was dancing. I have asked you to overlook my depravity on this occasion, and to say generously—I am sure you are generous, Miss Leigh—we will draw a veil over that unpleasant little incident and go on as we were before."

I had a notion that he was mocking me, but I was suddenly so happy that I did not care.

I was not going. The letter to Phillida need not be posted. I was not to leave in disgrace.

I inclined my head and I said: "I accept your apology, Mr. TreMellyn. We will forget this unpleasant and unfortunate incident."

Then I turned and went out of the room.

I found I was taking the stairs three at a time; my feet were almost dancing as they had been unable to resist dancing last night in the solarium.

The incident was over. I was going to stay. The whole house seemed to warm to me. I knew in that moment that if I had to leave this place I should be quite desolate.

I had always been given to self-analysis and I said to myself: Why this elation? Why would you be so wretched if you had to leave Mount Mellyn?

I had the answer ready: Because there is some secret here. Because I want to solve it. Because I want to help those two bewildered children, for Alvean is as bewildered as poor little Gillyflower.

But perhaps that was not the only reason. Perhaps I was a little more than interested in the master of the house.

Perhaps had I been wise I should have recognized the danger signals. But I was not wise. Women in my position rarely are.

·ঌৡৢয়·

That day Alvean and I took our riding lesson as usual. It went off well and the only remarkable thing about it was that I wore the new riding habit. It was different from the other, for it consisted of the tight-fitting dress of lightweight material and with it was a jacket, tailored almost like a man's.

I was delighted that Alvean showed no signs of fear after her small mishap of the day before, and I said that in a few days' time we might attempt a little jumping.

We arrived back at the house and I went to my room to change before tea.

I took off the jacket, thinking of the shock these things had given me in the night, and I laughed at my fears, for I was in very high spirits that day. I slipped out of the dress with some difficulty (Alice had been just that little bit more slender than I), put on my gray cotton—Aunt Adelaide had warned me that it was advisable not to wear the same dress two days running—and was about to hang up the riding habit in the cupboard when I felt something in the pocket of the coat.

I thrust in my hand in surprise, for I was sure I had had my hands in the pockets before this and nothing had been there.

There was nothing actually in the pocket now but there was something beneath the silk lining. I laid the jacket on the bed and, examining it, soon discovered the concealed pocket. I merely had to unhook it and there it was; in it was a book, a small diary.

My heart beat very fast as I took it out because I knew that this belonged to Alice.

I hesitated a moment but I could not resist the impulse to look inside. Indeed, I felt in that moment that it was my duty to look inside.

On the flyleaf was written in a rather childish hand "Alice Tre-Mellyn." I looked at the date. It was the previous year, so I knew that she had written in that diary during the last year of her life.

I turned the leaves. If I had expected a revelation of character I was soon disappointed. Alice had merely used this as a record for her appointments. There was nothing in this book to make me understand her more.

I looked at the entries: "Mount Widden to tea." "The Trelanders to dine." "C to Penzance." "C due back."

Still it was written in Alice's handwriting and that made it exciting to me.

I turned to the last entry in the book. It was under the twentieth of August. I looked back to July. Under the fourteenth was written: "Treslyns and Trelanders to dine at M.M." "See dressmaker about blue satin." "Do not forget to see Polgrey about flowers." "Send Gilly to dressmaker." "Take Alvean for fitting." "If jeweler has not sent brooch by sixteenth go to see him." And on the sixteenth: "Brooch not returned; must go along tomorrow morning. Must have it for dinner party at Trelanders on eighteenth."

It all sounded very trivial. What I had believed was a great discovery was nothing much. I put the book back into the pocket and went along to have tea in the schoolroom.

While Alvean and I were reading together a sudden thought struck me. I didn't know the exact date of her death, but it must have been soon after she was writing those trivial things in her diary. How odd that she should have thought it worth while to make those entries when she was planning to leave her husband and daughter for another man.

It suddenly became imperative to know the exact date of her death.

Alvean had had tea with her father because several people had come to pay duty calls and compliment Connan on last night's ball.

Thus I was free to go out alone. So I made my way down to Mellyn village and to the churchyard where I presumed Alice's remains would have been buried.

I had not seen much of the village before, as I had had little opportunity of going that far except when we went to church on Sunday, so it was an interesting tour of exploration.

I ran almost all the way downhill and was very soon in the village. I reminded myself that it would be a different matter toiling uphill on my way back.

The village in the valley nestled about the old church, the gray tower of which was half-covered in ivy. There was a pleasant little village green and a few gray stone houses clustered round it among which was a row of very ancient cottages which I guessed were of the same age as the church. I promised myself that I would make a closer examination of the village later. In the meantime I was most eager to find Alice's grave.

I went through the lich gate and into the churchyard. It was very quiet there at this time of the day. I felt I was surrounded by the stillness of death and I almost wished that I had brought Alvean with me. She could have pointed out her mother's grave.

How could I find it among these rows of gray crosses and headstones, I wondered as I looked about me helplessly. Then I thought: The TreMellyns would no doubt have some grand memorial to their dead; I must look for the most splendid vault, and I am sure I shall quickly find it that way.

I saw a huge vault of black marble and gilt not far off. I made for this and quickly discovered it to be that of the Nansellock family.

A sudden thought occurred to me. Geoffry Nansellock would lie here, and he died on the same night as Alice. Were they not found dead together?

I discovered the inscription engraved on the marble. This tomb contained the bones of defunct Nansellocks as far back as the middle seventeen hundreds. I remembered that the family had not been at Mount Widden as early as there had been TreMellyns at Mount Mellyn.

It was not difficult to find Geoffry's name, for his was naturally the last entry on the list of the dead.

He had died last year, I saw, on the seventeenth of July.

I was all eagerness to go back and look at the diary and check up that date.

I turned from the tomb and as I did so, I saw Celestine Nansellock coming toward me.

"Miss Leigh," she cried. "I thought it was you."

I felt myself flush because I remembered seeing her last night among the guests in the solarium, and I wondered what she was thinking of me now.

"I took a stroll down to the village," I answered, "and found myself here."

"I see you're looking at my family's tomb."

"Yes. It's a beautiful thing."

"If such a thing can be beautiful. I come here often," she volunteered. "I like to bring a few flowers for Alice."

"Oh, yes," I stammered.

"You saw the TreMellyn's vault, I suppose?"

"No."

"It's over here. Come and look."

I stumbled across the long grass to the vault which rivaled that of the Nansellocks in its magnificence.

On the black slab was a vase of Michaelmas daisies—large perfect blooms that looked like mauve stars.

"I've just put them there," she said. "They were her favorite flowers."

Her lips trembled, and I thought she was going to burst into tears.

I looked at the date and I saw that it was that on which Geoffry Nansellock had died.

I said: "I shall have to go back now."

She nodded. She seemed too moved to be able to speak. I thought then: She loved Alice. She seems to have loved her more than anyone else.

It was on the tip of my tongue to tell her about the diary I had discovered, but I hesitated. The memory of last night's shame was too near to me. I might be reminded that I was, after all, only the governess. And what right had I, in any case, to meddle in their affairs?

I left her there and as I went away I saw her sink to her knees. I turned again later and saw that her face was buried in her hands and her shoulders were heaving.

I hurried back to the house and took out the diary. So on the sixteenth of July last year, on the day before she was supposed to have eloped with Geoffry Nansellock, she had written in her diary that if her brooch was not returned on the next day she must go along to the jeweler, as she needed it for a dinner party to be held on the eighteenth!

That entry had not been made by a woman who was planning to elope.

I felt that I had almost certain proof in my hands that the body which had been found with Geoffry Nansellock's on the wrecked train was not Alice's.

I was back at the old question. What had happened to Alice? If she was not lying inside the black marble vault, where was she?

5

I felt I had discovered a vital clue but it took me no further. Each day I woke up expectant, but the days which passed were very like one another. Sometimes I pondered on several courses of action. I wondered whether I would go to Connan TreMellyn and tell him that I had seen his wife's diary and that it clearly showed she had not been planning to leave.

Then I told myself I did not quite trust Connan TreMellyn, and there was one thought concerning him which I did not want to explore too thoroughly. I had already begun to ask myself the question: Suppose Alice was not on the train, and something else had happened to her, who would be most likely to know what that was? Could it be Connan TreMellyn?

There was Peter Nansellock. I might discuss this matter with him, but he was too frivolous; he turned every line of conversation toward the flirtatious.

There was his sister. She was the most likely person. I knew that she had been fond of Alice; they must have been the greatest friends. Celestine was clearly the one in whom I could best confide. And yet I hesitated. Celestine belonged to that other world into which, I had been clearly shown on more than one occasion, I had no right to intrude. It was not for me, a mere governess, to set myself up as investigator.

The person in whom I might confide was Mrs. Polgrey, but again I shrank from doing this. I could not forget her spoonfuls of whisky and her attitude toward Gilly.

So, I decided that for the time being I would keep my suspicions to myself. October was upon us. I found the changing seasons delightful in this part of the world. The blustering southwest wind was warm and damp, and it seemed to carry with it the scent of spices from Spain. I had never seen so many spiders' webs as I did that October. They draped themselves over the hedges like gossamer cloth sewn with brilliants. When the sun came out it was almost as warm as June. "Summer do go on a long time in Cornwall," Tapperty told me.

The sea mist would come drifting in, wrapping itself about the gray stone of the house so that from the arbor in the south gardens it would sometimes be completely hidden. The gulls seemed to screech on a melancholy note on such days as though they were warning us that life was a sorrowful affair. And in the humid climate the hydrangeas continued to flower—blue, pink, and yellow—in enormous masses of bloom such as I should not have expected to find outside a hothouse. The roses went on flowering, and with them the fuchsias.

When I went down to the village one day I saw a notice outside the church to the effect that the horse show date was fixed for the first of November.

I went back and told Alvean. I was delighted that she had lost none of her enthusiasm for the event. I had been afraid that, as the time grew near, her fear might have returned.

I said to her: "There are only three weeks. We really ought to get in a little more practice."

She was quite agreeable.

We could, I suggested, rearrange our schedule. Perhaps we could ride for an hour both in the mornings and in the afternoons.

She was eager. "I'll see what can be done," I promised.

Connan TreMellyn had gone down to Penzance. I discovered this quite by accident. Kitty told me, when she brought in my water one evening.

"Master have gone off this afternoon," she said. " 'Tis thought he'll be away for a week or more."

"I hope he's back in time for the horse show," I said.

"Oh, he'll be back for that. He be one of the judges. He'm always here for that."

I was annoyed with the man. Not that I expected him to tell me he was going; but I did feel he might have had the grace to say good-by to his daughter.

I thought a good deal about him and I found myself wondering whether he had really gone to Penzance. I wondered whether Lady Treslyn was at home, or whether she had found it necessary to pay a visit to some relative.

Really! I admonished myself. Whatever has come over you? How can you entertain such thoughts? It's not as though you have any proof!

I promised myself that while Connan TreMellyn was away there was no need to think of him, and that would be a relief.

I was not entirely lying about that. I did feel relaxed by the thought that he was out of the house. I no longer felt it necessary to lock my door; but I continued to do so, purely on account of the Tapperty girls. I did not want them to know that I locked it for fear of the master—and although they were quite without education, they were sharp enough where such matters were concerned.

"Now," I said to Alvean, "we will concentrate on practicing for the horse show."

I procured a list of the events. There were two jumping contests for Alvean's age group, and I decided that she should take the elementary one, for I felt that she had a good chance of winning a prize in that; and of course the whole point of this was that she *should* win a prize and astonish her father.

"Look, miss," said Alvean, "there's this one. Why don't *you* go in for this?"

"Of course I shall do no such thing."

"But why not?"

"My dear child, I am here to teach you, not to enter for competitions."

A mischievous look came into her eyes. "Miss," she said, "I'm going to enter you for that. You'd win. There's nobody here can ride as well as you do. Oh, miss, you must!"

She was looking at me with what I construed as shy pride, and I felt a thrill of pleasure. I enjoyed her pride in me. She wanted me to win.

Well, why not? There was no rule about social standing in these contests, was there?

I fell back on my stock phrase for ending an embarrassing discussion.

"We'll see," I said.

❧

One afternoon we were riding close to Mount Widden and met Peter Nansellock.

He was mounted on a beautiful bay mare, the sight of which made my eyes glisten with envy.

He came galloping toward us and pulled up, dramatically removing his hat and bowing from the waist.

Alvean laughed delightedly.

"Well met, dear ladies," he cried. "Were you coming to call on us?"

"We were not," I answered.

"How unkind! But now you are here, you must come in for a little refreshment."

I was about to protest when Alvean cried: "Oh, do let's, miss. Yes, please. Uncle Peter, we'll come in."

"I had hoped you would call before this," he said reproachfully.

"We had received no definite invitation," I reminded him.

"For you there is always welcome at Mount Widden. Did I not make that clear?"

He had turned his mare and we all three walked our horses side by side. He followed my gaze, which was fixed on the mare.

"You like her?" he said.

"Indeed I do. She's a beauty."

"You're a real beauty, are you not, Jacinth my pet?"

"Jacinth. So that's her name."

"Pretty, you're thinking. Pretty name for a pretty creature. She'll go like the wind. She's worth four of that lumbering old cart horse you're riding, Miss Leigh."

"Lumbering old cart horse? How absurd! Dion is a very fine horse."

"Was, Miss Leigh. *Was!* Do you not think that the creature has seen better days? Really, I should have thought Connan could have given you something better from his stables than poor old Dion."

"It was not a matter of his giving her any horse to ride," said Alvean in hot defense of her father. "He does not know what horses we ride, does he, miss? These are the horses which Tapperty said we could have."

"Poor Miss Leigh! She should have a mount worthy of her. Miss Leigh, before you go, I would like you to take a turn on Jacinth. She'll quickly show you what it feels like to be on a good mount again."

"Oh," I said lightly, "we're satisfied with what we have. They serve my purpose—which is to teach Alvean to ride."

"We're practicing for the horse show," Alvean told him. "I'm going in for one of the events, but don't tell Papa; it's to be a surprise."

Peter put his finger to his lips. "Trust me. I'll keep your secret."

"And miss is entering for one of the events too. I've made her!"

"She'll be victorious," he cried. "I'll make a bet on it."

I said curtly: "I am not at all sure about this. It is only an idea of Alvean's."

"But you must, miss!" cried Alvean. "I insist."

"We'll both insist," added Peter.

We had reached the gates of Mount Widden which were wide open. There was no lodge here as at Mount Mellyn. We went up the drive—where the same types of flowers grew in profusion—the hydrangeas, fuchsias, and fir trees which were indigenous to this part of the country.

I saw the house, gray stone as Mount Mellyn was, but much smaller and with fewer outbuildings. I noticed immediately that it was not so well cared for as what in that moment I presumptuously called "our" house and I felt an absurd thrill of pleasure because Mount Mellyn compared so favorably with Mount Widden.

There was a groom in the stables and Peter told him to take charge of our horses. He did so and we went into the house.

Peter clapped his hands and shouted: "Dick! Where are you, Dick?"

The houseboy, whom I had seen when he had been sent over to Mount Mellyn with messages, appeared; and Peter said to him: "Tea, Dick. At once, in the library. We have guests."

"Yes, master," said Dick and hurried away.

We were in a hall which seemed quite modern when compared with our own hall. The floor was tessellated and a wide staircase at one end of the hall led to a gallery lined with oil paintings, presumably of the Nansellock family.

I laughed at myself for scorning the place, which was very much larger, and much grander than the vicarage in which I had spent my childhood. But it had a neglected air—one might almost say one of decay.

Peter took us into the library, a huge room the walls of which were lined with books on three sides. I noticed that the furniture was dusty and that dust was visible in the heavy curtains. What they need, I thought, is a Mrs. Polgrey with her beeswax and turpentine.

"I pray you sit down, dear ladies," said Peter. "It is to be hoped that tea will not long be delayed, although I must warn you that meals are not served with the precision which prevails in our rival across the cove."

"Rival?" I said in surprise.

"Well, how could there fail to be a little rivalry? Here we stand, side by side. But the advantages are all with them. They have the grander house, and the servants to deal with it. Your father, dear Alvean, is a man of property. We Nansellocks are his poor relations."

"You are not our relations," Alvean reminded him.

"Now is that not strange? One would have thought that, living side by side for generations, the two families would have mingled and become one. There must have been charming TreMellyn girls and charming Nansellock men. How odd that they did not join up and become relations! I suppose the mighty TreMellyns always looked down their arrogant noses at the poor Nansellocks and went farther afield to make their marriages. But now there is the fair Alvean. How maddening that we have no boy of your age to marry you, Alvean. *I* shall have to wait for you. There is nothing for it but that."

Alvean laughed delightedly. I could see that she was quite fascinated by him. And I thought: Perhaps he is more serious than he pretends. Perhaps he has already begun courting Alvean in a subtle way.

Alvean began to talk about the horse show and he listened attentively. I occasionally joined in, and so the time passed until tea was brought to us.

"Miss Leigh, will you honor us by pouring out?" Peter asked me.

I said I should be happy to do so, and I placed myself at the head of the tea table.

Peter watched me with attention which I found faintly embarrassing because it was not only admiring but contented.

"How glad I am that we met," he murmured as Alvean handed him his cup of tea. "To think that if I had been five minutes earlier or five minutes later, our paths might not have crossed. What a great part chance plays in our lives."

"Possibly we should have met at some other time."

"There may not be much more time left to us."

"You sound morbid. Do you think that something is going to happen to one of us?"

He looked at me very seriously. "Miss Leigh," he said, "I am going away."

"Where, Uncle Peter?" demanded Alvean.

"Far away, my child, to the other side of the world."

"Soon?" I asked.

"Possibly with the New Year."

"But where are you going?" cried Alvean in dismay.

"My dearest child, I believe you are a little hurt at the thought of my departure."

"Uncle, where?" she demanded imperiously.

"To seek my fortune."

"You're teasing. You're always teasing."

"Not this time. I have heard from a friend who was at Cambridge with me. He is in Australia, and there he has made a fortune. Gold! Think of it, Alvean. You too, Miss Leigh. Lovely gold . . . gold which can make a man . . . or woman . . . rich. And all one has to do is pluck it out of the ground."

"Many go in the hope of making fortunes," I said, "but are they all successful?"

"There speaks the practical woman. No, Miss Leigh, they are not all successful; but there is something named Hope which, I believe, springs eternal in the human breast. All may not have gold but they can all have Hope."

"Of what use is Hope if it is proved to be false?"

"Until she is proved false she can give so much pleasure, Miss Leigh."

"Then I wish that your hopes may not prove false."

"Thank you."

"But I don't want you to go, Uncle Peter."

"Thank *you,* my dear. But I shall come back a rich man. Imagine it. Then I shall build a new wing on Mount Widden. I will make a house as grand as—no, grander than—Mount Mellyn. And in the years to come people will say it was Peter Nansellock who saved the family fortunes. For, my dear young ladies, someone has to save them . . . soon."

He then began to talk of his friend who had gone to Australia a penniless young man and who, he was sure, was now a millionaire, or almost.

He began planning how he would rebuild the house, and we both joined in. It was a pleasant game—building a house in the mind, to one's own desires.

I felt exhilarated by his company. He at least, I thought, has never made me feel my position. The very fact of his poverty—or what to him seemed poverty—endeared him to me.

It was an enjoyable tea time.

Afterward he took us out to the stables and both he and Alvean insisted on my mounting Jacinth, and showing them what I could do with her. My saddle was put on her, and I galloped her and jumped with her, and she responded to my lightest touch. She was a delicious creature and I envied him his possession of her.

"Why," he said, "she has taken to you, Miss Leigh. Not a single protest at finding a new rider on her back."

I patted her fondly and said: "She's a beauty."

And the sensitive creature seemed to understand.

We then mounted our horses, and Peter came to the gates of Mount Mellyn with us, riding Jacinth.

As we went up to our rooms I decided that it had indeed been a very enjoyable afternoon.

Alvean came to my room and stood for a while, her head on one side. She said: "He likes you, I think, miss."

"He is merely polite toward me," I replied.

"No, I think he likes you rather specially . . . in the way he liked Miss Jansen."

"Did Miss Jansen go to tea at Mount Widden?"

"Oh yes. I didn't have riding lessons with her, but we used to walk over there. And one day we had tea just as we did this afternoon. He'd just bought Jacinth then and he showed her to us. He said he was going to change her name to make her entirely his. Then he said her name was to be Jacinth. That was Miss Jansen's name."

I felt foolishly deflated. Then I said: "He must have been very sorry when she left so suddenly."

Alvean was thoughtful. "Yes, I think he was. But he soon forgot all about her. After all . . ."

I finished the sentence for her: "She was only the governess, of course."

⁂

It was later that day when Kitty came up to my room to tell me that there was a message for me from Mount Widden.

"And something more too, miss," she said; it was clearly something which excited her, but I refrained from questioning her since I should soon discover what this was.

"Well," I said, "where is the message?"

"In the stables, miss." She giggled. "Come and see."

I went to the stables, and Kitty followed me at a distance.

When I arrived there I saw Dick, the Mount Widden houseboy; and, to my astonishment, he had the mare, Jacinth, with him.

He handed me a note.

I saw that Daisy, her father, and Billy Trehay were all watching me with amused and knowing eyes.

I opened the note and read it.

[It said] Dear Miss Leigh, you could not hide from me your admiration for Jacinth. I believe she reciprocates your feelings. That is why I am making you a present of her. I could not bear to see such a fine and graceful rider as yourself on poor old Dion. So pray accept this gift.

> *Your admiring neighbor,*
> *Peter Nansellock.*

In spite of efforts to control myself I felt the hot color rising from my neck to my forehead. I knew that Tapperty found it hard to repress a snigger.

How could Peter be so foolish! Was he laughing at me? How could I possibly accept such a gift, even if I wanted to? Horses had to be fed and stabled. It was almost as though he had forgotten this was not my home.

"Is there an answer, miss?" asked Dick.

"Indeed there is," I said. "I will go to my room at once, and you may take it back with you."

I went with as much dignity as I could muster in front of such an array of spectators back to the house, and in my room I wrote briefly:

Dear Mr. Nansellock,

Thank you for your magnificent gift which I am, of course, quite unable to accept. I have no means of keeping a horse here. It may have escaped you that I am employed in this house as a governess. I could not possibly afford the upkeep of Jacinth. Thank you for the kind thought.

> *Yours truly,*
> *Martha Leigh.*

I went straight back to the stables. I could hear them all laughing and talking excitedly as I approached.

"Here you are, Dick," I said. "Please take this note to your master with Jacinth."

"But . . ." stammered Dick, "I was to leave her here."

I looked straight into Tapperty's lewd old face. "Mr. Nansellock," I said, "is fond of playing jokes."

Then I went back to the house.

❧

The next day was a Saturday and Alvean asked that, since it was a half holiday, if we could not take the morning off and go to the moors. Her Great-aunt Clara had a house there, and she would be pleased to see us.

I considered this. I thought it would be rather pleasant to get away from the house for a few hours. I knew that they must all be talking about me and Peter Nansellock.

I guessed that he had behaved with Miss Jansen as he was behaving with me, and it amused them all to see the story of one governess turning out so much like another.

I wondered about Miss Jansen. Had she perhaps been a little frivolous? I pictured her stealing, whatever she was supposed to have stolen, that she might buy herself fine clothes to appear beautiful in the sight of her admirer.

And he had not cared when she was dismissed. A fine friend he would be!

We set out after breakfast. It was a beautiful day for riding, for the October sun was not too fierce and there was a soft southwest wind. Alvean was in high spirits, and I thought this would be a good exercise in staying power. If she could manage the long ride to her great-aunt's house and back without fatigue I should be delighted.

I felt it was pleasant to get away from the watchful eyes of the servants, and it was delightful to be in the moorland country.

I found that the great tracts of moor fitted my mood. I was enchanted by the low stone walls, the gray boulders, and the gay little streams which trickled over them.

I warned Alvean to be watchful of boulders, but she was sure-seated and alert now, so I did not feel greatly concerned.

We studied the map which would guide us to Great-aunt Clara's house—a few miles south of Bodmin. Alvean had traveled there in a carriage once or twice and she thought she would know the road; but the moor was the easiest place in the world in which to lose oneself, and I thought we could profit by the occasion to learn a little map-reading.

But I had left a great deal of my severity behind and I found myself laughing with Alvean when we took the wrong road and had to retrace our steps.

But at length we reached the "House on the Moors" which was the picturesque name of Great-aunt Clara's home.

And a charming house it was, set there on the outskirts of a moorland village. There was the church, the little inn, the few houses, and the House on the Moors which was like a small manor house.

Great-aunt Clara lived here with three servants to minister to her wants, and when we arrived there was great excitement as we were quite unexpected.

"Why, bless my soul if it b'aint Miss Alvean!" cried an elderly housekeeper. "And who be this you have brought with 'ee, my dear?"

"It is Miss Leigh, my governess," said Alvean.

"Well now! And be there just the two of you? And b'aint your papa here?"

"No. Papa has gone to Penzance."

I wondered then whether I had been wrong in acceding to Alvean's wishes, and had forgotten my position by imposing myself on Great-aunt Clara without first asking permission.

I wondered if I should be banished to the kitchen to eat with the servants. Such a procedure did not greatly disturb me, but I would rather have done that than sit down with a haughty, disapproving old woman.

But I was soon reassured. We were taken into a drawing room and there was Great-aunt Clara, a charming old lady seated in an armchair, white-haired, pink-cheeked, with bright friendly eyes. There was an ebony stick beside her, so I guessed she had difficulty in walking.

Alvean ran to her and she was warmly embraced.

Then the lively blue eyes were on me.

"So you are Alvean's governess, my dear," she said. "Well, that is nice. And how thoughtful of you to bring her to see me. It is particularly fortunate, for I have my grandson staying with me and I fear he grows a little weary of having no playmate of his own age. When he hears Alvean has arrived he'll be quite excited."

I did not believe that the grandson could be any more excited than Great-aunt Clara herself. She was certainly charming to me, so much so that I forgot my diffidence and I really did feel like a friend calling on a friend, rather than a governess bringing her charge to see a relative.

Dandelion wine was brought out and we were pressed to take a glass. There were wine cakes with it and I must say I found the wine delicious. I allowed Alvean to take a very small glass of it but when I had taken mine I wondered whether I had been wise, for it was certainly potent.

Great-aunt Clara wished to hear all the news of Mount Mellyn; she was indeed a garrulous lady, and I thought it was because she lived a somewhat lonely life in her house on the moors.

The grandson appeared—a handsome boy a little younger than Alvean—and the pair of them went off to play, although I warned Alvean not to go too far away as we must be home before dark.

As soon as Alvean had left us I saw that Great-aunt Clara was eager for a real gossip; and whether it was that I had taken her potent dandelion wine or whether I believed her to be a link with Alice, I am not sure; but I found her conversation fascinating.

She spoke of Alice as I had not until now heard her spoken of—with complete candor; and I quickly realized that from this gossipy lady I was going to discover a great deal more than I could from anyone else.

As soon as we were alone she said: "And now tell me how things really are at Mount Mellyn."

I raised my eyebrows as though I did not fully comprehend her meaning.

She went on: "It was such a shock when poor Alice died. It was so sudden. Such a tragic thing to happen to such a young girl—for she was little more than a girl."

"Is that so?"

"Don't tell me you haven't heard what happened."

"I know very little about it."

"Alice and Geoffry Nansellock, you know. They went off together . . . eloped. And then this terrible accident."

"I have heard that there was an accident."

"I think of them—those two young people—quite often, in the dead of the night. And then I blame myself."

I was astonished. I did not understand how this gentle talkative old lady could blame herself for Alice's infidelity to her husband.

"One should never interfere in other people's lives. Or should one? What do you think, my dear? If one can be helpful . . ."

"Yes," I said firmly, "if one can be helpful I think one should be forgiven for interference."

"But how is one to know whether one is being helpful or the reverse?"

"One can only do what one thinks is right."

"But one might be doing right and yet be quite unhelpful?"

"Yes, I suppose so."

"I think of her so much . . . my poor little niece. She was a sweet creature. But, shall I say, not equipped to face the cruelties of fate."

"Oh, was she like that?"

"I can see that you, Miss Leigh, are so good for that poor child. Alice would be so happy if she could see what you've done for her. The last time I saw her she was with her . . . with Connan. She was not nearly so happy . . . so relaxed as she is today."

"I'm so glad of that. I am encouraging her to ride. I think that has done her a world of good." I was loth to interrupt that flow of talk from which I might extract some fresh evidence about Alice. I was afraid that at any moment Alvean and the grandson would return, and I knew that in their presence there would be no confidences. "You were telling me about Alvean's mother. I am sure you have nothing with which to reproach yourself."

"I wish I could believe that. It worries me sometimes. Perhaps I shouldn't weary you. But you seem so sympathetic, and you are there, living in the house. You are looking after little Alvean like . . . like a mother. It makes me feel very grateful to you, my dear."

"I am paid for doing it, you know." I could not resist that remark, and I thought of the smile it would have brought to Peter Nansellock's lips.

"There are some things in this world which cannot be bought. Love . . . devotion . . . they are some of them. Alice stayed with me before her marriage. Here . . . in this house. It was so convenient, you see. It was only a few hours' ride from Mount Mellyn. It gave the young people a chance to know each other."

"The young people?"

"The engaged pair."

"Did they not know each other then?"

"The marriage had been arranged when they were in their cradles. She brought him a lot of property. They were well matched. Both rich, both of good families. Connan's father was alive then and, you know, Connan was a wild boy with a will of his own. The feeling was that they should be married as soon as possible."

"So he allowed this marriage to be arranged for him?"

"They both took it as a matter of course. Well, she stayed with me several months before the wedding. I loved her dearly."

I thought of little Gilly and I said: "I think a great many people loved her dearly."

Great-aunt Clara nodded; and at that moment Alvean and the grandson came in.

"I want to show Alvean my drawings," he announced.

"Well, go and get them," said his grandmother. "Bring them down and show her here."

I believed that she realized she had talked a little too much and was afraid of her own garrulity. It was clear to me that she was the sort of woman who could never keep a secret; how could she when she was ready to confide secret family history to me, a stranger?

The grandson returned with his portfolio, and the children sat at the table. I went over to them and I was so proud of Alvean's attempts at drawing that I determined again to speak to her father about drawing lessons at the first opportunity.

Yet as I watched, I felt frustrated. I was sure that Great-aunt Clara had been on the point of confiding something to me which was of the utmost importance.

Aunt Clara gave us luncheon and we left immediately after. We found our way back with the utmost ease, but I was determined to ride out again, and that before long, to the House on the Moors.

⋖§§⋗

When I was strolling through the village one day I passed the little jeweler's shop there. But perhaps that was scarcely the term to use when describing it. There were no valuable gems in the window; a few silver brooches and plain gold rings, some engraved with the word *Mizpah,* or studded with semiprecious stones, such as turquoises, topazes, and garnets. I guessed that the villagers bought their engagement and wedding rings here and that the jeweler made a living by doing repairs.

I saw in the window a brooch in the form of a whip. It was of silver, and quite tasteful, I decided, although it was by no means expensive.

I wanted to buy that whip for Alvean and give it to her the night before the horse show, telling her that it was to bring her luck.

I opened the door and went down the three steps into the shop.

Seated behind the counter was an old man wearing steel-rimmed spectacles. He let his glasses fall to the tip of his nose as he peered at me.

"I want to see the brooch in the window," I said. "The silver one in the form of a whip."

"Oh yes, miss," he said, "I'll show it to you with pleasure."

He brought it from the window and handed it to me.

"Here," he said, "pin it on and have a look at it." He indicated the little mirror on the counter. I obeyed him and decided that the brooch was neat, not gaudy, and in the best of taste.

As I was looking at it I noticed a tray of ornaments with little tickets attached to them. They were clearly jewelry which he had received for repair. Then I wondered whether this was the jeweler to whom Alice had brought her brooch last July.

The jeweler said to me: "You're from Mount Mellyn, miss?"

"Yes," I said; and I smiled encouragingly. I was becoming very ready to talk to anyone who I thought might have any information to offer me on this subject which appeared to obsess me. "As a matter of fact I want to give the brooch to my pupil."

Like most people in small villages he was very much interested in those living around him.

"Ah," he said, "poor motherless little girl. It's heartening to think she has a kind lady like yourself to look after her now."

"I'll take the brooch," I told him.

"I'll find a little box for it. A nice little box makes all the difference when it be a matter of a present, don't you agree, miss?"

"Most certainly."

He bent and from under the counter brought a small cardboard box which he began to stuff with cotton wool.

"Make a little nest for it, miss," he said with a smile.

I fancied that he was loth to let me go.

"Don't see much of them from the Mount these days. Mrs. Tre-Mellyn, her was often in."

"Yes, I suppose so."

"See a little trinket in the window and she'd buy it . . . sometimes for herself, sometimes for others. Why, she was in here the day she died."

His voice had sunk to a whisper and I felt excitement grip me. I thought of Alice's diary which was still in the concealed pocket of her habit.

"Really?" I said encouragingly.

He laid the brooch on the cotton wool and looked at me. "I thought 'twas a little odd at the time. I remember it very clearly. She came in here and said to me: 'Have you got the brooch done, Mr. Pastern? It's very important that I should have it. I'm anxious to wear it tomorrow. I'm going to a dinner party at Mr. and Mrs. Trelanders', and Mrs. Trelander gave me that brooch as a Christmas present, so you see it's most important I should wear it to show her I appreciate it.'" His eyes were puzzled as they looked into mine. "She were a lady who talked like that. She'd tell you where she was going, why she wanted a thing. I couldn't believe my ears when I heard she'd left home that very evening. Didn't seem possible that she could have been telling me about the dinner party she was going to the next day, you see."

"No," I said, "it was certainly very strange."

"You see, miss, there was no need for her to say anything to me like. If she'd said it to some, it might seem as though she was trying to pull the wool over their eyes. But why should she say such a thing to me, miss? That's what I've been wondering. Sometimes I think of it . . . and still wonder."

"I expect there's an answer," I said. "Perhaps you misunderstood her."

He shook his head. He did not believe that he had misunderstood. Nor did I. I had seen the entry in her diary and what I had read there confirmed what the jeweler had said.

⋘⧈⋙

Celestine Nansellock rode over the next day to see Alvean. We were about to go for our riding lesson, and she insisted on coming with us.

"Now, Alvean," I said, "is the time to have a little rehearsal. See if you can surprise Miss Nansellock as you hope to surprise your father."

We were going to practice jumping, and we rode down through the Mellyn village and beyond.

Celestine was clearly astonished by Alvean's progress.

"But you've done wonders with her, Miss Leigh."

We watched Alvean canter round the field. "I hope her father is going to be pleased. She has entered for one of the events in the horse show."

"He'll be delighted, I'm sure."

"Please don't say anything to him beforehand. We do want it to be a surprise."

Celestine smiled at me. "He'll be very grateful to you, Miss Leigh. I'm sure of that."

"I'm counting on his being rather pleased."

I was conscious of her eyes upon me as she smiled at me benignly. She said suddenly: "Oh, Miss Leigh, about my brother Peter. I did want to speak to you confidentially about that matter of Jacinth."

I flushed faintly, and I was annoyed with myself for doing so.

"I know he gave you the horse and you returned it as too valuable a gift."

"Too valuable a gift to accept," I answered, "and too expensive for me to be able to maintain."

"Of course. I'm afraid he is very thoughtless. But he is the most generous man alive. He's rather afraid he has offended you."

"Please tell him I'm not offended, and if he thinks awhile he will understand why I can't accept such a gift."

"I explained to him. He admires you very much, Miss Leigh, but there was an ulterior motive behind the gift. He wanted a good home for Jacinth. You know that he plans to leave England."

"He did mention it."

"I expect he will sell some of the horses. I shall keep a couple for myself, but there is no point in keeping an expensive stable with only myself at the house."

"No, I suppose not."

"He saw you on Jacinth and thinks you'd be a worthy mistress for her. That was why he wanted you to have her. He's very fond of that mare."

"I see."

"Miss Leigh, you would like to possess a horse like that?"

"Who wouldn't?"

"Suppose I asked Connan if it could be taken into his stables and kept there for you to ride. How would that be?"

I replied emphatically: "It is most kind of you, Miss Nansellock, and I do appreciate your desire—and that of your brother—to please me. But I do not wish for any special favors here. Mr. TreMellyn has a full and adequate stable for the needs of us all. I should be very much against asking for special favors for myself."

"I see," she said, "that you are very determined and very proud."

She leaned forward and touched my hand in a friendly manner. There was a faint mist of tears in her eyes. She was touched by my position, and understood how desperately I clung to my pride because it was my only possession.

I thought her kind and considerate, and I could understand why Alice had made a friend of her. I felt that I too could easily become her friend, for she had never made me in the least conscious of my social position in the house.

One day, I thought, I'll tell her what I've discovered about Alice. But not yet. I was, as her brother had said, as spiky as a hedgehog. I did not think for a moment that I should be rebuffed by Celestine Nansellock, but just at this time I was not going to run any risk.

Alvean joined us, and Celestine complimented her on her riding. Then we went back to the house, and tea, over which I presided, was served in the punch room.

I thought what a happy afternoon that was.

◆⟨§⟩◆

Connan TreMellyn came back the day before the horse show. I was glad he had not returned before, because I was afraid that Alvean might betray her excitement.

I was entered for one of the early events in which points were scored, particularly for jumping. It was what they called a mixed event which meant that men and women competed together.

Tapperty, who knew I was going to enter, wouldn't hear of my riding on Dion.

"Why, miss," he said, the day before the show, "if you'd have took Jacinth when she was offered you, you would have got first prize. That mare be a winner and so would you be, miss, on her back. Old Dion, he's a good old fellow, but he ain't no prize winner. How'd you say to taking Royal Rover?"

"What if Mr. TreMellyn objected?"

Tapperty winked. "Nay, he'd not object. He'll be riding out to the horse show on May Morning, so old Royal 'ull be free. I'll tell 'ee what, just suppose master was to say to me, 'Saddle up Royal Rover for me, Tapperty.' Right, then I'd saddle the Rover for him and it would be May Morning for you, miss. Nothing 'ud please master more than for to see his horse win a prize."

I was anxious to show off before Connan TreMellyn and I agreed to Tapperty's suggestion. After all, I was teaching his daughter to ride and that meant that I could, with the approval of his head stable man, make my selection from the stables.

The night before the horse show I presented Alvean with the brooch.

She was extremely delighted.

"It's a whip!" she cried.

"It will pin your cravat," I said, "and I hope bring you luck."

"It will, miss. I know it will."

"Well, don't rely on it too much. Remember luck only comes to those who deserve it." I quoted the beginning of an old rhyme which Father used to say to us.

> *"Your head and your heart keep boldly up,*
> *Your chin and your heels keep down."*

I went on; "And when you take your jump, remember . . . go with Prince."

"I'll remember."

"Excited?"

"It seems so long in coming."

"It'll come fast enough."

That night when I went in to say good night to her I sat on her bed and we talked about the horse show.

I was a little anxious about her because she was too excited, and I tried to calm her down. I told her she must go to sleep, for if she did not she would not be fresh for the morning.

"But how does one sleep, miss," she asked, "when sleep won't come?"

I realized then the magnitude of what I had done. A few months before, when I had come to this house, this girl had been afraid to mount a horse; now she was looking forward to competing at the horse show.

That was all well and good. I would have preferred her interest not to have been centered so wholeheartedly on her father. It was his approval which meant so much to her.

She was not only eager; she was apprehensive, so desperately did she long for his admiration.

I went to my room and came back with a book of Mr. Longfellow's poems.

I sat down by her bed and began to read to her, for I knew of nothing so able to turn the mind to peace than his narrative poem, "Hiawatha."

I often quoted it when I was trying to sleep and then I would feel myself torn from the events of this world in which I lived, and in my imagination I would wander along through the primeval forests with the "rushings of great rivers . . . and their wild reverberations."

The words flowed from my lips. I knew I was conjuring up visions for Alvean. She had forgotten the horse show . . . her fears and her hopes. She was with the little Hiawatha sitting at the feet of the good Nokomis and—she slept.

✦✦✦

I woke up on the day of the horse show to find that the mist had penetrated my room. I got out of bed and went to the window. Little wisps of it encircled the palm trees, and the feathery leaves of the evergreen pines were decorated with little drops of moisture.

"I hope the mist lifts before the afternoon," I said to myself.

But all through the morning it persisted, and there were anxious looks and whispers throughout the house where everyone was thinking of the horse show. Most of the servants were going to the show. They always did, Kitty told me, because the master had special interest in it as one of the judges, and Billy Trehay and some of the stable boys were entrants.

"It do put master in a good mood to see his horses win," said Kitty; "but they say he's always harder on his own than on others."

Immediately after luncheon Alvean and I set out; she was riding Black Prince and I was on Royal Rover. It was exhilarating to be on a good horse, and I felt as excited as Alvean; I fear I was just as eager to shine in the eyes of Connan TreMellyn as she was.

The horse show was being held in a big field close to the village church, and when we arrived the crowds were already gathering.

Alvean and I parted company when we reached the field and I discovered that the event in which I was competing was one of the first.

The show was intended to start at two-fifteen, but there was the usual delay, and at twenty past we were still waiting to begin.

The mist had lifted slightly, but it was a leaden day; the sky was like a gray blanket and everything seemed to have accumulated a layer of moisture. The sea smell was strong but the waves were silent today and the cry of the gulls was more melancholy than ever.

Connan arrived with the other judges; there were three of them, all local worthies. Connan, I saw, had come on May Morning, as I expected, since I had been given Royal Rover.

The village band struck up a traditional air and everyone stood still and sang.

It was very impressive, I thought, to hear those words sung with such fervor in that misty field:

> *"And shall they scorn Tre Pol and Pen,*
> *And shall Trelawny die?*
> *Then twenty thousand Cornish men*
> *Will know the reason why."*

A proud song, I thought, for an insular people; and they stood at attention as they sang. I noticed little Gillyflower standing there, singing with the rest, and I was surprised to see her; she was with Daisy and I hoped the girl would look after her.

She saw me and I waved to her, but she lowered her eyes at once; yet I could see that she was smiling to herself and I was quite pleased.

A rider came close to me and a voice said: "Well, if it is not Miss Leigh herself!"

I turned and saw Peter Nansellock; he was mounted on Jacinth.

"Good afternoon," I said, and my eyes lingered on the perfections of Jacinth.

I was wearing a placard with a number on my back which had been put there by one of the organizers.

"Don't tell me," said Peter Nansellock, "that you and I are competitors in this first event."

"Are you in it then?"

He turned, and I saw the placard on his back.

"I haven't a hope," I said.

"Against me?"

"Against Jacinth," I answered.

"Miss Leigh, you could have been riding her."

"You must have been mad to do what you did. You set the stables talking."

"Who cares for stable boys?"

"I do."

"Then you are not being your usual sensible self."

"A governess has to care for the opinions of all and sundry."

"You are not an ordinary governess."

"Do you know, Mr. Nansellock," I said lightly, "I believe all the governesses in your life were no ordinary governesses. If they had been, perhaps they would have had no place in your life."

I gave Royal Rover a gentle touch on the flank and he responded immediately.

I did not see Peter again until he was competing. He went before I did. I watched him ride round the field. He and Jacinth seemed like one animal. Like a centaur, I thought. Were they the creatures with the head and shoulders of a man and the body of a horse?

"Oh, perfect," I exclaimed aloud as I watched him take the jumps and canter gracefully round the field. And who couldn't, I said to myself maliciously, on a mare like that!

A round of applause followed him as he finished his turn.

Mine did not come until some time later.

I saw Connan TreMellyn in the judges' stand. And I whispered: "Royal Rover, help me. I want you to beat Jacinth. I want to win this prize. I want to show Connan TreMellyn that there is one thing I can do. Help me, Royal Rover."

The sensitive ears seemed to prick up as Royal Rover moved daintily forward and I knew that he heard me, and would respond to the appeal in my voice.

"Come on, Rover," I whispered. "We can do it."

And we went round as faultlessly, I hoped, as Jacinth had. I heard the applause burst out as I finished, and walked my horse away.

We waited until the rest of the competitors were finished and the results were called. I was glad that they were announced at the end of each event. People were more interested immediately after they had seen a performance. The practice of announcing all winners at the end of the meeting I had always thought to be a sort of anticlimax.

"This one is a tie," Connan was saying. "Two competitors scored full marks in this one. It's most unusual, but I am happy to say that the winners are a lady and a gentleman: Miss Martha Leigh on Royal Rover, and Mr. Peter Nansellock on Jacinth."

We trotted up to take our prizes.

Connan said: "The prize is a silver rose bowl. How can we split it? Obviously we cannot do that, so the lady gets the bowl."

"Of course," said Peter.

"But you get a silver spoon," Connan told him. "Consolation for having tied with a lady."

We accepted our prizes, and as Connan gave me mine he was smiling, very well pleased.

"Good show, Miss Leigh. I did not know anyone could get so much out of Royal Rover."

I patted Royal Rover and said, more for his hearing than anyone else's: "I couldn't have had a better partner."

Then Peter and I trotted off; I with my rose bowl, he with his spoon.

Peter said: "If you had been on Jacinth you would have been the undisputed winner."

"I should still have had to compete against you on something else."

"Jacinth would win any race . . . just look at her. Isn't she perfection? Never mind, you got the rose bowl."

"I shall always feel that it is not entirely mine."

"When you arrange your roses you will always think: Part of this belonged to that man . . . what was his name? He was always charming to me, but I was a little acid with him. I'm sorry now."

"I rarely forget people's names, and I feel I have nothing to regret in my conduct toward you."

"There is a way out of this rose bowl situation. Suppose we set up house together. It could have a place of honor there. 'Ours,' we could say, and both feel happy about it."

I was angry at this flippancy, and I said: "We should, I am sure, feel far from happy about everything else."

And I rode away.

⌘

I wanted to be near the judges' stand when Alvean appeared. I wanted to watch Connan's face as his daughter performed. I wanted to be close when she took her prize—which I was sure she would, for she was eager to win and she had worked hard. The jumps should offer no difficulty to her.

The elementary jumping contest for eight-year-olds began and I was feverishly impatient, waiting for Alvean's turn, as I watched those little girls and boys go through their performances. But there was no Alvean. The contest was over and the results announced.

I felt sick with disappointment. So she had panicked at the last moment. My work had been in vain. When the great moment came her fears had returned.

When the prizes were being given I went in search of Alvean, but I could not find her, and as the more advanced jumping contest for the eight-year-old group was about to begin, it occurred to me that she must have gone back to the house. I pictured her abject misery because after all our talk, all our practice, her courage had failed her at the critical moment.

I wanted to get away, for now my own petty triumph meant nothing to me, and I wanted to find Alvean quickly, to comfort her if need be, and I felt sure she would need my comfort.

I rode back to Mount Mellyn, hung up my saddle and bridle, gave Royal Rover a quick rub down and a drink, and left him munching an armful of hay in his stall while I went into the house.

The back door was unlatched and I went in. The house seemed very quiet. I guessed that all but Mrs. Polgrey were at the horse show. Mrs. Polgrey would probably be in her room having her afternoon doze.

I went up to my room and called Alvean as I went.

There was no answer, so I hurried through the schoolroom to her room which was deserted. Perhaps she had not come back to the house. I then remembered that I had not seen Prince in the stables. But then I had forgotten to look in his stall.

I came back to my room and stood uncertainly at the window. I thought: I'll go back to the horse show. She's probably still there.

And as I stood at the window I knew that someone was in Alice's apartments. I was not sure how I knew. It may only have been a shadow across the windowpane. But I was certain that someone was there.

Without thinking very much of what I would do when I discovered who was there, I ran from my room through the gallery to Alice's rooms. My riding boots must have made a clatter along the gallery. I threw open the door of the room and shouted: "Who is here? Who is it?"

No one was in the room, but in that fleeting second I saw the communicating door between the two rooms close.

I had a feeling that it might be Alvean who was there, and I was sure that Alvean needed me at this moment. I had to find her, and any fear I might have had disappeared. I ran across the dressing room and opened the door of the bedroom. I looked round the room. I ran to the curtains and felt them. There was no one there. Then I ran to the other door and opened it. I was in another dressing room and the communicating door—similar to that in Alice's—was open. I went through and immediately I knew that I was in Connan's bedroom, for I saw the cravat, which he had been wearing that morning, flung on the dressing table. I saw his dressing gown and slippers.

The sight of these made me blush and realize that I was trespassing in a part of the house where I had no right to be.

But someone other than Connan had been there before me. Who was it?

I went swiftly across the bedroom, opened the door and found myself in the gallery.

There was no sign of anyone there so I went slowly back to my room.

Who had been in Alice's room? Who was it who haunted the place?

"Alice," I said aloud. "Is it you, Alice?"

Then I went down to the stables. I wanted to get back to the horse show and find Alvean.

ᦌᦒᦌ

I had saddled Royal Rover and was riding out of the stable yard when I saw Billy Trehay hurrying toward the house.

He said: "Oh, miss, there's been an accident. A terrible accident."

"What?" I stammered.

"It's Miss Alvean. She took a toss in the jumping."

"But she wasn't in the jumping!" I cried.

"Yes she were. In the eight-year-olds. Advanced Class. It was the high jump. Prince stumbled and fell. They went rolling over and over . . ."

For a moment I lost control of myself; I covered my face with my hands and cried out my protest.

"They were looking for you, miss," he said.

"Where is she then?"

"She were down there in the field. They'm afraid to move her. They wrapped her up and now they'm waiting for Dr. Pengelly to come. They think she may have broken some bones. Her father's with her. He kept saying, 'Where's Miss Leigh?' And I saw you leave so I came after you. I think perhaps you'd better be getting down there, miss . . . since he was asking for you like."

I turned away and rode as fast as I dared down the hill into the village, and as I rode I prayed, and scolded:

"Oh God, let her be all right. Oh Alvean, you little fool! It would have been enough to take the simple jumps. That would have pleased him enough. You could have done the high jumps next year. Alvean, my poor, poor child." And then: "It's his fault. It's all his fault. If he had been a human parent this wouldn't have happened."

And so I came to the field. I shall never forget what I saw there: Alvean lying unconscious on the grass, and the group round her and others standing about. There would be no more competitions that day.

For a moment I was terrified that she had been killed.

Connan's face was stern as he looked at me.

"Miss Leigh," he said, "I'm glad you've come. There's been an accident. Alvean——"

I ignored him and knelt beside her.

"Alvean . . . my dear . . ." I murmured.

She opened her eyes then. She did not look like my arrogant little pupil. She was just a lost and bewildered child.

But she smiled.

"Don't go away . . ." she said.

"No, I'll stay here."

"You did go . . . before . . ." she murmured, and I had to bend low to catch her words.

And then I knew. She was not speaking to Martha Leigh, the governess. She was speaking to Alice.

6

Dr. Pengelly had arrived on the field and had diagnosed a broken tibia; but he could not say whether any further damage had been done. He set the fractured bone and drove Alvean back to Mount Mellyn in his carriage while Connan and I rode back together in silence.

Alvean was taken to her room and given a sedative by the doctor.

"Now," he said, "there is nothing we can do but wait. I'll come back again in a few hours' time. It may be that the child is suffering acute shock. In the meantime we will keep her warm and let her sleep. She should sleep for several hours, and at the end of that time we shall know how deeply she has suffered from this shock."

When the doctor had left, Connan said to me: "Miss Leigh, I want to have a talk with you. Come to the punch room . . . now, will you please?"

I followed him there and he went on:

"There is nothing we can do but wait, Miss Leigh. We must try to be calm."

I realized that he could never have seen me agitated as I was now, and he had probably considered me incapable of such deep feeling.

Impulsively I said: "I find it hard to be as calm about my charge as you are about your daughter, Mr. TreMellyn."

I was so frightened and worried that I wanted to blame someone for what had happened, so I blamed him.

"Whatever made the child attempt such a thing?" he demanded.

"You made her," I retorted. *"You!"*

"I! But I had no idea that she was so advanced in her riding."

I realized later that I was on the verge of hysteria. I believed that

Alvean might have done herself some terrible injury and I felt almost certain that a child of her temperament would never want to ride again. I believed I had been wrong in my methods. I should not have tried to overcome her fear of horses; I had tried to win my way into her affections by showing her the way to win those of her father.

I could not rid myself of a terrible sense of guilt, and I was desperately trying to. I was saying to myself: This is a house of tragedy. Who are you to meddle in the lives of these people? What are you trying to do? To change Alvean? To change her father? To discover the truth about Alice? What do you think you are? God?

But I wouldn't blame myself entirely. I was looking for a scapegoat. I was saying to myself: He is to blame. If he had been different, none of this would have happened. I'm sure of that.

I had lost control of my feelings and on the rare occasions when people like myself do that, they usually do it more completely than those who are prone to hysterical outbursts.

"No," I cried out, "of course you had no idea that she was so advanced. How could you when you had never shown the slightest interest in the child? She was breaking her heart through your neglect. It was for that reason that she attempted this thing of which she was not capable."

"My dear Miss Leigh," he murmured. "My dear Miss Leigh." And he was looking at me in complete bewilderment.

I thought to myself: What do I care! I shall be dismissed, but in any case I have failed. I had hoped to do the impossible—to bring this man out of his own selfishness to care a little for his lonely daughter. And what have I done—made a complete mess of it and perhaps maimed the child for life. A fine one I was to complain of the conduct of others.

But I continued to blame him, and I no longer cared what I said.

"When I came here," I went on, "it did not take me long to understand the state of affairs. That poor motherless child was starved. Oh, I know she had her broth and her bread and butter at regular intervals. But there is another starvation besides that of the body. She was starved of the affection which she might expect from a parent and, as you see, she was ready to risk her life to win it."

"Miss Leigh, please, I beg of you, do be calm, do be reasonable. Are you telling me that Alvean did that——"

But I would not let him speak. "She did that for you. She thought it would please you. She has been practicing for weeks."

"I see," he said. Then he took his handkerchief from his pocket and wiped my eyes. "You did not realize it, Miss Leigh," he went on almost tenderly, "but there are tears on your cheeks."

I took the handkerchief from him and angrily wiped my tears away.

"They are tears of anger," I said.

"And of sorrow. Dear Miss Leigh, I think you care very much for Alvean."

"She is a child," I said, "and it was my job to care for her. God knows, there are few others to do it."

"I see," he answered, "that I have been behaving in a very reprehensible manner."

"How could you . . . if you had any feeling? Your own daughter! She lost her mother. Don't you see that because of her loss she needed special care?"

Then he said a surprising thing: "Miss Leigh, you came here to teach Alvean, but I think you have taught me a great deal too."

I looked at him in astonishment; I was holding his handkerchief a few inches from my tear-stained face; and at that moment Celestine Nansellock came in.

She looked at me in some surprise, but only for a second. Then she burst out: "What is this terrible thing I've heard?"

"There's been an accident, Celeste," said Connan. "Alvean was thrown."

"Oh, no!" Celestine uttered a piteous cry. "And what . . . and where . . . ?"

"She's in her room now," Connan explained. "Pengelly's set the leg. Poor child. At the moment she is asleep. He gave her something to make her sleep. He's coming again in a few hours' time."

"But how badly . . . ?"

"He's not sure. But I've seen accidents like this before. I think she'll be all right."

I was not sure whether he meant that or whether he was trying to soothe Celestine who was so upset. I felt drawn toward her; she was the only person, I believed, who really cared about Alvean.

"Poor Miss Leigh is very distressed," said Connan. "I think she fancies it is her fault. I do want to assure her that I don't think that at all."

My fault! But how could I be blamed for teaching the child to ride? And having taught her, what harm was there in her entering for a competition? No, it was his fault, I wanted to shout. She would have been contented to do what she was capable of but for him.

I said with defiance in my voice: "Alvean was so anxious to impress her father that she undertook more than she could do. I am sure that had she believed her father would be content to see her victorious in the elementary event, she would not have attempted the advanced."

Celestine had sat down and covered her face with her hands. I thought fleetingly of the occasion when I had seen her in the churchyard, kneeling by Alice's grave. I thought: Poor Celestine, she loves Alvean as her own child because she has none of her own and perhaps believes she never will have.

"We can only wait and see," said Connan.

I rose and said: "There is no point in my remaining here. I will go to my room."

But Connan put out a hand and said almost authoritatively: "No, stay here, Miss Leigh. Stay with us. You care for her deeply, I know."

I looked down at my riding habit—Alice's riding habit—and I said: "I think I should change."

It seemed that in that moment he looked at me in a new light—and perhaps so did Celestine. If they did not look at my face I must have appeared to be remarkably like Alice.

I knew it was important that I change my clothes, for in my gray cotton dress with its severe bodice I should be the governess once more and that would help me to control my feelings.

Connan nodded. He said: "But come back when you've changed, Miss Leigh. We have to comfort each other, and I want you to be here when the doctor returns."

So I went to my room and took off Alice's riding habit and put on my own gray cotton.

I was right. The cotton did help to restore my equilibrium. I began to wonder, as I buttoned the bodice, what I had said, in my outburst, to Connan TreMellyn.

The mirror showed me a face that was ravaged by grief and anxiety, eyes which burned with anger and resentment, and a mouth that was tremulous with fear.

I sent for hot water. Daisy wanted to talk, but she saw that I was too upset to do so and she went quickly away.

I bathed my face and when I had done so I went down to the punch room and rejoined Connan and Celestine, there to await the coming of Dr. Pengelly.

కోస్తిఖ

It seemed a long time before the doctor returned. Mrs. Polgrey made a pot of strong tea and Connan, Celestine, and I sat together drinking it. I did not feel astonished then, but I did later, because the accident seemed to have made them both forget that I was merely the governess. But perhaps I mean it made Connan forget; Celestine had always treated me without that condescension which I thought I had discerned in others.

Connan seemed to have forgotten my outburst and treated me with a courtly consideration and a new gentleness. I believed he was anxious that I should not blame myself in any way, and he knew that the reason I had turned on him so vehemently was that I wondered whether I had been at fault.

"She'll get over this," he said. "And she'll want to ride again. Why, when I was little older than she I had an accident which I'm sure was worse than this one. I got it in the collarbone and was unable to ride for weeks. I could scarcely wait to get back on a horse."

Celestine shivered. "I shall never have a moment's peace if she rides again after this."

"Oh, Celeste, you would wrap her in cotton wool. And then what would happen? She would go out and catch her death of cold. You must not coddle children too much. After all, they've got to face the world. They must be prepared for it in some way. What does the expert have to say to that?"

He was looking at me anxiously. I knew he was trying to keep up our spirits. He knew how deeply Celestine and I felt about this, and he was trying to be kind.

I said: "I believe one shouldn't coddle. But if children are really set against something I don't think they should be forced to do it."

"But she was not forced to ride."

"She did it most willingly," I answered. "But I cannot be sure whether she did it from a love of riding or from an intense desire to please you."

"Well," he said almost lightly, "is it not an excellent thing that a child should seek to please a parent?"

"But it should not be necessary to risk a life for the sake of a smile."

My anger was rising again and my fingers gripped the cotton of my skirt as though to remind me that I was not in Alice's riding habit now. I was the governess in my cotton gown, and it was not for me to press forward my opinions.

Both Celestine and Connan were surprised by my remark, and I went on quickly: "For instance, Alvean's talents may lie in another direction. I think she has artistic ability. She has done some good drawings. Mr. TreMellyn, I have been going to ask you for some time whether you would consider letting her have drawing lessons."

There was a tense silence in the room and I wondered why they both looked so startled.

I blundered on: "I am sure there is great talent there, and I do not feel that it should be ignored."

Connan said slowly: "But, Miss Leigh, you are here to teach my daughter. Why should it be necessary to engage other teachers?"

"Because," I replied boldly, "I believe she has a special talent. I believe it would be an added interest in her life if she were to be given drawing lessons. These should be given by a specialist in the art. She is good enough for that. I'm merely a governess, Mr. TreMellyn. I am not an artist as well."

He said rather gruffly: "Well, we shall have to go into this at some other time."

He changed the subject, and shortly afterward the doctor arrived.

I waited outside in the corridor while Connan and Celestine were with Alvean and the doctor.

A hundred images of disaster crowded into my mind. I imagined that she died of her injuries. I saw myself leaving the place, never to return. If I did that I should feel that my life had been incomplete in some way. I realized that if I had to go away I should be a very unhappy woman. Then I thought of her, maimed for life, more difficult than she had been previously, a wretched and unhappy little girl; and myself devoting my life to her. It was a gloomy picture.

Celestine joined me.

"This suspense is terrible," she said. "I wonder whether we ought to get another doctor. Dr. Pengelly is sixty. I am afraid . . ."

"He seemed efficient," I said.

"I want the best for her. If anything happens to her . . ."

She was biting her lips in her anguish, and I thought how strange it was that she, who always seemed so calm about everything else, should be so emotional over Alice and her daughter.

I wanted to put my arm about her and comfort her, but of course, remembering my position, I did no such thing.

Dr. Pengelly came out with Connan, and the doctor was smiling.

"Injuries," he said, "a fractured tibia. Beyond that . . . there's very little wrong."

"Oh, thank God!" cried Celestine, and I echoed her words.

"A day or so and she'll be feeling better. It'll just be a matter of mending that fracture. Children's bones mend easily. There's nothing for you two ladies to worry about."

"Can we see her?" asked Celestine eagerly.

"Yes, of course you can. She's awake now, and she asked for Miss Leigh. I'm going to give her another dose in half an hour, and that will ensure a good night's sleep. You'll see a difference in her in the morning."

We went into the room. Alvean was lying on her back looking very ill, poor child; but she gave us a wan smile when she saw us.

"Hello, miss," she said. "Hello, Aunt Celestine."

Celestine knelt by the bed, took her hand and covered it with kisses. I stood on the other side of the bed and the child's eyes were on me.

"I didn't do it," she said.

"Well, it was a good try."

Connan was standing at the foot of the bed.

I went on: "Your father was proud of you."

"He'll think I was silly," she said.

"No, he doesn't," I cried vehemently. "He is here to tell you so."

Connan came round to the side of the bed and stood beside me.

"He's proud of you," I said. "He told me so. He said it didn't matter that you fell. He said all that mattered was that you tried; and you'd do it next time."

"Did he? Did he?"

"Yes, he did," I cried; and there was an angry note in my voice because he still said nothing and the child was waiting for him to confirm my words.

Then he spoke. "You did splendidly, Alvean. I *was* proud of you."

A faint smile touched those pale lips. Then she murmured: "Miss . . . oh miss . . ." And then: "Don't go away, will you. Don't *you* go away."

I sank down on my knees then. I took her hand and kissed it. The tears were on my cheeks again.

I cried: "I'll stay, Alvean. I'll stay with you always." I looked up and saw Celestine watching me from the other side of the bed. I was aware of Connan, standing beside me. Then I amended those words, and the governess in me spoke. "I'll stay as long as I'm wanted," I said firmly.

Alvean was satisfied.

❦

When she was sleeping we left her and as I was about to go to my room, Connan said: "Come into my library a moment with us, Miss Leigh. The doctor wants to discuss the case with you."

So I went into the library with him, Celestine, and the doctor, and we talked of the nursing of Alvean.

Celestine said: "I shall come over every day. In fact I wonder, Connan, whether I shouldn't come over and stay while she's ill. It might make things easier."

"You ladies must settle that," answered Dr. Pengelly. "Keep the child amused. We don't want her getting depressed while those bones are knitting together."

"We'll keep her amused," I said. "Any special diet, Doctor?"

"For a day or so, light invalid foods. Steamed fish, milk puddings, custards, and so on. But after a few days let her have what she wants."

I was almost gay, and this swift reversal of feeling made me slightly lightheaded.

I listened to the doctor's instructions and Connan's assurance that there was no need for Celestine to stay at the house; he was sure Miss Leigh would manage and it would be wonderfully comforting for Miss Leigh to know that in any emergency she could always ask for Celestine's help.

"Well Connan," said Celestine, "perhaps it's as well. People talk. And if I stayed here . . . Oh, people are so ridiculous. But they are always ready to gossip."

I saw the point. If Celestine lived at Mount Mellyn, people would begin to couple her name with Connan's; whereas the fact that I, an employee of the same age, lived in the house aroused no comment. I was not of the same social standing.

Connan laughed and said: "How did you come over, Celeste?"

"I rode over on Speller."

"Right. I'll ride back with you."

"Oh, thank you, Connan. It's nice of you. But I can go alone if you'd rather . . ."

"Nonsense! I'm coming." He turned to me. "As for you, Miss Leigh, you looked exhausted. I should advise you to go to bed and have a good night's sleep."

I was sure I could not rest, and my expression must have implied this, for the doctor said: "I'll give you a draught, Miss Leigh. Take it five minutes before retiring for the night. I think I can promise you a good night's sleep."

"Thank you," I said appreciatively, for I suddenly realized how exhausted I was.

I believed that tomorrow I should wake up, my usual calm self, able to cope with whatever new situation should be the result of all that had happened today.

◀§ဥ▶

I went to my room, where I found a supper tray waiting for me. It contained a wing of cold chicken, appetizing enough on most occasions, but tonight I had no appetite.

I toyed with it for a while and ate a few mouthfuls, but I was too upset to eat.

I thought it would be an excellent idea to take Dr. Pengelly's sleeping draught and retire for the night.

I was about to do so when there was a knock on my door.

"Come in," I called, and Mrs. Polgrey came. She looked distraught. No wonder, I thought. Who in this household isn't?

"It's terrible," she began.

But I cut in quickly: "She'll be all right, Mrs. Polgrey. The doctor said so."

"Oh yes, I heard the news. It's Gilly, miss, I'm worried about her."

"Gilly!"

"She didn't come back from the show, miss. I haven't seen her since this afternoon."

"Oh, she's wandering about somewhere, I expect. I wonder if she saw . . ."

"I can't understand it, miss. I can't understand her being at the show. She's afeared of going near the horses. You could have knocked me down with a feather when I heard she was there. And now . . . she's not come in."

"But she does wander off alone, doesn't she?"

"Yes, but she'll always be in for her tea. I don't know what can have become of her."

"Has the house been searched?"

"Yes, miss. I've looked everywhere. Kitty and Daisy have helped me. So's Polgrey. The child's not in the house."

I said: "I'll come and help look for her."

So instead of going to bed, I joined in the search for Gillyflower.

I was very worried because on this day of tragedy I was prepared for anything to happen. What could have happened to little Gilly? I visualized a thousand things. I thought she might have wandered onto the beach and been caught by the tide, and I pictured her little body thrown up by the waves in Mellyn Cove as her mother's had been eight years ago.

That was morbid. No, Gilly had gone wandering and had fallen asleep somewhere. I remembered that I had seen her often in the woods. But she would not be lost if she were in the woods. She knew every inch of them.

I nevertheless made my way to the woods, calling "Gilly! Gilly!" as I went; and the mist, which was rising again with the coming of evening, seemed to catch my voice and muffle it as though it were in cotton wool.

I searched those woods thoroughly because my intuition told me that she was there, and that she was not lost but hiding.

I was right. I came across her lying in a clearing surrounded by small conifers.

I had seen her in this spot once or twice and I guessed it was a haven to her.

"Gilly!" I called. "Gilly!" And as soon as she heard my voice she sprang to her feet. She was poised to run but she hesitated when I called to her: "Gilly, it's all right. I'm here all alone and I won't hurt you."

She looked like a wild fairy child, her extraordinary white hair hanging damply about her shoulders.

"Why, Gilly," I said, "you'll catch cold, lying on that damp grass. Why are you hiding, Gilly?"

Her big eyes watched my face, and I knew that it was fear of something which had driven her to this refuge in the woods.

If only she would talk to me! If only she would explain.

"Gilly," I said, "we're friends, aren't we? You know that. I'm your friend—as Madam was."

She nodded and the fear slipped from her face. I thought: She has seen me in Alice's riding clothes and I believe, in her confused little mind, she has bracketed us together in some way.

I put my arm about her; her dress was damp and I could see the mist on her pale brows and lashes.

"Why, Gilly, you are cold."

She allowed me to cuddle her. I said: "Come on, Gilly, we're going back. Your grandmamma is very anxious. She is wondering what has become of you."

She allowed me to lead her from the clearing, but I was aware of the reluctant drag of her feet.

I kept my arm firmly about her, and I said: "You were at the horse show this afternoon."

She turned to me and as she buried her face against me, her little hands gripped the cloth of my dress. I was conscious of her trembling.

Then in a flash of understanding I began to see what had happened. This child, like Alvean, was terrified of horses. Of course she was. Had she not been almost trampled to death by one?

I believed that as Alvean had been suffering from temporary shock, so was this child; but the shock which had come to her was of longer duration, and she had never known anyone who had been able to help her fight the darkness which had descended upon her.

In that misty wood I felt like a woman who has a mission. I was not going to turn my face from a poor child who needed help.

She was suffering from a return of that earlier shock. This afternoon she had seen Alvean beneath a horse's hoofs as she herself had been—after all, it had happened only four years ago.

At that moment I heard the sound of horse's hoofs in the wood, and I shouted: "Hello, I've found her."

"Hello! Coming, Miss Leigh." And I was exhilarated—almost unbearably so—because that was Connan's voice.

I guessed that he had returned from Mount Widden to discover that Gilly was lost and that he had joined the search party. Perhaps he knew that I had come to the woods and had decided to join me.

He came into sight and Gilly shrank closer to me, keeping her face hidden.

"She's here," I called. He came close to us and I went on: "She is exhausted, poor child. Take her up with you."

He leaned forward to take her, but she cried out: "No! No!"

He was astonished to hear her speak, but I was not. I had already discovered that in moments of stress she did so.

I said: "Gilly. Go up there with the master. I'll walk beside you and hold your hand."

She shook her head.

I went on: "Look! This is May Morning. She wants to carry you because she knows you're tired."

Gilly's eyes turned to look at May Morning, and, in the fear I saw there, was the clue.

"Take her," I said to Connan, and he stooped and swung her up in his arms and set her in front of him.

She tried to fight, but I kept talking to her soothingly. "You're safe up there. And we'll get back more quickly. You'll find a nice bowl of bread and milk waiting for you, and then there'll be your warm cosy bed. I'll hold your hand all the time and walk beside you."

She no longer struggled but kept her hand in mine.

And so ended that strange day, with Connan and myself bringing in the lost child.

When she was lifted from the horse and handed to her grandmother, Connan gave me a smile which I thought was infinitely charming. That was because it held none of the mockery which I had seen hitherto.

I went up to my room, exultation wrapped about me as the mist wrapped itself about the house. It was tinged with melancholy but the joy was so strong that the mingling of my feelings was difficult to understand.

I knew of course what had happened to me. Today had made it very clear. I had done a foolish thing—perhaps the most foolish thing I had ever done in my life.

I had fallen in love for the first time, and with someone who was quite out of my world. I was in love with the master of Mount Mellyn, and I had an uneasy feeling that he might be aware of it.

On the table by my bed was the draught which Dr. Pengelly had given me.

I locked my door, undressed, drank the draught, and went to bed.

But before I got into bed I looked at myself in my pink flannelette nightdress, primly buttoned up to the throat. Then I laughed at the incongruity of my thoughts and said aloud in my best governess's tones: "In the morning, after the good night's rest Dr. Pengelly's potion will give you, you'll come to your senses."

❦

The next few weeks were the happiest I had so far spent in Mount Mellyn. It soon became clear that Alvean had suffered no great harm. I was delighted to find that she had lost none of her keenness for

riding and asked eager questions about Black Prince's slight injuries, taking it for granted that she would soon ride him again.

We resumed school after the first week; she was pleased to do so.
I also taught her to play chess, and she picked up the game with
astonishing speed; and if I handicapped myself by playing without
my Queen she was even able to checkmate me.

But it was not only Alvean's progress which made me so happy. It
was the fact that Connan was in the house; and what astonished me
was that, although he made no reference to my outburst on the day of
the accident, he had clearly noted it and would appear in Alvean's
room with books and puzzles which he thought would be of interest
to her.

In the first days I said to him: "There is one thing that pleases her
more than all the presents you bring: that is your own company."

He had answered: "What an odd child she must be to prefer me to
a book or a game."

I smiled at him and he returned my smile; and again I was aware of
that change in his expression.

Sometimes he would sit down and watch our game of chess. Then
he would range himself on Alvean's side against me. I would protest
and demand that I be allowed to have my Queen back.

Alvean would sit smiling, and he would say: "Look, Alvean. We'll
put our bishop there, and that'll make our dear Miss Leigh look to her
defenses."

Alvean would giggle and throw me a triumphant glance, and I
would be so happy to be with the two of them that I grew almost careless and nearly lost the game. But not quite. I never forgot that between Connan and me there was a certain battle in progress and I
always wanted to prove my mettle. Though it was only a game of
chess I wanted to show him I was his match.

He said one day: "When Alvean's movable we'll drive over to
Fowey and have a picnic."

"Why go to Fowey," I asked, "when we have a perfect picnic beach
here?"

"My dear Miss Leigh"—he had acquired a habit of calling me his
dear Miss Leigh—"do you not know that other people's beaches are
more exciting than one's own?"

"Oh yes, Papa," cried Alvean. "Do let's have a picnic."

She was so eager to get well for the picnic that she ate all the food
which was brought to her and talked of the expedition continually. Dr.
Pengelly was delighted with her; so were we all.

I said to Connan one day: "But you are the real cure. You have made her happy because at last you let her see that you are aware of her existence."

Then he did a surprising thing. He took my hand and lightly kissed my cheek. It was very different from that kiss which he had given me on the night of the ball. This was swift, friendly, passionless yet affectionate.

"No," he said, "it is you who are the real cure, my dear Miss Leigh."

I thought he was going to say something more. But he did not do so. Instead, he left me abruptly.

❦

I did not forget Gilly. I determined to fight for her as I had for Alvean, and I thought the best way of doing so was to speak to Connan about it. He was in that mood, I believed, to grant me what I asked. I should not have been surprised if, when Alvean was about again, he had changed to his old self—forgetful of her, full of mockery for me. So I decided to strike my blow for Gilly while I had a chance of success.

I boldly went down to the punch room, when I knew he was there one morning, and asked if I might speak to him.

"But of course, Miss Leigh," he replied. "It is always a pleasure to speak with you."

I came straight to the point. "I want to do something for Gilly."

"Yes?"

"I do not believe she is half-witted. I think that no one has made any attempt to help her. I have heard about her accident. Before that, I understand, she was quite a normal little girl. Don't you see that it might be possible to make her normal once again?"

I saw a return of that mockery to his eyes as he said lightly: "I believe that as with God, so with Miss Leigh, all things are possible."

I ignored the flippancy. "I am asking your permission to give her lessons."

"My dear Miss Leigh, does not the pupil you came here to teach take up all your time?"

"I have a little spare time, Mr. TreMellyn. Even governesses have that. I would be ready to teach Gilly in my own time, providing of course you do not expressly forbid it."

"If I forbade you I am sure you would find some way of doing it,

so I think it would be simpler if I say: Go ahead with your plans for
Gilly. I wish you all success."

"Thank you," I said; and turned to go.

"Miss Leigh," he called. I stood waiting.

"Let us go on that picnic soon. I could carry Alvean, if necessary,
to and from the carriage."

"That would be excellent, Mr. TreMellyn. I'll tell her at once. I
know it will delight her."

"And you, Miss Leigh, does it delight you?"

For a moment I thought he was coming toward me and I started
back. I was suddenly afraid that he would place his hands on my
shoulders and that at his touch I might betray myself.

I said coolly: "Anything which is going to be so good for Alvean
delights me, Mr. TreMellyn."

And I hurried back to Alvean to tell her the good news.

~§~

So the weeks passed—pleasurable, wonderful weeks which I sometimes felt could never be repeated.

I had taken Gilly to the schoolroom and had even managed to teach
her a few letters. She delighted in pictures and quickly became absorbed in them. I really believed she enjoyed our lessons, for she
would present herself at the schoolroom each day at the appointed
time.

She had been heard to speak a few words now and then, and I
knew that the whole household was watching the experiment with
amusement and interest.

When Alvean was well enough to take lessons in the schoolroom
I should have to be prepared for opposition. Alvean's aversion to
Gilly was apparent. I had brought the child into the sick room on one
occasion and Alvean had immediately become sulky. I thought: When
she is quite well I shall have to reconcile her to Gilly. But that was
one of the problems of the future. I knew very well that when life
returned to normal I could not expect these days of pleasure to
continue.

There were plenty of visitors for Alvean. Celestine was there every
day. She brought fruit and other presents for her. Peter came and she
was always pleased to see him.

Once he said to her: "Do you not think I am a devoted uncle to call
and see you so often, Alvean?"

She had retorted: "Oh, but you don't come to see me only, do you, Uncle Peter. You come mainly for miss."

He had replied in characteristic style: "I come to see you both. How fortunate I am to have two such charming ladies on whom to call."

Lady Treslyn called with expensive books and flowers for Alvean, but Alvean received her sullenly and would scarcely speak to her.

"She is an invalid still, Lady Treslyn," I explained; and the smile which was flashed upon me almost took my breath away, so beautiful was it.

"Of course I understand," Lady Treslyn told me. "Poor child! Mr. TreMellyn tells me that she has been brave and you have been wonderful. I tell him how lucky he is to have found such a treasure. 'They are not easy to come by,' I said. I reminded him of how my last cook walked out in the middle of a dinner party. She was another such treasure."

I bowed my head and hated her—not because she had linked me in her mind with her cook, but because she was so beautiful, and I knew that rumors persisted about her and Connan and I feared that there was truth in them.

Connan seemed different when this woman was in the house. I felt that he scarcely saw me. I heard the sounds of their laughter and I wondered sadly what they said to each other. I saw them in the gardens and I told myself there was an unmistakable intimacy in the very way they walked together.

Then I realized what a fool I had been, for I had been harboring thoughts which I would not dare express, even to myself. I tried to pretend they did not exist. But they did—and in spite of my better sense they kept intruding.

I dared not look into the future.

Celestine one day suggested that she should take Alvean over to Mount Widden for the day and look after her there.

"It would be a change," she said.

"Connan," she added, "you shall come to dinner, and you can bring her back afterward."

He agreed to do so. I was disappointed not to be included in the invitation; which showed what a false picture I had allowed myself to make of the situation during these incredible weeks. Imagine me—the governess—invited to dine at Mount Widden!

I laughed at my own foolishness, but there was a note of bitterness and sadness. It was like waking up to a chilly morning after weeks of sunshine so brilliant that you thought it was going to last for ever; it was like the first gathering of storm clouds in a summer sky.

❧

Connan drove Alvean over in the carriage and I was left alone without any definite duties for the first time since I arrived here.

I gave Gilly her lesson but I did not believe in taxing the child too much, and when I had returned her to her grandmother I wondered what I was going to do.

Then an idea struck me. Why should I not go for a ride, a long ride? Perhaps on the moors.

I immediately remembered that day when Alvean and I had ridden to her Great-aunt Clara. I began to feel rather excited. I was remembering the mystery of Alice again, which I had forgotten during those halcyon weeks of Alvean's convalescence. I began to wonder whether I had been so interested in Alice's story because I needed some interest to prevent me from brooding on my own.

I thought to myself, Great-aunt Clara will want to hear how Alvean is getting on. In any case she had treated me with the utmost friendliness and had made it clear that I should be welcomed any time I called. Of course it would be different, calling without Alvean; but then I believed that she had been more interested in talking to me than to the child.

So I made up my mind.

I went to Mrs. Polgrey and said: "Alvean will be away all day. I propose to take a day's holiday."

Mrs. Polgrey had become very fond of me since I had taken such an interest in Gilly. She really did love the child, I believed. It was merely because she had assumed that Gilly's strangeness had been the price which had to be paid for her parents' sins that she had accepted her as *non compos mentis*.

"And none deserves a holiday more, miss," she said to me. "Where are you going?"

"I think I'll go on to the moors. I'll take luncheon at an inn."

"Do you think you should, miss, by yourself?"

I smiled at her. "I am very well able to take care of myself, Mrs. Polgrey."

"Well, there be bogs on the moor and mists and the Little People, some say."

"Little People indeed!"

"Ah, don' 'ee laugh at 'em, miss. They don't like people to laugh at 'em. There's some as say they've seen 'em. Little gnomelike men in sugar-loaf hats. If they don't like 'ee they'll lead 'ee astray with their fairy lanterns, and afore you knows where you be, you'm in the middle of a bog that sucks 'ee down and won't let 'ee go however much you do struggle."

I gave a shiver. "I'll be careful, and I wouldn't dream of offending the Little People. If I meet any I'll be very polite."

"You'm mocking, miss, I do believe."

"I'll be all right, Mrs. Polgrey. Don't have any fears about me."

I went to the stables and asked Tapperty which horse I could have today.

"There's May Morning if you'd like her. She be free."

I told him I was going to the moors. "A good chance to see the country," I added.

"Trust you, miss. Bain't much you miss." And he laughed to himself as though enjoying some private joke.

"You be going with a companion, miss?" he asked slyly.

I said that I was going alone, but I could see that he did not believe me.

I felt rather angry with him because I guessed that his thoughts were on Peter Nansellock. I believed that my name had been coupled with his since he had been so foolish as to send Jacinth over for me.

I wondered too if my growing friendship with Connan had been noted. I was horrified at the possibility. Oddly enough I could bear to contemplate their sly remarks, which I was sure were exchanged out of my hearing, about Peter and me; it would be a different matter if they talked in that way of me and Connan.

How ridiculous! I told myself as I walked May Morning out of the stables and down to the village.

There is nothing to talk about between you and Connan. But there is, I answered myself; and I fell to thinking of those two occasions when he had kissed me.

I looked across the cove at Mount Widden. Wistfully I hoped that I should meet Connan coming back. But I didn't, of course; he would stay there with Alvean and his friends. Why should I imagine that he would want to come back to be with me? I was letting this foolish habit of daydreaming get the better of my common sense.

But I continued to hope until I had left the village well behind me and I came to the first gray wall and boulders of the moor.

It was a sparkling December morning and there were great golden patches of gorse dotted over the moor.

I could smell the peaty soil, and the wind which had veered a little to the north was fresh and exhilarating.

I wanted to gallop across the moor with that wind in my face. I gave way to my desire and while I did so I imagined that Connan was riding beside me and that he called to me to stop that he might tell me what a difference I had made to his life as well as Alvean's, and that, incongruous as it seemed, he was in love with me.

In this moorland country it was possible to believe in fantastic dreams; as some told themselves that these tracts of land were inhabited by the Little People, so I told myself that it was not impossible that Connan TreMellyn would fall in love with me.

At midday I arrived at the House on the Moor. It was very like that other occasion; the elderly housekeeper came out to welcome me and I was taken into Great-aunt Clara's sitting room.

"Good day to you, Miss Leigh! And all alone today?"

So no one had told her of Alvean's accident. I was astonished. I should have thought Connan would have sent someone over to explain, since the old lady was obviously interested in her great-niece.

I told her about the accident and she looked very concerned. I hastily added that Alvean was getting on well and would soon be about again.

"But you must be in need of some refreshment, Miss Leigh," she said. "Let us have a glass of my elderberry wine; and will you stay to luncheon?"

I said it was most kind of her to invite me and if it were not causing too much inconvenience, I should be delighted to do so.

We sipped our elderberry wine, and once more I was conscious of that heady feeling which I had experienced after her dandelion wine on the previous occasion. Luncheon consisted of mutton with caper sauce exceedingly well cooked and served; and afterward we retired to the drawing room for what she called a little chat.

This was what I had been hoping for, and I was not to be disappointed.

"Tell me," she said, "how is dear little Alvean? Is she happier now?"

"Why . . . yes, I think she is very much happier. In fact I think she has been more so since her accident. Her father has been attentive, and she is very fond of him."

"Ah," said Great-aunt Clara, "her father." She looked at me, and her bright blue eyes showed her excitement. I knew she was one of those women who cannot resist talking; and since she spent so much of her time with only her own household, the coming of a visitor was an irresistible temptation.

I was determined to make the temptation even more irresistible. I said tentatively: "There is not the usual relationship between them, I fancy."

There was a slight pause, and then she said quickly: "No. I suppose it is inevitable."

I did not speak. I waited breathlessly, afraid that she might change her mind. She was hovering on the edge of confidences and I felt that she could give me some vital clue to the situation at Mount Mellyn, to the story of the TreMellyns which I was beginning reluctantly to admit might very well become my story.

"I sometimes blame myself," she said, as though she were talking to herself; and indeed her blue eyes looked beyond me as though she were looking back over the years and was quite unconscious of my presence.

"The question is," she went on, "how much should one interfere in the lives of others?"

It was a question which had often interested me. I had certainly tried to interfere in the lives of the people I had met since I entered Mount Mellyn.

"Alice was with me after the engagement," she went on. "Everything could have changed then. But I persuaded her. You see, I thought *he* was the better man."

She was being a little incoherent, and I was afraid to ask her to elucidate lest I break the spell. She might remember that she was betraying confidences to a young woman who was more curious than she should be.

"I wonder what would have happened if she had acted differently then. Do you ever play that game with yourself, Miss Leigh? Do you ever say: Now if at a certain point I—or someone else—had done such and such . . . the whole tenor of life for that person would have changed?"

"Yes," I said. "Everybody does. You think that things would have been different for your niece and for Alvean?"

"Oh yes . . . for her—Alice—more than most. She had come to a real turning point. A crossroads, one might say. Go this way and you have such and such a life. Go that way and everything will be quite different. It frightens me sometimes because if she had turned to the right instead of the left . . . as it were . . . she might be here today. After all, if she had married Geoffry there would not have been any need to run away with him, would there?"

"I see you were in her confidence."

"Indeed yes. I'm afraid I had quite a big part in shaping what happened. That's what alarmed me. Did I do right?"

"I am sure you did what you thought was right, and that is all any of us can do. You loved your niece very much, did you not?"

"Very much. My children were boys, you see, and I'd always wanted a girl. Alice used to come and play with my family . . . three boys and no girl. I used to hope that she might marry one of them. Cousins though. Perhaps that would not have been good. I didn't live in this house then. We were in Penzance. Alice's parents had a big estate some few miles inland. That's her husband's now of course. She had a good fortune to bring to a husband. All the same, perhaps it would not have been good for cousins to marry. In any case they were set on the marriage with the TreMellyns."

"So that was *arranged.*"

"Yes. Alice's father was dead, and her mother—she was my sister— had always been very fond of Connan TreMellyn—the elder I mean. There have been Connans in that family for centuries. The eldest son was always given the name. I think my sister would have liked to marry the present Connan's father, but other marriages were arranged for them, and so they wanted their children to marry. They were betrothed when Connan was twenty and Alice, eighteen. The marriage was to take place a year later."

"So it was indeed a marriage of convenience."

"How odd it is! Marriages of convenience often turn out to be marriages of inconvenience, do they not? They thought it would be a good idea if she came to stay with me. You see, I was within a few hours' riding distance from Mount Mellyn, and the young people could meet often like that . . . without her staying at the house. Of course you might say: Why did not her mother take her to stay at Mount Mellyn? My sister was very ill at that time and not able to travel. In any case it was arranged that she should stay with me."

"And I suppose Mr. TreMellyn rode over to see her often."

"Yes. But not as often as I should have expected. I began to suspect that they were not as well matched as their fortunes were."

"Tell me about Alice," I said earnestly. "What sort of girl was she?"

"How can I explain her to you? The word 'light' comes to my mind. She was lighthearted, light-minded. I do not mean she was light in her morals—which is a sense in which some people use the word. Although of course, after what happened . . . But who shall judge? You see, he came over here to paint. He did some beautiful pictures of the moors."

"Who? Connan TreMellyn?"

"Oh, dear me no! Geoffry. Geoffry Nansellock. He was an artist of some reputation. Did you not know that?"

"No," I said. "I know nothing of him except that he was killed with Alice last July twelvemonth."

"He came over here often while she was with me. In fact he came more often than Connan did. I began to understand how matters stood. There was something between them. They would go off together and he'd have his painting things with him. She used to say she was going to watch him at work. She would be a painter herself perhaps one day. But of course it was not painting they did together."

"They were . . . in love?" I asked.

"I was rather frightened when she told me. You see, there was going to be a child."

I caught my breath in surprise. Alvean, I thought. No wonder he could not bring himself to love her. No wonder my statement that she possessed artistic talent upset him and Celestine.

"She told me two weeks before the day fixed for her wedding. She was almost certain, she said. She did not think she could be mistaken. She said, 'What shall I do, Aunt Clara? Shall I marry Geoffry?'

"I said: 'Does Geoffry want to marry you, my dear?' And she answered: 'He would have to, would he not, if I told him?'

"I know now that she should have told him. It was only right that she should. But her marriage was already arranged, Alice was an heiress and I wondered whether Geoffry had hoped for this. You see the Nansellocks had very little and Alice's fortune would have been a blessing to them. I wondered . . . as one does wonder. He had a certain reputation too. There had been others who had found themselves in Alice's condition, and it was due to him. I did not think she would be very happy with him for long."

There was silence, and I felt as though vital parts of a puzzle were being fitted together to give my picture meaning.

"I remember her . . . that day," the old lady continued. "It was in this very room. I often go over it. She talked to me about it . . . unburdening herself as I'm unburdening myself to you. It's been on my conscience for the last year . . . ever since she died. You see, she said to me: 'What shall I do, Aunt Clara? Help me. . . . Tell me what I should do.'

"And I answered her. I said: 'There's only one thing you can do, my dear; and that is go on with your marriage to Connan TreMellyn. You're betrothed to him. You must forget what happened with Geoffry Nansellock.' And she said to me: 'Aunt Clara, how can I forget? There'll be a living reminder, won't there?' Then I did this terrible thing. I said to her: 'You must marry. Your child will be born prematurely.' Then she threw back her head and laughed and laughed. It was hysterical laughter. Poor Alice, she was near breaking point."

Great-aunt Clara sat back in her chair; she looked as though she had just come out of a trance. I really believe she had been seeing not me sitting opposite her, but Alice.

She was now a little frightened because she was wondering whether she had told me too much.

I said nothing. I was picturing it all; the wedding which would have been a ceremonial occasion; the death of Alice's mother almost immediately afterward; and Connan's father's death the following year. The marriage had been arranged to please them and they had not lived long to enjoy it. And Alice was left with Connan—my Connan—and Alvean, the child of another man, whom she had tried to pass off as his. She had not succeeded—that much I knew.

He had kept up the pretense that Alvean was his daughter, but he had never accepted her as such in his mind. Alvean knew it; she admired him so much; but she suspected something was wrong and she was uncertain; she longed to be accepted as his daughter. Perhaps he had never really discovered whether she was or not.

The situation was fraught with drama. And yet, I thought, what good can come of brooding on it? Alice is dead; Alvean and Connan are alive. Let them forget what happened in the past. If they were wise they would try to make happiness for each other in the future.

"Oh my dear," sighed Great-aunt Clara, "how I talk! It is like living it all again. I have wearied you." A little fear crept into her voice. "I have talked too much and you, Miss Leigh, have played no part in all this. I trust you will keep what I have said to yourself."

"You may trust me to do so," I assured her.

"I knew it. I would not have told you otherwise. But in any case, it is all so long ago. It has been a comfort to talk to you. I think about it all sometimes during the night. You see, it might have been right for her to marry Geoffry. Perhaps she thought so, and that was why she tried to run away with him. To think of them on that train! It seems like the judgment of God, doesn't it?"

"No," I said sharply. "There were many other people on that train who were killed. They weren't all on the point of leaving their husbands for other men."

She laughed on a high note. "How right you are! I knew you had lots of common sense. And you don't think I did wrong? You see, I sometimes tell myself that if I had persuaded her not to marry Connan, she wouldn't have. That is what frightens me. I pointed the way to her destiny."

"You must not blame yourself," I said. "Whatever you did you did because you thought it was best for her. And we, after all, make our own destinies. I am sure of that."

"You do comfort me, Miss Leigh. You will stay and have tea with me, won't you?"

"It is kind of you, but I think I should be back before dark."

"Oh yes, you must be back before dark."

"It grows dark so early at this time of year."

"Then I must not be selfish and keep you. Miss Leigh, when Alvean is well enough, you will bring her over to see me?"

"I promise I shall."

"And if you yourself feel like coming over before that . . ."

"Depend upon it, I shall come. You have given me a very pleasant and interesting time."

The fear came back into her eyes. "You will remember it was in confidence?"

I reassured her. I knew that this charming old lady's greatest pleasure in life must have been sharing confidences, telling a little more than was discreet. Well, I thought, we all have our little vices.

She came to the door to wave me on when I left.

"It's been so pleasant," she reiterated. "And don't forget." She put her finger to her lips and her eyes sparkled.

I imitated the gesture and, waving, rode off.

I was very thoughtful on the way home. This day I had learned so much.

I was nearly at Mellyn village when the thought struck me that Gilly was Alvean's half-sister. I remembered then the drawings I had seen of Alvean and Gilly combined.

So Alvean knew. Or did she merely fear? Was she trying to convince herself that her father was not Geoffry Nansellock—which would make her Gilly's half-sister? Or did her great desire for Connan's approval really mean that she was longing for him to accept her as his daughter?

I felt a great desire to help them all out of this morass of tragedy into which Alice's indiscretion had plunged them.

I can do it, I told myself. I will do it.

Then I thought of Connan with Lady Treslyn, and I was filled with disquiet. What absurd and impossible dreams I was indulging in. What chance had I—the governess—of showing Connan the way to happiness?

~§§~

Christmas was rapidly approaching, and it brought with it all that excitement which I remembered so well from the old days in my father's vicarage.

Kitty and Daisy were constantly whispering together; Mrs. Polgrey said they nearly drove her crazy, and that their work was more skimped than usual, though that had to be seen to be believed. She went about the house sighing "Nowadays . . ." and shaking her head in sorrow. But even she was excited.

The weather was warm, more like the approach of spring than of winter. On my walks in the woods I noticed that the primroses had begun to bloom.

"My dear life," said Tapperty, "primroses in December be nothing new to we. Spring do come early to Cornwall."

I began to think about Christmas presents and I made a little list. There must be something for Phillida and her family, and Aunt Adelaide; but I was mainly concerned with the people at Mount Mellyn. I had a little money to spend, since I used very little and had saved most of what I had earned since I had taken my post at Mount Mellyn.

One day I went into Plymouth and did my Christmas shopping. I went on Royal Rover and left him at a well-known hostelry where he would be looked after until I was ready to return.

I bought books for Phillida and her family and had them sent direct to her; I bought a scarf for Aunt Adelaide and that was sent direct too. I spent a long time choosing what I would give the Mellyn household. Finally I decided on scarves for Kitty and Daisy, red and green which would suit them, and a blue one for Gilly to match her eyes. For Mrs. Polgrey I bought a bottle of whisky which I was sure would delight her more than anything else, and for Alvean some handkerchiefs in many colors with A embroidered on them.

I was pleased with my purchases. I was beginning to grow as excited about Christmas as Daisy and Kitty.

The weather continued very mild, and on Christmas Eve I helped Mrs. Polgrey and the girls to decorate the great hall and some of the other rooms.

The men had been out the previous day and brought in ivy, holly, box, and bay. I was shown how the pillars in the great hall were entwined with these leaves and Daisy and Kitty taught me how to make Christmas bushes; they were delightedly shocked by an ignorance like mine. I had never before heard of a Christmas bush! We took two wooden hoops—one inserted into the other—and this ball-like framework we decorated with evergreen leaves and furze; then we hung oranges and apples on it; and I must say this made a pretty show. These we hung in some of the windows.

The biggest logs were carried in for the fireplaces; then the servants' hall was decorated in exactly the same manner as the great hall, and the house was filled with laughter.

"We do have our ball here while the family be having theirs," Daisy told me; and I wondered to which ball I should go. Perhaps to neither. A governess's position was somewhere in between, I supposed.

"My life!" cried Daisy. "I can scarcely wait for the day. Last Christmas was a quiet one . . . had to be on account of the house being in mourning. But we in the servants' hall managed pretty well. There was dash-an-darras and metheglin to drink, and Mrs. Polgrey's sloe gin had to be tasted to be believed. There was mutton and beef, I remember, and hog's pudding. No feast in these parts ain't complete without hog's pudding. You ask Father!"

All through Christmas Eve the smell of baking filled the kitchen and its neighborhood. Tapperty, with Billy Trehay and some of the boys from the stables, came to the door just to smell it. Mrs. Tapperty was up at the house all day working in the kitchen. I scarcely recognized the usually calm and dignified Mrs. Polgrey. She was bustling about, her face flushed, purring, stirring, and talking ecstatically of pies which bore the odd name of squab and lammy, giblet, muggety, and herby.

I was called in to help. "Do 'ee keep your eye on that saucepan, miss, and should it come to the boil tell I quickly." Mrs. Polgrey's dialect became more and more broad as the excitement grew, and I could scarcely understand the language which was being bandied about in the kitchen that Christmas.

I was smiling fatuously at a whole batch of pasties which had just come out of the oven, golden-brown pastry with the smell of savory meats and onions, when Kitty came in shouting: "M'am, the curl singers be here."

"Well, bring 'em, bring 'em in, ye daftie," cried Mrs. Polgrey, forgetting dignity in the excitement and wiping her hand across her sweating brow. "What be 'ee waiting for? Don't 'ee know, me dear, that it be bad luck to keep curl singers waiting?"

I followed her into the hall, where a company of village youths and girls had gathered. They were already singing when we arrived, and I then understood that the "curl" singers were carol singers.

They rendered "The Seven Joys of Mary," "The Holly and the Ivy," "The Twelve Days of Christmas," and "The First Noel." We all joined in.

Then the leader of the group began to sing:

> *"Come let me taste your Christmas beer*
> *That is so very strong,*
> *And I do wish that Christmas time,*
> *With all its mirth and song,*
> *Was twenty times as long."*

Then Mrs. Polgrey signed to Daisy and Kitty, who were already on their way, I guessed, to bring refreshment to the party after this gentle reminder.

Metheglin was served to the singers with blackberry and elderberry wine, and into their hands were thrust great pasties, some containing meat, some fish. The satisfaction was evident.

And when they had finished eating and drinking, a bowl—tied with red ribbons and decorated with furze—was handed to Mrs. Polgrey who very majestically placed some coins into it.

When they had gone Daisy said: "Well, now that lot have come a-gooding, what's to be next?"

She delighted in my ignorance, of course, when I had to ask what "a-gooding" meant.

"My dear life, you don't know all, miss, do 'ee now? To go a-gooding means to go collecting for Christmas wine or a Christmas cake. What else?"

I realized that I had a great deal to learn concerning the habits of the Cornish, but I did feel that I was enjoying their way of celebrating Christmas.

"Oh, miss, I forgot to tell 'ee," cried Daisy. "There be a parcel in your room. I took it up just afore them come a-gooding, and forgot to tell 'ee till now." She was surprised because I lingered. "A parcel, miss! Don't 'ee want to see what it is? 'Twas so size, and 'twas a box like as not."

I realized that I had been in a dream. I felt that I wanted to stay here forever, and learn all the customs of this part of the world. I wanted to make it my part of the world.

I shook myself out of that dream. What you really want, I told my-self, is some fairytale ending to your story. You want to be the mis-tress of Mount Mellyn. Why not admit it?

I went up to my room, and there I found Phillida's parcel.

I took out a shawl of black silk on which was embroidered a pat-tern in green and amber. There was also an amber comb of the Span-ish type. I stuck the comb in my hair and wrapped the shawl about me. I was startled by my reflection. I looked exotic, more like a Spanish dancer than an English governess.

There was something else in the parcel. I undid it quickly and saw that it was a dress—one of Phillida's which I had greatly admired. It was of green silk, the same shade of green as in the shawl. A letter fell out.

Dear Marty,

How is the governessing? Your last letter sounded as though you found it intriguing. I believe your Alvean is a little horror. Spoiled child, I'll swear. Are they treating you well? It sounded as if that side of it was not too bad. What is the matter with you, by the way? You used to write such amusing letters. Since you've been in that place you've become uncommunicative. I suspect you either love it or hate it. Do tell.

The shawl and comb are my Christmas gift. I hope you like them because I spent a lot of time choosing. Are they too frivolous? Would you rather have had a set of woolen underwear or some improving book? But I heard from Aunt Adelaide that she is sending you the former. There is a distinctly governessy flavor in your letters. All sound and fury, Marty my dear, signifying nothing. I am wondering whether you'll be sitting down to dine with the family this Christmas or presiding in the servants' hall. I'm sure it will be the former. They couldn't help but ask you. After all, it is Christmas. You'll dine with the family even if there's one of those dinner parties where a guest doesn't turn up and they say, "Send for the governess. We cannot be thir-teen." So our Marty goes to dine in my old green and her new scarf and comb, and here she attracts a millionaire and lives happy ever after.

Seriously, Marty, I did think you might need something for the festivities. So the green gown is a gift. Don't think of it as a cast-off. I love the thing and I'm giving it to you, not because I'm tired of it, but because it always suited you better than me.

I shall want to hear all about the Christmas festivities. And, dear sister, when you're the fourteenth at the dinner table don't freeze likely suitors with a look or give them one of your clever retorts. Be a nice gentle girl and, kind lady, I see romance and fortune in the cards for you.

Happy Christmas, dear Marty, and do write soon sending the real news. The children and William send their love. Mine to you also.

Phillida.

I felt rather emotional. It was a link with home. Dear Phillida, she did think of me often then. Her shawl and comb were beautiful, even if a little incongruous for someone in my humble position; and it was good of her to send the dress.

I was startled by a sudden cry. I spun round and saw Alvean at the door which led to the schoolroom.

"Miss!" she cried. "So it's you!"

"Of course. Who did you think it was?"

She did not answer, but I knew.

"I've never seen you look like that, miss."

"You've never seen me in a shawl and comb."

"You look . . . pretty."

"Thank you, Alvean."

She was a little shaken. I knew who she had thought it was standing in my room.

I was the same height as Alice, and if I were less slender that would not be obvious with the silk shawl round me.

❧

Christmas Day was a day to remember all my life.

I awoke in the morning to the sounds of excitement. The servants were laughing and talking together below my window.

I opened my eyes and thought: Christmas Day. And then: My first Christmas at Mount Mellyn.

Perhaps, I said to myself, trying to throw a cold douche over my exuberance which somehow made me apprehensive because it was so great, it will be not only your first but your last.

A whole year lay between this Christmas and the next. Who could say what would happen in that time?

I was out of bed when my water was brought up. Daisy scarcely stopped a moment, she was so full of excitement.

"I be late, miss, but there be so much to do. You'd better hurry now or you'll not be in time to see the wassail. They'll be coming early, you can depend on that. They know the family 'ull be off to church, so they mustn't be late."

There was no time to ask questions so I washed and dressed and took out my parcels. Alvean's had already been put by her bed the previous night.

I went to the window. The air was balmy and it had that strong tang of spices in it. I drew deep breaths and listened to the gentle rhythm of the waves. They said nothing this morning; they merely swished contentedly. This was Christmas morning when for a day all troubles, all differences might be shelved.

Alvean came to my room. She was carrying her embroidered handkerchiefs rather shyly. She said: "Thank you, miss. A happy Christmas!"

I put my arms about her and kissed her, and although she seemed a little embarrassed by this demonstration, she returned my kiss.

She had brought a brooch so like the silver whip I had given her that I thought for a moment that she was returning my gift.

"I got it from Mr. Pastern," she said. "I wanted one as near mine as possible, but not too near, so that we shouldn't get them mixed up. Yours has got a little engraving on the handle. Now we'll each have one when we go riding."

I was delighted. She had not ridden since her accident, and she could not have shown me more clearly that she was ready to start again.

I said: "You could not have given me anything I should have liked better, Alvean."

She was very pleased, although she murmured in an offhand way: "I'm glad you like it, miss." Then she left me abruptly.

This, I told myself, is going to be a wonderful day. It's Christmas.

My presents proved to be a great success. Mrs. Polgrey's eyes glistened at the sight of the whisky; as for Gilly, she was delighted with her scarf. I suppose the poor child had never had anything so pretty before; she kept stroking it and staring at it in wonder. Daisy and Kitty were pleased with their scarves too; and I felt I had been clever in my choice.

Mrs. Polgrey gave me a set of doilies with a coy whisper: "For your bottom drawer, me dear." I replied that I would start one immediately, and we were very gay. She said that she would make a cup of tea and we'd sample my whisky, but there wasn't the time.

"My dear life, when I think of all there has to be done today!"

The wassail singers arrived in the morning and I heard their voices at the door of the great hall.

> *"The master and mistress our wassail begin*
> *Pray open your door and let us come in*
> *With our wassail, wassail, wassail.*
> *And joy come to our jolly wassail."*

They came into the hall, and they also carried a bowl into which coins were dropped; all the servants crowded in and, as Connan entered, the singing grew louder and the verse was repeated.

"The master and the mistress . . ."

I thought: Two years ago Alice would have stood there with him. Does he remember? He showed no sign. He sang with them and ordered that the stirrup cup, the dash-an-darras, be brought out with the saffron cake and pasties and gingerbread, which had been made for the occasion.

He moved nearer to me.

"Well, Miss Leigh," he said under cover of the singing, "what do you think of a Cornish Christmas?"

"Very interesting."

"You haven't seen half yet."

"I should hope not. The day has scarcely begun."

"You should rest this afternoon."

"But why?"

"For the feasting this evening."

"But I . . ."

"Of course you will join us. Where else would you spend your Christmas Day? With the Polgreys? With the Tappertys?"

"I did not know. I wondered whether I was expected to hover between the great hall and the servants' hall."

"You look disapproving."

"I am not sure."

"Oh come, this is Christmas. Do not wonder whether you should be sure or not. Just come. By the way, I have not wished you a merry Christmas yet. I have something here . . . a little gift. A token of my gratitude, if you like. You have been so good to Alvean since her accident. Oh, and *before* of course, I have no doubt. But it has been brought to my notice so forcibly since . . ."

"But I have only done my duty as a governess."

"And that is something you would always do. I know it. Well, let's say this is merely to wish you a merry Christmas."

He had pressed a small object into my hand, and I was so overcome with pleasure that I felt it must show in my eyes and betray my feelings to him.

"You are very good to me," I said. "I had not thought . . ."

He smiled and moved away to the singers. I had noticed Tapperty's eyes on us. I wondered whether he had seen the gift handed to me.

I wanted to be alone, for I felt so emotionally disturbed. The small case he had pressed into my hand was demanding to be opened. I could not do so here.

I slipped out of the hall and ran up to my room.

It was a small, blue plush case, the sort which usually contained jewelry.

I opened it. Inside, on oyster-colored satin, lay a brooch. It was in the form of a horseshoe, and it was studded with what could only be diamonds.

I stared at it in dismay. I could not accept such a valuable object. I must return it of course.

I held it up to the light and saw the flash of red and green in the stones. It must be worth a great deal of money. I possessed no diamonds, but I could see that these were fine ones.

Why did he do it? If it had been some small token I should have been so happy. I wanted to throw myself onto my bed and weep.

I could hear Alvean calling me. "Miss, it's time for church. Come on, miss. The carriage is waiting to take us to church."

I hastily put the brooch into its box and put on my cape and bonnet as Alvean came into the room.

⋘⧸⧷⋙

I saw him after church. He was going across to the stables and I called after him.

He hesitated, looked over his shoulder and smiled at me.

"Mr. TreMellyn. It is very kind of you," I said as I ran up to him, "but this gift is far too valuable for me to accept."

He put his head on one side and regarded me in the old mocking manner.

"My *dear* Miss Leigh," he said lightly. "I am a very ignorant man, I fear. I have no notion how valuable a gift must be before it is acceptable."

I flushed hotly and stammered: "This is a very valuable ornament."

"I thought it so suitable. A horseshoe means luck, you know. And you have a way with horses, have you not?"

"I . . . I have no occasion to wear such a valuable piece of jewelry."

"I thought you might wear it to the ball tonight."

For a moment I had a picture of myself dancing with him. I should be wearing Phillida's green silk dress, which would compare favorably with those of his guests because Phillida had a way with clothes. I would wear my shawl, and my diamond brooch would be proudly flaunted on the green silk, because I treasured it so much, and I treasured it because he had given it to me.

"I feel I have no right."

"Oh," he murmured, "I begin to understand. You feel that I give the brooch in the same spirit as Mr. Nansellock offered Jacinth."

"So . . ." I stammered, "you knew of that?"

"Oh, I know most things that go on here, Miss Leigh. You returned the horse. Very proper and what I would expect of you. Now the brooch is given in a very different spirit. I give it to you for a reason. You have been good to Alvean. Not only as a governess but as a woman. Do you know what I mean? There is more to the care of a child, is there not, than arithmetic and grammar? You gave her that little extra. The brooch belonged to Alvean's mother. Look upon it like this, Miss Leigh: it is a gift of appreciation from us both. Does that make it all right?"

I was silent for a few moments. Then I said: "Yes . . . that is different, of course. I accept the brooch. Thank you very much, Mr. TreMellyn."

He smiled at me—it was a smile I did not fully understand because it seemed to hold in it many meanings.

I was afraid to try to understand.

"Thank you," I murmured again; and I hurried back to the house.

I went up to my room and took out the brooch. I pinned it on my dress, and immediately my lavender cotton took on a new look.

I would wear the diamonds tonight. I would go in Phillida's dress and my comb and shawl, and on my breast I would wear Alice's diamonds.

So on this strange Christmas Day I had a gift from Alice.

❧

I had dined in the middle of the day in the small dining room with Connan and Alvean, the first meal I had taken with them in this intimacy. We had eaten turkey and plum pudding and had been waited on by Kitty and Daisy. I could feel that certain significant looks were being directed toward us.

"On Christmas Day," Connan had said, "you could not be expected to dine alone. Do you know, Miss Leigh, I fear we have treated you rather badly. I should have suggested that you should go home to your family for Christmas. You should have reminded me."

"I felt I had been here too short a time to ask for a holiday," I answered. "Besides . . ."

"In view of Alvean's accident, you felt you should stay," he murmured. "It is good of you to be so thoughtful."

Conversation in the small dining room was animated. The three of us discussed the Christmas customs, and Connan told us stories of what had happened in previous years; how on one occasion the wassailers had arrived late, so that the family had gone to church and they had to wait outside and serenade them all the way home.

I imagined Alice with him then. I imagined her sitting in the chair I now occupied. I wondered what the conversation was like then. I wondered if now, seeing me there, he was thinking of Alice.

I kept reminding myself that it was merely because it was Christmas that I was sitting here. That after the festivities were over I should revert to my old place.

But I was not going to think of that now. Tonight I was going to the ball. Miraculously I had a dress worthy of the occasion. I had a comb of amber and a brooch of diamonds. I thought: Tonight I shall mingle with these people on my own terms. It will be quite unlike that occasion when I danced in the solarium.

I took Connan's advice that afternoon and tried to rest so that I might stay fresh until the early morning. Much to my surprise I did manage to sleep. I must have slept lightly, for I dreamed, and as so often in this house, my dreams were of Alice. I thought that she came to the ball, a shadowy wraith of a figure whom no one but I could see, and she whispered to me as I danced with Connan: "This is what I want, Marty. I like to see this. I like to see you sitting in my

chair at luncheon. I like to see your hand in that of Connan. You
. . . Marty . . . you . . . not another . . ."

I awoke with reluctance. That was a pleasant dream. I tried to
sleep again, tried to get back to that half-world where ghosts came
back from the tomb and told you that they longed for you to have all
that you most wanted in life.

Daisy brought me a cup of tea at five o'clock. On Mrs. Polgrey's
instructions, she told me.

"I've brought 'ee a piece of Mrs. Polgrey's fuggan to take with
it," she said, indicating a slice of raisin cake. "If there's more you do
want, 'tis only for you to say."

I said: "This will be ample."

"Then you'll be wanting to get ready for the ball, will 'ee not,
miss?"

"There's plenty of time," I told her.

"I'll bring 'ee hot water at six, miss. That'll give 'ee plenty of time
to dress. The master 'ull be receiving the guests at eight. That's how
it always was. And don't 'ee forget—'tis but buffet supper at nine, so
there's a long time to go afore you get more to eat. Are you sure you
wouldn't like something more than that there piece of fuggan?"

I was sure I was going to find it difficult to eat what she had
brought, so I said: "This is quite enough, Daisy."

"Well, 'tis for you to say, miss."

She stood at the door a moment, her head on one side, watching
me. Speculatively? Was she regarding me with a new interest?

I pictured them in the servants' hall, Tapperty leading the conversation.

Were they always wondering what new relationship had begun—or
was about to begin—between the master of the house and the governess?

I was at the ball in Phillida's green dress with the tight, low-cut
bodice and the billowing skirt. I had dressed my hair differently,
piling it high on my head; it was necessary to do so in order to do
justice to the comb. On my dress sparkled the diamond brooch.

I was happy. I could mingle with the guests as one of them. No
one would know, unless told, that I was only the governess.

I had waited until the ballroom was full before I went down. Then
I could best mingle with the guests. I had only been there a few
minutes when Peter was at my elbow.

"You look dazzling," he said.

"Thank you. I am glad to surprise you."

"I'm not in the least surprised. I always knew how you could look, given the chance."

"You always know how to pay the compliment."

"To you I always say what I mean. One thing I have not yet said to you, and that is 'A happy Christmas.' "

"Thank you. I wish you the same."

"Let us make it so for each other. I have brought no gift for you."

"But why should you?"

"Because it is Christmas, and a pleasant custom for friends to exchange gifts."

"But not for——"

"Please . . . please . . . no reminders of governessing tonight. One day I am going to give you Jacinth, you know. She is meant for you. I see Connan is about to open the ball. Will you partner me?"

"Thank you, yes."

"It's the traditional dance, you know."

"I don't know it."

"It's easy. You only have to follow me." He began humming the tune to me. "Haven't you seen it done before?"

"Yes, through the peep in the solarium at the last ball."

"Ah, that last ball! We danced together. But Connan cut in, didn't he?"

"It was somewhat unconventional."

"Very, for our governess. I'm really rather surprised at her."

The music had begun, and Connan was walking into the center of the hall holding Celestine by the hand. To my horror I realized that Peter and I would have to join them and dance those first bars with them.

I tried to hold back, but Peter had me firmly by the hand.

Celestine was surprised to see me there, but if Connan was, he gave no sign. I imagined that Celestine reasoned: It is all very well to ask the governess, since it is Christmas, but should she immediately thrust herself into such a prominent position?

However, I believed her to be of too sweet a nature to show her astonishment after that first start of surprise. She gave me a warm smile.

I said: "I shouldn't be here. I don't really know the dance. I didn't realize——"

"Follow us," said Connan.

"We'll look after you," echoed Peter.

And in a few seconds the others were falling in behind us.

Round the hall we went to the tune of the "Furry Dance."

"You're doing excellently," said Connan with a smile as our hands touched.

"You will soon be a Cornishwoman," added Celestine.

"And why not?" demanded Peter. "Are we not the salt of the earth?"

"I am not sure that Miss Leigh thinks so," replied Connan.

"I am becoming very interested in all the customs of the country," I added.

"And in the inhabitants, I hope," whispered Peter.

We danced on. It was simple enough to learn, and when it was over I knew all the movements.

As the last bars were played I heard someone say: "Who is the striking-looking young woman who danced with Peter Nansellock?"

I waited for the answer to be: "Oh, that's the governess."

But it was different: "I've no idea. She certainly is . . . unusual."

I was exultant. I doubt that I had ever been so happy in my life.

I knew that in the time to come I should treasure every minute of that wonderful evening, for I was not only at the ball, I was a success at the ball.

I did not lack partners; and even when I was forced to admit that I was the governess, I continued to receive the homage due to an attractive woman. What had happened to change me? I wondered. Why couldn't I have been like this at Aunt Adelaide's parties? But if I had, I should never have come to Mount Mellyn.

Then I knew why I had not been like this. It was not only the green dress, the amber comb, and the diamond brooch; I was in love, and love was the greatest beautifier of all.

Never mind if I was ridiculously, hopelessly in love. I was like Cinderella at the ball, determined to enjoy myself until the stroke of twelve.

A strange thing happened while I was dancing. I was with Sir Thomas Treslyn, who turned out to be a courteous old gentleman, a little wheezy during the dance, so I suggested that he might prefer to sit out the rest of it. He was very grateful to me and I felt quite fond of him. I was ready to be fond of everyone that night.

He said: "I'm getting a little too old for the dance, Miss . . . er . . ."

"Leigh," I said. "Miss Leigh. I'm the governess here, Sir Thomas."

"Oh indeed," he said. "I was going to say, Miss Leigh, it is extremely kind of you to think of my comfort when you must be longing to dance."

"I'm quite happy to sit for a while."

"I see that you are kind as well as very attractive."

I remembered Phillida's instructions and accepted the compliments nonchalantly as though I had been accustomed to them all my life.

He was relaxed and confidential. "It's my wife who likes to come to these affairs. She has so much vitality."

"Ah yes," I said, "she is very beautiful."

I had noticed her, of course, the very moment I entered the ballroom; she was in pale mauve chiffon over an underskirt of green; she evidently had a passion for chiffon and such clinging materials, and it was understandable considering her figure; she wore many diamonds. The mauve toning down the green was exquisite and I wondered whether my own vivid emerald was not a little blatant compared with hers. She looked outstandingly beautiful, as she would in any assembly.

He nodded, a little sadly I thought.

And as I sat talking, my eyes, wandering round the hall, went suddenly to the peep high in the wall, that star-shaped opening which merged so perfectly into the murals that none would have guessed it was there.

Someone was watching the ball through the peep, but it was impossible to see who it was.

I thought: Of course it is Alvean. Did she not always watch the ball through the peep? Then I was suddenly startled for, as I was sitting there, watching the dancers, I saw Alvean. I had forgotten that this was a special occasion—Christmas Day—and just as, on such a day, the governess might come to the ball, so might Alvean.

She was dressed in a white muslin dress with a wide blue sash and I saw that she wore the silver whip pinned to the bodice of her dress. All these things I noticed with half my attention. I looked swiftly up to the peep. The face, unrecognizable, indefinable, was still there.

❧

Supper was served in the dining room and the punch room. There was a buffet in both rooms and guests helped themselves, for according to custom the servants on this day of days were having their own ball in their own hall.

I saw that these people who so rarely waited on themselves now found it quite good fun to do so. Dishes piled on dishes were the results of all that kitchen activity: small pies of various kinds, called here pasties—not the enormous ones which were eaten frequently in the kitchen, but dainty ones. There were slices of beef, and chicken and fish of various descriptions. There was a great bowl of hot punch; another of mulled wine; there were mead, whisky, and sloe gin.

Peter Nansellock, with whom I had had the supper dance, led me into the punch room. Sir Thomas Treslyn was already there with Celestine, and Peter led me to the table at which they were sitting.

"Leave it to me," he said. "I'll feed you all."

I said: "Allow me to help you."

"Nonsense," he replied. "You remain with Celeste." He whispered banteringly: "You're not the governess tonight, Miss Leigh; you're a lady like the rest of them. Don't forget it; then no one else will."

But I was determined that I would not be waited on and I insisted on going to the buffet with him.

"Pride," he murmured, slipping his hand through my arm. "Wasn't that the sin by which fell the angels?"

"It may have been ambition; I am not sure."

"Well, I'll warrant you're not without a dash of that either. Never mind. What will you eat? Perhaps it is as well you came. Our Cornish food often seems odd to you foreigners from the other side of the Tamar."

He began loading one of the trays which had been put there in readiness.

"Which sort of pie will you have? Giblet, squab, nattling, or muggety? Ha, here's taddage too. I can recommend the squab: layers of apple and bacon, onions and mutton and young pigeon. The most delicious Cornish fare."

"I'm ready to try it," I said.

"Miss Leigh," he went on, "Martha . . . has anyone ever told you that your eyes are like amber?"

"Yes," I answered.

"Has anyone ever told you you're beautiful?"

"No."

"Then that oversight should be and is rectified immediately."

I laughed and at that moment Connan came into the room with Lady Treslyn.

She sat down with Celestine, and Connan came over to the buffet.

"I am enlightening Miss Leigh about our Cornish food. She doesn't know what a 'fair maid' is. Is that not odd, Con, seeing that she is one herself?"

Connan looked excited; his eyes smiling into mine were warm. He said: "Fair maids, Miss Leigh, is another name for pilchards served like this with oil and lemon." He took a fork and put some on two plates. "It is a contraction of the old Spanish *Fumado,* and we always say here that it is food fit for a Spanish Don."

"A relic, Miss Leigh," interrupted Peter, "of those days when the Spaniards raided our shores and took too great an interest in another kind of fair maid."

Alvean had come in and was standing beside me. I thought she looked tired.

"You should be in bed," I said.

"I'm hungry," she told me.

"After supper we'll go up."

She nodded and with sleepy pleasure she piled food on a plate.

We sat round the table, Alvean, Peter, Celestine, Sir Thomas, Connan, and Lady Treslyn.

It seemed like a dream that I should be there with them. Alice's brooch glittered on my dress, and I thought: Thus, two years ago, she would have sat . . . as I am sitting now. Alvean would not have been here then; she would have been too young to have been allowed to come, but apart from that and the fact that I was in Alice's place, it must have been very like other occasions. I wondered if any of the others thought this.

I remembered the face I had seen at the peep, and what Alvean had said on the night of that other ball. I could not remember the exact words but I knew that it had been something about her mother's love of dancing and how, if she came back, she would come to a ball. Then Alvean had half hoped to see her among the dancers. . . . What if she watched from another place? I thought of that ghostly solarium in moonlight and I said to myself: Whose face did I see at the peep?

Then I thought: Gilly! What if it were Gilly? It must have been Gilly. Who else could it have been?

My attention was brought back to the group at the table when Connan said: "I'll get you some more whisky, Tom." He rose and went to the buffet. Lady Treslyn got up quickly and went to him. I found it difficult to take my eyes from them. I thought how distinguished they looked—she in green shaded mauve draperies, the most beautiful woman at the ball, and he, surely the most distinguished of the men.

"I'll help you, Connan," she said and I heard them laughing together.

"Look out," said Connan, "we're spilling it."

They had their backs to us, and as I watched them I thought that with the slightest provocation I could have burst into tears because now I clearly saw the ridiculousness of my hopes.

She had slipped her arm through his as they came back to the table. The intimate gesture wounded me deeply. I suppose I had drunk too much of the mead, or metheglin as they called it. Mead. It was such a soft and gentle name. But the mead which was made at Mount Mellyn was very potent.

I said to myself coldly: It is time you retired.

As he gave the glass to Sir Thomas—who emptied it with a speed which surprised me—I noticed that there were smudges of shadow under Alvean's eyes, and I said: "Alvean, you look tired. You should be in bed."

"Poor child!" cried Celestine at once. "And she only just recovering . . ."

I rose. "I will take Alvean to bed now," I said. "Come along, Alvean."

She was half-asleep already and made no protest but rose meekly to her feet.

"I will say good night to you all," I said.

Peter rose to his feet. "We'll see you later," he said.

I did not answer. I was desperately trying not to look at Connan, for I felt he was not aware of me; that he would never be aware of anyone when Lady Treslyn was near.

"Au revoir," said Peter, and as the others echoed the words absent-mindedly I went out of the punch room, holding Alvean by the hand.

I felt as Cinderella must have felt with the striking of the midnight hour.

My brief glory was over. Lady Treslyn had made me realize how foolish I had been to dream.

❦

Alvean was asleep before I left her room. I tried not to think of Connan and Lady Treslyn while I went to my room and lighted the candles on my dressing table. I looked attractive; there was no doubt of it. Then I said to myself: Anyone looks attractive by candlelight.

The diamonds winked back at me, and I was immediately reminded of the face I had seen at the peep.

I thought afterward that I must have drunk too freely of the metheglin, because on impulse I went down to the landing below my own. I could hear the shouts coming from the servants' hall. So they were still merrymaking down there. The door to Gilly's room was ajar, and I went in. There was enough moonlight for me to see that the child was in her bed, but sitting up, awake.

"Gilly," I said.

"Madam!" she cried and her voice was joyful. "I knew you'd come tonight."

"Gilly, you know who this is." What had made me say such a foolish thing?

She nodded.

"I'm going to light your candle," I said, and I did so.

Her eyes regarded my face with that blank blue stare, and came to rest on the brooch. I sat on the edge of the bed. I knew that when I had first come in she had thought I was someone else.

She was contented though, which showed the confidence she was beginning to feel in me.

I touched the brooch and said: "Once it was Mrs. TreMellyn's."

She smiled and nodded.

I said: "You spoke when I came in. Why do you not speak to me now?"

She merely smiled.

"Gilly," I said, "were you at the peep in the solarium tonight? Were you watching the dancers?"

She nodded.

"Gilly, say Yes."

"Yes," said Gilly.

"You went up there all alone? You weren't afraid?"

She shook her head and smiled.

"You mean No, don't you, Gilly? Say No."

"No."

"Why weren't you afraid?"

She opened her mouth and smiled. Then she said: "Not afraid because . . ."

"Because?" I said eagerly.

"Because," she repeated.

"Gilly," I said. "Were you alone up there?"

She smiled and I could get her to say no more.

After a while I kissed her and she returned my kiss. She was fond of me, I knew. I believed that in her mind she confused me with someone else, and I knew who that person was.

⋘⟨§⟩⋙

Back in my room I did not want to take off my dress. I felt that as long as I wore it, I could still hope for what I knew to be impossible.

So I sat by my window for an hour or so. It was a warm night and I was comfortable with my silk shawl about me.

I heard some of the guests coming out to their carriages. I heard the exchange of good-bys.

And while I was there I heard Lady Treslyn's voice. Her voice was low and vibrant, but she spoke with such intensity that I caught every syllable and I knew to whom she was speaking.

She said: "Connan, it can't be long now. It won't be long."

⋘⟨§⟩⋙

Next morning, when Kitty brought my water, she did not come alone. Daisy was with her. I heard their rather raucous voices mingling and, in my half-waking state, thought they sounded like the gulls.

"Morning, miss."

They wanted me to wake up quickly; they had exciting news, I saw that in their faces.

"Miss—" they were both speaking together, both determined to be the one to impart the startling information—"last night . . . or rather this morning . . ."

Then Kitty rushed on ahead of her sister: "Sir Thomas Treslyn was taken bad on the way home. He were dead when they got to Treslyn Hall."

I sat up in bed, looking from one excited face to the other.

One of the guests . . . dead! I was shocked. But this was no ordinary death, no ordinary death.

I realized, no less than Kitty and Daisy, what such news could mean to Mount Mellyn.

7

Sir Thomas Treslyn was buried on New Year's Day.

During the preceding week gloom had settled on the house, and it was all the more noticeable because it followed on the heels of the Christmas festivities. All the decorations had been left about the house, and there was divided opinion as to which was the more unlucky—to remove them before Twelfth Night or to leave them up and thereby show a lack of respect.

They all appeared to consider that the death touched us closely. He had died between our house and his own; our table was the last at which he had sat. I realized that the Cornish were a very superstitious people, constantly on the alert for omens, eager to placate supernatural and malignant powers.

Connan was absent-minded. I saw very little of him, but when I did he seemed scarcely aware of my presence. I imagined he was considering all that this meant to him. If he and Lady Treslyn had been lovers there was no obstacle now to their regularizing their union. I knew that this thought was in the minds of many, but no one spoke of it. I guessed that Mrs. Polgrey would consider it unlucky to do so until Sir Thomas had been buried for some weeks.

Mrs. Polgrey called me to her room and we had a cup of Earl Grey laced with a spoonful of the whisky I had given her.

"This is a shocking thing," she said. "Sir Thomas to die on Christmas Day as he did. Although 'tweren't Christmas Day but Boxing Day morning," she added in a slightly relieved tone, as though this made the situation a little less shocking. "And to think," she went on, reverting to her original gloom, "that ours was the last house he rested in, my food were the last that passed his lips! The funeral is a bit soon, do you not think, miss?"

I began to count the days on my fingers. "Seven days," I said. "They could have kept him longer, seeing it's winter."

"I suppose they feel that the sooner it's over, the sooner they'll recover from the shock."

She herself looked shocked indeed. I think she thought it was disrespectful or unlucky to suggest that anyone would want to recover quickly from his grief.

"I don't know," she said, "you hear tales of people being buried alive. I remember years ago, when I was a child, there was a smallpox epidemic. People panicked and buried quick. It was said that some was buried alive."

"There is surely no doubt that Sir Thomas is *dead*."

"Some seem dead and are not, after all. Still, seven days should be long enough to tell. You'll come to the funeral with me, miss?"

"I?"

"But why not? I think we should show proper respect to the dead."

"I have no mourning clothes."

"My dear life, I'll find a bonnet for 'ee. I'll give 'ee a black band to sew on your cloak. Reckon that 'ud be all right if we was just at the grave. 'Twouldn't do for 'ee to go into the church like, but then 'twouldn't be right either . . . you being the governess here, and them having so many friends as will attend to fill Mellyn Church to the full."

So it was agreed that I should accompany Mrs. Polgrey to the churchyard.

இ§ஃ

I was present when Sir Thomas's body was lowered into the tomb.

It was an impressive ceremony, for the funeral had been a magnificent one in accordance with the Treslyns' rank in the duchy. Crowds attended, but Mrs. Polgrey and I hovered only in the distance. I was glad of this; she deplored it.

It was enough for me to see the widow in flowing black draperies, yet looking as beautiful as she ever had. Her lovely face was just visible among the flowing black, which seemed to become her even as green and mauve had on the night of the Christmas ball. She moved with grace and she looked even more slender in her black than in the brilliant colors I had seen her wear—intensely feminine and appealing.

Connan was there, and I thought how elegant and distinguished he looked; I tried to fathom the expression on his face that I might discover his feelings. But he was determined to hide those feelings from the world; and I thought, in the circumstances, that was just as well.

I watched the hearse with the large waving black plumes and I saw the coffin, carried by six bearers and covered with velvet palls of deep purple and black, taken into the church. I saw the banks of flowers and the mourners in their deathly black, the only color being the white handkerchiefs which the women held to their eyes—and they had wide black borders.

A cold wind had swept the mists away and the winter sun shone brightly on the gilt of the coffin as it was lowered into the grave.

There was a deep silence in the churchyard, broken only by the sudden cry of gulls.

It was over and the mourners, Connan, Celestine, and Peter among them, went back to their carriages which wound their way to Treslyn Hall.

Mrs. Polgrey and I returned to Mount Mellyn, where she insisted on the usual cup of tea and its accompaniment.

We sat drinking, and her eyes glittered. I knew she was finding it difficult to restrain her tongue. But she said nothing of the effect this death might have on us all at Mount Mellyn. So great was her respect for the dead.

જ્ક્ષેટ

Sir Thomas was not forgotten. I heard his name mentioned often during the next few weeks. Mrs. Polgrey shook her head significantly when the Treslyns were mentioned, but her eyes were sharp and full of warning.

Daisy and Kitty were less discreet. When they brought my water in the mornings they would linger. I was a little cunning, I think. I longed to know what people were saying but I did not want to ask; yet I managed to draw them out without, I hoped, seeming to do so.

It was true they did not need a lot of encouragement.

"I saw Lady Treslyn yesterday," Daisy told me one morning. "Her didn't look like a widow, in spite of the weeds."

"Oh? In what way?"

"Don't 'ee ask me, miss. She was quite pale and not smiling, but I could see something in her face . . . if you do get my meaning."

"I'm afraid I don't."

"Kit were with me. She said the same. Like as though she were waiting and content because she wouldn't have to wait long. A year though. Seems a long time to *me*."

"A year? What for?" I asked, although I knew very well what for. Daisy looked at me and giggled.

" 'Twon't do for them to be seeing too much of each other for a bit, will it, miss? After all, him dying here . . . almost on our doorstep. 'Twould seem as though they'd almost willed him to it."

"Oh Daisy, that's absurd. How could anybody?"

"Well, that's what you can't say till you know, 'twould seem."

The conversation was getting dangerous. I dismissed her with "I must hurry. I see I'm rather late."

When she had gone, I thought: So there is talk about them. They are saying he was willed to die.

As long as that's all they say, that won't do much harm.

I wondered how careful they were being. I remembered hearing Phillida say that people in love behaved like ostriches. They buried their heads in the sand and thought, because they saw no one, no one saw them.

But they were not two young inexperienced lovers.

No, I thought bitterly, it is clear that both are very experienced. They knew the people among whom they lived. They would be careful.

It was later that day, when I was in the woods, that I heard the sound of horses' hoofs walking nearby and then I heard Lady Treslyn say: "Connan. Oh, Connan!"

They had met then . . . and to meet as near the house as this was surely foolish.

In the woods their voices carried. The trees hid me, but snatches of their conversation came to me.

"Linda! You shouldn't have come."

"I know . . . I know . . ." Her voice fell and I could not hear the rest.

"To send that message . . ." That was Connan. I could hear him more clearly than her, perhaps because I knew his voice so well. "Your messenger will have been seen by some of the servants. You know how they gossip."

"I know, but——"

"When did this come . . . ?"

"This morning. I had to show it to you right away."

"It's the first?"

"No, there was one two days ago. That's why I had to see you, Connan. No matter what . . . I'm frightened."

"It's mischief," he said. "Ignore it. Forget it."

"Read it," she cried. "Read it."

There was a short silence. Then Connan spoke. "I see. There's only one thing to be done . . ."

The horses had begun to move. In a few seconds they might come past the spot where I was. I hurried away through the trees.

I was very uneasy.

That day Connan left Mount Mellyn.

"Called away to Penzance," Mrs. Polgrey told me. "He said he was unsure how long he would be away."

I wondered if his sudden departure had anything to do with the disquieting news which Lady Treslyn had brought to him that morning in the woods.

❧

Several days passed. Alvean and I resumed our lessons and Gilly too came to the schoolroom.

I would give Gilly some small task while I worked with Alvean, such as trying to make letters in a tray of sand or on a slate or counting beads on an abacus. She was contented to do this and I believed that she was happy in my company, that from me she drew a certain comfort which had its roots in security. She had trusted Alice and she was transferring that trust to me.

Alvean had rebelled at first, but I had pointed out the need to be kind to those less fortunate than ourselves, and at length I had worked on her sympathy so that she accepted Gilly's presence, although a little sullenly. But I had noticed that now and then she would throw a glance at the child, and I was sure that at least she was very interested in her.

Connan had been away a week and it was a cold February morning when Mrs. Polgrey came into the schoolroom. I was very surprised to see her, for she rarely interrupted lessons; she was holding two letters in her hand and I could see that she was excited.

She made no excuses for her intrusion but said: "I have heard from the master. He wants you to take Miss Alvean down to Penzance at once. Here is a letter for you. No doubt he explains more fully in that."

She handed me the letter and I was afraid she would see that my hand shook a little as I opened it.

My dear Miss Leigh, [*I read*]

I shall be here for a few weeks, I think, and I am sure you will agree that it would be very desirable for Alvean to join me here. I do not think she should miss her lessons, so I am asking you to bring her and be prepared to stay for a week or so.

Perhaps you could be ready to leave tomorrow. Get Billy Trehay to drive you to the station for the 2.30 train.

Connan TreMellyn.

I knew that the color had rushed to my face. I hoped I had not betrayed the extreme joy which took possession of me.

I said: "Alvean, we are to join your father tomorrow."

Alvean leaped up and threw herself into my arms, a most unusual display, but it moved me deeply to realize how much she cared for him.

This helped me to regain my own composure. I said: "That is for tomorrow. Today we will continue with our lessons."

"But, miss, there's our packing to do."

"We have this afternoon for that," I said primly. "Now let us return to our work."

I turned to Mrs. Polgrey. "Yes," I said, "Mr. TreMellyn wishes me to take Alvean to him."

She nodded. I could see that she thought it very strange, but this was because he had never before shown such interest in the child.

"And you're leaving tomorrow?"

"Yes. Billy Trehay is to be given instructions to drive us to the station in time for the two-thirty train."

She nodded.

When she had gone I sat down in a daze. I could not concentrate any more than Alvean could. It was some time before I remembered Gilly. She was looking at me with that blank expression in her eyes which I had dreamed of banishing.

Gilly understood more than one realized.

She knew that we were going away and that she would be left behind.

‌‌❧

I could scarcely wait to begin my packing. Alvean and I had luncheon together in the schoolroom but neither of us was interested in food, and immediately after the meal we went to our rooms to do the packing.

I had very little to pack. My gray and lavender dresses were clean, for which I was thankful, and I would wear my gray merino. It was not very becoming but it would be too difficult to pack.

I took out the green silk dress which I had worn at the Christmas ball. Should I take it? Why not? I had rarely possessed anything so becoming, and who knew, there might be an occasion when I could wear it.

I took out my comb and shawl, stuck the comb in my hair and let the shawl fall negligently about my shoulders.

I thought of the Christmas ball—that moment when Peter had taken my hand and had drawn me into the "Furry Dance." I heard the tune in my head and began to dance, for the moment really feeling I was in the ballroom and that it was Christmas night again.

I had not heard Gilly come in, and I was startled to see her standing watching me. Really, the child did move too silently about the house.

I stopped dancing, flushing with embarrassment to have been caught in such silly behavior. Gilly was regarding me solemnly.

She looked at the bag on my bed and the folded clothes beside it, and immediately my pleasure left me, for I understood that Gilly was going to be very unhappy if we went away.

I stooped down and put my arms about her. "It'll only be for a little while, Gilly."

She screwed her eyes up tightly and would not look at me.

"Gilly," I said, "listen. We'll soon be back, you know."

She shook her head and I saw tears squeeze themselves out of her eyes.

"Then," I went on, "we'll have our lessons. You shall draw me more letters in the sand, and soon you will be writing your name."

But I could see that she refused to be comforted.

She tore herself from me and ran to the bed and began pulling the things out of my trunk.

"No, Gilly, no," I said. I lifted her up in my arms and went to a chair. I sat for a while rocking her. I went on: "I'm coming back, you know, Gilly. In less than no time I'll be here. It will seem as though I've never been away."

She spoke then: "You won't come back. She . . . she . . ."

"Yes, Gilly, yes?"

"She . . . went."

For the moment I forgot even the fact that I was going to Connan, because I was certain now that Gilly knew something, and what she knew might throw some light on the mystery of Alice.

"Gilly," I said, "did she say good-by to you before she went?"

Gilly shook her head vehemently, and I thought she was going to burst into tears.

"Gilly," I pleaded, "try to talk to me, try to tell me. . . . Did you see her go?"

Gilly threw herself at me and buried her face against my bodice. I held her tenderly for a moment, then withdrew myself and looked into her face; but her eyes were tightly shut.

She ran back to the bed and again started to pull the things out of my trunk.

"No!" she cried. "No . . . no . . ."

Swiftly I went to her. "Look, Gilly," I said, "I'm coming back. I'll only be away a short time."

"She stayed away!"

We were back at that point where we started. I did not believe I could discover anything more from her at this stage.

She lifted her little face to mine and all the blankness had gone from the eyes; they were tragic.

I saw in that moment how much my care of her had meant to her, and that it was impossible to make her understand that if I went away it was not forever. Alice had been kind to her and Alice had gone. Her experiences had taught her that that was the way of life.

A few days . . . a week in the life of Gilly . . . would be like a year to most of us. I knew then that I could not leave Gilly behind.

Then I asked myself what Connan would say if I arrived with both children.

I believed that I could adequately explain my reasons. However, I was not going to leave Gilly behind. I could let Mrs. Polgrey know that the master expected the two children; she would be pleased;

she trusted Gilly with me, and she had been the first to admit that the child had improved since I had tried to help her.

"Gilly," I said. "I'm going away for a few days. Alvean and you are coming with me." I kissed her upturned face. And I repeated because she looked so bewildered: "You are coming with me. You'll like that, won't you."

It was still some seconds before she understood, and then she shut her eyes tightly and lowered her head; I saw she smiled. That moved me more than any words could have done.

I felt I was ready to brave Connan's displeasure to bring such happiness to this poor child.

❦

The next morning we set out early, and the whole household turned out to see us go. I sat in the carriage with a child on either side of me, and Billy Trehay in TreMellyn livery sat jauntily in the driver's seat talking to the horses.

Mrs. Polgrey stood, her arms folded across her bosom, and her eyes were on Gilly. It was clear that she was delighted to see her little granddaughter riding with Alvean and me.

Tapperty stood with his daughters on either side of him; and their twinkling eyes, all so much alike, were full of speculation.

I did not care. I felt so lightheaded as we drove off that it was all I could do to prevent myself breaking into song.

It was a bright sunny morning with a slight frost in the air which sparkled on the grass, and there was a thin layer of ice on the ponds and streams.

We rattled along at a good speed over the rough roads. The children were in high spirits; Alvean chattered a good deal, and Gilly sat contentedly beside me. I noticed that she clutched my skirt with one hand, and the gesture filled me with tenderness for her. I was deeply aware of my responsibility toward this child.

Billy was talkative, and when we passed a grave at a crossroads, he uttered a prayer for the poor lost soul who was buried there.

"Not that the soul will rest, me dears. A person who meets death that way never rests. 'Tis the same if they meet death any way violent like. They can't stay buried underground. They *walks.*"

"What nonsense!" I said sharply.

"Them that knows no better call wisdom nonsense," retorted Billy, piqued.

"It seems to me that many people have too lively imaginations."

The children's eyes I noticed were fixed on my face.

"Why," I said quickly as we passed a cob cottage with beehives in the garden, "look at those hives! What's that over them?"

" 'Tis black crepe," said Billy. "It means death in the family. Bees would take it terrible hard if they weren't told of the death and helped to share in the mourning."

I was glad when we arrived at the station.

We were met at Penzance by a carriage and then began the journey to Penlandstow. It was growing dark when we turned into a drive and I saw a house loom up before us. There was a man on the porch with a lantern who called out: "They be here. Run and tell master. He did say to let him know the minute they did come."

We were a little stiff and both children were half-asleep. I helped them down and as I turned, I saw Connan standing beside me. I could not see him very clearly in the dim light but I did know that he was very pleased to see me. He took my hand and pressed it warmly.

Then he said an astonishing thing. "I've been anxious. I visualized all sorts of mishaps. I wished I'd come and brought you here myself."

I thought: He means Alvean, of course. He is not really talking to me.

But he was facing me, and smiling; and I felt I had never been quite so happy in the whole of my life.

I began: "The children . . ."

He smiled down at Alvean.

"Hello, Papa," she said. "It's lovely to be here with you."

He laid a hand on her shoulder, and she looked up at him almost pleadingly, as though she were asking him to kiss her. That, it seemed, was asking too much.

He merely said: "I'm glad you've come, Alvean. You'll have some fun here."

Then I brought Gilly forward.

"What . . ." he began.

"We couldn't leave Gilly behind," I said. "You know you gave me your permission to teach her."

He hesitated for a moment. Then he looked at me and laughed. I knew in that moment that he was so pleased to see me—me, not the others—that he would not have cared whom I brought with me as long as I came myself.

It was no wonder that as I walked into Alice's old home I felt as though I were entering an enchanted place.

꧁꧂

During the next two weeks I seemed to have left behind me the cold hard world of reality and stepped into one of my own making, and that everything I desired was to be mine.

From the moment I arrived at Penlandstow Manor I was treated, not as a governess, but as a guest. In a few days I had lost my sensitivity on this point and, when I had cast that off, I was like the high-spirited girl who had enjoyed life in the country vicarage with her father and Phillida.

I was given a pleasant room next to Alvean's and when I asked that Gilly should be put near me this was done.

Penlandstow was a house of great charm which had been built in the Elizabethan era. It was almost as large as Mount Mellyn and as easy to lose oneself in.

My room was large and there were padded window seats upholstered in red velvet, and dark red curtains. My bed was a four-poster hung with silk embroidered curtains. The carpet was of the same deep red, and this would have given warmth to the room even if there had not been a log fire burning in the open grate.

My bag was brought up to this room and one of the maids proceeded to unpack while I stood by the fire watching the blue flames dart among the logs.

The maid curtsied when she had laid my things on the bed, and asked if she might put them away. This was not the manner in which to treat a governess, I thought. Kind and friendly as Daisy and Kitty had been, they had not been ready to wait on me like this.

I said I would put my things away myself but would like hot water to wash.

"There be a little bathroom at the end of the landing, miss," I was told. "Shall I show it to 'ee and bring 'ee hot water up there?"

I was taken along to the room in which there was a big bath; there was also a hip bath.

"Miss Alice had the room done afore her married and went away," I was told; and with a little shock I remembered that I was in Alice's old home.

When I had washed and changed my dress—I put on the lavender cotton—I went along to see Alvean. She had fallen asleep on her bed, so I left her. Gilly was also asleep in her room. And when I returned to my own the maid who had shown me the bathroom came in and said that Mr. TreMellyn had asked that, when I was ready, I would join him in the library.

I said I was ready then and she took me to him.

"It is indeed pleasant to see you here, Miss Leigh," he said.

"It will be very agreeable for you to have your daughter here——" I began.

And he interrupted me with a smile. "I said it was pleasant to see you here, Miss Leigh. I meant exactly that."

I flushed. "That is kind of you. I have brought certain of the children's lesson books along. . . ."

"Let us give them a little holiday, shall we? Lessons I suppose there must be, if you say so, but need they sit at their desks all the time?"

"I think their lessons might be curtailed on an occasion like this."

He came and stood close to me. "Miss Leigh," he said, "you are delightful."

I drew back startled, and he went on: "I'm glad you came so promptly."

"Those were your orders."

"I did not mean to order, Miss Leigh. Merely to request."

"But . . ." I began; and I was apprehensive because he seemed different from the man I had known. He was almost like a stranger— a stranger who fascinated me no less than that other Connan Tre- Mellyn, a stranger who frightened me a little, for I was unsure of myself, unsure of my own emotions.

"I was so glad to escape," he said. "I thought you would be too."

"Escape . . . from what?"

"From the gloom of death. I hate death. It depresses me."

"You mean Sir Thomas. But—"

"Oh, I know. A neighbor merely. But still it did depress me. I wanted to get right away. I am so glad you have joined me . . . with Alvean and the other child."

I said on impulse: "I hope you did not think it was presumptuous of me to bring Gillyflower. She would have been heartbroken if I had not brought her."

Then he said a thing which set my senses swimming: "I can under- stand her being heartbroken if she had to part from you."

I said quickly: "I suppose the children should have a meal of some sort. They are exhausted and sleeping now. But I do feel they need some refreshment before they go to bed. It has been a tiring day for them."

He waved a hand. "Order what you wish for them, Miss Leigh. And when you have seen to them, you and I will dine together."

I said: "Alvean dines with you . . . does she not?"

"She will be too tired tonight. We will have it alone."

So I ordered what I wanted for the children, and I dined with Connan in the winter parlor. It was a strange and exhilarating experience to dine with that man in candlelight. I kept telling myself that it could not be real. If ever anything was the stuff that dreams were made of, this was.

He talked a great deal; there was no sign of the taciturn Connan that evening.

He told me about the house, that it had been built in the shape of an E as a compliment to the Queen who had been reigning when it was built. He drew the shape to show me. "Two three-sided court-yards," he said, "and a projecting center block, if you see what I mean. We are in the central block now. The main feature of it is the hall, the staircase and the gallery, and these smaller rooms such as the winter parlor which, I think you will agree, is ideally suited for a small company."

I said I thought it was a delightful house, and how fortunate he was to possess two such magnificent places.

"Stone walls do not bring satisfaction, Miss Leigh. It is the life one lives within those walls which is of the greatest importance."

"Yet," I retaliated, "it is some comfort to have charming surroundings in which to live one's life."

"I agree. And I cannot tell you how glad I am that you find my homes so charming."

When we had eaten he took me to the library and asked me if I would play a game of chess with him. I said I would be delighted.

And we sat there in that beautiful room with its carved ceiling and thick piled carpet, lighted by lamps the bowls of which were made of artistically painted china of oriental origin. I was happier than I had ever dreamed I could be.

He had set out the ivory pieces on the board, and we played in silence.

It was a deep, contented silence, or so it seemed to me. I knew I should never forget the flickering firelight, the ticking of the gilded clock which looked as though it might have belonged to Louis XIV, as I watched Connan's strong lean fingers on the ivory pieces.

Once, as I frowned in concentration, I was conscious of his eyes fixed on me and, lifting them suddenly, I met his gaze. It was of amusement and yet of speculation. In that moment I thought: He has asked me here for a purpose. What is it?

I felt a shiver of alarm, but I was too happy to entertain such feelings.

I moved my piece and he said: "Ah!" And then: "Miss Leigh, oh my dear Miss Leigh, you have, I think, walked straight into the trap I have set for you."

"Oh . . . no!" I cried.

He had moved a knight which immediately menaced my King. I had forgotten that knight.

"I believe it is . . ." he said. "Oh no, not entirely. Check, Miss Leigh. But not checkmate."

I saw that I had allowed my attention to wander from the game. I sought hurriedly to save myself, but I could not. With every move the inevitable end was more obvious.

I heard his voice, gentle, full of laughter. "Checkmate, Miss Leigh."

I sat for a few seconds staring at the board. He said: "I took an unfair advantage. You were tired after the journey."

"Oh no," I said quickly. "I suspect you are a better player than I am."

"I suspect," he replied, "that we are very well matched."

I retired to my room soon after that game.

I went to bed and tried to sleep, but I couldn't. I was too happy. I kept going over in my mind his reception of me, our meal together, his words: "We are very well matched."

I even forgot that the house in which I now lay had been Alice's home—a fact which at one time would have seemed of the utmost interest to me—I forgot everything but that Connan had sent for me and, now that I was here, seemed so delighted to have me.

❦

The next day was as pleasant and unpredictable as the first. I did a few lessons with the children in the morning and in the afternoon Connan took us for a drive. How different it was riding in his carriage from jogging along behind Tapperty or Billy Trehay.

He drove us to the coast and we saw St. Michael's Mount rising out of the water.

"One day," he said, "when the spring comes, I'll take you out there and you can see St. Michael's chair."

"Can we sit in it, Papa?" asked Alvean.

"You can if you are prepared to risk a fall. You'll find your feet dangling over a drop of seventy feet or so. Nevertheless, many of your sex think it worth while."

"But why, Papa, why?" demanded Alvean, who was always delighted when she had his undivided attention.

"Because," he went on, "there is an old saying that if a woman can sit in St. Michael's chair before her husband, she will be the master of the house."

Alvean laughed with pleasure and Gilly, whom I had insisted on bringing with us, stood there smiling.

Connan looked at me. "And you, Miss Leigh," he said, "would you think it worth while to try?"

I hesitated for a second, and then met his gaze boldly. "No, Mr. TreMellyn, I don't think I should."

"Then you would not desire to be the master in the house?"

"I do not think that either a husband or his wife should be master in that sense. I think they should work together and if one has an opinion which he or she feels to be the only right one, he or she should adhere to it."

I flushed a little. I imagined how Phillida would smile if she heard that.

"Miss Leigh," said Connan, "your wisdom puts our foolish folklore to shame."

We drove back in the winter sunshine and I was happy.

⊷⚜❧

I had been in Penlandstow a week, and I was wondering how much longer this idyllic interlude could last when Connan spoke to me of what was in his mind.

The children were in bed and Connan had asked me if I would join him in a game of chess in the library. There I found him, the pieces set out on the board, sitting looking at them.

The curtains had been drawn and the fire burned cheerfully in the great fireplace. He rose as I entered and I quickly slipped into my place opposite him.

He smiled at me and I thought his eyes took in every detail of my appearance in a manner which I might have found offensive in anyone else.

I was about to move King's pawn when he said: "Miss Leigh, I did not ask you down here to play. There is something I have to say to you."

"Yes, Mr. TreMellyn?"

"I feel I have known you a very long time. You have made such a difference to us both—Alvean and myself. If you went away, we should miss you very much. I am certain that we should both want to ensure that you do not leave us."

I tried to look at him and failed because I was afraid he would read the hopes and fears in my eyes.

"Miss Leigh," he went on, "will you stay with us . . . always?"

"I . . . I don't understand. I . . . can't believe . . ."

"I am asking you to marry me."

"But . . . but that is impossible."

"Why so, Miss Leigh?"

"Because . . . because it is so incongruous."

"Do you find me incongruous . . . repulsive? Do please be frank."

"I . . . No indeed not! But I am the governess here."

"Precisely. That is what alarms me. Governesses sometimes leave their employment. It would be intolerable for me if you went away."

I felt I was choking with my emotions. I could not believe this was really happening to me. I remained silent. I dared not try to speak.

"I see that you hesitate, Miss Leigh."

"I am so surprised."

"Should I have prepared you for the shock?" His lips twitched slightly at the corner. "I am sorry, Miss Leigh. I thought I had managed to convey to you something of my feelings in this matter."

I tried to picture it all in those few seconds—going back to Mount Mellyn as the wife of the master, slipping from the role of governess to that of mistress of the house. Of course I would do it and in a few months they would forget that I had once been the governess. Whatever else I lacked I had my dignity—perhaps a little too much of it, according to Phillida. But I thought that a proposal would have been made in a different way. He did not take my hand; he did not touch me; he merely sat at the table watching me in an almost cool and calculating manner.

He went on: "Think of how much good this could bring to us all, my dear Miss Leigh. I have been so impressed by the manner in which you have helped Alvean. The child needs a mother. You would supply that need . . . admirably."

"Should two people marry for the sake of a child, do you think?"

"I am a most selfish man. I never would." He leaned forward across the table and his eyes were alight with something I did not understand. "I would marry for my own satisfaction."

"Then . . ." I began.

"I confess I was not considering Alvean alone. We are three people, my dear Miss Leigh, who could profit from this marriage. Alvean needs you. And I . . . I need you. Do you need us? Perhaps you are more self-sufficient than we are, but what will you do if you do not marry? You will go from post to post, and that is not a very pleasant life. When one is young, handsome, and full of spirit it is tolerable . . . but sprightly governesses become aging governesses."

I said acidly: "Do you suggest that I should enter into this marriage as an insurance against old age?"

"I suggest only that you do what your desires dictate, my dear Miss Leigh."

There was a short silence during which I felt an absurd desire to burst into tears. This was something I had longed for, but a proposal of marriage should have been an impassioned declaration, and I could not rid myself of the suspicion that there was something other than Connan's love for me which had inspired it. It seemed to me as though he were offering me a list of reasons why we should marry, for fear I should discover the real one.

"You put it on such a practical basis," I stammered. "I had not thought of marriage in that way."

His eyebrows lifted and he laughed, looking suddenly very gay. "How glad I am. I thought of you always as such a practical person, so I was trying to put it to you in the manner in which I felt it would appeal to you most."

"Are you seriously asking me to marry you?"

"I doubt if I have ever been so serious in my life as I am at this moment. What is your answer? Please do not keep me in suspense any longer."

I said I must have time to consider this.

"That is fair enough. You will tell me tomorrow?"

"Yes," I said. "I will tell you tomorrow."

I rose and went to the door. He was there before me. He laid his fingers on the door handle and I waited for him to open it, but he did no such thing. He stood with his back to the door and caught me up in his arms.

He kissed me as I had never been kissed, never dreamed of being kissed; so that I knew there was a life of the emotions of which I was totally ignorant. He kissed my eyelids, my nose, my cheeks, my mouth, and my throat until he was breathless, and I was too.

Then he laughed.

"Wait until the morning!" he mocked. "Do I look the sort of man who would wait until the morning? Do you think I am the sort of man who would marry for the sake of his daughter? No, Miss Leigh . . ." he mocked again, "my dear, *dear* Miss Leigh . . . I want to marry you because I want to keep you a prisoner in my house. I don't want you to run away from me because, since you came, I have thought of little else but you, and I know I am going on thinking of you all my life."

"Is this true?" I whispered. "Can this be true?"

"Martha!" he said. "What a stern name for such an adorable creature! And yet, how it fits!"

I said: "My sister calls me Marty. My father did too."

"Marty," he said. "That sounds helpless, clinging . . . feminine. You can be a Marty sometimes. For me you will be all three. Marty, Martha, and Miss Leigh, my very dear Miss Leigh. You see you *are* all three, and my dearest Marty would always betray Miss Leigh. I knew from her that you were interested in me. Far more interested than Miss Leigh would think proper. How enchanting! I shall marry not one woman but three!"

"Have I been so blatant?"

"Tremendously so . . . adorably so."

I knew that it was foolish to pretend. I gave myself up to his embrace, and it was wonderful beyond my imaginings.

At length I said: "I have a terrible feeling that I shall wake up in my bed at Mount Mellyn and find I have dreamed all this."

"Do you know," he said seriously, "I feel exactly the same."

"But it is so different for you. You can do as you will . . . go where you will . . . dependent on no one."

"I am independent no longer. I depend on Marty, Martha, my dear Miss Leigh."

He spoke so seriously that I could have wept with tenderness. The changing emotions were almost too much for me to bear.

This is love! I thought. The emotion which carries one to the very heights of human experience and, because it can carry one so high, one is in continual danger of falling; and one must never forget, the higher the delight, the more tragic the fall.

But this was not the moment to think of tragedy. I loved, and miraculously I was loved. I had no doubt in that library of Penlandstow that I was loved.

For love such as this, one would be prepared to risk everything.

He put his hands on my shoulders and looked long into my face.

He said: "We'll be happy, my darling. We'll be happier than either you or I ever dreamed possible."

I knew that we should be. All that had gone before would give us a finer appreciation of this joy we could bring each other.

"We should be practical," he said. "We should make our plans. When shall we marry? I do not like delay. I am the most impatient man alive, where my own pleasures are concerned. We will go home tomorrow, and there we will announce our engagement. No, not tomorrow . . . the day after. I have one or two little commitments here tomorrow. And as soon as we are home we will give a ball to announce our engagement. I think that in a month after that we should be setting out on our honeymoon. I suggest Italy, unless you have any other ideas?"

I sat with my hands clasped. I must have looked like an ecstatic schoolgirl.

"I wonder what they will think at Mount Mellyn."

"Who, the servants? You may be sure they have a pretty shrewd idea of the way things are; servants have, you know. Servants are like detectives in the house. They pick up every little clue. You shiver. Are you cold?"

"No, only excited. I still believe I'm going to wake up in a moment."

"And you like the idea of Italy?"

"I would like the idea of the North Pole in some company."

"By which, my darling, I hope you mean mine."

"That was my intention."

"My dear Miss Leigh," he said, "how I love your astringent moods. They are going to make conversation throughout our lives so invigorating." I had an idea then that he was making comparisons between Alice and me, and I shivered again as I had when he made that remark about the detectives.

"You are a little worried about the reception of the news," he went on. "The servants . . . the countryside. Who cares? Do you? Of course you do not. Miss Leigh has too much good sense for that. I am longing to tell Peter Nansellock that you are to be my wife. To tell the truth, I have been somewhat jealous of that young man."

"There was no need to be."

"Still, I was anxious. I had visions of his persuading you to go to Australia with him. That was something I should have gone to great lengths to prevent."

"Even so far as asking me to marry *you?*"

"Farther than that if the need had arisen. I should have abducted you and locked you up in a dungeon until he was far away."

"There was no need for the slightest apprehension."

"Are you quite sure? He is very handsome, I believe."

"Perhaps he is. I did not notice."

"I could have killed him when he had the effrontery to offer you Jacinth."

"I think he merely enjoys being outrageous. He probably knew I should not accept it."

"And I need not fear him?"

"You need never fear anyone," I told him.

Then once more I was in that embrace, and I was oblivious of all but the fact that I had discovered love, and believed, as doubtless hosts of lovers have before, that there was never love such as that between us two.

At length he said: "We'll go back the day after tomorrow. We'll start making arrangements immediately. In a month from now we'll be married. We'll put up the banns as soon as we return. We will have a ball to announce our engagement and invite all our neighbors to the wedding."

"I suppose it must be done in this way?"

"Tradition, my darling. It is one of the things we have to bow down to. You'll be magnificent, I know. You're not nervous?"

"Of your country neighbors, no."

"You and I will open the ball this time together, dearest Miss Leigh."

"Yes," I said; and I pictured myself in the green dress wearing the amber comb in my hair with the diamond horseshoe glittering on the green background.

I had no qualms about taking my place in his circle.

Then he began to talk of Alice. "I have never told you," he said, "of my first marriage."

"No," I answered.

"It was not a happy one."

"I'm sorry."

"A marriage which was arranged. This time I shall marry my own choice. Only one who has suffered the first can realize the joy of the second. Dearest, I have not lived the life of a monk, I fear."

"I guessed it."

"I am a most sinful man, as you will discover."

"I am prepared for the worst."

"Alice . . . my wife . . . and I were most unsuited, I suppose."

"Tell me about her."

"There is little to tell. She was a gentle creature, quiet, anxious to please. She seemed to have little spirit. I understood why. She was in love with someone else when she married me."

"The man she ran away with?" I asked.

He nodded. "Poor Alice! She was unfortunate. She chose not only the wrong husband but the wrong lover. There was little to choose between us . . . myself and Geoffry Nansellock. We were of a kind. In the old days there was a tradition of the *droit de seigneurs* in these parts. Geoffry and I did our best to maintain that."

"You are telling me that you have enjoyed many love affairs."

"I am a dissolute, degenerate philanderer. I am going to say *was*. Because from this moment I am going to be faithful to one woman for the rest of my life. You do not look scornful or skeptical. Bless you for that. I mean it, dearest Marty, I swear I mean it. It is because of those experiences of the past that I know the difference between them and this. This is love."

"Yes," I said slowly, "you and I will be faithful together because that is the only way we can prove to each other the depth and breadth of our love."

He took my hands and kissed them, and I had never known him so serious. "I love you," he said. "Remember that . . . always remember it."

"I intend to."

"You may hear gossip."

"One does hear gossip," I admitted.

"You have heard of Alice and that Alvean is not my daughter? Oh, darling, someone told you and you do not want to betray the teller. Never mind. You know. It is true. I could never love the child. In fact, I avoided the sight of her. She was an unpleasant reminder of much that I wished to forget. But when you came I felt differently. You made me see her as a lonely child, suffering from the sins of grown-up people. You see, you changed me, Marty dear. Your coming

changed the whole household. That is what confirms me in my belief
that with us it is going to be different from anything that has ever
happened to me before."

"Connan, I want to make that child happy. I want to make her
forget that there is a doubt as to her parentage. Let her be able to
accept you as her father. It is what she needs."

"You will be a mother to her. Then I must be her father."

"We are going to be so happy, Connan."

"Can you see into the future?"

"I can see into ours, for our future is what we make it, and I intend
that it shall be one of complete happiness."

"And what Miss Leigh decides shall be, will be. And you will
promise me not to be hurt if you hear gossip about me?"

"You are thinking of Lady Treslyn, I know. She has been your
mistress." The words seemed to come from my lips involuntarily.
I was astonished that I could speak of such matters. Yet I had to
know the truth, and so strong was my emotion that I seemed to have
thrown all sense of propriety aside.

He nodded.

Then I said: "She will never be again. That is all over."

He kissed my hand. "Have I not sworn eternal fidelity?"

"But Connan," I said, "she is so beautiful and she will still be
there."

"But I am in love," he answered, "for the first time in my life."

"And you were not in love with her?"

"Lust, passion," he answered, "they sometimes wear the guise
of love; but when one meets true love one recognizes it for what it
is. Dearest, let us bury all that is past. Let us start afresh from this
day forth—you and I—for better for worse. . . ."

I was in his arms again. "Connan," I said, "I am not dreaming,
am I? Please say I am not dreaming."

It was late when I left him. I went to my room in a haze of happiness. I was afraid to sleep for fear I should wake up and find that it
had all been a dream.

❦

In the morning I went to Alvean's room and told her the news.

For a few seconds a satisfied smile appeared at the corners of her
mouth; then she assumed indifference, but it was too late. I knew
that she was pleased.

"You'll stay with us all the time now, miss," she said.

"Yes," I assured her.

"I wonder if I shall ever ride as well as you."

"Probably better. You'll be able to have more practice than I ever could."

Again that smile touched her lips. Then she was serious.

"Miss," she said, "what shall I call you? You'll be my stepmother, won't you?"

"Yes, but you can call me what you like."

"Not miss!"

"Well, hardly. I shan't be miss any more."

"I expect I shall have to call you Mamma." Her mouth hardened a little.

"If you do not like that you could call me Martha in private. Or Marty. That's what my father and sister always called me."

"Marty," she repeated. "I like that. It sounds like a horse."

"What could be better praise," I cried, and she regarded my amusement with continued seriousness.

I went to Gilly's room.

"Gilly," I said, "I'm going to be Mrs. TreMellyn."

The blankness left the blue eyes and her smile was dazzling.

Then she ran to me and buried her head in my bodice. I could feel her body shaking with laughter.

I could never be quite sure what was going on among all the shadowy vagueness of Gilly's mind, but I knew she was contented. She had bracketed me with Alice in her mind and I felt that she was less surprised than I or Alvean, or anyone else, would be.

To Gilly it was the most natural thing in the world that I should take Alice's place.

I believe that, from that moment, for Gilly I became Alice.

❦

It was a merry journey home. We sang Cornish songs all the way to the station. I had never seen Connan so happy. I thought: This is how it will be all the rest of our lives.

Alvean joined in the singing, so did Gilly; and it was astonishing to hear that child, who scarcely ever spoke, singing quietly as though to herself.

We sang the "Twelve Days of Christmas." Connan had a rich baritone voice which was very pleasant to hear and I felt I had reached the very peak of happiness as he sang the first lines.

"The first day of Christmas my true love sent to me
A partridge in a pear tree."

We went through the song and I had difficulty in remembering all the gifts after the five gold rings; and we laughed together hilariously while we argued as to how many maids there were a-milking, and how many geese a-laying were sent.

"But they were not very sensible things," said Alvean, "except of course the five gold rings. I think he was pretending he loved her more than he really did."

"But he was her true love," I protested.

"How could she be sure?" asked Alvean.

"Because he told her so," answered Connan.

"Then he ought to have given her something better than a partridge in a pear tree. I expect the partridge flew away and the pears were those hard ones which are used for stewing."

"You must not be hard on lovers," Connan cried. "All the world loves them, and you have to keep in step."

And so we laughed and bantered until we boarded the train.

Billy Trehay met us with the carriage and I was astonished when we reached the house, for I then realized that Connan must have sent a message to arrive before we did. He wanted me to be received with honors. Even so I was unprepared for the reception which was waiting for us in the hall.

The servants were all there—the Polgreys and Tapperty families and others from the gardens and stables, and even the village boys and girls who came to help and whom I scarcely knew.

They were lined up ceremoniously, and Connan took my arm as we entered the hall.

"As you know," he said, "Miss Leigh has promised to marry me. In a few weeks' time she will be your mistress."

The men bowed and the women curtsied, but I was conscious, as I smiled at them and walked along the line with Connan, that there was a certain wariness in their eyes.

As I had guessed, they were not ready to accept me as mistress of the house . . . yet.

❦

There was a big fire in my room and everything looked cosy and welcoming. Daisy brought my hot water. She was a little remote, I thought. She did not stop and chat with me as she had hitherto.

I thought: I will regain their confidence, but of course I had to remember that as the future mistress of the house, I must not gossip as I once had.

I dined with Connan and Alvean and afterward I went up with Alvean; when I had said good night to her I joined Connan in the library.

There were so many plans to make, and I gave myself up to the complete joy of contemplating the future.

He asked me if I had written to my family, and I told him that I had not yet done so. I still could not quite believe this was really happening to me.

"Perhaps this token will help you to remember," he said. Then he took a jewel case from a drawer in the bureau and showed me a beautiful square-cut emerald set in diamonds.

"It's . . . quite beautiful, far too beautiful for me."

"Nothing is too beautiful for Martha TreMellyn," he said, and he took my left hand and put the ring on the third finger.

I held it out and stared at it.

"I never thought to possess anything so lovely."

"It's the beginning of all the beautiful things I shall bring to you. It's the partridge in the pear tree, my darling."

Then he kissed my hand, and I told myself that whenever I doubted the truth of all that was happening to me, I could look at my emerald and know I was not dreaming.

❦

Next morning when I went down Connan had gone out on business, and after I had given Alvean and Gilly their lessons—for I was eager that everything should go on as before—I went to my room, and I had not been there for more than a few minutes when there was a discreet knock.

"Come in," I said, and Mrs. Polgrey entered.

She looked a little furtive, and I knew that something significant had happened.

"Miss Leigh," she said, "there will be things which we have to discuss. I was wondering if you would come to my room. I have the kettle on. Could you drink a cup of tea?"

I said I would like that. I was very anxious that there should be no difference in our relationship which, from my point of view, had always been a very pleasant and dignified one.

In her room we drank tea. There was no suggestion of whisky this time, and this secretly amused me although I made no reference to it. I should be the mistress of the house, and it was very different for *her* to know of the teatippling than the governess.

She again congratulated me on my engagement and told me how delighted she was. "In fact," she said, "the whole household is delighted." She asked me then if I intended to make changes, and I answered that, while the household was so efficiently run by herself, I should make none at all.

This was a relief to her, I could see, and she settled down to come to the point.

"While you've been away, Miss Leigh, there's been a bit of excitement in these parts."

"Oh?" I said, feeling that we were now coming to the reason for my visit.

"It's all along of the sudden death of Sir Thomas Treslyn."

My heart had begun to leap in a disconcerting manner.

"But," I said, "he is buried now. We went to his funeral."

"Yes, yes. But that need not be the end, Miss Leigh."

"I don't understand, Mrs. Polgrey."

"Well, there's been rumors . . . nasty rumors, and letters have been sent."

"To . . . to whom?"

"To her, Miss Leigh . . . to the widow. And, it seems, to others . . . and as a result they're going to dig him up. There's going to be an examination."

"You mean . . . they suspect someone poisoned him?"

"Well, there's been these letters, you see. And him dying so sudden. What I don't like is that he was here last. . . . It's not the sort of thing one likes to have connected with the house. . . ."

She was looking at me oddly. I thought I saw speculation in her eyes.

I wanted to shut from my mind all the unpleasant thoughts which kept coming to me.

I saw again Connan and Lady Treslyn in the punch room together, their backs toward me . . . laughing together. Had Connan loved me then? One would not have thought so. I thought of the words they had spoken in my hearing when the party was over. "It will not be long . . . now." She had said that . . . and to him. And then there was the conversation I had partly overheard in the woods.

What did this mean?

There was a question that hammered in my brain. But I would not let my mind dwell on it.

I dared not. I could not bear to see all my hopes of happiness shattered. I had to go on believing, so I would not ask myself that question.

I looked expressionlessly into Mrs. Polgrey's face.

"I thought you'd want to know," she said.

8

I was afraid, more afraid than I had ever been since I came to this house.

The body of Sir Thomas Treslyn, who had died after supping at Mount Mellyn, was to be exhumed. People were suspicious of the manner in which he died and, as a result, there had been anonymous letters. Why should they be suspicious? Because his wife wanted him out of the way; and it was known that Connan and Linda Treslyn had been lovers. There had been two obstacles to their union—Alice and Sir Thomas. Both had died suddenly.

But Connan had no wish to marry Lady Treslyn. He was in love with me.

A terrible thought had struck me. Did Connan know that there was to be this exhumation? Had I been living in a fool's paradise? Was my wonderful dream-come-true nothing but a living nightmare?

Was I being used by a cynic? Why did I not use the harsher word? Was I being used by a *murderer?*

I would not believe it. I loved Connan. I had sworn to be faithful to him all my life. How could I make such a vow when I believed the worst of him at the first crisis?

I tried to reason with myself. You're crazy, Martha Leigh. Do you really think that a man such as Connan TreMellyn could suddenly fall in love with *you!*

Yes, I do. I do, I retorted hotly.

But I was a frightened woman.

❧

I could see that the household was divided between two topics of conversation: the exhumation of Sir Thomas and the proposed marriage of the master and the governess.

I was afraid to meet the stern eyes of Mrs. Polgrey, the lewd ones of Tapperty, and the excited ones of his daughters.

Did they, as I had begun to do, connect these two events?

I asked Connan what he thought of the Treslyn affair.

"Mischief-makers," he said. "They'll have an autopsy and find he died a natural death. Why, his doctor has been attending him for years and has always told him that he must expect to go off like that."

"It must be very worrying for Lady Treslyn."

"She will not worry unduly. Indeed, since she has been pestered by letter writers she may well be relieved to have the matter brought to a head."

I pictured the medical experts. They would no doubt be men who knew the Treslyns and Connan. As Connan was going to marry me— and he was very eager to spread the news—was it possible that they would approach the matter in a different spirit from that in which they would if they believed Lady Treslyn was eager to marry again? Who could say?

I must drive away these terrible thoughts. I would believe in Connan. I had to; if I did not I must face the fact that I had fallen in love with a murderer.

The invitations for the ball had gone out hastily—too hastily, I thought. Lady Treslyn, being in mourning and with the autopsy pending, was of course not invited. It was to take place only four days after our return from Penlandstow.

Celestine and Peter Nansellock rode over the day before the ball.

Celestine put her arms about me and kissed me.

"My dear," she said, "how happy I am. I have watched you with Alvean and I know what this is going to mean to her." There were tears in her eyes. "Alice would be so happy."

I thanked her and said: "You have always been such a good friend to me."

"I was so grateful that at last the child had found a governess who really understood her."

I said: "I thought Miss Jansen did that."

"Miss Jansen, yes. We all thought so. It was a pity she was not honest. Perhaps, though, it was the temptation of a moment. I did all I could to help her."

"I'm so glad somebody did."

Peter had come up. He took my hand and kissed it lightly. Connan's look of displeasure made my heart beat fast with happiness, and I was ashamed of my suspicions.

"Fortunate Connan," cried Peter exuberantly. "No need to tell you how much I envy him, is there! I think I've made it clear. I've brought over Jacinth. I told you I'd make you a present of her, didn't I? Well, she's my wedding present. You can't object to that, can you?"

I looked at Connan. "A present for us both," I said.

"Oh no," said Peter. "She's for you. I'll think of something else for Con."

"Thank you, Peter," I said. "It's generous of you."

He shook his head. "Couldn't bear the thought of her going to anyone else. I feel sentimental about that mare. I want a good home for her. You know I'm going at the end of next week."

"So soon?"

"Everything has been speeded up. There's no point in delaying further." He looked at me significantly—"now," he added.

I saw that Kitty, who was serving us with wine, was listening with all attention.

Celestine was talking earnestly to Connan, and Peter went on: "So it's you and Con, after all. Well, you'll keep him in order, Miss Leigh. I'm sure of that."

"I am not going to be his governess, you know."

"I'm not sure. Once a governess, always a governess. I thought Alvean seemed not displeased by the new arrangement."

"I think she's going to accept me."

"I think you're an even greater favorite than Miss Jansen was."

"Poor Miss Jansen! I wonder what became of her."

"Celeste did something for her. She was rather worried about the poor girl, I think."

"Oh, I'm so glad."

"Helped her to find another place . . . with some friends of ours actually. The Merrivales who have a place on the edge of Dartmoor. I wonder how our gay Miss Jansen likes Hoodfield Manor. Finds it a bit dull, I should imagine, with Tavistock, the nearest town, quite six miles away."

"It was very kind of Celestine to help her."

"Well, that's Celestine all over." He lifted his glass. "To your happiness, Miss Leigh. And whenever you ride Jacinth, think of me."

"I shall . . . and of Jacinth's namesake, Miss Jansen."

He laughed. "And if," he went on, "you should change your mind . . ."

I raised my eyebrows.

"About marrying Connan, I mean. There'll be a little homestead waiting for you on the other side of the world. You'll find me ever faithful, Miss Leigh."

I laughed and sipped my wine.

◈

The next day Alvean and I went riding together, and I was mounted on Jacinth. She was a wonderful creature and I enjoyed every moment of the ride. I felt that this was another of the glorious things which were happening to me. I even had my own mount now.

The ball was a great success and I was surprised how ready the neighborhood was to accept me. The fact that I had been Alvean's governess was forgotten. I felt that Connan's neighbors were reminding each other that I was an educated young woman and that my family background was passably good. Perhaps those who were fond of him were relieved because he was engaged to be married, for they would not wish him to be involved in the Treslyn scandal.

The day after the ball Connan had to go away again on business.

"I neglected a great deal during our stay at Penlandstow," he said. "There were things I simply forgot to do. It is understandable. My mind was on other matters. I shall be away a week, I think, and when I come back it'll be but a fortnight before our wedding. You'll be getting on with your preparations, and darling, if there's anything you want to do in the house . . . if there's anything you want to change, do say so. It mightn't be a bad idea to ask Celestine's advice; she's an expert on old houses."

I said I would, because it would please her, and I wanted to please her.

"She was kind to me right from the first," I said. "I shall always have a soft feeling for her."

He said good-by and drove off while I stood at my window, waving. I did not care to do so from the porch because I was still a little shy of the servants.

When I went out of my room I found Gilly standing outside the door. Since I had told her that I was to be Mrs. TreMellyn she had taken to following me around. I was beginning to understand the way her mind worked. She was fond of me in exactly the same way that she had been fond of Alice, and with the passing of each day the two of us became in her mind merged into one. Alice had disappeared from her life; she was going to make sure that I did not.

"Hello, Gilly," I said.

She dropped her head in that characteristic way of hers and laughed to herself.

Then she put her hand in mine and I led her back to my room.

"Well, Gilly," I said, "in three weeks' time I am going to be married, and I am the happiest woman in the world."

I was really trying to reassure myself, for sometimes talking to Gilly was like talking to oneself.

I thought of what Connan had said about altering anything I wished to in the house, and I remembered that there were some parts of it which I had not even seen yet.

I suddenly thought of Miss Jansen and what I had been told about her having a different room from the one I occupied. I had never seen Miss Jansen's room and I decided that I would go along now and inspect it. I need have no qualms now about going to any part of the house I wished, for in a very short time I should be mistress of it.

"Come along, Gilly," I said. "We'll go and see Miss Jansen's room."

She trotted along contentedly by my side, and I thought how much more intelligent she was than people realized, for it was she who led me to Miss Jansen's room.

There was nothing very unusual about it. It was smaller than mine. But there was a rather striking mural. I was looking at this when Gilly tugged at my arm and drew me close to it. She pulled up a chair and stood on it. Then I understood. There, in this wall, was a peep like that in the solarium. I looked through it and saw the chapel. It was of course a different view from that to be seen in the solarium, as it was from the opposite side.

Gilly looked at me, delighted to have shown me the peep. We went back to my room, and clearly she did not want to leave me.

I could see that she was apprehensive. I understood, of course. Her somewhat confused mind had so clearly associated me with Alice that she expected me to disappear as Alice had done.

She was determined to keep an eye on me so that this should not happen.

❧

All through the night a southwest gale was blowing in from the sea. The rain which came with it was driven horizontally against our windows, and even the solid foundations of Mount Mellyn seemed to shake. It was one of the wettest nights I had known since my arrival in Cornwall.

The next day the rain continued; everything in my room—the mirrors, the furniture—was misty with damp. It was what happened often enough, Mrs. Polgrey told me, when the southwest wind came bringing rain with it, which it invariably did.

Alvean and I could not go out riding that day.

By the following morning the skies had cleared a little, and the heavy rain gave way to a light drizzle. Lady Treslyn called, but I did not see her. She did not ask for me; it was Mrs. Polgrey who told me she had called and that she had wished to see Connan.

"She seemed very distressed," said Mrs. Polgrey. "She'll not rest until this terrible business is over."

I felt sure that Lady Treslyn had come over to talk to Connan about his engagement to me and that she was probably distressed because he was not at home.

Celestine Nansellock also called. We had a chat about the house. She said she was pleased that I was becoming very interested in Mount Mellyn.

"Not only as a home," she said, "but as a house." She went on: "I have some old documents about Mount Mellyn and Mount Widden. I'll show them to you one day."

"You must help me," I told her. "It'll be fun discussing things together."

"You'll make some changes?" she asked.

"If I do," I assured her, "I shall ask your advice."

She left before luncheon, and in the afternoon Alvean and I went down to the stables for the horses.

We stood by while Billy Trehay saddled them for us.

"Jacinth be frisky today, miss," he told me.

"It's because she had no exercise yesterday." I stroked her muzzle and she rubbed against my hand to show she shared my affection.

We took our usual ride down the slope, past the cove and Mount Widden; then we went along the cliff path. The view here was particularly beautiful with the jagged coast stretched out before us and Rame Head lying in the water, hiding Plymouth and its Sound from view.

Some of the paths were narrow, cut into the cliffs at spots where it had been convenient to do so. Up and down we went; sometimes we were almost down to the sea; at others we climbed high.

It was not very easy going, for the rain had whipped up the mud and I began to feel a little anxious about Alvean. She sat firmly in her saddle—no novice now—but I was conscious of Jacinth's mood and I expected Black Prince's was not much different, although, of course, he hadn't Jacinth's fiery temperament. At times I had to rein her in firmly; a gallop would have been more to her taste than this necessarily slow careful walk along paths which were a good deal more dangerous than when we had come this way on our last ride.

There was one spot on this cliff path which was particularly narrow; above the path loomed the cliff face, dotted with bushes of gorse and brambles; below it, the cliff fell almost sheer to the sea. The path was safe enough ordinarily; but I felt a little nervous about Alvean's using it on a day like this.

I noticed that in places some of the cliff had fallen. This was continually happening. Tapperty had often said that the sea was gradually claiming the land, and that in his grandfather's day there had been a road which had now completely disappeared.

I thought of turning back, but if we did I would have to explain my fears to Alvean; and I did not want to do this while she was mounted.

No, I thought, we'll continue on this path until we can climb to the top road. Then we'll go home a roundabout way, but on firm land.

We had come to that danger spot and I noticed that the ground was even more slippery here, and that there had been a bigger fall of cliff than I had seen on other portions of the path.

I held Jacinth in and walked her slowly in front of Alvean and Black Prince, for we naturally had to go in single file.

I pulled up and looked over my shoulder, saying: "We're going very slowly along here. You just follow."

Then I heard it. I turned quickly as the boulder came tumbling down bringing in its wake shale, turf, and vegetation. It passed within a few inches of Jacinth. I stared, in fascinated horror, as it went hurtling down to the sea.

Jacinth reared. She was terrified and ready to plunge anywhere . . . over the cliff . . . down to the sea . . . to escape what had startled her.

It was fortunate for me that I was an experienced rider, and that Jacinth and I knew each other so well. Thus it was all over in a matter of seconds. I had her under control. She grew calm as I began to talk to her in a voice which was meant to be soothing but which shook a little.

"Miss! What happened?" It was Alvean.

"It's all over," I answered, trying to speak lightly. "You managed perfectly."

"Why, miss, I thought Black Prince was going to start a gallop." He would, I thought, if Jacinth had.

I was terribly shaken and afraid to show it, either to Alvean or Jacinth.

I suddenly felt the need to get off that dangerous path immediately. I glanced nervously up and said: "It's not safe to be on these paths . . . after the weather we've been having."

I don't know what I expected to see up there, but I was staring at the thickest of the bushes. Did I see a movement there, or did I imagine it? It would be easy for someone to hide up there. What if a boulder had become dislodged by the recent rains. What an excellent opportunity if someone wanted to be rid of me. It merely had to be rolled down at that moment when I was on the path—a perfect target. Alvean and I had made a habit of coming along this path at a certain time.

I shivered and said: "Let's get on. We'll get onto the top road and won't go back along the cliff path."

Alvean was silent; and when in a few minutes we were on the road she looked at me oddly. I saw that she was not unaware of the danger through which we had passed.

It was not until we were back in the house that I realized how alarmed I was. I was telling myself that a terrifying pattern was being formed. Alice had died: Sir Thomas Treslyn had died; and now I, who was to be Connan's wife, might easily have met my death on the cliff path this day.

I longed to tell Connan of my fears.

But I was a sensible, practical woman. Was I going to refuse to look facts in the face because I was afraid of what I might see there if I did so?

Suppose Connan had not really gone away. Suppose he had wanted an accident to happen to me while he was believed to be away from home. I thought of Lady Treslyn at the Christmas ball. I thought of her beauty, her sensuous, voluptuous beauty. Connan had admitted that she had been his mistress. Had been? Was it possible that anyone, knowing her, could want me?

The proposal had been so sudden. It had come at a time when his mistress's husband was about to be exhumed.

It was small wonder that the practical governess had become a frightened woman.

❧§§❧

To whom could I go for help?

There was Peter or Celestine . . . only those two, I thought. No, I could not betray these terrible suspicions of Connan to them. It was bad enough that I entertained them myself.

"Don't panic," I cautioned myself. "Be calm. Think of something you can do."

I thought of the house, vast and full of secrets, a house in which it was possible to peep from certain rooms into others. There might be peeps as yet undiscovered. Who could say? Perhaps someone was watching me now.

I thought of the peep in Miss Jansen's room and that set me thinking of her sudden dismissal. Then I was saying to myself: "Hoodfield Manor near Tavistock."

I wondered if Miss Jansen were still there. There was a good chance that she might be, for she must have gone there about the same time that I came to Mount Mellyn.

Why should I not try to meet her? She might have some light to throw on the secrets of this house.

I was desperately afraid, and at such times it is always comforting to take action.

I felt better when I had written the letter.

Dear Miss Jansen,

I am the governess at Mount Mellyn and I have heard of you. I should so like to meet you. I wonder if that would be possible. If so, I should like our meeting to be as soon as you can manage it.

Yours sincerely,

Martha Leigh.

I went out quickly to post the letter before I could change my mind. Then I tried to forget it.

I longed for a message from Connan. There was none. Each day I looked for his return. I thought: When he comes home I am going to tell him of my fears, because I must do so. I am going to tell him of what happened on the cliff path. I am going to ask him to tell me the truth. I am going to say to him: Connan, why did you ask me to marry you? Was it because you love me and want me to be your wife, or was it because you wished to divert suspicion from yourself and Lady Treslyn?

The devilish scheme which I had invented seemed to gain credibility with every passing moment.

I said to myself: Perhaps Alice died by accident, and that gave them the idea of ridding themselves of Sir Thomas, who was the only obstacle to their marriage. Did they slip something into his whisky? Why not? And it could not have been merely by chance that the boulder came hurtling down at that precise moment. Now there was to be an exhumation of Sir Thomas and the countryside knew of the relationship between Connan and Lady Treslyn. So Connan became engaged to the governess in order to divert suspicion. The governess is now an obstacle even as Alice was, even as Sir Thomas was. So the governess could have an accident on her newly acquired mare to which it might be said that she had not yet grown accustomed.

The road is clear for the guilty lovers and all they need do is wait until scandal has blown over.

How could I imagine such things of the man I loved? Could one love a man and think such thoughts of him?

I do love him, I told myself passionately. So much that I would rather meet death at his hands than leave him and be forced to endure an empty life without him.

❧

Three days later there was a letter from Miss Jansen, who said she was eager to meet me. She would be in Plymouth the following day and if I would meet her at the White Hart, which was not far from the Hoe, we might have luncheon together.

I told Mrs. Polgrey that I was going into Plymouth to shop. That seemed plausible enough since my wedding was due to take place in three weeks' time.

I made straight for the White Hart.

Miss Jansen was already there—an extremely pretty, fair-haired girl. She greeted me with pleasure and told me that Mrs. Plint, the innkeeper's wife, had said that we might have luncheon together in a small room of our own.

We were conducted to this private room and there took stock of each other.

The innkeeper's wife talked with enthusiasm of duck and green peas and roast beef, but neither of us was very much interested in food.

We ordered roast beef, I think it was, and as soon as we were alone, Miss Jansen said to me: "What do you think of Mount Mellyn?"

"It's a wonderful old place."

"One of the most interesting houses I ever saw," she replied.

"I did hear, from Mrs. Polgrey I think, that old houses specially interested you."

"They do. I was brought up in one. However, the family fortunes declined. That's what happens to so many of us who become governesses. I was sorry to leave Mount Mellyn. You have heard why I went?"

"Y-yes," I said hesitantly.

"It was a very distressing affair. I was furiously angry to be unjustly accused."

She was so frank and sincere that I believed her, and I made that clear.

She looked pleased; and then the food was brought in.

As we sat eating in a somewhat desultory way she told me of the affair.

"The Treslyns and the Nansellocks had been having tea at the house. You know the Treslyns and the Nansellocks of course?"

"Oh yes."

"I mean, I expect you know quite a lot about them. They are such friends of the family, are they not?"

"Indeed yes."

"I had been treated rather specially." She flushed slightly, and I thought: Yes, you are so pretty. Connan would have thought so. I was aware of a flash of not so much jealousy as uneasiness as I wondered whether in the years to come I was going to be continually jealous of Connan's appreciation of the attractive members of my sex.

She went on: "They had called me in to tea because Miss Nansellock wanted to ask some questions about Alvean. She did dote on that child. Does she still?"

"Indeed yes."

"She is such a kind person. I don't know what I should have done without her."

"I am so glad somebody was kind to you."

"I think that she looks upon Alvean as her child. There was a rumor that Miss Nansellock's brother was the father of Alvean, which would make her Miss Nansellock's niece. Perhaps that is why——"

"She certainly does feel strongly about Alvean."

"So I was called down to talk to her, and I was given tea and chatted with them—as though I were a guest as they were. I think that Treslyn woman resented it . . . she resented my presence there altogether. Perhaps they were a little too attentive to me—I mean Mr. Peter Nansellock and Mr. TreMellyn. Lady Treslyn has a hot temper, I am sure. In any case I believe she arranged the whole thing."

"She couldn't be so vile!"

"Oh, but I am sure she could, and she was. You see, she was wearing a diamond bracelet and the safety chain had broken. It had caught in the upholstery of the chair, I think. She said, 'I won't wear it. I'll take it down to old Pastern to get it repaired as soon as we leave.' She took it off and put it on the table. I left them at tea and went to the schoolroom to do some work with Alvean. It was while we were there that the door was thrown open and they all stood there looking at me accusingly.

"Lady Treslyn said something about having a search made because her diamond bracelet was missing. She was truculent. One would have thought she was already the mistress of the house. Mr. TreMellyn said very kindly that Lady Treslyn was asking that my room be searched, and he hoped I would not object. I was very angry and I said: 'Come on, search my room. Nothing will satisfy me but that you should.'

"So we all went into my room, and there in a drawer, hidden under some of my things was the diamond bracelet.

"Lady Treslyn said I was caught red-handed, and she was going to have me sent to prison. The others all pleaded with her not to make a scandal. Finally they agreed that if I went at once the matter would be forgotten. I was furious. I wanted an enquiry. But what could I do? They had found the thing there, and whatever I had to say after that, they wouldn't believe me."

"It must have been terrible for you." I began to shiver.

She leaned across the table and smiled in a kindly way at me. "You are afraid that they may do something similar to you. Lady Treslyn is determined to marry Connan TreMellyn."

"Do you think so?"

"I do. I am sure there was something between them. He was, after all, a widower and not the sort of man, I think, to live without women. One knows his sort."

I said: "I suppose he made advances to you?"

She shrugged her shoulders. "At least Lady Treslyn imagined that I might be a menace, and I am sure she chose that way to get rid of me."

"What a foul creature she is! But Miss Nansellock was kind."

"Very kind. She was with them, of course, when they found the bracelet; and when I was packing she came to my room. She said: 'I'm very distressed, Miss Jansen, that this should have happened. I know they found the bracelet in your drawer, but you didn't put it there, did you?' I said: 'Miss Nansellock, I swear I didn't.' I can tell you, I was hysterical. It had all happened so suddenly. I didn't know what was to become of me. I had very little money and I would have to go to some hostel to look for work, and I knew I could not expect a testimonial. I shall never forget her kindness to me. She asked me where I was going and I gave her this address in Plymouth. She said: 'I know the Merrivales are going to want a governess in a month or so. I am going to see that you get that job.' She lent me some money, which I have now paid back, although she did not want me to do so; and that's how I lived until I went to the Merrivales. I have written, thanking Miss Nansellock, but how can one thank people adequately who do so much for one in such dire need?"

"Thank goodness, there was someone to help."

"Heaven knows what would have become of me if she had not been there. Ours is a precarious profession, Miss Leigh. We are at the mercy of our employers. No wonder so many of us become meek and downtrodden." She brightened. "I try to forget all that. I'm going to be married. He is a doctor who looks after the family. In six months' time my governessing days will be over."

"Congratulations! As a matter of fact, I too am engaged to be married."

"How wonderful!"

"To Connan TreMellyn," I added.

She stared at me in astonishment. "Why . . ." she stammered, "I wish you the best of luck."

I could see that she was a little embarrassed and trying to remember what she had said about Connan. I felt too that she thought I should need that good luck.

I could not explain to her that I would rather have one stormy year with Connan than a lifetime of peace with anyone else.

"I wonder," she said after a pause, "why you wanted to see me."

"It is because I had heard of you. They talk of you often. Alvean was fond of you and there are things I want to know."

"But you, who are soon to be a member of the family, will know so much more than I can tell you."

"What did you think of Gilly—Gillyflower?"

"Oh, poor little Gilly. A strange, mad Ophelia-like creature. I always felt that one day we should find her floating on the stream with rosemary in her hands."

"The child had a shock."

"Yes, the first Mrs. TreMellyn's horse nearly trampled her to death."

"You must have gone there soon after the death of Mrs. Tre-Mellyn."

"There were two others before me. I heard they left because the house was too spooky. The house couldn't be too spooky for me!"

"Oh yes, you're an expert on old houses?"

"Expert! Indeed I'm not. I just love them. I've seen a great many and I've read a great deal about them."

"There was a peep in your room. Gilly showed it to me the other day."

"Do you know, I lived in that room three weeks without knowing it was there."

"I'm not surprised. The peeps are so cleverly concealed in the murals."

"That's an excellent way of doing it. Do you know those in the solarium?"

"Oh yes."

"One overlooking the hall, the other, the chapel. I think there's a reason for that. You see, the hall and the chapel would be the most important parts of the house at the time that was built."

"You know a great deal about periods and so on. At what period was Mount Mellyn built?"

"Late Elizabethan. At the time when people had to keep the presence of priests in their houses secret. I think that's why they had all these peeps and things."

"How interesting."

"Miss Nansellock is an expert on houses. That was something we had in common. Does she know we're meeting?"

"No one knows."

"You mean, you came here without telling even your future husband?"

Confidences trembled on my lips. I wondered if I dared share them with this stranger. I wished it were Phillida sitting opposite me. Then I could have poured out my heart to her; I could have listened to her advice, which I was sure would be good.

But, although I had heard Miss Jansen's name mentioned so much since I had come to Mount Mellyn, she was still a stranger to me. How could I say to a stranger: I suspect the man I am engaged to marry of being involved in a plot to murder me.

No! It was impossible.

But, I reasoned, she had suffered accusation and dismissal. There was a kind of bond between us.

How far, I asked myself, are hot-blooded people prepared to go for the satisfaction of their lust?

I could not tell her.

"He is away on business," I said. "We are to be married in three weeks' time."

"I wish you the best of luck. It must have happened very suddenly."

"It was August when I went to the house."

"And you had never met before?"

"Living in the same house one quickly gets to know people."

"Yes, I suppose that is so."

"And you yourself must have become engaged in almost as short a time."

"Oh yes, but . . ."

I knew what she was thinking. Her pleasant country doctor was a very different person from the master of Mount Mellyn.

I went on quickly: "I wanted to meet you because I believed you had been falsely accused. I am sure that many people at the house think that."

"I'm glad."

"When Mr. TreMellyn returns I shall tell him that I have seen you, and I shall ask if something can be done."

"It is of little consequence now. Dr. Luscombe knows what happened. He is very indignant. But I have made him see that no good purpose could be served by bringing up the matter again. If Lady Treslyn ever tried to make more mischief, then something could be done. But she won't; her only desire was to get rid of me, and that she did . . . quite effectively."

"What a wicked woman she is! She did not consider the effect on you. But for the kindness of Miss Nansellock . . ."

"I know. But don't let's talk of it. You will tell Miss Nansellock that you have seen me?"

"Yes, I will."

"Then tell her that I am engaged now to Dr. Luscombe. She will be so pleased. And there's something else I would like her to know. Perhaps you'll be interested too. It's about the house. That house will soon be your home, won't it? I envy you the house. It's one of the most interesting places I've ever seen."

"What were you going to tell me to pass on to Miss Nansellock?"

"I've been doing a little research on architecture, and so on, of the Elizabethan period, and my fiancé arranged for me to see Cotehele, the Mount Edgcumbe's place. They were delighted to let me see it because they are understandably proud of it. It's more like Mount Mellyn than any house I've ever seen. The chapel is almost identical, even to the lepers' squint. But the squint at Mount Mellyn is much bigger, and the construction of the walls is slightly different. As a matter of fact, I've never seen a squint quite like that at Mount Mellyn before. Do tell Miss Nansellock. She would be most interested, I'm sure."

"I'll tell her. I expect she'll be more interested to hear that you are so happy and that you are going to marry."

"Don't forget to tell her too that I remember I owe it all to her. Give her my kindest regards and my best thanks."

"I will," I said.

We parted, and on my journey home I felt that I had obtained from Miss Jansen some fresh light on my problem.

There was no doubt that Lady Treslyn arranged for Miss Jansen's dismissal. Miss Jansen was very pretty indeed. Connan admired her and Alvean was fond of her. Connan would consider marriage because he would want sons; and Lady Treslyn, possessive as a tigress, was not going to allow him to marry anyone but herself.

I believed now that Lady Treslyn was planning to remove me as she had removed Miss Jansen; but because I was already engaged to Connan she would have to use more drastic methods in my case.

But Connan did not know of this attempt on my life.

I refused to believe that of him and, refusing, I felt a great deal happier.

Moreover, I had made up my mind. When Connan came back I was going to tell him everything—all I had discovered, all I feared.

The decision brought me great comfort.

⋧§⋦

Two days passed and still Connan had not returned.

Peter Nansellock came over to say good-by. He was leaving late that night for London on his way to join the ship which would carry him to Australia.

Celestine was with him when he came to say good-by. They thought Connan would have returned by now. As a matter of fact, while they were there a letter arrived from Connan. He was coming back if possible late that night; if not, as early as possible next day.

I felt tremendously happy.

I gave them tea and, as we talked, I mentioned Miss Jansen.

I saw no reason why I should not do so in front of Peter because it was he who had told me that Celestine had found her a job with the Merrivales.

"I met Miss Jansen the other day," I began.

They were both startled.

"But how?" asked Peter.

"I wrote and asked her to meet me."

"What made you do that?" asked Celestine.

"Well, she had lived here, and there was a mystery about her, and I thought it would be rather interesting, so, as I was going to Plymouth . . ."

"A charming creature," mused Peter.

"Yes. You'll be pleased to hear that she's engaged to be married."

"How interesting," cried Celestine, her face growing pink. "I'm delighted."

"To the local doctor," I added.

"She'll make an excellent doctor's wife," said Celestine.

"Her husband's male patients will all be in love with her," put in Peter.

"That could be disconcerting," I replied.

"But good for business," murmured Peter. "Did she send us greetings?"

"Particularly to your sister." I smiled at Celestine. "She is so grateful to you; you were wonderful to her. She says she'll never forget."

"It was nothing. I could not let that woman do what she did and stand by doing nothing."

"You think Lady Treslyn deliberately planted that theft on her? I know Miss Jansen does."

"There is not a doubt of it," said Celestine firmly.

"What an unscrupulous woman she must be!"

"I believe that to be so."

"Well, Miss Jansen is happy now, so good came out of evil. By the way, I have a special message for you. It's about the house."

"What house?" asked Celestine with great interest.

"This one. Miss Jansen has been to Cotehele and has been comparing their squint, in the chapel, with ours. She says ours is quite unique."

"Oh really! That's very interesting."

"It's bigger, she says—I mean ours is. And there's something about the construction of the walls."

"Celestine is aching to go down and have a look at it," said Peter. She smiled at me. "We'll look at it together sometime. You're going to be the mistress of the house, so you ought to take an interest in it."

"I'm becoming more and more interested. I'm going to ask you to teach me lots about it."

She smiled at me warmly. "I'll be glad."

I asked Peter what train he was catching, and he answered that it would be the ten o'clock from St. Germans.

"I'll ride to the station," he said, "and stable the horse there. The baggage has gone on ahead of me. I shall go alone. I don't want any fond farewells at the station. After all, I shall no doubt be home this time next year—with a fortune. Au revoir, Miss Leigh," he went on. "I'll come back one day. And if you do feel like coming with me . . . it's not too late even now."

He spoke flippantly, and his eyes were full of mischief. I wondered what he would say if I suddenly agreed to his proposal, if I suddenly told him that I was filled with terrible doubts about the man I had promised to marry.

I went down to the porch to say my last farewells. The servants were there, for Peter was a great favorite. I guessed that he had bestowed many a sly kiss on Daisy and Kitty, and they were sad to see him go.

He looked very handsome in the saddle and beside him Celestine seemed insignificant.

We stood waving to them.

His last words were: "Don't forget, Miss Leigh . . . if you should change your mind!"

Everybody laughed and I joined in with them. I think we all felt a little sad that he was going.

⊷⧉⊷

As we were going back into the house, Mrs. Polgrey said to me: "Miss Leigh, could I have a word with you?"

"But certainly. Shall I come to your room?"

She led the way there.

"I've just had word," she said. "The result of the autopsy. Death through natural causes."

I felt floods of relief sweeping over me.

"Oh, I'm so pleased about that."

"So are we all. I can tell you, I didn't like the things that were being said . . . and him dying after he'd had supper here."

"It seems as though it was all a storm in a teacup," I said.

"Something like that, Miss Leigh. But there you are—people talk and something has to be done."

"Well, it must be a great relief to Lady Treslyn."

She looked a little embarrassed and I guessed she was wondering what she had said to me in the past about Connan and Lady Treslyn. It must have been disconcerting to discover that I was going to be Connan's wife. I decided to sweep aside her embarrassment forever, and said: "I hoped you were going to offer me a cup of your special Earl Grey."

She was pleased and rang for Kitty.

We talked of household affairs while the kettle boiled, and when tea was made she tentatively brought out the whisky and when I nodded, a teaspoonful was put into each cup. I felt then that we had indeed resumed the old friendly relationship.

I was glad, because I could see this made her happy, and I wanted everyone about me to be as happy as I was.

I kept telling myself: If Lady Treslyn really did attempt to kill me by sending that boulder crashing down in front of me when I was mounted on Jacinth, Connan knew nothing about it. Sir Thomas died a natural death, so there was nothing to hide; he had no reason to ask me to marry him except the one which he gave me: he loves me.

৶ঔৡৢ

It was nine o'clock and the children were in bed. It had been a warm and sunny day and there were signs of spring everywhere.

Connan was coming home either tonight or tomorrow and I was happy.

I wondered what time he would arrive. Perhaps at midnight. I went to the porch to look for him because I had imagined I heard horses' hoofs in the distance.

I waited. The night was still. The house always seemed very quiet at times like this, for all the servants would be in their own quarters.

I guessed that Peter would be on his way to the station by now. It was strange to think that I might never see him again. I thought of our first meeting in the train; he had begun by playing his mischievous tricks on me even then.

Then I saw someone coming toward me. It was Celestine, and she had come by way of the woods, not along the drive as usual.

She was rather breathless.

"Why, hello," she said. "I came to see you. I felt so lonely. Peter's gone. It's rather sad to think that I shan't see him for a long time."

"It does make one sad."

"He played the fool a great deal, of course, but I am very fond of him. Now I've lost both my brothers."

"Come in," I said.

"Connan's not back, I suppose?"

"No. I don't think he can possibly be here before midnight. He wrote that he had business to attend to this morning. I expect he'll arrive tomorrow. Won't you come in?"

"Do you know, I rather hoped you'd be alone."

"Did you?"

"I wanted to have a look at the chapel . . . that squint, you know. Ever since you gave me Miss Jansen's message I've been eager to see it. I didn't say so in front of Peter. He's apt to laugh at my enthusiasm."

"Do you want to have a look at it now?"

"Yes, please. I've got a theory about it. There may be a door in the paneling which leads to another part of the house. Wouldn't it be fun if we could discover it and tell Connan about it when he arrives?"

"Yes," I agreed, "it would."

"Let's go now then."

We went through the hall and, as we did so, I glanced up at the peep, because I had an uncanny feeling that we were being watched. I thought I saw a movement up there, but I was not sure, and said nothing.

We went along to the end of the hall, through the door, down the stone steps, and were in the chapel.

The place smelled damp. I said: "It smells as though it hasn't been used for years." And my voice echoed weirdly through the place.

Celestine did not answer. She had lighted one of the candles which stood on the altar. I watched the long shadow which the flickering light threw against the wall.

"Let's get into the squint," she said. "Through this door. There is another door in the squint itself which opens onto the walled garden. That was the way the lepers used to come in."

She carried the candle high and I found that we were in a small chamber.

"This is the place," I said, "which is bigger than most of its kind."

She did not answer. She was pressing different parts of the wall. I watched her long fingers at work.

Suddenly she turned and smiled at me. "I've always had a theory that somewhere in this house there is a priest's hole . . . you know, the hidey hole of the resident priest into which he scuttled when the Queen's men arrived. As a matter of fact, I know that one TreMellyn did toy with the idea of becoming a Catholic. I'll swear there is a priest's hole somewhere. Connan would be delighted if we found it. He loves this place as much as I do . . . as much as you're going to. If I found it . . . it would be the best wedding present I could give him, wouldn't it? After all, what can you give people who have all they want?"

She hesitated, and her voice was high with excitement. "Just a minute. There's something here." I came close to her, and caught my breath with amazement, for the panel had moved inward and shown itself as a long narrow door.

She turned to look at me and she looked unlike herself. Her eyes were brilliant with excitement. She put her head inside the aperture and was about to go forward when she said: "No, you first. It's going to be your house. You should be the first to enter it."

I had caught her excitement. I knew how pleased Connan would be.

I stepped ahead of her and was aware of an unrecognizable pungent odor.

She said: "Have a quick look. It's probably a bit foul in there. Careful. There are probably steps." She held the candle high, and I saw there were two of them. I went down those steps and, as I did so, the door shut behind me.

"Celestine!" I cried in terror. But there was no answer. "Open that door," I screamed. But my voice was caught and imprisoned in the darkness, and I knew that I was a prisoner too–Celestine's prisoner.

The darkness shut me in. It was cold and eerie–foul, evil. Panic seized me. How can I explain such terror? There are no words to describe it. Only those who have suffered it could understand.

Thoughts–hideous thoughts–seemed to be battering on my brain. I had been a fool. I had been trapped. I had accepted what seemed obvious, I had walked the way she who wished to be rid of me had directed; and like a fool I had asked no questions.

My fear numbed my brain as it did my body.

I was terrified.

I mounted the two steps. I beat my fists against what now seemed to be a wall. "Let me out! Let me out!" I cried.

But I knew that my voice would not be heard beyond the lepers' squint. And how often did people go to the chapel?

She would slip away . . . no one would know she had even been in the house.

I was so frightened I did not know what to do. I heard my own voice sobbing out my terror, and it frightened me afresh because, for the moment, I did not recognize it as my own.

I felt exhausted and limp. I knew that one could not live for long in this dark, damp place. I pulled at the wall until I tore my nails and I felt the blood on my hands.

I began to look about me because my eyes were becoming familiar to the gloom. Then I saw that I was not alone.

Someone had come here before me. What was left of Alice lay there. At last I had found her.

"Alice," I screamed. "Alice. It is you then? So you were here in the house all the time?"

There was no answer from Alice. Her lips had been silent for more than a year.

I covered my face with my hands. I could not bear to look. There was the smell of death and decay everywhere.

I wondered: How long did Alice live after the door had closed on *her?* I wanted to know because so long I might expect to live.

I think I must have fainted for a long time and I was delirious when I came to. I heard a voice babbling; it must have been my own because it could not have belonged to Alice.

I was mercifully only half-conscious. But it was as though a part of me understood so much.

During that time I spent in the dark and gruesome place I was not sure who I was. Was I Martha? Was I Alice?

Our stories were so much alike. I believed the pattern was similar. They had said she ran away with Geoffry. They would say I had run away with Peter. Our departure had been cleverly timed. "But why," I said, "but why . . . ?"

I knew whose shadow I had seen on the blind. It was hers . . . that diabolical woman. She had known of the existence of that little diary which I had discovered in Alice's coat pocket and she was searching for it because she knew it could provide one of those small clues which might lead to discovery.

I knew that she did not love Alvean, that she had tricked us all with her gentle demeanor. I knew that she was incapable of loving anyone. She had used Alvean as she had used others, as she was going to use Connan.

It was the house that she loved.

I pictured her during those delirious moments looking from her window at Mount Widden across the cove—coveting a house as fiercely as man ever coveted woman or woman, man.

"Alice," I said. "Alice we were her victims . . . you and I."

And I fancied Alice talked to me . . . told me of the day Geoffry had caught the London train and how Celestine had come to the house and told her of the great discovery in the chapel.

I saw Alice . . . pale, pretty, fragile Alice crying out in pleasure at the discovery, taking those fatal steps forward to death.

But it was not Alice's voice I heard. It was my own.

Yet I thought she was with me. I thought that at last I had found her, and that we had comfort to offer each other as I waited to go with her into the shadowy world which had been hers since she was led by Celestine Nansellock into the lepers' squint.

There was a blinding light in my eyes. I was being carried.

I said: "Am I dead then, Alice?"

And a voice answered: "My darling . . . my darling . . . you are safe."

It was Connan's voice, and it was his arms which held me.

"Are there dreams in death then, Alice?" I asked.

I was conscious of a voice which whispered: "My dearest . . . oh, my dearest . . ." And I was laid upon a bed, and many people stood about me.

Then I saw the light glinting on hair which looked almost white. "Alice, there is an angel."

Then the angel answered and said: "It's Gilly. Gilly brought them to you. Gilly watched and Gilly saw. . . ."

And oddly enough it was Gilly who brought me back to the world of reality. I knew that I was not dead, that some miracle had happened; that it was in truth Connan's arms which I had felt about me, Connan's voice I heard.

I was in my own bedroom from the window of which I could see the lawns and the palm trees and the room which had once been Alice's, on the blind of which I had seen the shadow of Alice's murderer who had sought to kill me too.

I called out in terror. But Connan was beside me.

I heard his voice, tender, soothing, loving. "It's all right, my love . . . my only love. I'm here . . . I'm with you forevermore."

AFTERWARD

This is the story I tell my great-grandchildren. They have heard it many times, but there is always a first time for some.

They ask for it again and again. They play in the park and in the woods; they bring me flowers from the south gardens, a tribute to the old lady who can always charm them with the story of how she married their great-grandfather.

To me it is as clear as though it happened yesterday. Vividly I remember my arrival at the house and all that preceded those terrifying hours I spent in the dark with dead Alice.

The years which followed with Connan have often been stormy ones. Connan and I were both too strong-willed, I suppose, to live in perpetual peace; but they were years in which I felt I had lived life richly, and what more could one ask than that?

Now he is old, as I am, and three more Connans have been born since that day we married in Mellyn church—our son, grandson, and great-grandson. I was glad I was able to give Connan children. We had five sons and five daughters, and they in their turn were fruitful.

When the children hear the story they like to check all the details. They want every incident explained.

Why was it believed that the woman who died in the train was Alice? Because of the locket she wore. But it was Celestine who identified the locket as one which, she said, she had given Alice, but which, of course, she had never seen before in her life.

She had been eager that I should accept Jacinth when Peter had first offered the mare to me—I suppose because she feared it was just possible that Connan might be interested in me and therefore she was ready to encourage the friendship between myself and Peter; and it was she who later, discovering the loosened boulder on the cliff, had lain in wait for me and attempted to kill or maim me.

She was the sender of the anonymous letters to Lady Treslyn and the public prosecutor, commenting on the suspicious circumstances of Sir Thomas's death. She had believed that if there was a big enough scandal, marriage between Connan and Lady Treslyn would have been impossible for years. She had reckoned without Connan's feelings for me; thus when she knew that I was engaged to marry him, she immediately planned to remove me. She failed to do this on the cliff path; therefore I was to join Alice; the fact that Peter was leaving for Australia on that day must have made her decide on this method. The whole household knew that Peter's attitude to me had been a flirtatious one, and it would appear that I had run away with him.

It was Celestine who had put the diamond bracelet in Miss Jansen's room because the governess was learning too much about the house and the knowledge would inevitably lead her to the lepers' squint and Alice. She had worked on Lady Treslyn's jealousy of the pretty young governess, for she had known Lady Treslyn to be a vindictive woman who, given the opportunity, would bring all her malice to bear on Miss Jansen.

She was in love—passionately in love with Mount Mellyn and she wanted to marry Connan only because thus she would be mistress of the house. After discovering the secret of the squint, she had kept it to herself, and had chosen her opportunity to murder Alice. She knew of the love affair between Alice and her brother Geoffry; she knew that Alvean was his child. It worked out so easily because she had waited for her opportunity. If it had not been possible to make it appear that Alice had gone on the train with Geoffry, she would have found some other way of disposing of her as she had intended to dispose of me through Jacinth.

But she had reckoned without Gilly. Who would have thought that a poor simple child should play such a big part in this diabolical plan? But Gilly had loved Alice as later she was to love me. Gilly had known Alice was in the house, for Alice had made a habit of coming to say good night to her when she did the same to Alvean; she had always done it before she went out to a dinner party. Because she had never forgotten, Gilly did not believe she had forgotten this time. Gilly therefore continued to believe that Alice had never left the house, and had gone on looking for her. It was Gilly's face which I had seen at the peep. Gilly knew all the peeps in the house and used them frequently, because she was always watching for Alice.

Thus she had seen Celestine and me enter the hall, from the solarium. I imagined her crossing the room and looking through the peep on the other side of the room so that she saw us enter the chapel. We crossed to the squint, but that side of the chapel could not easily be seen from the solarium squint. Gilly then sped along to Miss Jansen's room, where from that peep she could have a good view of the squint. She was just in time to see us disappearing through the door, and waited for us to come out. She waited and waited, for Celestine naturally left by the door to the courtyard and slipped away so that, since she believed that no one had seen her come into the house except me, she could let it appear that she had not been there at all.

Thus, while I lived through that period of horror in Alice's death-chamber, Gilly was standing on her stool in Miss Jansen's room, watching the door to the lepers' squint.

Connan returned at eleven and expected the household to give him a welcome.

Mrs. Polgrey received him. "Go and tell Miss Leigh that I am here," he said. He must have been a little piqued because he was—and still is —the sort of man who demands the utmost affection and attention, and the fact that I could be sleeping when he came home was inconceivable to him.

I pictured the scene: Mrs. Polgrey reporting that I was not in my room, the search for me, that terrible moment when Connan believed what Celestine had intended he should believe.

"Mr. Nansellock came over this afternoon to say good-by. He caught the ten o'clock from St. Germans. . . ."

I have wondered often how long it would have been before they discovered that I had not run away with Peter. I could imagine what might have happened. Connan's losing that belief in life which I believed I was beginning to bring back to him, perhaps continuing his *affaire* with Linda Treslyn. But it would not have led to marriage, Celestine would have seen to that. And in time she would have found some way of making herself mistress of Mount Mellyn; insidiously she would have made herself necessary to Alvean and to him.

How strange, I thought, that all this might have come to pass and the only two who could have told the truth would have been two skeletons behind the walls of the lepers' squint. Who would have believed that even at this day the story of Alice and Martha would never have been known had not a simple child, born in sorrow, living in shadow, led the way to the truth.

Connan has told me often of the uproar in the house when I was missing. He told me of the child, who came and stood patiently beside him, waiting to be heard; how she tugged at his coat and sought for the words to explain.

"God forgive us," he says, "it was some time before we would listen to her, and so we delayed bringing you out of that hellish place."

But she had led them there . . . through the door into the lepers' squint.

She had seen us, she said.

And for a moment Connan had thought that Peter and I had left the house together, slipping out that way so that we should not be noticed.

It was dusty in the squint—for no one had entered it since Alice had gone there with her murderer; but in the dust on the wall was the mark of a hand, and when Connan saw it he began to take Gilly seriously.

It was not easy to find the secret spring to the door even if it had been known that it was there. There was an agonizing search of ten minutes while Connan was ready to tear the walls down.

But they found it and they found me. They found Alice too.

❦

They took Celestine to Bodmin where she was eventually to be tried for the murder of Alice. But before the trial could take place she was a raving lunatic. At first I believed this was yet another scheme of hers. It may have started that way, but she did not die until twenty years after, and all that time she spent locked away from the world.

Alice's remains were buried in the vault where those of an unknown woman lay. Connan and I were married three months after he had brought me out of the darkness. That experience had affected me even more than I realized at the time, and I suffered from nightmares for a year or more. It was a great shock to have been buried alive even though one's tomb was opened before life was extinguished.

Phillida came to my wedding with William and the children. She was delighted. So was Aunt Adelaide, who insisted that the wedding take place from her town house. Thus Connan and I had a smart London wedding. Not that we cared, but it pleased Aunt Adelaide who, for some reason, seemed to have the idea in her head that it was all her doing.

And so we honeymooned, as we had originally intended, in Italy and then we came home to Mount Mellyn.

I dream over the past when I have told the story to the children. I think of Alvean happily married to a Devonshire squire. As for Gilly, she never left me. She is with me now. At any moment she will appear on the lawn with the eleven o'clock coffee which on warm days we take in that arbor in the south gardens where I first saw Lady Treslyn and Connan together.

I must confess that Lady Treslyn continued to plague me during the first years of my married life. I discovered that I could be a jealous woman—and a passionate one. Sometimes I think Connan liked to tease me, in repayment, he said, for the jealousy he had felt of Peter Nansellock.

But she went to London after a few years, and we heard that she married there.

Peter came back some fifteen years after he left. He had acquired a wife and two children but no fortune; he was however as gay and full of vitality as ever. In the meantime Mount Widden had been sold; and later one of my daughters married the owner, so the place has become almost as much home to me as Mount Mellyn.

Connan said he was glad when Peter went back, and I laughed at the thought of his ever feeling he needed to be jealous. When I told him this, he replied: "You're even more foolish about Linda Treslyn."

That was one of those moments when we both knew that there was no one for us but each other.

And so the years passed and now, as I sit here thinking of it all, Connan is coming down the path from the gardens. In a moment I shall hear his voice.

Because we are alone he will say: "Ah, my dear Miss Leigh . . ." as he often does in his most tender moments. That is to remind me that he does not forget those early days; and there will be a smile on his lips which tells me that he is seeing me, not as I am now, but as I was then, the governess somewhat resentful of her fate, desperately clinging to her pride and her dignity—falling in love in spite of herself —his dear Miss Leigh.

Then we shall sit in the warm sunshine, thankful for all the good things which life has brought us.

Here he comes and Gilly is behind him . . . still a little different from other people, still speaking rarely, singing as she works, in that off-key voice that makes us think she is a little out of this world.

As I watch her I can see so clearly the child she once was, and I think of the story of Jennifer, the mother who one day walked into the sea, and how that story was part of my story, and how delicately and intricately our lives were woven together.

Nothing remains, I thought, but the earth and the sea which are here just as they were on the day Gilly was conceived, on the day Alice walked unheeding into her tomb, on the day I felt Connan's arms about me and I knew that he had brought me back to life.

We are born, we suffer, we love, we die, but the waves continue to beat upon the rocks; the seed time and the harvest come and go, but the earth remains.

Kirkland Revels

1

I met Gabriel and Friday on the same day, and strangely enough I lost them together; so that thereafter I was never able to think of one without the other. The fact that my life became a part of theirs is, in a way, an indication of my character, because they both began by arousing some protective instinct in me; all my life up to that time I had been protecting myself and I think I felt gratified to find others in need of protection. I had never before had a lover, never before had a dog; and, when these two appeared, it was natural enough that I should welcome them.

I remember the day perfectly. It was spring, and there was a fresh wind blowing over the moors. I had ridden away from Glen House after luncheon and I could not at this time leave the house without a feeling that I had escaped. This feeling had been with me since I returned home from my school in Dijon; perhaps it had always been there, but a young woman senses these emotions more readily than a child.

My home was a somber place. How could it be otherwise when it was dominated by someone who was no longer there. I decided during the first days of my return that I would never live in the past. No matter what happened to me, when it was over I should not look back. Early in life—I was nineteen at this time—I had learned an important lesson. I determined to live in the present—the past forgotten, the future left to unfold itself.

Looking back I realize now that I was a ready victim for the fate which was awaiting me.

Six weeks before it happened, I had come home from school where I had been for the past four years. I had not returned home in all that time, for I lived in Yorkshire and it was a long and expensive journey halfway across France and England; my education was costly enough. During my school years I had dramatized my home to some extent, so the picture in my imagination was different from the reality. Hence the shock when I arrived.

I had traveled from Dijon in the company of my friend Dilys Heston-Browne and her mother; my father had arranged that this should be so, for it was unthinkable that a young lady should travel so far unchaperoned. Mrs. Heston-Browne had seen me safely to St. Pancras Station, put me in a first-class carriage and I had traveled alone from London to Harrogate, where I was to be met.

I had expected my father would be there. I had hoped my uncle would be. But that was ridiculous of me, for if Uncle Dick had been in England he would have come all the way to Dijon for me.

It was Jemmy Bell, my father's stableman, who was waiting for me with the trap. He looked different from the Jemmy I had known four years before, more wizened yet younger. That was the first little shock, discovering that someone whom I thought I knew so well was not quite what I had been imagining him.

Jemmy whistled when he saw the size of my trunk. Then he grinned at me. "By gow, Miss Cathy," he said, "looks like you've grown into a right grand young lady."

That was another reminder. In Dijon I had been Catherine or Mademoiselle Corder. Miss Cathy sounded like a different person.

He looked incredulously at my bottle-green velvet traveling coat with the leg-o'-mutton sleeves, and the straw hat which was tilted over my eyes and decorated with a wreath of daisies. My appearance startled him; he did not often see such fashionable clothes in our village.

"How is my father?" I asked. "I expected him to drive in to meet me."

Jemmy thrust out his lower lip and shook his head. "A martyr to gout," he said. "He can't abide the jolting. Besides . . ."

"Besides what?" I asked sharply.

"Well . . ." Jemmy hesitated. "He's just coming out of one of his bad turns. . . ."

I was conscious of a little tug of fear, remembering those bad turns which had been a feature of the old days. "Be quiet, Miss Cathy, your father's having one of his bad turns. . . ." They had descended upon the house, those bad turns, with a certain regularity, and when they were with us we tiptoed about the place and spoke in whispers. As for my father, he disappeared from view, and when he reappeared he was paler than usual, with deep shadows under his eyes; he did not seem to hear when he was spoken to; he had frightened me. While I had been away from home I had allowed myself to forget the bad turns.

I said quickly: "My uncle is not at home?"

Jemmy shook his head. " 'Tis more than six months since we've seen him. Happen it'll be eighteen more afore we do."

I nodded. Uncle Dick was a sea captain and he had written to me that he was off to the other side of the world, where he would be engaged for many months.

I felt depressed; I should have felt so much happier if he had been at home to welcome me.

We were trotting along roads which stirred my memories, and I thought of the house where I had lived until Uncle Dick had decided it was time I went away to school. I had endowed my father with Uncle Dick's personality; I had swept away the old cobwebs of time and let in the bright sunshine. The home I had talked of to my companions had been the home I wanted, not the one I knew.

But now the time for dreaming was over. I had to face what was— not what I wished it to be.

"You're quiet, Miss Cathy," said Jemmy.

He was right. I was in no mood to talk. Questions were on my lips but I did not ask them because I knew that the answers Jemmy would give me were not what I wanted. I had to discover for myself.

We went on driving through lanes which were sometimes so narrow that the foliage threatened to snatch my hat from my head. Soon the scenery would change; the neat fields, the narrow lanes, would give way to the wilder country; the horse would steadily climb and I should smell the open moors.

I thought of them now with a burst of pleasure and I realized that I had been a little homesick for them ever since I had left them.

Jemmy must have noticed that my expression brightened for he said: "Not long now, Miss Cathy."

And there was our village—it was little more. Glengreen—a few houses clustered round the church, the inn, the green and the cottages. On we went past the church to the white gates, through the drive, and there was Glen House, smaller than I had imagined it, with the Venetian blinds drawn down, the lace curtains just visible behind them. I knew that there would be heavy velour curtains at the windows to shut out the light.

If Uncle Dick had been at home he would have drawn back the curtains, pulled up the blinds, and Fanny would have complained that the sun was fading the furniture, and my father . . . he would not even have heard the complaint.

As I got out of the trap, Fanny who had heard us arrive came out to greet me.

She was a round tub of a Yorkshire woman who should have been jolly, but was not. Perhaps years in our house had made her dour.

She looked at me critically and said in her flat-voweled accent: "You've got thin while you've been away."

I smiled. It was an unusual greeting from someone who had not seen me for four years and who had been the only "mother" I could really remember. Yet it was what I expected. Fanny had never petted me; she would have felt it "daft," as she would call it, to show any demonstration of affection. It was only when she could be critical that she believed in giving vent to her feelings. Yet this woman had studied my creature comforts; she had made sure that I was adequately fed and clothed. I was never allowed any fancy frills and what she called falderols. She prided herself on plain speaking, on never disguising the truth, on always giving an honest opinion—which often meant a brutal one. I was by no means blind to Fanny's good points, but in the past I had yearned for a little show of affection however insincere. Now my memories of Fanny came rushing back to me. As she studied my clothes her mouth twitched in the way I well remembered. She, who found it difficult to smile in pleasure, could readily smirk in contemptuous amusement.

"Yon's what you wear over there, is it?" she said. Again there was that twitch of the lips.

I nodded coolly. "Is my father at home?"

"Why, Cathy . . ." It was his voice and he was coming down the staircase to the hall. He looked pale and there were shadows under his eyes; and I thought to myself, seeing him with the eyes of an adult for the first time: He looks bewildered, as though he does not quite belong in this house, or to this time.

"Father!"

We embraced but, although he endeavored to show some warmth, I was aware that it did not come from the heart. I had a strange feeling then that he was not pleased that I had come home, that he had been happy to be rid of me, that he would have preferred me to stay in France.

And there in our gloomy hall, before I had been home five minutes, I was oppressed by the house, and the longing to escape from it was with me.

If only Uncle Dick had been there to greet me, how different my homecoming would have been.

The house closed in on me. I went to my room where the sun was shining through the slats of the blinds. I pulled them up and light flooded the room; then I opened the window. Because my room was at the top of the house I had a view of the moor, and as I looked I felt myself tingling with pleasure. It had not changed at all; it still delighted me; I remembered how I had exulted to ride out there on my pony even though I always had to be accompanied by someone from the stables. When Uncle Dick was at the house we would ride together; we would canter and gallop with the wind in our faces; I remembered that we often stopped at the blacksmith's shop while one of the horses was shod—myself sitting there on a high stool, the smell of burning hoofs in my nostrils while I sipped a glass of Tom Entwhistle's homemade wine. It had made me a little dizzy and that had seemed a great joke to Uncle Dick.

"Captain Corder, you're a caution, that's what you are!" So said Tom Entwhistle many a time to Uncle Dick.

I had discovered that Uncle Dick wanted me to grow up exactly like himself; and as that was exactly what I wanted to do we were in accord.

My mind was wandering back to the old days. Tomorrow, I thought, I'll ride out onto the moors . . . this time alone.

How long that first day seemed! I went round the house into all the rooms—the dark rooms with the sun shut out. We had two middle-aged servants, Janet and Mary, who were like pale shadows of Fanny. That was natural perhaps because she had chosen them and trained them. Jemmy Bell had two lads to help him in the stables and they managed our garden too. My father had no profession. He was what was known as a gentleman. He had come down from Oxford with honors, had taught for a while, had had a keen interest in archaeology which had taken him to Greece and Egypt; when he had married, my mother had traveled with him, but when I was about to be born they had settled in Yorkshire, he intending to write works on archaeology and philosophy; he was also something of an artist. Uncle Dick used to say that the trouble with my father was that he was too talented; whereas he, Uncle Dick, having no talents at all, had become a mere sailor.

How often had I wished that Uncle Dick had been my father! My uncle lived with us in between voyages; it was Uncle Dick who

had come to see me at school. I pictured him as he had looked, standing in the cool white-walled reception room whither he had been
conducted by Madame la Directrice, legs apart, hands in pockets,
looking as though everything belonged to him. We were much alike
and I was sure that beneath that luxuriant beard was a chin as sharp
as my own.

He had lifted me in his arms as he used to when I was a child. I
believed he would do the same when I was an old woman. It was his
way of telling me that I was his special person . . . as he was mine.
"Are they treating you well?" he said, his eyes fierce suddenly, ready
to do battle with any who were not doing so.

He had taken me out; we had clip-clopped through the town in
the carriage he had hired; we had visited the shops and bought new
clothes for me, because he had seen some of the girls who were being
educated with me and had imagined they were more elegantly clad
than I. Dear Uncle Dick! He had seen that I had a very good allow-
ance after that, and it was for this reason that I had come home with
a trunk full of clothes all of a style which, the Dijon *couturière* had
assured me, came straight from Paris.

But as I stood looking out on the moor I knew that clothes could
have little effect on the character. I was myself, even in fine clothes
from Paris, and that was somebody quite different from the girls with
whom I had lived intimately during my years in Dijon. Dilys Heston-
Browne would have a London season; Marie de Freece would be introduced into Paris society. These two had been my special friends;
and before we parted we had sworn that our friendship would last
as long as we lived. Already I doubted that I should ever see them
again. That was the influence of Glen House and the moors. Here one
faced stark truth however unromantic, however unpleasant.

That first day seemed as though it would never end. The journey
had been so eventful, and here in the brooding quietness of the house
it was as though nothing had changed since I had left. If there appeared to be any change, that could only be due to the fact that I was
looking at life here through the eyes of an adult instead of those of a
child.

I could not sleep that night. I lay in bed thinking of Uncle Dick,
my father, Fanny, everyone in this house. I thought how strange it was
that my father should have married and had a daughter, and Uncle
Dick should have remained a bachelor. Then I remembered the quirk
of Fanny's mouth when she mentioned Uncle Dick, and I knew that
meant that she disapproved of his way of life and that she was se-

cretly satisfied that one day he would come to a bad end. I understood now. Uncle Dick had had no wife, but that did not mean he had not had a host of mistresses. I thought of the sly gleam I had seen in his eyes when they rested on Tom Entwhistle's daughter who, I had heard, was "no better than she should be." I thought of many glances I had intercepted between Uncle Dick and women.

But he had no children, so it was characteristic of him, greedy for life as he was, to cast his predatory eyes on his brother's daughter and treat her as his own.

I had studied my reflection at the dressing table before I got into bed that night. The light from the candles had softened my face so that it seemed—though not beautiful nor even pretty—arresting. My eyes were green, my hair black and straight; it felt heavy about my shoulders when I loosened it. If I could wear it so, instead of in two plaits wound about my head, how much more attractive I should be. My face was pale, my cheekbones high, my chin sharp and aggressive. I thought then that what happens to us leaves its mark upon our faces. Mine was the face of a person who had had to do battle. I had been fighting all my life. I looked back over my childhood to those days when Uncle Dick was not at home; and the greater part of the time he was away from me. I saw a sturdy child with two thick black plaits and defiant eyes. I knew now that I had taken an aggressive stand in that quiet household; subconsciously I had felt myself to be missing something, and because I had been away to school, because I had heard accounts of other people's homes, I had learned what it was that young child had sought and that she had been angry and defiant because she could not find it. I had wanted love. It came to me in a certain form only when Uncle Dick was home. Then I was treated to his possessive, exuberant affection; but the gentle love of a parent was lacking.

Perhaps I did not know this on that first night; perhaps it came later; perhaps it was the explanation I gave myself for plunging as recklessly as I did into my relationship with Gabriel.

But I did learn something that night. Although it was long before I slept I eventually dozed to be awakened by a voice, and I was not sure in that moment whether I had really heard that voice or whether it came to me from my dreams.

"Cathy!" said the voice full of pleading, full of anguish. "Cathy, come back."

I was startled—not because I had heard my name, but because of all the sadness and yearning with which it was spoken.

My heart was pounding; it was the only sound in that silent house. I sat up in bed, listening. Then I remembered a similar incident from the days before I had gone to France. The sudden waking in the night because I had thought I heard someone calling my name! For some reason I was shivering; I did not believe I had been dreaming. Someone *had* called my name.

I got out of bed and lighted one of the candles. I went to the window which I had opened wide at the bottom before going to bed. It was believed that the night air was dangerous and that windows should be tightly closed while one slept; but I had been so eager to take in that fresh moorland air that I had defied the old custom. I leaned out and glanced down at the window immediately below. It was still, as it had always been, that of my father's room.

I felt sobered because I knew what I had heard this night, and on that other night of my childhood, was my father's calling out in his sleep. And he called for Cathy.

My mother had been Catherine too. I remembered her vaguely— not as a person but a presence. Or did I imagine it? I seemed to re-member being held tightly in her arms, so tightly that I cried out be-cause I could not breathe. Then it was over, and I had a strange feeling that I never saw her again, that no one else ever cuddled me because when my mother did so I had cried out in protest.

Was that the reason for my father's sadness? Did he, after all those years, still dream of the dead? Perhaps there was something about me which reminded him of her; that would be natural enough and was almost certainly the case. Perhaps my homecoming had re-vived old memories, old griefs which would have been best forgotten.

How long were the days; how silent the house! Ours was a house-hold of old people, people whose lives belonged to the past. I felt the old rebellion stirring. *I* did not belong to this house.

I saw my father at meals; after that he retired into his study to write the book which would never be completed. Fanny went about the house giving orders with hands and eyes; she was a woman of few words but a click of her tongue, a puff of her lips, could be eloquent. The servants were in fear of her; she had the power to dismiss them; I knew that she held over them the threat of encroaching age to re-mind them that if she turned them out, there would be few ready to employ them.

There was never a spot of dust on the furniture; the kitchen was twice weekly filled with the fragrant smell of baking bread; the household was run smoothly. I almost longed for chaos.

I missed my school life which, in comparison with that in my father's house, seemed to have been filled with exciting adventures. I thought of the room I had shared with Dilys Heston-Browne; the courtyard below from which came the continual sound of girls' voices; the periodic ringing of bells which made one feel part of a lively community; the secrets, the laughter shared; the dramas and comedies of a way of life which in retrospect appeared desirably lighthearted.

There had been several occasions during those four years when I had been taken on holiday trips by people who pitied my loneliness. Once I went to Geneva with Dilys and her family, and at another time to Cannes. It was not the beauties of the lake which I remembered, nor that bluest of seas with the background of Maritime Alps; it was the close family feeling between Dilys and her parents, which she took for granted and which filled me with envy.

Yet, looking back, I realized that it was only now and then that the feeling of loneliness had come to me; for the most part I walked, rode, bathed and played games with Dilys and her sister as though I were a member of the family.

During one holiday when every other pupil had gone away, I was taken to Paris for a week by one of the mistresses. Very different this from holidaying with the lighthearted Dilys and her indulgent family, for Mademoiselle Dupont was determined that my cultural education should not be neglected. I laughed now to think of that breathless week; the hours spent in the Louvre among the old masters; the trip out to Versailles for a history lesson. Mademoiselle had decided that not a moment was to be wasted. But what I remembered most vividly from that holiday was hearing her talk of me to her mother; I was "the poor little one who was left at school during holidays because there was nowhere else for her to go."

I was sad when I heard that said of me and deeply conscious of that desperate aloneness. The unwanted one! The one who had no mother and whose father did not want her to come home for the holiday. Yet I forgot quickly, as one does when a child, and was soon lost in the enchantment of the Latin Quarter, the magic of the Champs Élysées and the shop windows of the rue de la Paix.

It was a letter from Dilys which made me recall those days with nostalgia. Life was wonderful for Dilys, being prepared for the London season.

"My dear Catherine, I have scarcely a moment. I've been meaning to write for *ages,* but there's always something to prevent me. I seem to be forever at the dressmaker's being fitted for this and that. You should see some of the dresses! Madame would *scream* her dismay. But Mother's determined that I shan't go unnoticed. She's making out lists of people who are to be asked to my first ball. Already, mind you! How I wish you could be here. Do tell me *your* news. . . ."

I could imagine Dilys and her family in their house in Knightsbridge—close to the park with the mews at the back. How different her life must be from mine!

I tried to write to her, but there seemed nothing to say that was not grim and melancholy. How could Dilys understand what it was like to have no mother to make plans for one's future, and a father who was so preoccupied with his own affairs that he did not even know I was there.

So I abandoned my letter to Dilys.

As the days passed I was finding the house more and more intolerable and spent a good deal of time out of doors, riding every day. Fanny smirked at my riding habit—the latest from Paris by the bounty of Uncle Dick—but I did not care.

One day Fanny said to me: "Your father's going off today." Her face was tightly shut, completely without expression, and I knew she had deliberately made it so. I could not tell whether she disapproved of my father's going away or not; all I knew was that she was holding in some secret which I was not allowed to share.

Then I remembered that there had always been those times when he went away and did not come home until the next day; and when he did come back we still did not see him because he shut himself away in his room and trays were taken up to him. When he emerged he looked ravaged and was more silent than ever.

"I remember," I said to Fanny. "So he still goes . . . away?"

"Regular," Fanny answered. "Once in t'month."

"Fanny," I asked earnestly, "where does he go?"

Fanny shrugged her shoulders as though to imply that it was no business of hers nor of mine; but I believed she knew.

I kept thinking about him all day, and wondering. Then it suddenly came to me. My father was not very old . . . perhaps forty, I was not sure. Women might still mean something to him although he had never married again. I thought I was worldly-wise. I had discussed life with my school friends, many of whom were French—always so much more knowledgeable in such matters than we English—and we thought ourselves very up-to-date. I decided that my father had a mistress whom he visited regularly but whom he would never marry because he could not replace my mother; and after visiting this woman he came back filled with remorse because, although she was long since dead, he still loved my mother and believed he had desecrated her memory.

He returned the following evening; the pattern was the same as I remembered it. I did not see him on his return; I only knew that he was in his room, that he did not appear for meals, and that trays were taken up to him.

When at length he did appear he looked so desolate that I longed to comfort him.

At dinner that evening I said to him: "Father, you are not ill, are you?"

"Ill?" His brows were drawn together in dismay. "Why should you think that?"

"Because you look so pale and tired—and as though you have something on your mind. I wondered if there's anything I can do to help. I'm not a child any more, you know."

"I'm not ill," he said, without looking at me.

"Then . . ."

I saw the expression of impatience cross his face, and hesitated. But I decided not to be thrust aside so easily. He was in need of comfort and it was the duty of his daughter to try to give it to him.

"Look here, Father," I said boldly, "I feel something is wrong. I might be able to help."

He looked at me then and the impatience had given way to coolness. I knew that he had deliberately put up a barrier between us and that he resented my persistence and construed it as inquisitiveness.

"My dear child," he murmured, "you are too imaginative."

He picked up his knife and fork and began paying more attention to his food than he had before I had spoken. I understood. It was a curt dismissal.

I had rarely felt so alone as I did at that moment.

After that our conversation became even more stilted, and often when I addressed him he did not answer. They said in the house that he was suffering from one of his "bad turns."

Dilys wrote again, complaining that I never told her what was happening to me. Reading her letters was like listening to her talking;

the short sentences, the underlining, the exclamation marks, gave
the impression of breathless excitement. She was learning to curtsy;
she was taking dancing lessons; the great day was approaching. It
was wonderful to have escaped from Madame and feel oneself no
longer a schoolgirl, but a young lady of fashion.

I tried again to write to her, but what could I say? Only this: I'm
desperately lonely. This house is a melancholy one. Oh Dilys, *you*
congratulate yourself because you have left your school days behind, and I am here in this sad house, wishing I were at school again.

I tore up that letter and went out to the stables to saddle my mare,
Wanda, whom I had taken for my own on my return. I felt as
though I were trapped in the web of my childhood, and that my life
was going on in the same dismal way forever.

And the day arrived when Gabriel Rockwell and Friday came into
my life.

I had ridden out onto the moors that day as usual and had galloped
over the peaty ground to the rough road when I saw the woman and
the dog; it was the pitiful condition of the latter which made me
slacken my speed. He was a thin pathetic-looking creature, and
about his neck was a rope which acted as a lead. I had always had
a special feeling for animals, and the sight of any one of them in
distress never failed to rouse my sympathy. The woman, I saw, was
a gypsy; this did not surprise me for there were many wandering
from encampment to encampment on the moors; they came to the
house selling clothes pegs and baskets or offering us heather which
we could have picked for ourselves. Fanny had no patience with
them. "They'll get nowt from me," she would say. "They're nobbut
lazy good-for-nothings, the lot of 'em."

I pulled up beside the woman and said: "Why don't you carry
him? He's too weak to walk."

"And what's that to you?" she demanded, and I was aware of her
sharp beady eyes beneath a tangle of graying black hair. Then her
expression changed; she had noticed my smart riding habit, my
well-cared-for horse, and I saw the cupidity leap into her eyes. I was
gentry, and gentry were for fleecing. "It's not a bite that's passed me
lips, lady, this day and last. And that's the gospel truth, without the
word of a lie."

She did not, however, look as though she were starving, but the
dog undoubtedly was. He was a little mongrel, with a touch of the
terrier, and in spite of his sad condition his eyes were alert; the manner
in which he looked at me touched me deeply because I fancied that

he was imploring me to rescue him. I was drawn to him in those first moments and I knew that I could not abandon him.

"It's the dog who looks hungry," I commented.

"Lord love you, lady, I haven't had a bite I could share with him these last two days."

"The rope's hurting him," I pointed out. "Can't you see that?"

"It's the only way I can get him along. I'd carry him, if I had the strength. With a little nourishment I'd get back me strength."

I said on impulse: "I'll buy the dog. I'll give you a shilling for him."

"A shilling! Why, lady, I couldn't bear to part with him. Companion of me sorrows, that's what he's been." She stooped to the dog, and the way in which he cowered betrayed the true state of affairs, so that I was doubly determined to get him. "Times is hard, ain't they, little 'un?" she went on. "But we've been together too long now for us to be parted for . . . a shilling."

I felt in my pockets for money. I knew she would finally accept a shilling for him because she would have to sell a great many clothes pegs to earn as much; but, being a gypsy, she was going to bargain first. Then to my dismay I discovered that I had come out without money. In the pocket of my habit was one of Fanny's patties, stuffed with meat and onions, which I had brought with me in case I should not return for luncheon; but it was hardly likely that the gypsy would exchange the dog for that. It was money she wanted; and her eyes had already begun to glisten at the thought of it.

She was watching me intently; so was the dog. Her eyes had grown crafty and suspicious, and the dog's were more appealing than ever.

I began: "Look here, I've come out without money . . ."

But even as I spoke her lips curled in disbelief. She gave a vicious jerk at the rope round the dog's neck and he gave a piteous yelp. "Quiet!" she snapped; and he cowered again, with his eyes on me.

I wondered whether I could ask the woman to wait at this spot while I rode home to get the money, or whether she would allow me to take the dog and she could call at Glen House for the money. I knew that was useless, for she would not trust me any more than I would trust her.

And it was then that Gabriel appeared. He was galloping across the moor towards the road, and at the sound of a horse's hoofs the woman and I turned to see who was coming. He was on a black horse which made him seem fairer than he actually was, but his fairness made an immediate impression; so did his elegance. His dark brown coat and breeches were of the finest material and cut; but as he came

nearer it was his face which attracted my attention and made it possible for me to do what I did. Looking back afterwards it seemed a
strange thing to do—to stop a stranger and ask him to lend me a shilling to buy a dog. But there he was, I told him afterwards, like a knight
in shining armor, a Perseus or Saint George.

There was a brooding melancholy about his delicate features
which immediately interested me, although this was not so apparent
on our first meeting as it was to become later.

I called to him as he came onto the road: "Stop a moment, please."
And even as I said it, I marveled at my temerity.

"Is anything wrong?" he asked.

"Yes. This dog is starving."

He pulled up and looked from me to the dog and the gypsy woman,
summing up the situation as he did so.

"Poor little fellow," he said. "He's in a bad way."

His voice was gentle, and I was immediately exhilarated because
I knew that I should not ask for help in vain.

"I want to buy him," I explained, "and I've come out without
money. It's most annoying and distressing. Will you please lend me
a shilling?"

"Look here," whined the woman, "I ain't selling him. Not for no
shilling, I ain't. He's my little dog, he is. Why should I sell him?"

"You were ready to for a shilling," I retorted.

She shook her head and pulled the dog towards her; and I again
felt that twinge of compassion as I saw the little animal's reluctance.
I looked pleadingly at the young man who smiled as he dismounted,
put his hand in his pocket and said: "Here's two shillings for the
dog. You can take it or leave it."

The woman could not hide her delight at so large a sum. She held
out a dirty hand for the money which, with a fastidious gesture, he
dropped into her palm. Then he took the rope from her, and she
moved away quickly as though she were afraid he would change his
mind.

"Thank you," I cried. "Oh, thank you."

The dog made a little whimpering sound which I felt to be pleasure.
"The first thing to be done is feed him," I said, dismounting.
"Fortunately I have a meat patty in my pocket."

He nodded and, taking the reins from my hands, led our horses
off the road while I picked up the dog who made a feeble attempt to
wag his tail. I sat down on the grass and took the patty from my

pocket; I fed the dog who ate ravenously while the young man stood by holding the horses.

"Poor little dog," he said. "He's had a bad time."

"I don't know how to begin to thank you," I told him. "What would have happened if you hadn't come along is unthinkable. She would never have given him to me."

"Don't let's brood on that," he said. "We have him now."

I was drawn towards him because I knew that he cared as much about the dog's fate as I did; and the dog, from that moment, became a bond between us.

"I shall take him home and look after him," I said. "Do you think he'll recover?"

"I am sure he will. He's a tough little mongrel, I imagine, but hardly the dog to spend his days on a lady's velvet cushion."

"He's my sort of dog," I replied.

"You should feed him regularly and often."

"It is what I intend to do. When I get him home I shall give him some warm milk—a little at a time."

The dog knew we were talking of him, but the effort of eating, together with the excitement, had been exhausting, and he lay very still. The young man's melancholy expression which I believed might well be habitual with him had lifted when he had bargained for the dog and had presented him to me, and I was anxious to know what could have happened to a young man, who was clearly blessed with a goodly share of the comforts of life, to have produced that melancholy. I was curious about him, and it was stimulating to discover this curiosity in myself at the very same time that I had acquired my interest in the dog. I was torn between two desires: I wanted to stay and learn more about the man, and at the same time I wanted to take the dog home and feed him. I knew, of course, that there must be no question what I did, for the dog was dangerously near death by starvation.

"I must be going," I said.

He nodded. "I'll carry him, shall I?" he replied; and, without waiting for my reply, he helped me to mount. He gave me the dog to hold while he mounted; then he took the little creature from me and tucking him under his arm said: "Which way?"

I showed him and we set out. In twenty minutes we had reached Glengreen, scarcely speaking on the way there. At the gates of Glen House we paused.

"He's really yours," I said. "You paid for him."

"Then I make a gift of him to you." His eyes smiled into mine. "But I shall retain rights in him. I shall want to know whether he lives or not. May I call and ask?"

"Of course."

"Tomorrow?"

"If you wish."

"And for whom shall I ask?"

"For Miss Corder . . . Catherine Corder."

"Thank you, Miss Corder. Gabriel Rockwell will call on you tomorrow."

Fanny was horrified by the presence of the dog. "Happen there'll be dog's hair all over t'place. Happen we'll be finding whiskers in t'soup and fleas in our beds."

I said nothing. I fed the dog myself . . . on bread and milk in small quantities, at intervals all through the rest of the day and once in the night. I found a basket and I took him to my bedroom. It was the happiest night since my return, and I wondered why I had never thought of asking for a dog when I was a child. Perhaps it was because I knew that Fanny would never have allowed me to have one.

What did it matter—I had him now.

He knew I was his friend right from the start. He lay in the basket too weak to move, but his eyes told me that he understood what I was doing was for his good. Those eyes, already loving, patiently followed me as I moved. I knew that he would be my friend as long as he lived. I wondered what to call him; he must have a name. I could not go on thinking of him as the gypsy's dog. Then I remembered that I had found him on a Friday and I thought: He'll be my dog Friday. And from then he had his name.

By the morning he was on the way to recovery. I waited for the coming of Gabriel for, now that my anxieties about the dog were over, I began to think more of the man who had shared the adventure. I was a little disappointed because he did not come in the morning, and I felt sad because I was afraid he might have forgotten us by now. I did want to say thank you to him, because I was sure Friday owed his life to his timely arrival.

He came in the afternoon. It was three o'clock, and I was in my room with the dog when I heard the sound of a horse's hoofs below. Friday's ears twitched and his tail moved as though he knew that the other one to whom he would be forever grateful was near.

I looked out of my window, standing well back so that he could not see me if he should chance to look up. He was certainly handsome but in a somewhat delicate way, not as we expected our men to be in Yorkshire. He had an aristocratic air. I had noticed this on the previous day but I had wondered whether I had imagined it because of the contrast he made with Friday's previous mistress.

I went hastily downstairs because I did not want him to be ungraciously received.

I was wearing a dark blue velvet afternoon dress—my best—because I was expecting him, and I had wound my plaits to form a coronet on the top of my head.

I went out into the drive just as he came up. He swept off his hat in a manner which I knew would be called "daft" by Fanny, but I thought it elegant and the height of courtesy.

"So you came!" I said. "Dog Friday will recover. I've christened him after the day on which he was found."

He had dismounted and at that moment Mary appeared. I made her call one of the stable boys to lead his horse round to the stable, and water and feed him.

"Come in," I said, and when Gabriel came into the hall, the house seemed brighter for his presence.

"Let me take you up to the drawing room," I said, "and I will ring for tea."

He followed me up the stairs while I told him how I was treating Friday. "I shall bring him down to show you. You will see a great improvement."

In the drawing room I pulled back the curtains and drew up the Venetian blinds. Now it seemed more cheerful—or perhaps that was due to Gabriel. When he sat in one of the armchairs and smiled at me, I was conscious that in my blue velvet with my neatly plaited hair I looked very different from the girl in the riding habit.

"I'm glad you were able to save him," he said.

"*You* did that."

He looked pleased and I rang the bell which was almost immediately answered by Janet.

She stared at my visitor and, when I told her to bring tea, she looked as though I were asking for the moon.

Five minutes later Fanny came in; she had an indignant air and I felt angry with her. She would have to realize that I was now the mistress of the house.

"So it's visitors," said Fanny ungraciously.

"Yes, Fanny, we have a visitor. Pray see that tea is not long delayed."

Fanny pursed her lips; I could see that she was trying to make some retort, but I turned my back on her and said to Gabriel: "I trust you did not have to ride far."

"From the Black Hart Inn in Tomblersbury."

I knew Tomblersbury. It was a small village, rather like our own, some five or six miles away.

"You are staying at the Black Hart?"

"Yes, for a short while."

"You must be on holiday."

"You could call it that."

"Your home is in Yorkshire, Mr. Rockwell? But I am asking too many questions."

I was aware that Fanny had left the room. I could imagine her going to the kitchen or perhaps to my father's study. She would consider it most unseemly for me to entertain a gentleman alone. Let her! It was time she—and my father—understood that the life I was called upon to live was not only exceedingly lonely but one unsuitable for a young lady of my education.

"No," he replied, "please ask me as many questions as you like. If I cannot answer them, I shall say so."

"Where is your home, Mr. Rockwell?"

"The house is called Kirkland Revels, and it is situated in the village—or rather on the outskirts of the village—of Kirkland Moorside."

"Kirkland Revels! That sounds joyous."

The expression which flitted across his face was enough to tell me that my remark had made him uncomfortable. It had told me something else: He was not happy in his home life. Was that the reason for that moodiness of his? I ought to have curbed my curiosity regarding his private affairs but I found it exceedingly difficult to do so.

I said quickly: "Kirkland Moorside . . . is that far from here?"

"Some thirty miles perhaps."

"And you are on holiday in this district, and you were taking a ride on the moors when . . ."

"When our little adventure occurred. You cannot be more glad than I am that it happened."

I felt reassured that the temporary awkwardness was past and I said: "If you will excuse me, I will bring Friday down to show you."

When I returned with the dog, my father was in the room. I guessed Fanny had insisted on his joining us and that even he had been conscious of the proprieties. Gabriel was telling him how we had acquired the dog and my father was being charming; he listened attentively and I was pleased that he manifested an interest even though I did not believe he really felt it.

Friday, in his basket, too weak to rise, made an effort to do so; his pleasure was obvious at the sight of Gabriel, whose long, elegant fingers gently stroked the dog's ear.

"He's fond of you," I said.

"But you'll have first place in his heart."

"I saw him first," I reminded him. "I shall keep him with me always. Will you let me pay you what you gave the woman?"

"I wouldn't hear of it," he told me.

"I should like to feel that he is all mine."

"So he is. A gift. But I admit to an interest. If I may, I shall call again to inquire after his health."

"It is not a bad idea to have a dog in the house," said my father, as he came to stand beside us and look down into the basket.

We were standing thus when Mary brought in the tea wagon. There were hot crumpets as well as bread and butter and cakes; and as I sat behind the silver teapot, I thought this was my happiest afternoon since I had returned from France; I was as contented as I had been when Uncle Dick came home.

I did not realize until later that this was because I now had something in the house which I could love. I had Friday. I did not think at this stage that I had Gabriel too. That came later.

During the next two weeks Gabriel called regularly at Glen House; and at the end of that first week Friday was fully restored to health. His wounds had healed and good food regularly taken had done the rest.

He slept in his basket in my room and followed me wherever he could. I talked to him continuously. The house had changed; my life had changed because of him.

He wanted to be not only my companion but my defender. There was adoration in those limpid eyes when they looked into mine. He remembered that he owed his life to me; and because he was the faithful sort, that was something he would never forget.

We went for walks together—he and I. Only when I rode did I leave him behind, and when I returned he would fling himself at me in the sort of welcome I had only ever had from Uncle Dick.

Then there was Gabriel.

He continued to stay at the Black Hart. I wondered why. There was a lot I could not quite understand about Gabriel. There were times when he talked freely about himself, but even at such times I always had the impression that there was something he was holding back. I felt that he was on the verge of telling me, that he longed to tell me, and could never quite bring himself to do so; and that which he held back was some dark secret, perhaps something which he did not entirely understand himself.

We had become great friends. My father seemed to like him—at least he made no protests about his constant visits. The servants had grown used to him, and even Fanny, as long as we were properly chaperoned, made no complaints.

At the end of the first week he had said that soon he would be going home; but at the end of the second he was still with us. I had a feeling that he was deceiving himself in some way, that he was promising himself that he would go home and then making excuses not to.

I did not ask him questions about his home even though I longed to know more about him. This was something else I had learned. At school I had often been made uneasy by searching questions about *my* home; I had determined not to inflict the same discomfort on others. I would never probe, but always wait to be told.

So we talked about me, for Gabriel had no such reticence where I was concerned, and strangely enough, with him I did not mind. I told him about Uncle Dick who had always been a kind of hero to me, and I made him see Uncle Dick with his sparkling greenish eyes and black beard.

Gabriel said once when I had talked of my uncle: "You and he must be somewhat alike."

"There is a strong resemblance, I believe."

"He sounds like the sort of person who is determined to get the most out of life. I mean, he would act without first weighing up the consequences. Tell me, are you like that?"

"Perhaps I am."

He smiled. "I believe you are," he said; and there came into his eyes what I can only describe as a faraway look, by which I mean that he was seeing me, not as we were together at that moment, but in some other place, in some other situation.

I thought he was about to speak, but he remained silent and I did not press him, for I was already beginning to feel that too much probing, too many questions, disturbed him. I must wait, I knew intuitively, for him to tell me without prompting.

But I had discovered that there was something unusual about Gabriel, and that should have warned me not to allow myself to become too deeply involved. I had been so lonely; I found the atmosphere of my home so depressing; I longed for a friend of my own age; and the strangeness of Gabriel enthralled me.

So I refused to see any danger signals and we continued to meet.

We liked to ride onto the moors, tether our horses and stretch ourselves out in the shelter of a boulder, looking up at the sky, our arms behind our heads, talking in a dreamy, desultory way. Fanny would have considered this the height of impropriety, but I was determined to adhere to no conventions; I knew this attitude delighted Gabriel, and I learned later why it did so.

Each day I would ride out and meet him at some agreed spot because I could not bear the sly glances Fanny gave him when he called at the house. In our small and sheltered community it was not possible to meet a young man daily without causing a certain amount of speculation. I often wondered, during that early period of our acquaintance, whether Gabriel was aware of this; I also wondered whether he felt as embarrassed about it as I did.

I had not heard from Dilys for some weeks, so I supposed she was too immersed in her own affairs to have time to write. I did feel, however, that now I could write to her because I had something to tell her. I explained about our finding the dog, and how fond I had become of him; but what I really wanted to talk about was Gabriel. My affection for Friday was uncomplicated, but I could not quite understand my feelings for Gabriel.

He interested me, and I looked forward to our meetings with something more than the pleasure of a lonely girl who has at last found a friend; I realized that this was because I was constantly expecting some revelation which would startle me. There was certainly an air of mystery about Gabriel and I believed that again and again he was on the verge of confiding some secret which he longed to share with me and could not quite bring himself to do so. I had a conviction that he, like my father, was in need of comfort; and while my father repulsed me, Gabriel, when the time came, would welcome my desire to share whatever it was that was troubling him.

It was impossible, of course, to confide all this to the lighthearted Dilys, particularly when I was not at all sure of it myself. So I wrote a chatty, superficial letter, and felt pleased because something had happened to me which was worthy to be written about.

It was three weeks after we met when Gabriel seemed to come to a decision; and the day he began to talk to me about his home marked a change in our relationship.

We were lying stretched out on the moor and he pulled up handfuls of grass as he talked to me.

"I wonder what you would think of Kirkland Revels," he said.

"I am sure I should find it attractive. It's very old, is it not? Old houses have always been absorbingly interesting to me."

He nodded, and again there was that faraway look in his eyes.

"Revels," I murmured. "It's such a lovely name. It sounds as though the people who named it were determined to have a great deal of fun there."

He laughed mirthlessly, and there was a brief silence before he began to speak; then it was as though he were reciting a piece he had learned by heart.

"It was built in the middle of the sixteenth century. When Kirkland Abbey was dissolved, it was given to my ancestors. They took stones from the Abbey and with them built a house. Because it was used as a house in which to make merry—I must have had very merry ancestors—it was called Kirkland Revels in contrast to Kirkland Abbey."

"So the stones which built your house were once those of an ancient abbey!"

"Tons and tons of stone," he murmured. "There's still much of the old Abbey in existence. When I stand on my balcony I can look across to those gray and ancient arches. In certain lights you can imagine that they are not merely ruins . . . in fact it is difficult to believe they are. Then you can almost see the monks in their habits moving silently among the stones."

"How attractive it must be. You love it, do you not?"

"It has a fascination for all who see it. Don't all things as old as that? Imagine, although the house is a mere three hundred years old, the stones of which it is built date back to the twelfth century. Naturally everyone's impressed. You will be when . . ."

He stopped and I saw the slow smile curve his delicate lips.

I am forthright and had never been able to hedge, so I said: "Are you suggesting that I shall see it?"

The smile about his lips expanded. "I have been a guest in your home. I should like you to be one in mine."

Then it came bursting out: "Miss Corder, I shall have to go home soon."

"You don't want to, do you, Mr. Rockwell?"

"We are great friends, I believe," he said. "At least I feel we are."

"We have known each other but three weeks," I reminded him.

"But the circumstances were exceptional. Please call me Gabriel."

I hesitated, then I laughed. "What's in a name?" I asked. "Our friendship cannot be greater or less, whether I call you by your Christian or surname. What were you going to say to me, Gabriel?"

"Catherine!" he almost whispered my name as he turned on his side and leaned on his elbow to look at me. "You are right, I don't want to go back."

I did not look at him because I feared my next question was impertinent, but I could not prevent myself from asking it. "Why are you afraid to go back?"

He had turned away. "Afraid?" His voice sounded high-pitched. "Who said I was afraid?"

"Then I imagined it."

Silence fell between us for a few seconds, then he said: "I wish I could make you see the Revels . . . the Abbey. I wish . . ."

"Tell me about it," I said and added: "If you want to . . . but only if you want to."

"It's about myself I want to tell you, Catherine."

"Then please do."

"These have been the most interesting and happiest weeks of my life, and it is because of you. The reason I do not want to go back to the Revels is because it would mean saying good-by to you."

"Perhaps we should meet again."

He turned to me. "When?" he asked almost angrily.

"Some time perhaps."

"Some time! How do we know what time is left to us?"

"How strangely you talk . . . as though you thought that one . . . or both of us . . . might die tomorrow."

There was a faint flush in his cheeks which seemed to make his eyes burn brightly. "Who can say when death shall come?"

"How morbid you have grown. I am nineteen. You have told me that you are twenty-three. People of our ages do not talk of dying."

"*One* evidently does. Catherine, will you marry me?"

I must have looked shocked by this unexpected outburst, because he laughed and said: "You are looking at me as though I am crazy. Is it so strange that someone should want to marry you?"

"But I cannot take this seriously."

"You must, Catherine. I ask with the utmost seriousness."

"But how can you speak of marriage after such a short acquaintance?"

"It does not seem short. We have met every day. I know that you are all I want, and that is enough for me."

I was silent. In spite of Fanny's attitude I had not considered marriage with Gabriel. We were the best of friends and I should be desolate if he went away; but when I thought of marriage he seemed almost like a stranger. He aroused my curiosity and interest; he was unlike anyone I had ever known and, because of that certain mystery which shrouded his personality, he attracted me very much; but until this moment I had thought of him mainly as a person whom good fortune had sent my way at an important moment. There was so little I knew about him; I had never met any of his people. Indeed when they, or his home, briefly intruded into our conversation I was immediately conscious of Gabriel's withdrawing from me, as though there were secrets in his life which he was not prepared to share with me. In view of all this I thought it very strange that he should suddenly suggest marriage.

He went on: "Catherine, what is your answer?"

"It is No, Gabriel. There is so much we do not know about each other."

"You mean there is so much you do not know about me."

"Perhaps that is what I mean."

"But what do you want to know? We love horses; we love dogs; we find pleasure in each other's company; I can laugh and be happy with you. What more could I ask than to laugh and be happy for the rest of my life?"

"And with others . . . in your home . . . you cannot laugh and be happy?"

"I could never be completely happy with anyone else but you; I could never laugh so freely."

"It seems a flimsy structure on which to base a marriage."

"You are being cautious, Catherine. You feel I have spoken too soon."

I knew then how desolate I should be if he went away, and I said quickly: "Yes, that is it. This is too soon . . ."

"At least," he said, "I do not have to fear a rival. Do not say No,

Catherine. Think of how much I want this to be . . . and try to want it a little yourself."

I stood up. I was no longer in the mood to stay on the moors. He made no protest and we rode to the village where he said good-by to me.

When I reached the stables Friday was waiting there for me. He always knew when I had gone out riding and never failed to be in the stable yard watching for my return.

He waited patiently until I had given Wanda to one of the lads, then he flung himself at me, making sure that I was fully aware of his pleasure in my return. Many dogs have that lovable quality, but in Friday it was stronger than usual because it was touched by an extreme humility. He stood aside while my attention was given to others, waiting patiently until it was his turn. I believed that the memory of early wretchedness always remained with Friday, and that was why in all his exuberant affection there was that touch of deep humility and gratitude.

I lifted him in my arms and he sniffed my jacket with ecstasy.

I hugged him. I was growing more and more fond of him with every day, and my affection for him enhanced my feelings for Gabriel.

Even as I turned into the house I was wondering what marriage with Gabriel would be like. I was already beginning to believe that it was a state which I could contemplate without abhorrence.

What would my life in Glen House be like when Gabriel went away? I should ride Wanda, walk with Friday, but one could not be out of doors forever. The winter would come. Winters were harsh in the moorland country; there were days at a stretch when it was impossible to venture out unless one wanted to risk death in the blizzards. I thought of long dark days in the house—the weary monotonous round. It was true that Uncle Dick might come home; but his visits could not be of very long duration and I could remember from the past how life seemed doubly dull after he had left.

It occurred to me then that I needed to escape from Glen House. A way was being offered to me. If I refused to take it, might I not be regretful for the rest of my life?

Gabriel came to dine with us occasionally. My father always roused himself on such occasions and was a tolerable host. I could see that he did not dislike Gabriel. Fanny's lips would curl in a sardonic smile when Gabriel was in the house. I knew that she was thinking that he was making use of our hospitality while he was in the neighborhood, and that when the time came for him to leave he would do so and promptly forget us. Fanny, who was determined to give nothing, was always afraid that people were going to take something from her. There were sly references to my "hopes" regarding Gabriel. She had never married and believed that it was the woman who desired that state in cold blood because it meant that she must be fed and clothed for the rest of her life. As for the man who had to provide the food and clothing, he would naturally seek to "get what he wanted"—Fanny's expression—without giving more than he could help. Fanny's values were material. I longed to escape from them, and I knew that with each day I was withdrawing myself farther and farther from Glen House and feeling closer and closer to Gabriel.

May was with us and the days were warm and sunny; it was a joy to escape to the moors. Now we talked of ourselves and there was a certain feverishness about Gabriel. He always seemed to me like a man who was looking over his shoulder at some pursuer, while he was desperately conscious of passing time.

I made him tell me about his home, and he was willing enough to do so now. I felt this to be because he had already convinced himself that I would marry him and that it would not only be his home but mine.

In my imagination it was a hazy, gray edifice of ancient stones. I knew there was a balcony because Gabriel talked of it often; I pictured the scene from that balcony, for Gabriel had described it to me many times. The balcony was evidently a favorite spot of his. I knew that from it it was possible to see the river winding its way through the meadows; the woods, which in some places went down to the river's edge, and a quarter of a mile from the house those ancient piles of stone, those magnificent arches which the years had not been able to destroy; and across the wooden bridge, away beyond the river, the wild moorland country.

But what were houses compared with the people who lived in them? I learned by degrees that Gabriel, like myself, had no mother; she had been advanced in years when he was conceived, and when he came into the world she went out of it. Our motherlessness was a further bond between us.

He had a sister, fifteen years older than himself—a widow with a seventeen-year-old son; he also had a father who was very old.

"He was nearly sixty when I was born," Gabriel told me. "My mother was forty. Some of the servants used to say I was "the afterthought"; others used to say I killed my mother."

I was immediately angry because I knew how such careless comments could hurt a sensitive child. "How ridiculous!" I cried, my eyes flashing with anger as they always did over what I considered injustice. Gabriel laughed, took my hand and held it very tightly. Then he said seriously: "You see I cannot do without you. I need you . . . to protect me against the cruel things that are said of me."

"You are no longer a child," I replied somewhat impatiently; and when I analyzed my impatience I found it grew out of my desire to protect him. I wanted to make him strong enough not to be afraid.

"Some of us remain children until we die."

"Death!" I cried. "Why do you harp continually on death?"

"It's true that I do," he said. "It's because I am so anxious to live every minute of my life to the full."

I did not understand what he meant then; and I asked to hear more of the family.

"Ruth, my sister, rules the household and will do so until I marry. Then of course my wife will do that, because I am the only son and the Revels will one day be mine."

"When you speak of the Revels you do so in a tone of reverence."

"It is my home."

"And yet . . ." I was going to say: I believe you are glad to have escaped from it. "You are not eager to return."

He did not notice my interruption. He murmured as though to himself: "It ought to have been Simon . . ."

"Who is Simon?"

"Simon Redvers. A sort of cousin. A Rockwell through his grandmother who is my father's sister. You won't like him very much. But then you'll rarely meet. There isn't much communication between Kelly Grange and the Revels."

He was talking as though there was no doubt that I would marry him and that one day his house would be my home.

Sometimes I wondered whether there was not some subtlety in Gabriel. He gradually built up pictures in my mind, so that his home and family somehow came alive for me, and as the picture grew clearer in my mind it brought with it a fascination which was not altogether pleasant and yet no less impelling because of that—but rather more so.

I wanted to see that pile of gray stones which had been made into a house three hundred years ago; I wanted to see those ruins which from a balcony of the house would have the appearance, not of a ruin, but an ancient abbey because so much of the outer structure remained.

I was caught up in Gabriel's life. I knew that if he went away I should be desperately lonely and dissatisfied with my life. I should be continually regretful.

And one sunny day, when I had walked out of the house with Friday at my heels, I met Gabriel on the moor; and we sat with our backs against a boulder while Friday crouched before us on the grass his eyes going from one to the other, his head slightly cocked as though he listened to our conversation. This was complete happiness for him and we knew it was because we were together.

"There's something I haven't told you, Catherine," said Gabriel.

I felt relieved, because I knew that he was going to tell me something now which he had been trying to for a long time.

"I want you to say you'll marry me," he went on, "but so far you haven't said that. You don't dislike me; you're happy in my company. That's true, Catherine?"

I looked at him and saw again those lines between his brows; I saw the puzzled frustration there and I remembered those occasions when he had seemed to forget what it was that made him melancholy, when he threw off his moodiness and became gay. I felt a great desire then to chase the gloom out of his life, to make him happy as I had made Friday healthy.

"Of course I don't dislike you," I said, "and we're happy together. If you go away . . ."

"You'd miss me, Catherine, but not as much as I should miss you. I want you to come back with me. I don't want to go without you."

"Why are you so eager for me to go back with you?"

"Why? Surely you know. It's because I love you—because I never want to leave you again."

"Yes, but . . . is there another reason?"

"What other reason should there be?" he asked; but he did not meet my eyes as he said that, and I knew that there was a great deal about him and his home that I had to learn.

"You should tell me everything, Gabriel," I said on impulse.

He moved closer to me and put his arm about me. "You are right, Catherine. There are things you should know. I cannot be happy without you and . . . there cannot be long left to me."

I drew away from him. "What do you mean?" I demanded sharply.

He sat up and looking straight ahead said: "I cannot live more than a few years. I have received my sentence of death."

I was angry with him because I could not bear to hear his talk of dying. "Stop being dramatic," I commanded, "and tell me exactly what all this means."

"It's perfectly simple. I have a weak heart—a family complaint. I had an elder brother who died young. My mother died at my birth, but it was due to the same heart condition, aggravated by the strain of bringing me into the world. I could die tomorrow . . . next year . . . or in five years' time. It would apparently be extraordinary if I lived longer than that."

I yearned to comfort him and he knew how his words had affected me for he went on wistfully: "It would not be a great many years, Catherine."

"Don't talk like that," I said harshly; and I stood up, so overcome by my emotions that I could say no more. I started to walk quickly and Gabriel fell into step beside me. We were both silent, and Friday kept running ahead of us to look back at us anxiously, head on one side, while his eyes implored us to be gay.

That night I scarcely slept at all. I could think of nothing but Gabriel and his need of me. This was what had made him seem so different from any other person I had ever known, for I had never before known a person who was under a sentence of death. I kept hearing his voice saying: "I could die tomorrow . . . next year . . . or in five years' time. It would apparently be extraordinary if I lived longer than that." I kept seeing those melancholy eyes and remembering how at times he could be happy. And I could make him happy for what time was left to him—I alone. How could I forget that? How could I turn away from someone who needed me so much?

At this time I was so inexperienced that I did not know how to analyze my emotions. But I was sure that if Gabriel went away I should miss him. He had brought a new interest into my life, making me forget the gloominess of my home; it was so pleasant to be with someone who was really interested in me, after my father's indifference, with someone who admired me, after Fanny's criticism.

Perhaps I was not in love; perhaps pity was at the very root of my feelings for Gabriel; but by the morning I had made up my mind.

The banns were read in the village church and Gabriel went back to Kirkland Revels, I presumed to inform his family, while I began preparing for my wedding.

Before leaving, Gabriel had formally asked my father for my hand, and Father had been rather bewildered by the proceedings. He had hesitated, reminding Gabriel of my youth and the short time we had known each other; but I, who had been expecting he might do this, burst in on them and assured my father that I had quite made up my mind to marry.

Father looked worried and I knew that he was wishing that Uncle Dick were at home so that he could consult him; however, I had no real fear of opposition, and after a while Father said that as I seemed determined, he supposed I must have my way. Then he asked the conventional questions about Gabriel's standing which Gabriel was able to answer to his satisfaction; and it occurred to me for the first time that I must be marrying into a wealthy family.

I longed for the presence of Uncle Dick, because it seemed unthinkable that he should not be at my wedding. I believed that I could have talked to him of my feelings and that he would have helped me to come to a better understanding of them.

I told Gabriel how much I wanted Uncle Dick to come to the wedding, but he was so full of despair at the thought of postponement that I gave way. That desire in Gabriel to make the most of every hour touched me so deeply that I would let nothing stand in the way of the comfort he was sure I could bring him. Besides, although it was possible to write to Uncle Dick, one could never be sure when letters would reach him; and when I heard from him—he was not a good letter writer and wrote rarely—his letters never seemed to answer mine and I always wondered whether he had received them.

I could not resist writing to Dilys. "The most extraordinary thing has happened. I am going to be married! How strange that this should happen to me before you. It is the man I wrote to you about—the man who helped with the dog. He lives in Yorkshire in a wonderful old house near an abbey, and it has all happened so quickly that I don't quite understand how it has come about. I don't know whether I'm in love with him. I only know that I couldn't bear it if he went away and I never saw him again. Oh, Dilys, it's so exciting, because before it happened I was so wretched here. You've no idea what my home is like. I myself had forgotten during all those years I was away. It's a dark house . . . and I don't mean that there's just an absence of sunshine. . . . I mean the people in it live dark lives. . . ."

I tore that up. Was I crazy, trying to make Dilys understand what I did not myself? How could I explain to Dilys that I was going to marry Gabriel because, for some reason which I could not fully understand, I was sorry for him and I knew he needed my help; because I wanted desperately to love someone who belonged to me; because my father had repulsed me when I had tried to show affection and had mutely asked for little in return; because I wanted to escape from the house which was now my home.

Instead of that letter I sent a conventional little note inviting Dilys to my wedding.

Fanny was still skeptical. She thought it was a queer way to go about getting married. There were references to proverbs such as "Marry in haste, repent at leisure"; and she talked about "supping sorrow with a long spoon." Still, the thought of future disaster seemed to cheer her considerably and she was determined that my grand in-laws, if they came to the wedding, should have no complaints about the wedding feast.

Gabriel wrote regularly and his letters were ardent, but they spoke only of his devotion to me and his desire for our union; he did not let me know anything about his family's reactions.

I heard from Dilys that I had not given her enough notice of my wedding. She was so full of engagements that she could not possibly leave London. I realized then that our lives had taken such entirely different turnings that the intimacy which had once been ours was over.

Three days before our marriage was to take place, Gabriel came back and put up at the King's Head less than half a mile from Glen House.

When Mary came to my room to tell me that he was in the first-floor sitting room waiting to see me, I went down eagerly. He was standing with his back to the fireplace watching the door, and as soon as I opened it he strode towards me and we embraced. He looked excited, younger than he had when he had left, because some of the strain had gone from him.

I took his face in my hands and kissed it.

"Like a mother with a precious child," he murmured.

He had summed up my feelings. I wanted to look after him; I wanted to make what life was left to him completely happy. I was not passionately in love with him, but I did not attach great importance to this because passion was something I knew nothing about at that time. Yet I loved him nonetheless; and when he held me tightly against him, I knew that the kind of love I had for him was what he wanted.

I withdrew myself from his arms and made him sit down on the horsehair couch. I wanted to hear what his family's reactions were to the news of our engagement and how many were coming to the wedding.

"Well, you see," he said slowly, "my father is too infirm to make the journey. As for the others . . ." He shrugged his shoulders.

"Gabriel!" I cried aghast. "Do you mean that none of them is coming?"

"Well, you see, there's my Aunt Sarah. Like my father, she's too old to travel. And . . ."

"But there's your sister and her son."

He looked uneasy and I saw the frown between his eyes. "Oh, darling," he said, "what does it matter? It's not *their* wedding, is it?"

"But not to come! Does that mean they don't approve of our marriage?"

"Of course they'll approve. But the ceremony itself is not all that important, is it? Look, Catherine, I'm back with you. I want to be happy."

I could not bear to see the moody expression returning to his face, so I tried to hide my uneasiness. It was very strange. No members of his family at the wedding! This was most unusual; but when I looked back, everything that had led up to this wedding of ours was somewhat unusual.

I heard a scratching at the door. Friday knew that Gabriel had come, and was impatient to see him. I opened the door and he bounded straight into Gabriel's arms. I watched them together; Gabriel was laughing as Friday tried to lick his face.

I told myself that I must not expect Gabriel's family to behave conventionally, any more than Gabriel himself did; and I was relieved that Dilys had declined my invitation.

"Happen they think you're not good enough for 'em." That was Fanny's verdict.

I was not going to let Fanny see how the behavior of Gabriel's family disturbed me, so I merely shrugged my shoulders.

After the wedding Gabriel and I were going to have a week's holiday at Scarborough, and then we were going to Kirkland Revels. All in good time I should discover for myself what his family thought of the marriage; I must be patient until then.

My father gave me away, and I was married to Gabriel in our village church on a day in June about two months after we first met. I wore a white dress which had been made rather hurriedly by our village seamstress, and I had a white veil and a wreath of orange blossoms. There were very few guests at the reception, which was held in the drawing room at Glen House: the vicar and his wife, the doctor and his, and that was all.

Gabriel and I left immediately after our health had been drunk. It was a very quiet wedding; and we were both glad to leave our few guests and be driven to the station where we took the train for the coast.

I felt when we were alone together in that first-class compartment that we were like any bride and groom. Previously the unconventional manner of our marrying—at such short notice, so few guests and none of the bridegroom's family being present—had given the entire proceedings an unreality for me; but now that we were alone together I felt relaxed.

Gabriel held my hand, a smile of contentment on his face, which was gratifying. I had never seen him look so peaceful before and I knew then that that was what he had always lacked: peace. Friday was with us, for it was unthinkable that we could go away without him. I had procured a basket for him, for I was not sure how he would travel; I had chosen a loosely woven one so that he could see us, and I talked to him explaining that it would only be for a short time that he was thus confined. I had taken to talking to him, explaining everything, which had set Fanny's lips twitching. She thought I was "real daft" talking to a dog.

And so we reached our hotel.

During those first days of our honeymoon, I felt my love for Gabriel growing because he needed me so desperately to lift him out of those dark moods of melancholy which could quickly descend upon him; there was a wonderful gratification in being so important to another human being which I think at that time I mistook for being in love.

The weather was glorious, the days full of sunshine. We walked a good deal; the three of us—for Friday was always with us. We explored that glorious coast from Robin Hood's Bay to Flamborough Head; we marveled at those delightful little bays, the grandeur of the cliffs, the coves and glimpses of moorland beyond; we both enjoyed walking and did so frequently, and we hired horses and rode inland to explore the moors and compare them with our own of the West Riding. On that coast line there are occasionally to be found the crumbling walls of an ancient castle, and one day we found the remains of an old abbey.

Gabriel was attracted by the ruins; indeed I soon discovered that the fascination they had for him was morbid, and for the first time

since our marriage I saw a return to that moodiness which I had determined to abolish. Friday was quick to notice that Gabriel was losing
some of his honeymoon happiness. I saw him, on one occasion when
we were exploring the abbey ruins, rub his head against Gabriel's leg
while he looked up appealingly, as though to implore him to remember
that the three of us were together and therefore should be happy.

It was then that I felt little pinpricks of alarm stabbing my pleasure.
I said to him: "Gabriel, does this abbey remind you of Kirkland
Abbey?"

"There's always a similarity in old ruins," was the noncommittal
reply.

I wanted to ask more questions. I was certain that there was something which disturbed him, and it was in Kirkland Abbey and the
Revels.

I blundered on: "But, Gabriel, you would rather not have been
reminded."

He put his arm about me and I could see that he was desperately
trying to break out of the mood which had fallen on him.

Rapidly I changed the subject. "It looks as though it might rain,"
I said. "Do you think we should be getting back to the hotel?"

He was relieved that I was not going to ask questions to which he
would want to give evasive replies. Soon, I told myself, I should be
in my new home. There I might discover the reason for this strangeness in my husband. I would wait until then; and when I had made my
discovery I would eliminate whatever it was that troubled him; I
would let nothing stand in the way of his happiness for all the years
that were left to us.

2

The honeymoon was over. During the last day we had both been a little on edge. Gabriel had been silent and I had been a little exasperated with him. I could not understand why he could be gay one day and moody the next. Perhaps I was—although I would not admit this—a little nervous about facing the Rockwell family. Friday sensed our mood and lost some of his exuberance.

"There are three of us now, that's what he's telling us," I said to Gabriel; and that did seem to cheer him.

The journey across the North Riding was long because we had to change; and the afternoon was over by the time we reached Keighley.

A carriage was waiting for us—rather a grand one; and when the coachman saw me I fancied he was startled. I thought it rather strange that he should not have heard of Gabriel's wedding and surely he had not, for if he had why should he be surprised when a bridegroom arrived with his bride?

Gabriel helped me into the carriage while the coachman dealt with our luggage, taking covert looks at me as he did so.

I shall never forget that drive from the station. It took about an hour and before we reached our destination dusk had fallen.

So it was in the half-light that I first saw my new home.

We had passed over the moors which were wild and eerie in this light; but these moors were very like those which had been close to Glen House, and I felt at home on any moor. We had climbed high and although it was June there was a sharpness in the air. The peaty smell was in my nostrils and I felt my spirits rise in spite of my growing apprehension. I pictured myself riding on these moors—Gabriel and myself together. Now we were descending and the country was less wild although there was still the moorland touch about it. We were coming near the hamlet of Kirkland Moorside, close by which was my new home, Kirkland Revels.

The grass was more lush; we passed an occasional house; there were fields which were cultivated.

Gabriel leaned towards me. "If the light were better you might be able to see Kelly Grange from here—my cousin's place. Did I mention him—Simon Redvers?"

"Yes," I said, "you did." And I strained my eyes and thought I saw the faint outlines of a house away to the right.

On we went over the bridge; and it was then that I caught my first glimpse of the Abbey.

I saw the Norman tower, the outer shell of which was preserved; and walls clustered about it, so that it was impossible to see at this distance that it was a mere shell. It looked grand yet forbidding—although I wondered in that moment whether it was really so or whether the moods of my husband had made me imagine there was something to be feared.

We were driving along a road which was bordered on either side by massive oaks, and suddenly we were in the clear and there before me was the house.

I caught my breath, for it was beautiful. The first thing that struck me was its size. It looked like a massive oblong of stone. I discovered later that it was built round a courtyard, and that although it was of Tudor origin, it had been restored through the later centuries. The windows were mullioned and about them were fantastic carvings of devils and angels, pitchforks and harps, scrolls and Tudor roses. This was indeed an historic baronial hall. I thought then how small Glen House must have seemed to Gabriel when he had visited us.

About a dozen stone steps, worn away in the center, led to a great portico of massive stone carved in a way similar to the space round the windows. There was a heavy oak door decorated with finely wrought iron; and even as I began to mount the steps the door opened and I met the first member of my new family.

She was a woman in her late thirties or early forties and her resemblance to Gabriel told me at once that she was his widowed sister, Ruth Grantley.

She looked at me for a few seconds without speaking and her glance was cool and appraising before she forced some warmth into it.

"How do you do? You must forgive us if we're surprised. We only heard this morning. Gabriel, it *was* perverse of you to be so secretive."

She took my hands and smiled, although it was a baring of the teeth rather than a smile. I noticed that her eyelashes were so fair that they were almost invisible. She was just that little bit fairer than Gabriel; and what struck me at once was her coldness.

"Come along in," she said. "I'm afraid you'll find us unprepared. It was such a surprise."

I said: "It must have been."

I looked at Gabriel questioningly. What could have been the point in not telling?

We stepped into the hall in which a log fire was blazing and I was immediately struck by the air of antiquity about the place. I could see that this had been preserved and was cherished. The walls were hung with tapestry which doubtless had been worked by members of this family centuries ago. In the center of the hall was a refectory table and on it were laid utensils of brass and pewter.

I looked around me.

"Well?" said Ruth.

"It's so . . . exciting to be here," I said.

She seemed a little gratified. She turned first to Gabriel. "Gabriel, why all this secrecy?" Then to me as she spread her hands deprecatingly: "He seems to have no reason for keeping us in the dark until this morning."

"I wanted to surprise you all," said Gabriel. "Catherine, you'll be tired. You'd like to go to our room."

"Of course you would," put in Ruth. "And meet the family later. I can tell you we're all very eager to make your acquaintance."

Her eyes glittered as her somewhat prominent teeth were bared once more. Friday barked suddenly.

"A dog too?" she said. "So you are fond of animals . . . Catherine?"

"Yes, very. I'm sure everyone will be fond of Friday." I was aware of a movement high in the wall and I looked up quickly to a gallery.

"That's the minstrels' gallery," Gabriel explained. "We sometimes use it when we have a ball."

"We adhere to old customs here, Catherine," said Ruth. "I hope you're not going to find us too old-fashioned."

"I am sure I shall enjoy old customs very much."

"I hope so. When there are traditions . . ."

I fancied her voice was a little sardonic and I wondered whether she was suggesting that I could not possibly understand the traditions which belonged to a family such as theirs.

Ruth's cool welcome was increasing my apprehension, and I wondered afresh what Gabriel's reason had been for withholding the news of our marriage.

A manservant appeared, to ask about our luggage, and Gabriel said: "Take it up to my room, William."

"Ay, master," was the answer.

He mounted the stairs with my trunk on his shoulder and Gabriel took my arm and we followed him. Ruth came after us and I could feel her eyes on my back, taking in every detail. I was never more pleased with Uncle Dick than at that moment. My smart traveling costume of dark blue gaberdine gave me confidence.

At the top of the flight of stairs was a door and Gabriel said: "That's the door to the minstrels' gallery." I hoped he would throw it open and that I should see whether someone were there, because I was certain that I had seen a movement in the gallery, and I wondered what member of the household had preferred to hide there to take a glimpse of me instead of coming down to welcome me.

It was a wide staircase of great beauty, but in the light of oil lamps it seemed full of shadows. I had an uncanny feeling as I went up that all the members of this family who had lived in the house over the last three hundred years were watching me with disapproval—the girl whom Gabriel had brought into the house without consulting his family.

"My rooms," Gabriel told me, "are at the top of the house. It's a long climb."

"Will you keep these rooms now that you have a wife?" asked Ruth from behind me.

"I certainly shall. Unless of course Catherine does not like them."

"I feel sure I shall."

"There are others to choose from if you are not satisfied," Ruth told me.

We had climbed to the second floor when a young man appeared. He was tall and slim and very like Ruth. He had cried: "Are they here yet, Mother? What's she . . ." before he saw us. He paused, not in the least embarrassed, laughing at himself, while his eyes went to me.

"This is Luke . . . my nephew," said Gabriel.

"My son," murmured Ruth.

"I am delighted to meet you," I said, and held out my hand.

"He took it and bowed over it so that a lock of his long fair hair fell forward over his face.

"The delight then is mutual," he said with a faint drawl. "It's amusing to have a wedding in the family."

He was very like his mother, and that meant that he was like Gabriel too. The same rather prominent, aristocratic features, the delicate fairness, the almost languid air.

"What do you think of the house?" he asked eagerly.

"She has been in it less than ten minutes and has not seen a tenth of it—and what she has seen has not been in daylight," his mother reminded him.

"Tomorrow I will take you on a tour of inspection," he promised me, and I thanked him.

He bowed once more and stood aside for us to pass; but when we went on he joined the procession and accompanied us to the rooms on the third floor which I gathered had always been Gabriel's.

We came to a circular gallery, and the feeling that I was being watched was stronger than ever; for here were the family portraits, life-sized; three or four rose-quartz lamps were burning and in this dim light the figures had the appearance of reality.

"Here we are," said Gabriel, and I felt the pressure on my arm; I heard Friday in his basket then; he whimpered faintly as though reminding me of his presence. I believed that Friday sensed my moods and knew that I felt as though I were being enclosed in an alien prison, and that I was resented here. Of course, I reminded myself, it was due to the fact that we had arrived in the twilight. It would have been quite different if we had come on a bright and sunny morning. There was too much atmosphere in these ancient houses; and at nightfall the shadows came to plague those whose imaginations were too vivid. I was in an extraordinary position. I was eventually to be the mistress of this house, and three days ago no one in it had been aware of my existence. No wonder I was resented.

I shook off the uncanny feeling, turned my back on the portraits and followed Gabriel through a door on the right and into a corridor. We went along this until we came to a door which Gabriel threw open. I gave a gasp of pleasure, for I was standing on the threshold of a charming room. The heavy red damask curtains had been drawn across the windows; a fire was burning in a big open fireplace and, on the mantelpiece which was of beautifully carved white marble, candles in gleaming silver candlesticks were burning and throwing a soft light about the room. I saw the four-poster bed with curtains to match those at the windows, the tallboy, the chairs with tapestry backs worked in gold and red; there were red rugs which seemed to be flecked with gold; and the general effect was of warmth. On a table was a bowl of red roses.

Gabriel looked at them and flushed. Then he said: "Thank you, Ruth."

"There was too little time to do much."

"This is a beautiful room," I said.

She nodded. "It's a pity you can't see the view from the window."

"She will in an hour or so," put in Gabriel. "The moon will be up then."

I felt my fears evaporating.

"I'm going to leave you now," said Ruth. "I'll have hot water sent up; and could you be ready to dine in three quarters of an hour?"

I said we could; and she and Luke left us. As the door shut on them Gabriel and I looked at each other in silence.

Then Gabriel said: "What's wrong, Catherine? You don't like it, do you?"

"It's so magnificent," I began. "I didn't imagine . . ." Then I could not restrain my resentment. "Why on earth didn't you tell them you were getting married!"

He flushed and looked distressed, but I was determined to know the truth.

"Well, I didn't want any fuss. . . ."

"Fuss!" I interrupted. "But I thought you went back to tell them."

"So I did."

"And you found you couldn't . . . when it came to the point?"

"There might have been opposition. I didn't want that."

"You mean they wouldn't have thought me worthy to marry into their family?" I knew that my eyes were flashing; I was both angry and miserable; this was such a disappointing beginning to my life in this house. I was hurt with Gabriel, and very depressed because I was realizing that the fact that my marriage had to be kept a secret until it was a *fait accompli* meant I was not going to live on very easy terms with my new family.

"Good heavens, no!" cried Gabriel emphatically. He caught me by the shoulders, but somewhat impatiently I freed myself. "They'll be delighted . . . once they know you. They don't like change, though. You know what families are."

"No," I retorted, "I don't. And they are distressed, which is natural. The idea of having me suddenly produced as a new member of the family! I can understand how they feel."

"But you don't understand, Catherine," Gabriel said pleadingly.

"Then tell me," I flashed at him. "Explain. Why does there have to be this mystery?"

He looked very unhappy. "But there is no mystery. It's simply that I didn't tell them. I didn't want fuss and bother. I wanted to marry you as quickly as possible so that we could be together and make the most of all the time that's left."

When he spoke like that all my anger disappeared. That softness, that desire to make him happy because he was afraid of something in life (perhaps it was of death) enveloped me. It was because of this desire that I had married him. I vaguely understood then that he was afraid of something in this house, and that he wanted an ally. I was to be that ally. I knew because, although I had been in Kirkland Revels less than half an hour, I was catching that fear.

"Friday's still in his basket," I said.

"I'll take him outside." He opened the basket and Friday jumped out, barking his pleasure to be free. There was a knock and I turned sharply, for the sound did not come from the door by which we had entered. I noticed then that there were two doors in this room.

A voice in a broad Yorkshire accent said: "Hot water, master."

The door was shut before I had a chance to see the owner of the voice.

"That's the old powder closet," said Gabriel indicating the door. "I use it for my ablutions. You'll find it useful. Lock both doors before you disrobe. One of the servants might come in."

He fastened the leash on Friday. "You don't want to lose yourself on your first evening, Friday," he said. And when he had gone I went into the powder closet and there I saw the hip bath, the cans of hot water, the soap and towels. A big mirror in an ornate gilded frame was fixed to the wall, and attached to this frame were two gilded candlesticks in which candles burned.

I looked at myself in the mirror. My eyes appeared to be more green than usual, and I found that they quickly strayed from my reflection and were looking over my shoulder, probing the shadowy corners of the powder room.

Old houses in twilight . . . Was it possible that in such places the presence of those long dead lingered?

What ridiculous thoughts for a sensible young Yorkshire woman to entertain.

I took off my costume and began to wash the stain of travel from my person. Tomorrow, in daylight, I should laugh at my fancies.

We dined that night in a pleasant room on the first floor.

Gabriel had explained that on ceremonial occasions dinner was served in the hall. That was because the hall had been used for that purpose when the house had been built. "The refectory table down there is as old as the house itself. But we have a small and more comfortable dining room for the family," he added.

It was a large room by Glen House standards; the curtains were drawn when I entered and there were candles on the table. I could see that living here was going to be a somewhat formal affair.

There were six of us at dinner. This was the family. Ruth and Luke I had already met. I now encountered Gabriel's father, Sir Matthew Rockwell, and his aunt, Miss Sarah Rockwell; they both seemed very old, being in their eighties.

As soon as I met Sir Matthew I began to feel happier because he was quite obviously pleased to see me. He had been very tall but stooped a little; his hair was plentiful and quite white; his face was ruddy but too much of the port wine shade to be healthy; and his blue eyes, embedded so deeply in folds of flesh that they had almost disappeared, were bright—one might say jaunty.

"Gabriel's lucky to have such a beautiful wife," he said. Surely this was flattery, for I was not beautiful and could not seem so even to old men of eighty. He kept my hand in his and then kissed it lingeringly. I guessed that he was not too old for gallantry; he gave the impression that he had enjoyed life and hoped the young members of his family would follow his example.

"You must sit beside me," he said. "I want to look at you and hear you tell me what you think of your new family."

So I sat beside him at the dinner table and every now and then he would lean towards me and pat my hand.

Aunt Sarah was quite different although I recognized the Rockwell features and fairness. Her blue eyes were vacant and she had an air of strain as though she were desperately trying to understand what was going on about her and could not quite catch up with it all.

I imagined her to be even older than her brother.

"Sarah," shouted Sir Matthew, "this is my new daughter."

Sarah nodded and gave him a smile that was sweet in its innocence. I wished I had met these older people first. Then I should have felt I was being warmly welcomed.

"What is your name?" she asked.

"Catherine," I told her.

She nodded; and whenever I looked up, I found her eyes upon me.

Sir Matthew wanted to hear about our meeting and the suddenness of our decision to marry. I told him about Friday.

"Gypsies," he said. "They can be brutal to their animals. I won't have them on my land. I must say it was a lucky day for Gabriel when he rode that way."

Luke said: "He was always going away . . . riding off . . . and we never knew when he was coming back."

"Why not?" said Gabriel. "It's the way to take a holiday. I hate making plans. You anticipate the pleasures of getting away and it invariably disappoints. No. Go as the spirit moves you . . . that's my motto."

"And look how well it turned out!" pointed out Sir Matthew, smiling at me.

"I must show Claire my tapestry. She'd like to see it," said Sarah.

There was a brief silence. Then Ruth said quietly: "This is Catherine, Aunt. Not Claire."

"Of course . . . of course . . ." murmured Sarah. "Are you interested in tapestry, dear?"

"I admire it, but I don't excel at it. I'm not very handy with my needle."

"I should think not," retorted Sir Matthew. "You don't want to strain those fine eyes of yours." He leaned towards me, his old hand caressing mine. "My sister is a bit forgetful. She wanders at times into the past." He grimaced. "No longer young . . . like myself alas!"

They talked of the house, of the country surrounding it, of the stables—which I was glad to hear were well stocked—of their neighbors, friends, county hunts and life generally in Kirkland Moorside; and I felt then that they were doing their best to make me welcome, and that perhaps it was the strangeness of Gabriel which had made me doubt this in the beginning.

Ruth said that before the end of the week there would be a dinner party to celebrate our marriage, and that she would have arranged it for this evening had there been time.

"There are certain people you must meet," she said. "They will be most eager to meet *you*."

"Whom do you propose to ask?" Gabriel put in quickly.

"Well . . . Simon, I suppose. After all, he's part of the family. We shall have to ask Hagar too, but I doubt whether she'll come. And I thought perhaps the vicar and his wife, and of course the Smiths."

Sir Matthew nodded. Then he turned to me. "We want you to feel at home, my dear, without delay."

I thanked him and when the meal was over, Ruth, Sarah and I retired to a nearby drawing room leaving the men to their port. I was glad that they did not leave us long, for I felt uncomfortable with Gabriel's sister and aunt.

Gabriel came to my side immediately and remarked that I looked tired.

"No doubt it has been a busy day," murmured Ruth. "We shall all understand if you retire early."

I said good night to the members of my new family and Gabriel and I went up to our room at the top of the house.

Friday came out of his basket to greet us as we entered the room. It was clear that he too was finding it difficult to adjust himself to his new surroundings.

"Well," said Gabriel, "the worst is over. You've met the family."

"Not all, apparently."

"The rest are on the fringe. These are the ones you'll have to live with. Before we retire I want to show you the view from the balcony."

"Oh yes . . . your balcony. Where is it?"

"At the end of our corridor. Come now."

He put his arm about me and we left our room and went to the end of the corridor where there was a door. He opened this and we stepped onto the balcony. The moon was high in the sky and it shone its light on the scene about us. I saw the Abbey ruins like a great ghost of its former self. I saw the dark river winding through the grassland and the black hump of the bridge, and beyond, away in the distance, the shadowy outline of the moor.

"It's beautiful," I breathed.

"When I'm away from here I dream of this view."

"I'm not surprised."

"Every night I come and look. I always have since I was a child. It has a fascination for me." He looked down suddenly. "Two of my ancestors threw themselves over parapets—not this one. There are three others in the house."

I felt a shiver run along my spine and I looked down into the dimness below.

"We're at the top of the house," said Gabriel. "It was certain death to leap over onto the flagstones below. The only two suicides in our history . . . and both chose the same method."

"Come along in," I said. "I'm tired."

But when we entered the room I felt my fear returning. Those moments on the balcony had done that, those chance words of Gabriel's. I was certainly strung up, which was unusual for me. But all would be well tomorrow, I promised myself.

During the next two days I explored the house and the surrounding country. I was fascinated—at times enchanted, at times repelled. I enjoyed being in the house during the daytime, and I was continually losing my way in it; but when dusk fell—I am ashamed to admit—the habit of looking furtively over my shoulder when I was alone persisted.

I had never stayed in such a large or ancient house; when one was alone the present seemed to merge into the past; it was because so much of the furniture had been in the house for centuries and one could not get away from the idea that this was exactly how it had looked hundreds of years ago, when other footsteps, other voices had been heard, other figures had made those long shadows on the walls.

It was absurd to be influenced by such fancies when the people in the house were normal enough; I had them all clearly docketed in my mind within those first days: Sir Matthew, jolly old squire fond of good food, wine and women, a typical country squire of this or any other century; Aunt Sarah, the spinster who had always lived at home, somewhat innocent, remembering the birthdays, the triumphs and failures of every member of the family, and only now that she was growing old forgetting to whom they had happened and thinking now and then that Gabriel's new wife was her sister-in-law, Claire, long-dead wife of Sir Matthew; there was Ruth who had been mistress of the house since her mother had died, and naturally enough mildly resented the intruder; there was Luke, a young man absorbed in his own affairs as most young men were. A normal family similar to those which were to be found in many households throughout the country.

I had tried to make myself pleasant and I was sure I was succeeding. Ruth of course was the most difficult to reassure; I did want her to know that I had no intention of ousting her from her position. Heaven knew this house was large enough for us to live our separate lives in it. Sir Matthew was master of the house and she was his daughter, who had been mistress of the place since she came of age, had continued to live here after her marriage, and naturally had remained when she became a widow. I wanted her to know that I considered she had more right to be the chatelaine of Kirkland Revels than I had.

She told me of the dinner party she was planning, and I candidly replied that she must go ahead with her plans, for I had come from a very small household and had done no housekeeping, having but a short while before my marriage been at school.

This seemed to please her and I felt happy.

During that first morning Gabriel was with his father; I guessed there were certain business matters concerning the estate which had to be discussed, particularly as Gabriel had been away from home so long. I assured him that I was well able to take care of myself.

I planned to take Friday for a walk, for I was eager to explore the country and in particular to have a look at the Abbey ruins. But on my way downstairs I met Luke. He grinned at me in a friendly way and stooped to have a word with Friday. Friday was delighted to be taken notice of and there was no doubt that he took a fancy to Luke right from the first.

"I like dogs," Luke told me.

"You have none?"

He shook his head. "Who'd look after them when I am away? I was often away . . . at school, you know. Now I'm in the transitory period. I have left school and shall shortly be going to Oxford."

"Surely there are plenty of people to look after a dog while you're away?"

"I don't see it. If you have a dog it's your dog and you can't trust anyone else to look after it. Have you seen the house yet?" he asked.

"Not all of it."

"I'll take you on a conducted tour. You ought to know it. You'll get lost if you don't. It's so easy to take the wrong turning. Shall I show it to you?"

I was anxious to be friends, and I felt it was best to accept his invitation. Moreover I was eager to see the house, so I decided the walk could wait until the tour was over.

I had had no idea of the size of the house. I reckoned there must be at least a hundred rooms. Each of the four parts which made up that rectangle of stone was like a house in itself, and it certainly was easy to lose oneself.

"The story goes," Luke told me, "that one of our ancestors married four wives and kept them in separate houses; and for a long time none of them knew of the existence of the other three."

"It sounds like Bluebeard."

"Perhaps the original Bluebeard was a Rockwell. There are dark secrets in our history, Catherine. You've no idea what a family you've married into!"

His light eyes regarded me with amusement which was not untinged with cynicism; and I was reminded of Gabriel's decision not to tell the family that he was going to marry me. Of course they regarded me as a fortune hunter, for not only would Gabriel inherit this house but also the means which would enable him to live in such a place, as well as the title which, as the only son of his baronet father, would be his when the old man died.

"I'm beginning to learn," I told him.

I went through those rooms in a state of bewilderment—there were so many, and all had the high windows, the lofty ceilings often decorated with exquisite carving, the paneled walls, the furniture of another age. I saw the great cellars, the kitchens, where I met some of the servants who also seemed to eye me with a certain suspicion; I saw the other three balconies so like that near our own room; I examined the massive stone pillars which supported them, and the faces of gargoyles which seemed to grimace at me from everywhere.

"How fond they seemed to be of these devils and grotesques," I said.

"They were to scare off intruders," Luke told me. "You must admit they're somewhat scarifying. 'Keep off,' they seem to be saying. 'The devils of Kirkland will get you if you don't look out.'"

"Surely they sometimes wanted to *welcome* visitors," I murmured lightly.

"We must have been an inhospitable crowd, sufficient unto ourselves perhaps."

When we reached the gallery he took me round, explaining who the subjects were. There was the first Sir Luke who had built the place, a fierce-looking gentleman in armor. There were Thomas, Mark, John, several Matthews and another Luke.

"We always have biblical names," he said. "It's a feature of the family. Always Matthew, Mark, Luke and John, Peter, Simon, anything you can think of . . . even down to the Angel Gabriel. I often call him Angel, though he doesn't like it much. I think that was going a bit too far. A nice down-to-earth Mark or John would have been so much better. Now that's Sir Luke . . . he died young. He jumped over the balcony in the west wing."

I stared at the young man in the picture; they were all so lifelike, those pictures, that the lips seemed to move as I watched.

"And that," went on Luke, "is John who, about a hundred years after, decided he'd die the same way. He jumped over the balcony in the north wing. Strange, isn't it? Although I think he got the idea from that Luke."

I turned away. This talk made me feel uneasy. I was not sure why.

As I moved towards a woman in a feathered Gainsborough-type hat, I heard Luke's voice at my elbow. "My great-great-great-grand-mother. Only I'm not sure of the number of greats." I went on walking along the gallery.

"Oh, and here's your father-in-law himself," he added.

A younger Sir Matthew looked back at me; his flowing cravat was the essence of elegance as was his green velvet jacket; his complexion was ruddy, rather than port wine, his eyes slightly bigger than they were now, and I was sure that I had not been mistaken when I had judged him to have been something of a rake in his day. And beside him was a woman whom I knew to be his wife; she was beautiful in a frail way and there was an expression of resignation on her face. Gabriel's mother, I thought, who had died soon after his birth. And there was a picture of Gabriel himself, looking young and innocent.

"You'll be beside him," said Luke. "You'll be captured like the rest and held prisoner on canvas . . . so that in two hundred years' time the new lady of the house will come to look at you and wonder about you."

I shivered, and was conscious of a great desire to escape from him, to get out of the house, if only for half an hour, because the talk of suicides had oppressed me.

"Friday is impatient for his walk," I said. "I think perhaps that I should take him now. It is very good of you to have taken so much trouble to show me everything."

"But I have not shown you *everything!* There is a great deal more for you to see."

"I shall enjoy it more another time," I replied firmly.

He bowed his head. "When," he murmured, "it will be my pleasure to continue with our tour."

I went down the staircase, and halfway, turned to look back. Luke was standing by the portraits, watching me, looking as though he had but to step up into one of those frames to become one of them.

The rest of the day I spent with Gabriel. We went for a ride in the afternoon, right out onto the moors; and when we came back it was time to change for dinner, and the evening was spent like the previous one.

Before we retired for the night Gabriel took me out to the balcony, and as we stood for a while admiring that superb view I remarked that I had not yet visited the Abbey ruins and decided that I would do so the next day.

During the morning which followed Gabriel was again with his father and I wandered off with Friday; this time I went to the Abbey.

As I approached those ancient piles I was struck with wonder. It was a sunny morning; and here and there the stone glistened as though it had been set with diamonds. I could have believed that this was not a ruin, for the great tower was intact and so was the wall which was facing me; it was not until I had come close that I realized there was no roof but the sky. The Abbey nestled in the valley close to the river and I guessed that it would be more sheltered from the storms than the Revels was. Now I saw clearly the high Norman tower, the ancient buttresses and the nave which, like the tower, was almost intact, apart from the fact that there was no roof. I was surprised at the vastness of the ruins and I thought how interesting it would be to make a plan of the Abbey and try to rebuild it in the imagination. Friday was running to and fro in great excitement as though he shared my emotions about the place. Here, I told myself, was a shell; yet there were enough stones to indicate which parts were the kitchens, for instance, the cloister, the nave, the transept, the monks' quarters.

It was necessary to tread warily, for here and there stones jutted dangerously out of the ground. I lost Friday for a moment and was immediately conscious of a panic which was quite ridiculous; equally so was my relief when, after I had called to him, he came running back to me.

I wondered from what part of the Abbey the stones had been taken to build the house. I wanted to learn something of the history of this house and the family to which I now belonged. I laughed at myself. There was so much I did not know about my own husband. Why was he so secretive with me? Why was there this constant feeling that he was hiding something from me?

I sat down on a ridge of stones, obviously all that was left of a room of some sort—the monks' dorter, I hazarded—and I told myself then that I had not thought enough of Gabriel since I had arrived here. Naturally Gabriel would be full of odd fancies; he was a young man who was afflicted with a disease of the heart which threatened his life. It was for that reason that he was moody. He was afraid of death—and I had thought it was something in the house, something in these old ruins which disturbed him! How should *I* feel if Death were round the corner, waiting for me? That was something which one could not imagine until it happened to one.

I would make Gabriel happy. Moreover I would not accept the inevitability of death as he seemed to. I would take such care of him that he would live on.

Friday's barking startled me out of my daydream. I called: "Friday! Friday!"

And as he did not come to me I went to look for him.

I found him in the hands of a strange man; he was struggling and, if he had not been so expertly held, he would have bitten those hands which imprisoned him.

"Friday," I called. Then the man who held him turned to look at me. He was of medium height and I was struck by his brilliant dark eyes and olive complexion.

He released the dog when he saw me, and taking off his hat bowed. Friday ran to me, barking furiously and, as I came forward, stood between me and the stranger as though to protect me.

"So the dog is yours, madam," said the man.

"Yes, what happened? He's usually so friendly."

"He was a little annoyed with me." I noticed the flash of very white teeth in that dark face. "He didn't understand that I probably saved his life."

"How was that?"

He turned and pointed to what I saw now was a well.

"He was perilously perched on the edge, looking down. If he had decided to explore further, that would have been the end of him."

"Then I have to thank you."

He inclined his head. "This was the monks' well. It's deep—and probably not very sweet down there."

I peered over into the darkness. I was looking down the narrow well, to what might have been water at the bottom.

"He's rather inquisitive," I said.

"I should put him on a lead when you bring him here again. And you will come here again, won't you? I can see this place intrigues you. You have a look in your eyes which betrays your interest."

"Surely everyone would be interested."

"Some more than others. May I introduce myself? I believe I know you. You are Mrs. Gabriel Rockwell, are you not?"

"But how did you know?"

He spread his hands and smiled again; it was a warm, friendly smile. "A simple deduction. I knew you were due to arrive and, as I know almost everyone in these parts, I put two and two together and tried a guess."

"Your guess was correct."

"Then welcome to our community. My name is Deverel Smith. Doctor. I am at the Revels almost every day, so we should have met sooner or later."

"I have heard you mentioned."

"Pleasantly, I hope?"

"Very much so."

"I'm an old friend of the family as well as the doctor; and of course Sir Matthew and Miss Rockwell are no longer young. They both need my services rather frequently. Tell me, when did you arrive?"

I told him and he listened gravely. I thought there was a foreign look about him but his name was as English as it could be; I supposed he seemed so dark because of the extreme fairness of my new relations.

He said: "I was going to call at the Revels today. Shall we walk back together?"

We did so and he made me feel that I had found a new friend.

He talked familiarly of the family, and when he spoke of Gabriel there was an anxious note in his voice. I knew what that meant and I wanted to speak to him about Gabriel's health, but I refrained from doing so. Later, I promised myself. He would be easy to talk to.

He told me that he had been invited to dine at the house on Saturday. "My daughter and I," he added.

I was astonished that he should have a daughter old enough to be invited to a dinner party. He saw my surprise and I liked him no less because he appeared to be pleased by it. I had thought he was somewhere in his mid-thirties, but decided he must be older than that.

"I have a seventeen-year-old daughter," he said. "She enjoys parties. My wife is not well enough to attend them, so she and I go together."

"I shall look forward to meeting her."

"Damaris is looking forward to meeting you." He smiled.

"Damaris! That is an unusual name."

"You like it? It's from the Bible. Just a brief mention . . . but it's there."

I remembered what Luke had said about biblical names, and I wondered if it was a custom in this part of the world to take names

from the Bible. I was about to mention this; then I remembered that
Madame la Directrice had said that my impetuosity often verged on
bad manners, so I restrained myself.

We went into the Revels together. The doctor sent one of the servants to tell Ruth he had arrived; and I went up to my room.

I wore a white gown on the night of the dinner party. It was the
only real evening dress I possessed, and I told myself that if entertaining at the Revels was going to be on a lavish scale I should have
to get some new clothes. The dress was of white chiffon and lace, very
simple, as became a young woman. I had no qualms about it because I knew that the few clothes I had were perfectly cut and would
appear elegant in any company. I did my hair in the coronet style
which Gabriel liked so much; then I waited for him to come in and
dress, for time was passing.

As he did not come, I wondered whether he was still out and I
went onto the balcony to see if he were in the grounds. He was nowhere in sight, but I heard the sound of voices coming from the
porch.

I was about to call out and ask if Gabriel was there when I heard
a deep masculine voice say: "So I gather, Ruth, you have not taken
to our little bride?"

I drew back feeling the hot color rush into my cheeks. I knew that
listeners are said never to hear good of themselves. Fanny had told
me that often enough; but how difficult it is, when you overhear yourself being discussed far from flatteringly, to refrain from listening.

"It's early yet," answered Ruth.

There was a laugh. "I've no doubt she found our Gabriel easy
prey."

I did not hear Ruth's reply to that, but the voice went on: "Why
did you let him stray so far from home? He was bound to find some
little fortune hunter sooner or later."

I was furiously angry. I wanted to lean over the balcony and tell
whoever was speaking to come out where I could see him; I wanted
to tell him that I had had no idea of Gabriel's position when I had
married him.

I stood still, my eyes blazing. Then he stepped backwards a little,
and by leaning over the parapet I saw him. His hair was light brown
and he seemed excessively broad. There was a resemblance to the
Rockwells there, but it was faint. He stepped forward suddenly into
the house and was lost to view. I hated him, whoever he was.

I was trembling as I went back to our bedroom. Gabriel was already there. He was out of breath and had clearly been hurrying.

"I forgot the time," he said. "I shall have to look sharp. Where have you been? Why, you're dressed already."

It was on the tip of my tongue to tell him what I had heard, but I changed my mind. It would upset him and he was breathless now. No, I would fight my own battles; I should have to teach this relative, whoever he was, a lesson. So I helped Gabriel dress and when we went down I met my enemy.

He was Simon Redvers, the cousin; he looked less broad when seen on the level. He was very tall, a fact I had not fully realized looking down at him.

Gabriel introduced me, and when he took my hand, those cynical eyes looked straight into mine and I knew exactly what he was thinking. His eyes were light brown and his skin deeply bronzed; his mouth was smiling slightly but his eyes were not. I knew my own were flashing with anger, for I had never found it easy to restrain my feelings and I could not get the sound of his words out of my ears.

"How do you do?" he said.

"I am well, thank you," I answered.

"I suppose I should congratulate you."

"Pray do not, unless you wish to."

He was faintly amused, and I could not resist saying: "I believe we have met before."

"I am certain we have not."

"You may not have been aware of the meeting."

"If it had taken place, I am convinced, I should remember."

I matched my smile with his. He was puzzled and he said: "It is the Rockwell resemblance, no doubt. You'll find it again and again in these parts."

I guessed he was referring to the amorous proclivities of his ancestors, and I thought this indelicate so I turned away.

There was fortunately a diversion created by the arrival of Dr. Smith and his daughter.

The doctor was already a friend. He came over to me and greeted me warmly. I was pleased to give my attention to him, but the girl who accompanied him immediately claimed it, and, I imagine, that of everyone in the room.

Damaris Smith was one of the loveliest creatures I had ever seen. She was of medium height and very dark—her hair smooth and silky with that blackness which has a sheen of blue in it, like a bird's wing.

Her eyes were black, long and languorous, her skin olive; and the shape of her face was a perfect oval; her lips were delicately formed yet sensuous; her teeth white; her nose almost aquiline, giving dignity as well as beauty. But it was not merely her face which caught and held the attention. It was her slim, lissome body also; all her movements were full of grace. She was a joy to look at. Dressed in white, as I was, she wore a gold belt about her tiny waist and in her ears were gold Creole earrings.

There was silence as she entered—the silence which was homage to her beauty.

I asked myself: Why did Gabriel marry me when there was such a goddess on his very doorstep?

The effect she had on everyone was apparent. Her father obviously adored her, for his eyes rarely left her; Luke, I imagined, was less nonchalant than usual; Simon Redvers seemed to watch her almost speculatively. Already I disliked him intensely, seeing in him a type I could never tolerate. He would be a man to scorn sentiment; he would be practical in the extreme; he would be unimaginative, believing everyone else looked at life with the same calculating gaze; there was great virility there. His personality was overpowering so that it dominated the company in its masculine way as Damaris's beauty did in the feminine. Sir Matthew's admiration was apparent; but then he admired all women, it seemed; and during that dinner party he divided his attention between myself and Damaris.

Damaris herself I did not fully understand; she was a quiet person, who had a smile for everyone and did not seek in the least to call attention to herself, which was of course unnecessary. The first impression she gave was that she was merely an innocent girl; I don't know what made me feel that that smooth, rather expressionless perfection was a mask.

The dinner was in honor of Gabriel and myself, and our health was drunk. Apart from the family there were the Smiths, Simon Redvers, the vicar and his wife and two other local people, neighbors, I gathered, rather than great friends.

I was asked what I thought of the house and the countryside, and Simon Redvers wanted to know how it compared with that part from which I had come. I answered that when not at school I had lived as close to the moor as they did, so that the change was not very great. I believe a note of asperity came into my voice when I addressed the man, that he noticed it and it amused him.

He, who was sitting next to me at dinner, leaned to me and said:

"You must have your portrait painted so that it can be added to those in the gallery."

"Is that necessary?"

"Indeed yes. Have you not seen the gallery? All the masters of Kirkland Revels are painted and hung with their wives beside them."

"There's plenty of time for that."

"You'll make a good subject."

"Thank you."

"Proud . . . strong . . . determined."

"So you read character?"

"When it is there for me to see."

"I had no idea that I had such a legible face."

He laughed. "It's unusual in one so young. Don't you agree that as one grows older fate . . . life . . . whatever you call it . . . is like a mischievous artist, gradually etching the lines of betrayal?" He gazed along the table; I refused to follow his gaze, but looked down at my plate. I thought his manners too candid, and I wanted him to know this. "I believe you doubt my word," he insisted.

"I believe what you say to be true, but is it not a little embarrassing—even impertinent—to test the theory on the present company?"

"You'll discover that I'm a blunt Yorkshireman; and they are not noted for their tact."

"Why speak of the future? I have already made the discovery."

I saw the smile touch his lips again; I thought it rather a brutal smile. He enjoyed baiting me because I was a worthy opponent. At least I had the satisfaction of knowing that; even if he did consider me a fortune hunter, he did not find me a simpering one. I came to the conclusion in that moment that he had a grudging admiration for me, partly because he believed I had endeavored to catch Gabriel, as he would put it, and had achieved my object. There was a ruthlessness in him which would always admire success.

I said impulsively: "You are Gabriel's cousin, or second cousin, are you not? Yet how unlike him you are! You are absolute opposites."

He gave me that cool, appraising smile again. I was telling him that I did not like him; and he was retaliating by implying that I would not have caught him as I had caught Gabriel. As if I should have wanted to! As if there had been any "catching" in our marriage!

"Talking of faces," he said, "you've looked at the gallery. What a splendid example of the revelations of physiognomy. You can see old Sir John who went on fighting for his King to the fury of Crom-

well. He lost us the Revels for a while, that one. You can see his ob-
stinate idealism in his face. Then there's Sir Luke, the gambler who
nearly gambled away our inheritance. And then there's that other
Luke, and John . . . the suicides. If you look long enough you can
read their histories in their faces. Take that Luke for instance. You
see the weakness of the mouth. You can imagine him, finding life
too difficult and standing there on the west balcony, and suddenly
. . . over . . ."

I realized then that the others at the table had become silent and
were listening to Simon.

Sir Matthew leaned forward and patted my arm. "Don't listen to
my nephew," he said. "He's telling you about our disreputable ancestors. Simon's annoyed because he's a Rockwell on the distaff side
. . . and the Revels is not for him."

I saw that inscrutable gleam in Simon's eyes and said: "I daresay
you have a pleasant residence of your own."

"Kelly Grange!" Sir Matthew almost spat out the words. "The
Redvers family were always jealous of the Revels." He pointed to
Simon. "His grandfather married one of my sisters but she wouldn't
stay away from the Revels. She was always coming back and bringing
first her son, then her grandson with her. Don't see you here so often
now, Simon."

"I must remedy that," said Simon; and he was smiling ironically
at me.

There was a deep chuckle from Sir Matthew which seemed to
shock the vicar and his wife.

So the conversation progressed and, in spite of my dislike of my
neighbor at the dinner table, I was a little sorry when it was over; I
enjoyed a battle, and I was enjoying mine with him—although it was
merely one of words. I told myself that I particularly disliked those
people who were ready to be critical before they knew the truth. I
was sure Simon Redvers was one of these.

After dinner the ladies retired to the drawing room and I tried to
get to know Damaris, but it was not easy; she was pleasant, but so
reserved that she made little effort to help with the conversation, and
I decided that a blank mind lay behind that lovely face. I was pleased
when the men joined us; and when Simon Redvers kept at Damaris's
side—rather to the chagrin of Luke—I was glad and gave myself up
to conversation with the vicar, who told me how the grounds of the
Revels were used for the Church annual garden party and that he and
his wife were trying to arrange to do a miracle play or a pageant in

the Abbey ruins next Midsummer Night's eve. He hoped that I would support their endeavors, and I told him that I should be delighted to do all I could.

It was shortly after dinner that Sir Matthew was taken ill. He lay back in his chair, his face a deeper purple than usual. Dr. Smith was immediately at his side, and with the help of Simon and Luke took Sir Matthew to his room. The incident naturally broke up the party, but when Dr. Smith rejoined us he told us that Sir Matthew would be all right. He was going back to his home for leeches. Sir Matthew always insisted on being bled in the manner his father had been before him.

"He'll be about again in a day or so," the doctor assured us before he left.

But the party spirit had gone and we sat on talking desultorily.

When Gabriel and I retired it was about eleven-thirty. He put his arms about me and told me that I had been a success and he was proud of me.

"I'm not sure that I was very popular with everybody," I said.

"Who could fail to be charmed?"

"That cousin of yours for one."

"Oh, Simon! He was born a cynic. He is jealous. He'd throw away Kelly Grange for the Revels any day. You wait till you see the Grange. It is not half the size of the Revels—it's an ordinary old manor house."

"I don't understand why his desire for the Revels should affect his attitude toward me."

"Perhaps he's jealous of me for more reasons than one."

"How absurd!"

At that moment Friday ran to the door and began barking furiously while he leaped at the door as though he would break it down.

"What on earth's the matter with him?" I cried.

Gabriel had turned pale. "Someone's out there," he whispered.

"It's evidently someone Friday doesn't like." I turned to Friday. "Be quiet, Friday."

But Friday for once ignored me; he continued to bark and jump frenziedly up at the door.

I picked him up and opened the door. "Who's there?" I called.

There was no answer, but Friday was struggling out of my arms.

"Something has disturbed him," I said. "I'm going to put him on his lead. I don't want him jumping over the balcony."

Still holding him I went back to the room for his lead and slipped it on; and when I set him down he tugged at it with all his might.

He dragged me along the corridor, but before we reached the balcony door he leaped at another to the left of it. I tried this and it opened easily. It was a large empty cupboard, and Friday ran into it and began sniffing round.

I opened the balcony door, and there was no one on the balcony either.

"You see, Friday," I said, "it's nothing. What is it that's bothering you?"

I returned with him to the bedroom. Gabriel had his back to me as I entered the room. When he turned I saw how pale he was; and a terrible thought came to me then: He was afraid of what was out there and he had let me go alone. Was the man I had married a coward?

It was a horrible thought which I discarded almost as soon as it entered my head.

"Much ado about nothing," I said lightly.

Friday appeared completely to have satisfied himself; when I took him off the lead, he leaped into his basket and curled up there.

As I prepared myself for bed I wondered what Gabriel had been so disturbed about.

Then I remembered the conversation at dinner and I asked myself whether Gabriel had thought it was a ghost prowling out there. The balcony certainly had a morbid attraction for him.

But in a house like this fancies came easily.

It was late during the next afternoon when I discovered that Friday was missing. I remembered then that I had not seen him since the morning. It had been a busy morning, for the guests of the previous night all paid duty calls to give conventional thanks.

I saw Simon Redvers ride up on a magnificent gray horse, and I decided to stay in my room until he had left; I did not see him leave and was afraid that I should find he was staying to luncheon; however, when I went down he had gone. Dr. Smith and Damaris had ridden over in his brougham—the doctor to see how Sir Matthew was after his attack, Damaris to pay her duty call. With all the guests arriving it seemed like a continuation of the party.

It was just before dinner when I began to be anxious about Friday's absence. Dinner was a solemn meal that evening and there was little conversation. Sir Matthew was still in his room and I guessed that everyone was worried on his account although they assured me that such turns were frequent.

When the meal was over and there was still no sign of Friday, I was really alarmed. I went up to our room; his basket, with the folded blanket, was neat and had clearly not been used by him. Was it possible that he was lost?

I wondered if he had been stolen, and when I thought of the ill treatment he had received at the hands of the gypsy woman I felt sick with worry. It was possible that there were gypsies not far from Kirkland Moorside, for the moor was always an attraction to them.

I slipped on a light coat and went downstairs, intending to ask Gabriel to come with me to look for him, but as I could not find him I went out alone, calling Friday as I did so.

I found my footsteps wandering towards the Abbey. At any other time I might have found it awe-inspiring; on this evening my thoughts were all for Friday.

I kept calling his name, straining my ears for an answering bark. There was nothing.

It was an uncanny experience to stand there among those ruins . . . alone. It had been a glorious day and there were signs of a fine day to follow. The old saying came into my head: Red sky at night, shepherds' delight.

Then suddenly the fear came to me. I felt that I was not alone; that through those narrow slits, which had once been windows, eyes watched me. The glow from the sky touched the stones so that they looked rosy; and the ridiculous fancy came to me that life was being breathed into them.

I did not know what had happened to me, but I expected to hear the chanting of monks as they walked down the nave. I felt my heart hammering as I looked up at the arches through which I glimpsed the blood-red sky. I imagined that somewhere, not far distant, I heard a stone dislodged and following that, a footstep.

"Who's there?" I called; and the hollow sound of my own voice startled me.

I looked about me. There was nothing but those piles of stones, those half-walls, those rectangles of brick within which the grass grew. Here a community of men had lived long ago and I could almost believe that I was moving back in time, that the half-walls would become walls in their entirety, that a roof would appear to shut out the sky and this nineteenth century.

I began to call Friday again, and I noticed that it had become considerably darker than when I had first entered the ruins. Evening skies change rapidly, and the red was now streaked with gray. The sun had disappeared and soon darkness would descend upon me . . . and the Abbey.

I tried to leave by the way I had come—at least I thought it was the way I had come, but after a few minutes I realized that I was in a section of the ruins which I had not visited before. I saw part of a staircase, leading down to darkness; I turned and hurried away; I tripped over a ridge of stone and only saved myself in time. I had a horrible fear of breaking an ankle and being forced to spend the night here . . . a prisoner. I began to feel faint at the thought of it.

This was most unlike myself. What is this? I demanded. Nothing but bricks and grass. Why be afraid? But what was the use? I *was* afraid.

I blundered on. My one thought, my great desire, was to escape from the ruins of Kirkland Abbey.

It was only now that I had lost my way that I became fully aware of the vastness of the place; and there was a time during that nocturnal adventure when I thought I should never find my way out of the maze of stone. With every passing second the light was fading and I was so anxious to get away from the place that I panicked and lost my sense of direction.

At length when I did escape I came out on the far side of the Abbey and it was now between me and the house.

Nothing would have induced me to go back the way I had come, which would have been difficult in any case, for I should have lost myself in that pile of stones. I ran on swiftly until I found a road. This I took and, guessing my direction, I hurried on, now and then breaking into a run.

As I came to a clump of trees through which the road wound, a figure emerged and for a moment I knew terror. Then it took on a familiar shape and a voice I knew said: "Hello! Have you got the devil at your heels?"

The note of mockery in that voice set annoyance swamping my fear.

"I lost my way, Mr. Redvers," I said. "But I think I'm on the right road now."

He laughed. "You are, but I can show you a short cut . . . if you'll allow me."

"Doesn't this road lead to the house?"

"It does . . . eventually. But if you cut through the trees here you come out about half a mile nearer. Will you allow me to escort you?"

"Thank you," I said stiffly.

We walked side by side and he fitted his step to mine.

"How did you come to be out alone at this hour?" he asked.

I told him that my dog had been out all the afternoon and evening, and I was anxious.

"You shouldn't wander too far alone," he reproved me. "You see how easy it is to lose yourself."

"Had it been day I should easily have found the right road."

"But it was not day. As for the dog, doubtless he has found a little companion somewhere. Dogs will be dogs."

I did not answer him; we had come through the trees and I saw the house. In five minutes we were there.

Gabriel, Ruth, Luke and Dr. Smith were in the grounds. They were all looking for me. The doctor had come in to see Sir Matthew and had heard that I had disappeared.

Gabriel was so anxious that he was almost angry with me for the first time in our lives.

I breathlessly explained that I had been looking for Friday, had got lost among the ruins and met Simon Redvers on the way back.

"You shouldn't have gone out alone at dusk," said Dr. Smith gently.

"One of us would have gone with you!" Luke reproved me.

"I know," I said and smiled with relief because I was so happy to be back. I turned to Simon Redvers. "Thank you, Mr. Redvers," I went on.

He bowed ironically. "Such a pleasure," he murmured.

"Has Friday come home?" I asked Gabriel.

He shook his head.

"He'll turn up tomorrow," Luke put in.

"I do hope so," I answered.

Gabriel put his arm through mine. "There's nothing else we can do tonight. And you look exhausted. Come along in."

They all seemed to be watching us. I turned and said: "Good night."

There was an echoing answer as Gabriel drew me into the house.

"I've never seen you look so white and tired," he told me.

"I thought I should never get back."

He laughed and put his arm about me. He said suddenly: "Wasn't that honeymoon of ours wonderful! But it was very short; we ought to have a longer one. I've often thought I'd like to go to Greece."

"'The isles of Greece, the isles of Greece! Where burning Sappho loved and sung,'" I quoted, and my voice had a high pitch to it. Although I was worried about Friday I was very relieved to be safe, which seemed unaccountably foolish.

"I'm going to tell them to bring you some hot milk. It'll make you sleep," said Gabriel.

"Gabriel, I can't stop wondering about Friday."

"He'll turn up. You go to our room and I'll go to the kitchen to tell them to bring that milk."

I went on up, thinking how gentle he was, how considerate to the servants. They had so many stairs in a house of this nature to contend with.

When I reached our room, the first thing I noticed was Friday's empty basket and I felt very unhappy.

I went into the corridor and called him once more. I tried to comfort myself that he was hunting rabbits. It was a favorite pastime of his and I had known him forget everything when pursuing it. It might be that in the morning he would come home.

I did realize there was nothing more I could do that night so I undressed and got into bed.

So exhausted was I that I was almost asleep when Gabriel came in. He sat by the bed and talked about our trip to Greece; he seemed really excited about it. But soon one of the servants came in with my milk on a tray.

I did not really want it but I drank it off to please Gabriel, and in a few minutes I fell into a deep sleep.

I was awakened by a banging on my door. Reluctantly I awoke; rarely had I slept so deeply. I sat up in bed to find Ruth standing in the room. Her eyes looked enormous, her face was the color of white paper.

"Catherine," she was saying. "Wake up! Wake up, *please!*" And I knew something terrible had happened.

I looked for Gabriel but there was no sign of him.

"It's Gabriel," said Ruth. "You must prepare yourself for a shock."

"What . . . has happened to Gabriel?" I asked as though I found the greatest difficulty in getting out the words.

"He is dead," she said. "He has killed himself."

I did not believe her. I felt as though I was struggling out of a fantastic world of dreams.

Gabriel . . . dead? It wasn't possible. Why, only a short while ago he had sat by my bed watching me drink my milk, talking of our trip to Greece.

"You'll have to know," she said looking at me steadily; and was it with a hint of accusation in her eyes? "He threw himself over the parapet of the balcony. One of the grooms has just found him."

"It can't be true."

"You'd better get dressed," she said.

I stumbled out of bed; my limbs were trembling; one thought kept hammering in my brain. This is not true. Gabriel did not kill himself.

3

So within a week of my coming to Kirkland Revels tragedy had struck the house.

I do not clearly remember the sequence of the events of that day, but I can recall the numbness which took possession of me, the certainty that something inevitable had taken place, something which had threatened me, warned me from the moment I entered the house.

I remember lying on my bed during that first morning. Ruth had insisted that I should, and it was at this time that I learned what a forceful character she had. Dr. Smith came and gave me a sedative; he said it was necessary, and I slept until the afternoon.

I joined them in the room which was known as the winter parlor . . . one of the smaller rooms on the first floor which looked onto the courtyard and which was so called because during the winter it could be kept warmer and more cosy than those rooms which were less sheltered. The entire family was there: Sir Matthew, Aunt Sarah, Ruth, Luke; and Simon Redvers had joined them. I was conscious of the gaze of everyone as I entered.

"Come here, my dear," said Sr. Matthew. "This is a terrible shock to us and especially to you, my dear child."

I went to him because I trusted him more than any of the others; and when I sat down beside him, Aunt Sarah came over and, taking the chair on the other side of me, placed her hand over mine and kept it there.

Luke had walked to the window. He was saying tactlessly: "It was exactly like the others. He must have remembered them. All the time we were talking of them, he must have been planning . . ."

I said sharply: "If you mean Gabriel committed suicide, I don't believe it. I don't believe it for a moment."

"This is so terrible for you, my dear," murmured Sir Matthew.

Aunt Sarah came a little closer and leaned against me. There was a faint odor of decay about her.

"What do you believe happened?" she asked; and her blue eyes were bright and eager with curiosity.

I turned away from her. "I don't know," I cried. "I only know he didn't kill himself."

"My dear Catherine," said Ruth sharply, "you're overwrought. We all have the utmost sympathy for you, but . . . you knew him such a short time. He is one of *us* . . . all his life he has belonged to us. . . ."

Her voice broke, but I did not believe she was sincerely sorry. And I thought: The house will pass to Luke now. Are you pleased about that, Ruth?

"Last night he talked about the holiday we should have," I insisted. "He talked of our going to Greece."

"Perhaps he didn't want you to guess what he planned," suggested Luke.

"He couldn't deceive me. Why should he talk of going to Greece if he were planning to . . . do that!"

Simon spoke then. His voice sounded cold and seemed to come from a long distance. "We do not always say that which is in our minds."

"But I knew . . . I tell you, I knew . . ."

Sir Matthew had put a hand to his eyes and I heard him murmur: "My son, my only son."

There was a knock on the door and William entered.

He looked at Ruth and said: "Dr. Smith is here, madam."

"Then bring him in," Ruth answered.

And in a few moments Dr. Smith came in. His eyes were sympathetic and it was to my side that he came.

"I cannot express my grief," he murmured. "And I am concerned for you."

"Please don't be," I replied. "I have suffered a great shock . . . but I shall be all right." I heard myself give a slightly hysterical laugh which horrified me.

The doctor laid his hand on my shoulder.

"I'm going to give you a sedative for tonight," he said. "You'll need it. Then when you wake up there'll be a night between you and all this. You'll be one step away from it."

Aunt Sarah spoke suddenly in a high, rather querulous voice: "She doesn't believe he killed himself, Doctor."

"No . . . no . . ." soothed the doctor. "It's hard to credit it. Poor Gabriel!"

Poor Gabriel! It seemed like an echo in that room, and it came from more than one of those present.

I found myself looking at Simon Redvers. "Poor Gabriel!" he said, and there was a cold glitter in his eyes as they met mine. I felt I wanted to shout at him: Are you suggesting that I had anything to do with this? Gabriel was happier with me than he had ever been in his life. He told me so repeatedly.

But I said nothing.

Dr. Smith said to me: "Have you been out today, Mrs. Rockwell?"

I shook my head.

"A little walk in the grounds would do you good. If you would allow me to accompany you, I should be glad."

It was clear that he had something to say to me alone, and I rose at once.

"You should wear your cloak," Ruth put in. "There's a chill in the air today."

A chill in the air, I thought; and a chill in my heart. What would happen next? My life seemed suspended between Glen House and Kirkland Revels and the future was like a thick fog all about me.

Ruth had rung the bell and eventually a servant appeared with my cloak. Simon took it from the maid and wrapped it about me. I looked over my shoulder and tried to read what I saw in his eyes, but that was impossible.

I was glad to escape from that room and be alone with the doctor.

We did not speak until we had left the house and were walking in the direction of the Abbey. It was difficult to believe that it was only the night before that I had lost my way.

"My dear Mrs. Rockwell," said Dr. Smith, "I could see that you wished to get away from the house. That was one reason why I suggested this walk. You feel bewildered, do you not?"

"Yes," I said. "But there is one thing of which I am certain."

"You think it impossible that Gabriel killed himself?"

"Yes, I do."

"Because you were happy together?"

"We were happy together."

"I think it may have been because Gabriel *was* happy with you that he found life intolerable."

"I do not understand you."

"You know that his health was precarious."

"He told me that before we married."

"Ah, I thought perhaps he might have kept it from you. His heart was weak and he might have died at any moment. But you knew that."

I nodded.

"It's a family weakness. Poor Gabriel, it struck him young. I had a conversation with him only yesterday about . . . his weakness. I am wondering now whether this had something to do with the tragedy. May I be frank with you? You are very young but you are a married woman, and I am afraid I must speak."

"Please do."

"Thank you. I was struck from the first by your good sense and I rejoiced that Gabriel had chosen so wisely. Yesterday Gabriel came to me and asked me some questions about . . . his married life."

I felt a flush rise to my cheeks and said: "Pray tell me what you mean."

"He asked me if the state of his heart made it dangerous for him to indulge in marital relations."

"Oh!" My voice sounded faint and I could not bring myself to look at the doctor. We had reached the ruins and I stared up at the Norman tower. "And . . . what was your answer?"

"I told him that in my opinion he would take a considerable risk if such relations did occur."

"I see."

He was trying to read my thoughts, but I would not look at him. What had happened between me and Gabriel should, I decided, be our secret. I felt embarrassed to be involved in such a discussion and, although I reminded myself that this man was a doctor, the discomfort persisted. But I could see what he was driving at, and he had no need to explain; but he did.

"He was a normal young man, apart from this weakness of the heart. He was proud. I realized when I warned him that I was giving him a shock—but I did not understand then how deeply it had affected him."

"And you think that this . . . warning . . . decided him?"

"It seems to me a logical deduction. What . . . is your opinion,

Mrs. Rockwell? In the past, has there been between you . . .
er . . ."

I touched a fragment of broken wall, and my voice was as cold
as the stones as I said: "I do not think that what you told my husband
would have made him wish to end his life."

The doctor seemed satisfied with that answer. "I should not have
liked to think that any words of mine . . ."

"You need have no qualms," I answered. "What you said to Gabriel was what any doctor would have said."

"I believe it may have been a reason . . ."

"Do you mind if we turn back?" I asked. "It seems to have grown
colder."

"Forgive me. I should not have brought you out. You feel cold
because of the shock you have suffered. I'm afraid I've behaved
brutally to you, discussing this . . . indelicate matter . . . just
when . . ."

"No, you have been kind to me. But I am shocked . . . and I cannot believe that only this time yesterday . . ."

"Time will pass. Believe me, I know what I'm talking about. You
are so young. You will go away from here . . . at least I suppose
you will. . . . You won't stay shut away here, will you?"

"I do not know what I shall do. I have not thought about it."

"Of course you have not. I was saying that you have your life before you. In a few years' time this will seem like a bad dream."

"Some bad dreams one never forgets."

"Oh come, you must not be morbid. You are so close to tragedy
that it overwhelms you. You will feel a little better tomorrow, and a
little better every day."

"You forget I have lost my husband."

"I know, but . . ." he smiled and laid his hand on my arm. "If
there is anything I can do to help you . . ."

"Thank you, Dr. Smith. I shall remember your kindness."

We had returned to the grounds and walked across the front lawns
in silence. As we approached the house I looked up at the balcony
and pictured what might have happened. Gabriel, sitting by my bed,
talking of the holiday we would have, making me drink my hot milk
and then, when I slept, coming quietly out onto the balcony and letting himself fall. I shivered. "I don't believe it; I can't believe it."

I did not realize that I had spoken aloud until Dr. Smith said: "You
mean you don't want to believe it. Sometimes the two are synony-

mous. Do not fret, Mrs. Rockwell. I hope you will look on me as something more than the family doctor. I have been on terms of close friendship with the Rockwells for years, and you are now a member of that family. So do please remember that if you need my advice at any time, I shall be very happy to give it."

I scarcely heard him; I thought the faces of the devils looked glee-ful, those of the angels sad.

As I went in a feeling of desolation came over me, and I said quickly: "Friday is still missing."

The doctor looked blank and I realized that he had probably not heard of the dog's disappearance, for in view of what had happened who would have thought to tell him?

"I must find him," I went on.

I left him and hurried to the servants' hall to ask if Friday had been seen. No one had seen him. I went through the house calling him.

But there was no response.

So I had lost Gabriel and Friday . . . together.

At the inquest the verdict was that Gabriel had taken his life while temporarily insane, in spite of my insistence that we had been plan-ning to go to Greece. Dr. Smith explained that he had been suffer-ing from a weakness of the heart which depressed him. It was his opinion that his marriage had brought home to him the magnitude of his infirmity and the consequent depression had forced him to act as he had done.

This seemed to be considered an adequate reason and the verdict was given without demur. I was present at the inquest although Dr. Smith had advised me against going.

"You will only distress yourself further," he said. Ruth agreed with him. But I had quickly recovered from my shock and I found a certain resentment mingling with my sorrow. Why, I kept asking myself, were they all so certain that Gabriel had killed himself?

I answered that myself. How else could he have died? By acci-dent? I tried hard to think of how it could have happened. Could he have leaned too far over the parapet and fallen? Was that possible?

It must be possible, because it was the only reasonable explanation.

Over and over again I tried to picture it. Suppose he went onto the balcony as he so frequently did. Suppose something below caught his attention. Friday! I thought excitedly. What if Friday had ap-peared down there and Gabriel had called to him and in his excite-ment leaned over too far?

They had already passed their verdict and they would not have believed me. They would have called me an hysterical bride.

I had written to my father to tell him of Gabriel's death, and he came to the funeral. I had been pleased when I heard that he was coming, believing that he would have some comfort to offer me. Childishly I had expected that my trouble might bring us closer together; but as soon as I saw him I realized how foolish I had been. He was as remote as ever.

He sought an opportunity to speak to me before we left for the church, but I was conscious all the time that to him it was a painful duty.

"Catherine," he asked, "what are your plans?"

"Plans!" I echoed blankly, for I had not considered my future. I had lost the only two who had loved me—for as each day passed I began to despair of finding Friday—and I could think of nothing but my loss.

My father seemed a little impatient. "Yes, yes. You'll have to decide what you're going to do now. I suppose you could stay here or come back . . ."

I had never felt quite so lonely in the whole of my life. I kept thinking of Gabriel's solicitude for me, his eagerness to be with me every minute of the night and day. I thought: If only Friday would suddenly come bounding up to me, leaping into my arms, I might have something to plan for.

I said stonily: "I have made no plans so far."

"Perhaps it's early yet," he replied in his weary voice, "but if you should want to come back, you must of course."

I turned away from him; I could not trust myself to speak.

How melancholy it was when the hearse and carriages arrived with the plumed horses and velvet palls and the mutes dressed in black from head to foot. Gabriel was buried in the Rockwell vault in which lay so many of his ancestors. I wondered if those others were there —the two who had died in the same way.

I returned with the rest of the family to the house and we solemnly drank wine and ate the funeral meats which had been prepared for us. I felt a stranger in my widow's weeds. I was so pale that I looked like a ghost, and there seemed no color in my face except that of my vivid green eyes. Surely mine was a most extraordinary fate—to be a bride and widow in less than two weeks.

My father left immediately after the funeral saying that he had a long journey ahead of him and adding that he would expect to hear from me what my plans were for the future. Had he shown me in some small way that he really wanted me, I should have been eager to go back with him.

I was drawn to Sir Matthew who had lost all his jauntiness since the tragedy. He was very kind to me and made me sit beside him when all the mourners, who were not members of the family, had gone.

"How do you feel, my dear," he asked me, "in this house full of strangers?"

"I do not feel anything but a numbness now, an emptiness," I told him.

He nodded. "If you wish to stay here," he said, "you would always be welcome. This was Gabriel's home and you were Gabriel's wife. If you want to go away, I shall understand, but I should be very sorry."

"You are kind to me," I said, and those words of kindness brought the tears, which till now I had not been able to shed, to my eyes.

Simon had come to stand beside me. He said: "You will go away from here. What is there here for you? It is so dull in the country, is it not?"

"I came from the country," I said.

"But after those years in France."

"I am surprised that you remember so much of my affairs."

"I have a very good memory. It is the only good thing about me. Yes, you will go away. You will be more free than you were . . . more free than you have ever been before." He changed the subject abruptly. "Those weeds become you."

I felt there was something behind his words, but I was too weary and too obsessed with thoughts of Gabriel to give him much of my attention.

I was glad when Luke came over to us and began to talk of other matters.

"It doesn't do to dwell on all this," he said. "We've got to forget. We've got to go on living."

I thought I detected a certain glitter in his eyes. He was, after all, the new heir. Was his grief for Gabriel rather superficial?

I was trying to hold off frightening notions which were creeping into my mind. I did not really believe that Gabriel had had an accident on the balcony. I did not believe that he had deliberately killed himself.

But what else was there to believe?

When Gabriel's will was read I learned that he had left me comfortably off, although not rich. I had an income which would make me independent. This was a surprise because, although I had known that Kirkland Revels would pass to Gabriel on his father's death, together with an income adequate for its upkeep, I had not realized that he had so much money of his own.

The fact of my new affluence cheered me a little, and this was only due to the promise of freedom which it held out.

A week passed and I was still at the Revels, each day hoping for the return of Friday even though the days passed without sign of him.

I knew that the family were waiting for me to come to a decision as to whether or not I was going to stay, and I found it difficult to make up my mind. This house was of great interest to me; I felt that there was so much I did not know and only by staying could I discover it. I had a right to live here; I was Gabriel's widow. His father clearly wanted me to stay and, I believed, so did Aunt Sarah; but I thought Ruth would have been relieved to see me go. I wondered why. Was it because she did not care to have another female in the house, or was there some other reason? As for Luke, he was friendly in a breezy manner; but I had a notion that he did not care either way. He was immersed in his own affairs, and try as he might he could not hide his new importance. He was the heir of Kirkland Revels and, in view of Sir Matthew's age and infirmity, it could not be many more years before he was its master.

The Smiths were frequently at the house now, and when the doctor visited Sir Matthew—which he did each day—he invariably made a point of seeing me too. He was always kind and solicitous; he made me feel as though I were a patient, and, during that unhappy time when I mourned for Gabriel, gave me a little of the comfort I so desperately needed. He seemed to be concerned about my health.

"You have suffered a great shock," he told me, "perhaps greater than you realize. We must see that you take care of yourself."

He was giving me that solicitude which I had sought in vain from my father, and I began to wonder whether one of the reasons why I lingered on at the house was because of Dr. Smith, for it seemed that he understood my grief and loneliness as no one else did.

Damaris often drove over with her father, always cool, always serene and beautiful. I could see that Luke was in love with her but it was impossible to know what her feelings for him were. She was inscrutable. If Luke had his way he would marry her, but they were both so young at present that I doubted whether Sir Matthew or Ruth would allow Luke to marry for some time. And who knew what could happen in three, four or five years?

I had a feeling that I was marking time. I had not recovered from that strange numbness which had come to me when I heard I was a widow, and I could make no plans until I was free of it. If I left Kirkland Revels, where should I go? Back to Glen House? I thought of those dark rooms made bright only by the filtering of light through the Venetian blinds. I thought of Fanny's pursed lips and my father's "bad turns." No, I was not eager to return to Glen House; yet I was not sure that I wanted to stay at the Revels. What I wanted was to clear away this ignorance which shut me in like a fog. I believed if I could do that I should understand . . . what?

I walked each day and my footsteps always seemed to lead me to the Abbey. I had found in the Revels library an old plan of the place as it must have been before the 1530s and the Dissolution, and it took my mind from morbid thoughts to attempt to reconstruct the old building on those ruins. The plan was a great help and I was able to identify certain landmarks. I was excited when I came upon what must have been the chapel of the nine altars, the monks' dorter, the gatehouse, the kitchens and bakehouses. I also discovered the fishponds. There were three of these, a grassy bank separating them from each other.

I wondered whether Friday had fallen into one of these and been drowned. Impossible. They could not be very deep and he would swim to the bank. Nevertheless I called him whenever I came to the Abbey, which I knew was foolish even as I did it; but I could not bear to face the fact that he was gone forever. I must continue to hope.

I remembered the day when I had first seen Dr. Smith at this spot and he had said that Friday ought to have been brought here on a lead. As soon as I had recovered sufficiently from the shock of Gabriel's death, I had gone to the old well to look for Friday, but there was no sign of him there.

One day returning from my walk I took a new route and consequently arrived at the back of the house instead of the front, so I entered through a door I had not hitherto used. I was in the east wing of the house—a part with which I was not yet familiar. All the wings, I discovered, were almost identical with each other, except that the main staircase which led down to the hall past the minstrels' gallery was in the south wing.

I mounted a flight of stairs to the third floor, knowing that there were communicating corridors between the wings, and I thought I should easily find my way to my own apartments. But this was not so, for I found myself in a maze of corridors and I was not sure which door communicated with the south wing.

I hesitated because I was afraid I might walk into someone's private room.

I knocked at several doors, opened them and found a bedroom or a sitting room, a sewing room, but not the corridor I was looking for.

I could either retrace my steps, leave the house and enter by the front door, or continue my search. I decided on the latter, realizing that it was the only thing to do, for how could I be sure that I could find my way out of such a maze?

In desperation I tried more doors only to be disappointed. At length when I knocked on one a voice said: "Come in." I entered and Aunt Sarah was standing so close to the door that she startled me and I jumped back.

She laughed and put out a thin hand with which she clutched my sleeve.

"Come in," she said. "I'd been expecting you, my dear."

She ran around me as I entered—she seemed more nimble than she was when with the rest of the family—and quickly shut the door as though she was afraid I would try to escape.

"I know," she said, "you've come to see my tapestries. That's it, isn't it?"

"I should greatly enjoy seeing your tapestries," I told her. "Actually I lost myself. I came in by the east door. I have never done that before."

She shook a finger at me as though I were a naughty child. "Ah, it's easy to lose your way . . . when you don't know. You must sit down."

I was not sorry to do so because I was quite tired from my walk.

She said: "It was sad about the little dog. He and Gabriel went together. Two of them . . . lost. That is sad."

I was surprised that she remembered Friday, and felt at a loss with her because it was perfectly obvious that at times her mind wandered, that she flitted from past to present in a manner which was disconcerting; but there were occasions when she was capable of unexpected clarity.

I noticed that the walls of this large room were hung with tapestry, all exquisitely worked in bright colors; I was looking at it in fascination when she noticed this and chuckled with pleasure.

"That's all my own tapestry," she said. "You see what a large space it covers . . . but there is so much more to be done. Perhaps I shall fill every bit of the walls . . . unless I die. I am very old. It would be sad if I died before I had finished all I had to do." The melancholy expression was replaced by a dazzling smile. "But that is in the hands of God, is it not? Perhaps if I ask Him in my prayers to let me live a little longer, He will. Do you still say your prayers, Claire? Come and look at my tapestry . . . come closer. And I will tell you all about it."

She had taken my hand; her fingers were restless and moved continually; they felt like claws.

"It's exquisite work," I said.

"You like it? Claire, you didn't work hard enough at yours. I have told you many times that it is easy . . . easy . . . if you persevere. I know you had a great deal to do. You used to say that Ruth was such a willful little thing. Mark was good though . . . and then there was a new one coming . . ."

I said gently: "You have forgotten, Aunt Sarah. I am not Claire. I am Catherine, Gabriel's widow."

"So you have come to see my tapestry, Catherine. It is time you did. I know you will like it . . . you more than any." She came close to me and peered into my face. "You will figure in my tapestry. I shall know when the time has come."

"I?" I asked bewildered.

"Here. Come close. Look. Do you recognize this?"

"It's the house."

She laughed gleefully and pulled me away from the tapestry I was studying, drawing me towards a cupboard which she pulled open. Stacks of canvases fell out. She picked them up laughing. She no longer seemed like an old woman, her movements were so agile. I saw that there was a cupboard within the cupboard, and this she opened to disclose skein upon skein of silks of all colors.

She stroked them lovingly. "I sit here and I stitch and stitch. I stitch what I see. First I draw it. I will show you my drawings. Once I thought I should be an artist and then I did my tapestry instead. It is so much better, do you not think so?"

"The tapestry is lovely," I told her. "I want to look at it more closely."

"Yes, yes."

"I want to see that one of the house. It is so real. That is the exact color of the stones."

"Sometimes it is not easy to find the right colors," she said, her face puckering.

"And the people . . . why, I recognize them."

"Yes," she said. "There is my brother . . . and my sister Hagar, and there is my niece Ruth and my nephew Mark—he died when he was fourteen—and Gabriel and Simon, and myself. . . ."

"They are all looking at the house," I said.

She nodded excitedly. "Yes," she said, "we are all looking at the house. Perhaps there should be more looking at the house. . . . You should be there now. . . . But I do not think you are looking at the house. Claire didn't look either. Neither Claire nor Catherine."

I was not sure what she meant and she did not explain, but went on: "I see a great deal. I watch. I saw you come. You didn't see me."

"You were in the minstrels' gallery."

"You saw me?"

"I saw someone."

She nodded. "From there you see so much . . . and are not always seen. Here is the wedding of Matthew and Claire."

I was looking at a picture of a church which I recognized as that of Kirkland Moorside; there were the bride and groom, the latter recognizable as Sir Matthew. It was astonishing how she had managed to convey a likeness with those tiny stitches. She was undoubtedly an artist.

"And Ruth's marriage. He was killed in a hunting accident when Luke was ten. Here it is."

Then I realized that here on the walls of this room was Rockwell history as seen through the eyes of this strange woman.

She must have spent years of her life recapturing these events and stitching them onto canvas.

I said: "You are a looker-on at life, Aunt Sarah."

Her face puckered again and she said almost tearfully: "You mean I haven't lived myself . . . only through others. Is that what you mean, Claire?"

"I am Catherine," I reminded her.

"Catherine," she said, "I have been happy looking on. See, I have this gallery . . . this tapestry gallery . . . and when I am dead people will look at it and they will know more of what happened to us than they can know from the picture gallery. I am glad I did my tapestry pictures instead of portraits. Portraits often have little to tell."

I walked round that room and I saw scenes from the life of Kirkland Revels—I saw Ruth's husband being carried on a stretcher from the hunting field, and the mourners about his bed. I saw the death of Mark, and in between each of these scenes was a picture of the house and those recognizable figures gazing at it.

I said: "I believe that is Simon Redvers, among those who look at the house."

She nodded. "Simon looks at the house because it could be his one day. If Luke were to die as Gabriel died, then the Revels would be Simon's. So you see he is looking at the house too."

She was studying me intently and from the pocket of her gown she took a small notebook; and while I watched she sketched a figure. She managed to suggest myself by a few deft strokes of her pencil.

"You are very clever," I said.

She looked at me sharply and asked: "How did Gabriel die?"

I was startled. "They said at the inquest . . ." I began.

"*You* said he did not kill himself."

"I said I did not believe he could have done it."

"Then how did he die?"

"I do not know. I only sense within me that he could not have done it."

"I sense things within me. You must tell me. We must discover. I must know for my picture."

I looked at the watch pinned to my blouse. It was a gesture which meant that I must be going.

"I shall soon have finished the one I am working on. Then I shall want to start it. You must tell me."

"What are you working on now?"

"Look," she said, and she drew me across the room to the window. There on a frame was the familiar picture of the house.

"You have done that one before."

"No," she said, "this is different. There is no Gabriel to look at the house now. Only Matthew, Ruth, Hagar, myself, Luke, Simon . . ."

I felt stifled suddenly by the room and the effort of trying to catch at her innuendoes. She was indeed a strange woman, for she managed to give the impression of innocence and wisdom . . . almost simultaneously.

I had had enough of symbols. I wanted to get to my room and rest. "I lost my way. Tell me how I can get back to the south wing."

"I will show you." She was like an eager child trotting at my side as she opened the door and we went into the corridor.

I followed her and when she opened another door I went through in her wake to find myself on a balcony similar to that of the tragedy.

"The east balcony," she said. "I thought you would like to see it. It is now the only one over which no one has fallen to death."

There was a strange curve of her lips which might have been a smile.

"Look over," she said. "Look over. See how far down it is." She shivered. And I felt her little agile body pressing me against the parapet. For a horrible moment I thought she was trying to force me over.

Then she said suddenly: "You don't believe he killed himself. You don't believe it."

I drew away from the parapet and moved towards the door. I felt relieved to step into the corridor.

She went on ahead of me and in a short time she had led me to the south wing.

She had now become like an old woman again and I imagined that the change came when she left the east for the south wing.

She insisted on accompanying me to my own rooms even though I told her I now knew the way.

At the threshold of my room I thanked her and told her how I had enjoyed seeing the tapestries. Her face lighted up; then she put her fingers to her lips.

"We must find out," she said. "Don't forget. There's the picture to do."

Then she smiled conspiratorially and went quietly away.

It was a few days later when I made my decision.

I was still using the rooms in which I had lived with Gabriel and I found little peace in them. I was sleeping badly—something that had never happened to me before; I would fall asleep as soon as I went to bed but in a few minutes I would awake startled as though someone were calling me. On the first few occasions I thought that this was indeed so and got out of bed to see who was outside my door. After a few times I was convinced that it was some sort of nightmare.

I would doze and be startled again; and so it went on until the early hours of the morning when I would be so exhausted that I actually slept.

It was always the same dream—someone calling my name.

Sometimes it seemed to be Gabriel's voice calling Catherine. At others it was the voice of my father calling Cathy. I knew I had been dreaming and that this was due to the shock I had suffered.

Outwardly I could seem calm enough, but inwardly I was beset by misgivings. Not only had I lost my husband but, if I had to accept the verdict that he had killed himself, I could only think that I had never really known him.

If only Friday had been with me I could have been happier. They were the two I had loved, and to have lost them both together was a double tragedy.

There was no one at the house with whom I could make a real friendship. Each day I asked myself: Why do you stay here? And the answer was: Where would you go if you left?

I was wandering among the Abbey ruins one golden afternoon, calling Friday as I did now and then, when I was startled by the unmistakable sound of footsteps.

Even in daylight I could be overawed by the place and it says a great deal for the state of my nerves that I should not have been entirely surprised to see the figure of a black-robed monk emerge from the cloister.

Instead I saw the contemporary and sturdy figure of Simon Redvers.

"So you still hope to find your dog," he said, as he came towards me. "Don't you think that if he were here he would lose no time in coming home?"

"I suppose so. It was rather foolish of me."

He looked surprised—to hear me admit my folly, I suppose. He had an idea that I was a very self-opinionated young woman.

"Strange . . ." he mused, "that he should have disappeared the day before . . ."

I nodded.

"What do you think happened to him?" he asked.

"He was either lost or stolen. Nothing else would have kept him away."

"Why do you come here looking for him?"

I was silent for a while, because I was not entirely sure why I did. Then I remembered the occasion when I had met Dr. Smith here, and how he had told me that I should not bring Friday to the ruins unless I did so on a lead.

I mentioned this to Simon.

"He was thinking of the well," I added. "In fact, he said Friday was in danger of toppling over. He stopped him in time. That was when I first met Dr. Smith. It was one of the first places I went to when I was looking for Friday."

"I should have thought the fishponds might have been more dangerous. Have you seen them? They are worth a visit."

"I think every part of these ruins is worth a visit."

"They interest you, do they not?"

"Would they not interest anyone?"

"Indeed not. They are so much a part of the past. So many people have no interest in the past . . . only in the present, or in the future."

I was silent and after a while he went on: "I congratulate you on your serenity, Mrs. Catherine. So many women in your position would have been hysterical; but then I suppose with you it was different. . . ."

"Different?"

He smiled at me and I was aware that there was no real warmth in that smile.

He shrugged his shoulders and went on almost brutally: "You and Gabriel—well, it was no *grande passion,* was it? . . . at least on your side."

I was so angry that I was unable to speak for a few seconds.

"Marriages of convenience are as one would expect them to be, convenient," he continued in what I can only call an insolent tone. "It was a pity though that Gabriel took his life before the death of his father . . . from your point of view of course."

"I . . . I do not understand you," I said.

"I am sure you do. Had he died after Sir Matthew, so much of that which he inherited from his father would have been yours. . . . Lady Rockwell instead of plain Mrs. . . . and there would have been other compensations. It must have been a great blow to you, and yet . . . you are the perfectly composed yet sorrowing widow."

"I think you are trying to insult me."

He laughed, but his eyes flashed angrily. "I looked on him as my brother," he said. "There are only five years between us. I could see what you had done to him. He thought you were perfect. He should have enjoyed his illusion for a little longer. He would not have lived very many years."

"What are you talking about?"

"Do you think that I could accept his death . . . just like that? Do you think I believe that he killed himself because of his weak heart? He had known about that for years. Why did he marry and then do this thing? Why? There has to be a reason. There always has to be a reason. Following so soon after his marriage, it is logical to believe that it had something to do with that event. I could see what he thought of you. I could imagine the effect disillusion would have on him."

"What do you mean by disillusion?"

"That you would know better than I. Gabriel was sensitive to a degree. If he discovered that he had been married . . . not for love . . . he would think life was no longer worth living, and so . . ."

"This is monstrous! You seem to think that he found me in the gutter, that he lifted me out of squalor. You are quite mistaken. I knew nothing of his father's precious house and title when I married him. He told me none of these things."

"Why did you marry him? For *love?*" He seized me suddenly by the shoulders and put his face close to mine. "You were not in love with Gabriel. Were you? Answer me." He shook me a little. I felt my fury rising against him, against his arrogance, against his certainty that he understood all.

"How dare you!" I cried. "Take your hands off me at once!"

He obeyed and laughed again. "At least I've shaken you out of your serenity," he said. "No," he added, "you were never what I should call in love with Gabriel."

"It may be," I answered curtly, "that your knowledge of such an emotion is slight. People who love themselves so deeply, as you evidently do, are rarely able to understand the affection which some are able to give to others."

I turned from him and walked away, my eyes on the ground, wary of any jutting stone which might trip me.

He made no attempt to follow me, for which I was grateful. I was trembling with rage.

So he was suggesting that I had married Gabriel for his money and the title which would eventually go with it; worse still, he believed that Gabriel had discovered this and that it had driven him to take his life. So in his eyes I was not only a fortune huntress but a murderess."

I left the ruins behind me and hurried towards the house.

Why had I married Gabriel? I kept asking myself. No, it was not love. I had married him for pity's sake . . . and perhaps because I had longed to escape from the gloom of Glen House.

In that moment I wanted nothing so much as to finish with this phase of my life. I wanted to put the Abbey, the Revels and the whole Rockwell family behind me forever. Simon Redvers had done this to me, but I could not help wondering whether he had whispered his suspicions to the others and they believed him.

As I entered the house I saw Ruth; she had come from the garden and carried a basket full of red roses, which reminded me of those which she had put in our room on our return from the honeymoon, and how pleased Gabriel had been with them. I thought of his pale delicate face flushed with pleasure, and I could not bear to remember Simon Redvers's hideous insinuation.

"Ruth," I said on impulse, "I've been thinking about my future. I don't think I should stay here . . . indefinitely."

She inclined her head and looked at the roses instead of me.

"So," I went on, "I will go back to my father's house while I make my plans."

"You know you always have a home here, if you wish it," she replied.

"Yes, I know. But here there is this unhappy memory."

She laid her hand on my arm. "We shall all have that, but I understand. You came here and almost immediately it happened. It is for you to decide."

I thought of Simon Redvers's cynical eyes and my anger threatened to choke me.

"I have decided," I said. "I shall write to my father tonight telling him I am coming. I expect to leave before the end of the week."

Jemmy Bell was at the station to meet me, and while we drove to Glen House through those narrow lanes and when I caught a glimpse of our moors, I could almost believe that I had dozed on the journey home from school and had imagined all that had happened to me between then and now.

It was so like that other occasion. Fanny greeted me while Jemmy took the trap round to the stables.

"Still thin as a rake," was Fanny's greeting; and her lips were tight and self-congratulatory; I knew she was thinking: Well, I didn't hope for much from that marriage.

My father was in the hall, and he embraced me, a little less absent-mindedly than usual.

"My poor child," he said, "this has been terrible for you."

Then he put his hands on my shoulders and drew back to look at me. There was sympathy in his eyes and I felt that for the first time there was a bond between us.

"You're home now," he said. "We'll look after you."

"Thank you, Father."

Fanny cut in with: "Warming pan's in your bed. There's been mist lately."

I realized that I was receiving an unusually warm welcome.

When I went up to my room, I stood at the window looking out to the moor, and was poignantly reminded of Gabriel and Friday. Why had I thought I could forget in Glen House more easily than I could at Kirkland Revels!

I slipped into the familiar pattern. There were meals with my father, when we both sought to find a topic for conversation. He did not speak very often of Gabriel, being determined, I was sure, not to raise the painful subject. So we were both relieved when those meals were over.

Two weeks after my arrival he went away again and came home melancholy. I felt I could not endure to live much longer in this house.

I rode and walked and once made my way to the spot where I had found Friday and Gabriel but the memory was now so painful that I decided I would not ride that way again. I must stop thinking of Gabriel and Friday if I were ever to be completely at peace again.

I think it was on that day that I made up my mind to rearrange my life. I was after all a young widow with some means. I could set up a house, engage a few servants and live a completely different life from that which I had lived with my father or my husband.

I wished that I had some real friend to advise me. If Uncle Dick had been at home I should have been able to confide in him. I had written to him to tell him that I was now a widow, but letters between us would always be inadequate.

I toyed with the idea of taking a sea trip. I might arrange to meet him in some port and tell him all that had happened to me. But even while I was considering this idea a possibility had occurred to me which excited me and made me feel that all the plans which had half formed in my mind would be cast aside if this were indeed true.

I was in an agony of doubt while I told no one of my suspicions. Several weeks passed and then I visited our doctor.

I shall always remember sitting there in his consulting room with the sun streaming through and the certainty that the story of my marriage to Gabriel was not ended, even though he might no longer play his part in it.

How can I express my emotions? I was about to undergo a wonderful experience.

He was smiling at me, because he knew my story and believed that this was the best possible thing that could happen to me.

"There is no doubt," he told me. "You are going to have a child."

All the rest of that day I hugged my secret to myself. My own child! I was impatient with the months of gestation which must ensue. I wanted my child . . . now.

My whole life was changed. I no longer brooded on the past. I believed that this was the consolation which Gabriel was giving to me, and that nothing had been in vain.

It was when I was alone in my room that I remembered this was Gabriel's child as well as mine and if it were a boy he would be the heir of Kirkland Revels.

Never mind, I told myself. There is no need for him to look to that inheritance. I have enough to give him. The Rockwells need never know that he is born. Let Luke take everything. What did I care?

But the thought tormented me. I did care. If I had a son I was going to call him Gabriel, and everything that I could give him must be his.

Next day during luncheon I told my father the news. He was startled, and then I saw the color come to his face so that it was pale pink—with pleasure, I believed.

"You are happier now," he said. "God bless you. This is the best thing that could happen to you."

I had never known him so talkative. He said that I must inform the Rockwell family immediately. He knew of the precarious state of Sir Matthew's health and I guessed he thought it would be awkward if Luke inherited his grandfather's title when it should really belong to my unborn son—if it was a son I carried.

I caught his excitement, and I went at once to my room and wrote to Ruth.

It was not an easy letter to write because Ruth had never been very friendly towards me and I could well imagine the consternation the news would cause her.

My letter was stilted but it was the best I could do.

Dear Ruth,

I am writing to tell you that I am going to have a child. My doctor has just assured me that there is no doubt of this; and I thought I should let the family know that there will shortly be a new member of it.

I hope Sir Matthew has recovered from his attack. I am sure he will be delighted to hear that there is a possibility of his having another grandchild.

I am in excellent health and I hope you are the same.

I send my very best wishes to all.

> *Your sister-in-law*
> *Catherine Rockwell.*

Ruth's reply came within two days.

Dear Catherine,

We are surprised and delighted by your news.

Sir Matthew says that you must come at once to the Revels because it is unthinkable that his grandchild should be born anywhere but here.

Please do not refuse his request that you should do so. He will be most unhappy if you do; and it is an old tradition with us that our children should be born in the house.

Please let me know by return when I may expect you. I will have everything ready for you.

> *Your sister-in-law, Ruth.*

There was also a letter from Sir Matthew. The handwriting was a little shaky but the welcome was indeed warm. He had missed me, he said; and there was nothing which could have delighted him more at this sad time than my news. I must not disappoint him. I must come back to Kirkland Revels.

I knew he was right. I had to go back.

Ruth and Luke drove to Keighley Station to meet me.

They greeted me with outward pleasure, but I was not at all sure that they were pleased to see me. Ruth was serene, but Luke, I thought, had lost a little of his breeziness. How did it feel, I wondered, to think yourself heir to something you must always have coveted, only to find that an intruder might be on the way? It depended, of course, on how strong was your covetousness.

Ruth made solicitous inquiries about my health while we drove to the house. I was filled with emotion as we left the moors and came to the old bridge, as I caught a glimpse of the Abbey ruins and the Revels itself.

We alighted and went through the portico, and I felt that the faces of the devils looked smug and evil, as though they were saying to me: Did you think you had escaped us?

But I felt strong as I entered the house. I had someone to love, to protect, and because of that someone the emptiness had gone from life and I was ready to be happy again.

4

When I entered the house Matthew and Sarah were waiting for me. They both embraced me and handled me with such care that I might have been a piece of porcelain; it made me smile.

"I don't break, you know," I said, and that started everything on the right note.

"Your news . . . your wonderful news!" murmured Sarah, wiping her eyes, although I saw no tears.

"This means so much to us all," Sir Matthew told me. "It is a great consolation."

"We've been telling her that," Ruth put in. "Haven't we, Luke?"

Luke smiled with a return of his camaraderie. "Have we, Catherine?" he asked.

I avoided answering by smiling at him.

"I expect Catherine is tired and would like to go to her room," said Ruth. "Shall I have tea sent up, Catherine?"

"That would be nice."

"Luke, ring for one of the maids. Come along, Catherine. Your trunk has already gone up."

Sir Matthew and Sarah followed Ruth and myself up the stairs.

"I've put you on the first floor of the south wing," Ruth explained. "You won't want too many stairs, and this is a very pleasant room."

"If you don't like it," Sir Matthew said hurriedly, "you must tell us, my dear."

"How kind you are!" I murmured.

"You could come near me." Sarah's voice was high-pitched with excitement. "That would be very nice . . . very nice indeed."

"I think the room I have chosen will be most suitable," said Ruth.

We passed the minstrels' gallery and went up the staircase to the first floor. We then went along a short corridor in which were two doors. Ruth opened the second of these to disclose my room.

It was an almost exact replica of that which I had shared with Gabriel, even to the powder closet, and I saw from the windows, which gave me a view of the lawns and of the Abbey, that it was in a similar position although two floors below.

"It is very pleasant," I said; I looked at the decorated ceiling from which cherubs, encircling the chandelier in the center, looked down upon me. My bed was a four-poster, as were almost all in the house, I believed; there were blue silk curtains about it, and these matched curtains of blue damask at the windows. My carpet was blue. There was an enormous fireplace, a wardrobe and several chairs, besides an oak chest over which hung a brass warming pan. There was a red glow in the highly polished brass which came from a bowl of red roses, put there I guessed by Ruth.

I smiled at her. "Thank you," I said.

She inclined her head in acknowledgment, but I could not help wondering whether she was really pleased to see me or would have been happier if, when I had left the Revels, I had gone out of her life forever. I was sure her welcome could not be wholehearted because of what the birth of a son to me would mean to Luke. She adored Luke, I was fully aware of that; and now that I was to be a mother myself I understood how ambitious one could become on behalf of one's children, and I felt no resentment against Ruth even if she did towards me.

"This should be convenient for you," she went on quickly.

"It is kind of you to take so much trouble."

Sir Matthew was beaming at me. "*You* are going to be put to a lot of trouble for us," he told me. "We are delighted . . . delighted. I've told Deverel Smith he's got to keep me alive by hook or by crook—by potions or spells—to see my new grandson."

"You have determined on the sex."

"Of course I have, my dear. Haven't a doubt of it. You were meant to be the mother of boys."

"I want you to come and see my tapestries, Hagar, my dear," murmured Sarah. "You will, won't you? I'll show you the cradle. All Rockwells use that cradle."

"It will have to be overhauled within the next months," Ruth put in practically. "And this is Catherine, Aunt Sarah."

"Of course it's Catherine," said Aunt Sarah indignantly. "We're good friends. She so liked my tapestry."

"I expect she would like to rest now."

"We must not tire her," agreed Sir Matthew.

Ruth nodded towards Aunt Sarah significantly, and Sir Matthew took his sister's arm.

"We shall be able to talk to her when she is rested," he said; and, smiling once more at me, he led his sister away.

Ruth sighed as the door shut on them. "I'm afraid she's becoming rather a trial. Her memory's so up and down. Sometimes she'll reel off all the dates of our births without an effort. It seems absurd that she can't remember to which of us she's talking."

"I suppose that happens when one grows older."

"I hope I escape that. There's a saying, 'Whom the gods love die young.' Sometimes I think it's true."

I immediately thought of Gabriel. Was he beloved of the gods? I did not think so.

"Please don't talk of dying," I said.

"I'm sorry. How silly of me. That tea should be along soon. I expect you need it, don't you?"

"It will be refreshing."

She went to the bowl of roses and began rearranging them.

"They remind me . . ." I began; and she looked at me interrogatively, so I had to go on. ". . . of those you put in the room when I first arrived here."

"Oh . . . I'm sorry. That was thoughtless of me, I suppose." I guessed she was thinking that they would have to be careful in future, that when a tragedy had happened it was necessary to be very tactful to avoid bringing back memories.

One of the maids came in with the tea; she bobbed a curtsy to me and I said, "Good afternoon, Mary-Jane."

Mary-Jane set the tea down on a table by the window and I thanked her.

"Mary-Jane will be your personal maid," Ruth said. "She will answer your bell."

I was pleased. Mary-Jane was a rather tall, fresh-faced young woman who I was sure would be honest and conscientious. Because I showed my pleasure she allowed me to see hers, and I believed I had a friend in the house.

Ruth went over to the tray. "She has brought two cups," she said. "Shall I join you?"

"Please do."

"Then you sit down, and I'll bring yours to you."

I took the chair near the bed because I did not wish, at this moment, to look out of the window. I kept thinking of Gabriel and telling myself that anyone looking out of this window at the time of his accident would have seen him falling.

Ruth handed me the cup of tea; then she brought a footstool and made me rest my feet.

"We're going to watch over you," she said, "all of us."

But I thought how cold her eyes were, and the note of friendship in her voice seemed forced.

Here I go! I thought. No sooner do I come to this house than my fancies grow. "We are going to watch over you." It could be ambiguous.

She went to the table by the window and sat down there. She talked of what had been happening during my absence. Sir Matthew had recovered from his attack, but he was getting too old for attacks nowadays, and Deverel Smith was worried. "Last week," she said, "he stayed all night. He's so good. He gives himself to his patients quite selflessly. There was no need for him to stay. We could have called him. But he insisted."

"Some doctors are very noble," I agreed.

"Poor Deverel, I don't think his home life is very happy."

"Really? I know little about his family."

"Damaris is the only child. Mrs. Smith must be a great trial to him. She is supposed to be an invalid. I would call her a hypochondriac. I imagine she indulges in illness as a way of attracting attention to herself."

"Does she never go out?"

"Rarely. She is supposed to be too ill. I imagine that the doctor has made his profession his whole life because of the state of his domestic affairs. Of course he dotes on Damaris."

"She is so very beautiful. Is her mother like her?"

"There is a resemblance, but Muriel was never half as beautiful as her daughter."

"If she were half as beautiful she would be extremely attractive."

"Yes, indeed. I'm so sorry for Damaris. I planned to give a ball for her, and for Luke too. But of course now that we are in mourning that is out of the question . . . for this year at least."

"She is fortunate to have such a good friend in you."

"We are fortunate to have such a good doctor. Would you care for more tea?"

"No, thank you. I have had enough."

"I expect you want to unpack. Would you care for me to send Mary-Jane along to help you?"

I hesitated. Then I said I would; and she went out and shortly afterwards Mary-Jane appeared with another of the maids who took the tea tray away leaving Mary-Jane with me.

I watched Mary-Jane kneeling by my trunk taking out my clothes.

"I shall have to buy some new clothes soon," I said. "These will not fit me."

Mary-Jane smiled. "Yes, madam," she said.

She was about my height and it occurred to me that she might like some of my clothes when I grew too large for them. I would give them to her.

"You look pleased, Mary-Jane."

"It's t'news, madam. And I'm right glad to see you back."

There was no doubt of her sincerity, and it made me happy.

The house was beginning to have that odd effect on me; I had only been in it an hour or so and I was already looking round for friends . . . and enemies.

"It'll be a long time to wait," I said.

"Yes, madam. My sister's expecting. Hers will be born in five months' time. We're hoping for a boy . . . though if it's a girl, reckon we won't fret about that."

"Your sister, Mary-Jane? So you have a family."

"Oh yes, madam. Etty's husband works up at Kelly Grange, and they've a fine cottage on t'estate. At t'lodge, madam, and all their firewood free. It's her first . . . I get down to see her when I can."

"I'm sure you do. You must let me know how she gets on. We have something in common, Mary-Jane."

She smiled. "Time was, our Etty got terrible scared. The first . . . that's what it is. But they both was scared. . . . Jim as well. First she's scared she's going to die; then she wonders whether the baby's going to be a wreckling. Yes, scared our Ett was, that when t'baby was born it 'ud be short of something. But Jim asked the doctor to see her and he put her right. He was wonderful to her. He's a wonderful man . . . the doctor."

"Dr. Smith?"

"Oh . . . ay. He's kind. Don't care nowt whether you be gentry or poor folk. He said: 'Don't you fret, Mrs. Hardcastle—baby won't be a wreckling or nowt like it. There's every sign it'll be bonny.' That set our Ett to rights."

"We are fortunate," I said, "to have such a good doctor to look after us."

She smiled. And I felt happier at the sight of her, shaking out my clothes and hanging them in the wardrobe. With her not uncomely person and her bright Yorkshire good sense she brought normality into the room.

After dinner that first evening we were all assembled in one of the sitting rooms on the first floor—not far from my own room—when Dr. Smith was announced.

"Bring him up," said Ruth; and as the door closed on the servant, she said to me: "He comes at all times. He's so attentive."

"He fusses too much," grumbled Sir Matthew. "I'm all right now."

As Dr. Smith came into the room he was, I was sure, looking for me.

"I'm so pleased to see you, Mrs. Rockwell," he said.

"You know the reason why she's returned, eh?" Sir Matthew asked.

"Indeed I do. I prophesy that by the end of the week there won't be one person in the village who doesn't know it. I can assure you that it makes me happy . . . very happy."

"You are not alone in that," said Sir Matthew.

"We are going through the nursery together," announced Sarah like a young child who has been promised a special treat.

"In fact," put in Luke—and was his voice mildly sardonic?—"we are preparing to join in the chorus while Catherine sings the 'Magnificat.'"

There was a slightly shocked silence at this irreverence but Dr. Smith said quickly: "We must take great care of Mrs. Rockwell."

"We are all determined to do that," Ruth assured him.

The doctor came over to me and took my hand briefly in his. There was a certain magnetism about this man, of which I think I had been aware before but which now struck me forcibly. He was outstandingly handsome in his dark way, and I knew that he was capable of deep feeling. I guessed that, disappointed in his marriage as he must be, he sublimated his desire for a wife's affection in his devotion to his patients. I noticed that Sir Matthew, although complaining of his overzealousness, was nevertheless pleased to see him, and it was clear to me that the old man felt comforted by his presence. I remembered what Mary-Jane had said of his kindness to her sister. The people of this neighborhood perhaps should thank that unsatisfactory wife of his since his devotion to their needs was the stronger because of her.

"I know you are so fond of riding," he said, "but I don't think I should indulge in it too frequently . . . not after this month at any rate."

"I won't," I promised.

"You'll be a good and sensible young lady, I am sure of that."

"Have you been visiting Worstwhistle today?" asked Ruth.

"I have," said the doctor.

"And it has depressed you. That place always does." Ruth turned to me. "Dr. Smith gives his services free, not only to patients who cannot afford to pay, but to this . . . hospital."

"Oh come," cried the doctor laughing, "don't make a saint of me. Someone has to look in on those people now and then. . . . And don't forget, if I have poor patients here I also have rich ones. I fleece the rich to help the poor."

"A regular Robin Hood," said Luke.

Dr. Smith turned to Sir Matthew. "Well, sir," he said, "I'm going to have a look at you today."

"You think it's necessary?"

"I think that since I am here . . ."

"Very well," said Sir Matthew rather testily, "but first of all you must join us in a toast. I'm going to have some of my best champagne brought up from the cellars. Luke, ring the bell."

Luke did so and Sir Matthew gave the order.

The wine was brought, the glasses filled.

Sir Matthew lifted his glass and cried: "To my grandson." He put his arm about me while we all drank.

Very soon after that the doctor went with Sir Matthew to his room and I went to mine. Mary-Jane, determined to be a real lady's maid, was turning down the bed for me.

"Thank you, Mary-Jane."

"Is there anything else you'll be wanting, madam?"

I did not think there was, so I said good night to her, but as she went to the door I called: "By the way, Mary-Jane, do you know a place called Worstwhistle?"

She stopped short and stared at me.

"Why yes, madam. It's some ten miles off on the way to Harrogate."

"What sort of place is it, Mary-Jane?"

"It's the place where mad people go."

"Oh, I see. Good night, Mary-Jane."

The next morning I was awakened by Mary-Jane who came in to draw the curtains and bring my hot water.

It was comforting to wake up and see her pleasant face. She was looking a little surprised because there had been no need to draw the curtains. I had pulled them back before getting into bed; and I had opened the window. Mary-Jane shared the belief that night air was "dangerous."

I told her that I always slept with my window open, except in the depth of winter; and I was sure that she had decided I should need a great deal of looking after.

I took my bath in the powder room and went along to the first-floor dining room for breakfast. I felt quite hungry. Two mouths to feed now, I reminded myself, as I took eggs, bacon and deviled kidneys from the chafing dish on the sideboard.

I knew the routine. Breakfast was taken between eight and nine, and one helped oneself.

I rang for hot coffee and when it was brought to me I was joined by Luke. Later Ruth appeared and solicitously asked if I had had a good night and liked my room.

Had I any plans for the day? they wanted to know. Luke was going to Ripon and would be delighted to buy anything I needed. I thanked him and told him that I should need things, but I had not yet decided what.

"There's plenty of time before the happy event," he said; and his mother murmured his name indulgently, because she thought it was somewhat indelicate to refer to the birth of my child. I did not mind. It was something I wanted to think of continually.

I told them that I would take a little walk during the morning; I was longing to have a look at the Abbey again.

"The place appeals strongly to you," remarked Luke. "I believe it's the main reason why you wanted to come back here."

"It would interest anyone," I answered.

"You must not exhaust yourself," Ruth warned me.

"I feel very well, so I don't think there's any danger of that."

"All the same you have to remember to take care."

The conversation turned to the affairs of the neighborhood; the effort of the vicar to raise money for the upkeep of the church, the bazaars and jumble sales he was organizing for this purpose, the ball which a friend was giving and which we could not attend as we were in mourning.

The sun streamed through the windows of that pleasant room and there was certainly nothing eerie about Kirkland Revels that morning. Even the Abbey, which I visited a few hours later, appeared to be nothing but a pile of ruins.

So that was a pleasant walk. I felt serene, ready to accept the theory that Gabriel had killed himself because of his illness. It seemed strange that I should feel more contented to believe that, but I did; perhaps it was because I was afraid of the alternative.

I came back through the Abbey ruins. It was very quiet—peaceful was the word to describe it this morning. This was merely a shell; the brilliant sunshine falling onto the grass floors, exposing the crumbling walls, defied that sense of the supernatural. I thought back to the evening when I had walked here and panicked, and I laughed at my folly.

Luncheon was a quiet meal which I shared with Ruth and Luke, Sir Matthew and Aunt Sarah taking theirs in their rooms.

Afterwards I went to my room and began making out a list of the things I should need. It was early, yet I was so impatient for the birth of my child that I could not wait. While I was thus engaged there was a knock on my door and when I called "Come in," Sarah stood on the threshold, smiling as though we were a pair of conspirators.

"I want to show you the nursery," she said. "Will you come with me?"

I rose without reluctance, for I was eager to see the nursery.

"It's in my wing," she went on. "I often go up to the nursery." She giggled. "That's why they say I'm in my second childhood."

"I'm sure they don't say that," I told her, and her face puckered a little.

"They do," she said. "I like it. If you can't be in your first child-hood, the next best thing is to be in your second."

"I should love to see the nursery," I said. "Please show me now."

Her face was smooth and happy again. "Come along."

We mounted the staircase to the top floor. I felt an involuntary tremor as I passed that corridor which led to our old room and the front of the house, for my memories of Gabriel and even of poor little Friday, which I was constantly trying to suppress, were as vivid as they had ever been; but Aunt Sarah did not seem to notice my mood; she was intent on leading me into the east wing and the nursery.

I was struck once more by the change in her as we entered her section of the house; she seemed almost girlish and very happy.

"Right at the top," she murmured, as she led the way up a short flight of stairs. "The schoolroom, the day nursery, the night nursery, Nanny's quarters and those of the undernursemaid." She opened a door and said in a hushed voice: "This is the schoolroom."

I saw a large room with three windows, all of which were fitted with window seats; the slightly sloping ceiling told me that we were immediately below the roof. I found my eyes fixed on the windows which had bars across them in accordance with nursery tradition. My child would be safe up here.

There was a large table close to one of the windows and beside it a long form. I went over to this table and saw the cuts and scratches on it; it must have been used by many generations of Rockwells.

"Look," cried Sarah. "Can you read that?"

I leaned forward and saw the name Hagar Rockwell carved there with a penknife.

"She always put her name on everything." Sarah laughed on a gleeful note. "If you went through this house peering into cupboards and such places you would see her name. Our father said she ought to have been the boy instead of Matthew. She used to bully us all . . . especially Matthew. She was annoyed with him for being the boy. Of course if she had been the boy . . . she would be here now, wouldn't she? And Simon would have been . . . But perhaps that's not exactly right . . . because he's a Redvers. Oh dear, it's a little complicated, is it not? But she was not the son, and so it was Matthew."

"Hagar is Simon Redvers's grandmother?" I asked.

Sarah nodded. "She thinks the world of him." She came close to me. "She'd like to see him here . . . but she won't now, will she? There's the child . . . and there's Luke too . . . both before Simon. The child first. . . . I shall have to get some more silks."

"You're thinking that my child will make his appearance on your tapestries."

"Are you going to call him Gabriel?"

I was astonished and I wondered how she had guessed my thoughts. She was studying me, her head on one side; now she looked infinitely wise as simple people sometimes do.

"It may not be a boy," I said.

She merely nodded as though there was no doubt of it.

"Little Gabriel will take big Gabriel's place," she said. "Nobody can stop him, can they?" Her face puckered suddenly. *"Can* they?" she repeated.

"If the child is a boy he will take his father's place."

"But his father died. He killed himself . . . they said so. Did he kill himself?" She had caught my arm and held it tightly. "You said he didn't. Who did? Tell me, please tell me."

"Aunt Sarah," I said quickly, "when Gabriel died I was distraught. Perhaps I did not know what I said. He must have killed himself."

She dropped my arm and looked at me reproachfully.

"I'm disappointed in you," she said, pouting. Then her mood changed at once. "We all sat at that table. Hagar was the cleverest of us all—and the eldest—so you see it would have been best . . . Then Simon would have been . . . Our governesses did not like her though. They all liked Matthew. He was the favorite. All women liked Matthew. I was the stupid one. I could not learn my lessons."

"Never mind," I soothed. "You could draw beautifully; and your tapestry work will be here for years and years after we are all dead."

Her face lightened. Then she began to laugh. "I used to sit here, Matthew there . . . and Hagar at that end of the table. Our governess was always at the other end. Hagar said she should sit at the head of the table because she was the eldest. She could do everything . . . except drawing and needlework. I beat her there. Hagar was a tomboy. You should have seen her on horseback. She used to ride to hounds with our father. She was his favorite. Once she climbed up to the window nearly at the top of the Abbey tower. She could not get down and they had to send two of the gardeners with ladders. She was sent to her room for a whole day on bread and water; but she did not care. She said it was worth it." She came close to me and whispered: "She said: 'If you want to do something, do it and then think about paying for it afterwards—and if you've done it, you must not mind what you have to pay for it.' "

"She was a forceful character, your sister Hagar."

"Our father liked to take her round the estate with him. He was sorry when she married John Redvers. Then the trouble started with Matthew. He was sent down from Oxford. There was a young woman there. I remember that day. The girl came here to see Father. I watched them from where they couldn't see me; I heard it all."

"From the minstrels' gallery," I said.

She giggled. "They did not think to look up there."

She sat down at the table in that place which she had occupied to learn her lessons; and I knew that the reason for her youthfulness in this part of the house was due to the fact that here she relived her youth. I was sure that all her memories of the past would be flawless; it was only in the present that she was uncertain whether she was talking to Catherine or Claire, Gabriel's or Matthew's wife.

"Trouble," she brooded, "always trouble about women. He was well into his thirties before he married, and they went more than ten years without a child. Then Ruth was born. All that time Hagar thought it would be *her* son Peter who'd be master of Revels. Then Mark and Gabriel were born. Poor little Mark! But there was still Gabriel left. Then Luke was born . . . so you see Hagar was not happy about that." She rose from the table. She took me to the cupboard and showed me the marks on the wall there. There were three lines marked with the initials H., M. and S.

"Her Majesty's Ship," I murmured.

"Oh no," said Sarah earnestly. "Hagar, Matthew and Sarah. Those were our heights. Matthew shot up past her after that, and then Hagar wouldn't measure any more. I want to show you the night and day nurseries."

I followed her from the schoolroom and with her explored that part of the house which had been the children's domain through the centuries. I noticed with satisfaction that all the windows were barred. In the day nursery was a great oak chest, and this Sarah opened. In here were stored the Rockwell christening robes and she brought them out reverently for my inspection.

They were beautifully made of white silk and lace which I guessed was priceless.

"I must examine them," she said. "I may have to mend part of the lace. The last time they were used was for Luke. That's nearly eighteen years ago. He was not a good baby. None of our babies were good babies. I shall take these to my room. I shall allow no one to touch them except myself. I shall have them ready for you when you need them."

"Thank you, Aunt Sarah."

I looked at the watch pinned to my bodice and saw that it was four o'clock.

"It's tea time," I said. "I had no idea. How quickly the time passes when one is interested!"

She did not answer me; she was clutching the christening robe to her breast, and I believed that in her imagination she was already nursing the baby—or perhaps some other baby from the past—Ruth, Mark, Gabriel or Luke.

"I am going down to tea," I told her; but she did not answer me.

It was some days later when Ruth came to my room with a letter.

"One of the servants from Kelly Grange brought this over," she said.

"For me?" I asked astonished.

"Undoubtedly for you. 'Mrs. Gabriel Rockwell'—it says it distinctly on the envelope."

Ruth was smiling as though she were amused when she handed this to me, and as she did not attempt to go, I murmured, "Excuse me," and read it.

It was formal; almost like a command.

> *If Mrs. Gabriel Rockwell will call at Kelly Grange on Friday at 3:30 Mrs. Hagar Rockwell-Redvers will be pleased to receive her.*

Because I had already crossed swords with Mrs. Hagar Redvers's grandson, I was prepared to do so with her. I flushed faintly with annoyance.

"A royal command?" asked Ruth with a smile.

I passed the invitation to her.

"It's characteristic of my Aunt Hagar," she said. "I really believe she's of the opinion that she is head of the family. She wants to inspect you."

"I have no intention of being inspected," I retorted rather sharply. "The inspection in any case would be rather useless at this stage."

"She's very old," said Ruth apologetically. "She's older than my father. She can't be far off ninety. You'll have to go carefully with her."

I said quickly: "I have decided that I shall not go to call on Friday."

Ruth shrugged. "The servant's waiting," she said. "My aunt will expect a reply."

"She shall have that," I answered; and I sat down at my writing table and wrote:

> *Mrs. Gabriel Rockwell regrets that she is unable to call on Mrs. Hagar Rockwell-Redvers at Kelly Grange on Friday at 3:30.*

Ruth took the note from me. She was clearly amused.

I stood at my window watching the messenger from Kelly Grange ride away, and I thought: So it is from his grandmother that he gets his arrogance.

Early the following week I was on the front lawn when Simon Redvers rode up to the house.

He leaped from his horse, lifted his hat to greet me, then shouted to one of the grooms as though he were the master of this house and its servants.

"Mrs. Catherine," he said, "I am pleased to find you at home because it was to see you that I have ridden over from the Grange."

I had not seen him since my return and I thought he looked larger, and more arrogant than ever. I endeavored to look as dignified as possible as I said: "Pray tell me what your business is with me."

As soon as his horse was taken from him he came towards me; he was smiling almost ingratiatingly.

"May I say that it is a great pleasure to see you here again?"

"You may say it if you wish to."

"You are still angry with me."

"I have not forgotten certain remarks you made to me before I left."

"Do you harbor resentments then?"

"If they are as insulting as those you made, yes."

"I am sorry about that because I have come to apologize."

"Indeed!"

"Mrs. Catherine, I am a forthright Yorkshireman, and you are a Yorkshire woman, and therefore forthright also. We are no dandified southerners to wrap up our thoughts in pretty phrases. I cannot pretend to possess the manners and style of a gentleman of London."

"I am sure it would be useless for you to make such a pretense."

He laughed. "You have a sharp tongue, Mrs. Catherine."

I was not altogether displeased by his method of addressing me. I found Mrs. Rockwell formal, and naturally I did not wish him to use my christian name alone.

"I can only hope that it will be a match for yours on those occasions when we are obliged to meet."

"I hope those occasions will be many, and that while we sharpen our tongues we shall also sharpen our wits."

"What did you wish to say to me?"

"I wished to ask your pardon for certain unmannerly remarks I made at our last meeting. I have come to offer my congratulations, and to wish you good health and happiness."

"So you have changed your mind concerning me?"

"I hope I shall not do that, because I always admired you. But I sincerely ask your pardon. May I explain my feelings? Let us say that I was angered by the loss of one who was as my brother. I am the type who loses control of his tongue in anger, Mrs. Catherine. One of my less worthy traits, of which I fear there are many."

"Then let us say no more of the incident."

"So you will forgive and forget?"

"Forgiveness is so much easier to grant than forgetfulness. I promise you the first. The second . . . I hope will come."

"You are gracious, Mrs. Catherine, beyond my deserts. Now I am going to ask a favor of you."

"Ah!" I said.

"Not for myself," he added hastily, "but for my grandmother. She has asked you to visit her."

"It was scarcely a request."

He laughed. "You must forgive her methods. She is used to authority. It is a great grief to her that she has not seen you, and it would give her much pleasure if you would pass over the manner of her asking and remember that she is a very old lady, rarely able to leave the house."

"Did she send you to give this second command?"

"She has no idea that I have come. She was hurt by your refusal of her invitation and I am going to ask you to allow me to take you there tomorrow. I will drive over for you and take you to her. Will you allow me to do this?"

I hesitated.

"Oh come," he urged. "Remember she is old; she is lonely; she is greatly interested in the family and you are now a member of it. Please say yes. Please, Mrs. Catherine."

He suddenly seemed attractive; his eyes, screwed up against the sunlight had lost their boldness; I noticed his strong teeth which looked very white against his sun-bronzed skin. He was a little like Gabriel without any of Gabriel's delicacy; and as I looked at him I found myself relenting.

He saw the change in my mood immediately. "Oh thanks," he cried, and his face was creased in smiles such as I had not seen there before. He's really fond of that old grandmother, I thought; and I almost liked him because he was fond of someone other than himself.

He went on exuberantly: "You'll like her. You can't fail to do so.

And she will like you . . . though she may be a little chary of showing it just at first. Like you, she's a strong character."

This was the second time a man had referred to my strength, and I felt weakened suddenly. There was even a prickle in my eyes which suggested tears.

I was horrified at the idea of shedding tears, particularly before this man!

I said hurriedly to hide my embarrassment: "Very well. I will come."

"That's wonderful. I shall call for you tomorrow at two o'clock. I am now going back to tell her that you have agreed to call and see her."

He did not wait for any more. He was shouting to the groom and seemed to have forgotten me.

Yet I liked him for it; and liking him, I was prepared not to dislike his grandmother, which previously I am afraid I had made up my mind to do.

The next day Simon Redvers called at the Revels promptly at two o'clock; he came in a phaeton drawn by two of the handsomest horses I had ever seen. I sat beside him during the journey which was under two miles.

"I could have walked," I said.

"And deprived me of the pleasure of taking you?" The mocking note was back in his voice, but the antagonism between us had considerably lessened. He was pleased with me because I had agreed to see his grandmother, and as his obvious affection for her had softened me towards him, we could not hate each other so wholeheartedly.

Kelly Grange was a manor house which I guessed to be less than a hundred years old—very modern when compared with the Revels. It was of gray stone and surrounded by fertile land. We drove up to a pair of massive wrought-iron gates through which I saw an avenue of chestnut trees. From the lodge a woman, who was clearly with child, came out to open the gates for us.

Simon Redvers touched his hat with his whip in acknowledgment and she bobbed a curtsy.

I smiled, and her eyes rested on me with speculation.

"Now I wonder," I said as we drove on, "if that could be Mary-Jane's sister."

"It's Etty Hardcastle. Her husband works on the land for us."

"Then it would be. Mary-Jane is my personal maid and she has told me of her sister."

"In a place like this, you find everyone is related to everyone else. There! What do you think of the Grange? A pale shadow, eh, of the Revels."

"It's very attractive."

"It has its points. Kelly Grange can offer you more in the way of comfort than the Revels, I do assure you. Wait until the winter and compare them. Our great fires keep the house warm. There are many draughty spots in the Revels. You'd need all the coal of Newcastle to keep that place warm in the winter."

"It is so much easier with a smaller place."

"Yet we are not exactly cramped. However, you shall see for yourself."

The wheels crunched on a gravel drive and soon we had drawn up before the front porch, on either side of which were marble statues of women, decently draped, holding baskets in which geraniums and lobelias had been planted. There was a long marble seat on each side of the porch.

The door was opened by a parlormaid before we had reached it and I guessed that she had heard the sound of wheels in the drive. As we alighted, and the coachman drove off in the phaeton, I imagined this house full of servants all alert to anticipate Simon's needs.

We went into a tiled hall from which rose a wide staircase. The house was built around this hall and standing in it one could look up to the roof.

It was a large house of its kind but it seemed small and intimate when compared with the Revels.

Simon turned to me. "If you will wait here a moment, I will go and tell my grandmother that you have arrived."

I watched him mount the stairs to the first-floor gallery, knock at a door and enter. In a few minutes he appeared and beckoned. I went up.

Simon stood aside for me to pass him and said with a certain amount of ceremony which may have held its mockery—I was not entirely sure of this—"Mrs. Gabriel Rockwell!"

I entered. It was a room crowded with heavy furniture; thick plush curtains as well as lace ones were held back by ornate brass fittings. There was a table in the center of the room as well as several occasional tables; there was a horsehair sofa, a grandfather clock, many chairs, cabinets containing china, a whatnot, an epergne filled with white and red roses.

But all this I took in at a glance, for it was the woman in the high-backed chair who demanded my attention.

This was Hagar Redvers, Rockwell-Redvers as she called herself, the autocrat of the schoolroom who had remained an autocrat all her life.

It was evident that she was tall, although she was sitting down; her back was very straight; her chair was no soft and comfortable one, but had a hard carved wood back; her white hair was piled high on her head and on it was a white lace cap. There were garnets in her ears and her dress of lavender-colored satin was high at the throat where a lace collar was held in place by a garnet brooch to match the stones in her ears. An ebony stick with a gold top leaned against her chair; I gathered she needed it when she walked. Her eyes were bright blue; another version of Gabriel's eyes, but there was none of Gabriel's gentleness there; there was none of his delicacy in this woman. Her hands, resting on the carved wooden arms of the chair, must have been beautiful in her youth; they were still shapely, and I saw diamonds and garnets there.

For a few seconds we took the measure of each other. I, being conscious of a faint hostility, held my head a little higher than I normally should have done, and perhaps my voice held a trace of haughtiness as I said: "Good afternoon, Mrs. Rockwell-Redvers."

She held out a hand as though she were a queen and I a subject. I had a feeling that she expected me to go down on my knees before her. Instead I coolly took the hand, bowed over it and relinquished it.

"It was good of you to come this afternoon," she said. "I had hoped you would come before."

"It was your grandson who suggested that I should come this afternoon," I told her.

"Ah!" Her lips twitched a little, I fancied with amusement. "We must not keep you standing," she said.

Simon brought a chair for me and set it before the old lady. I was very close to her and facing what light could come through the lace curtains; she had her own face in shadow and I felt that even in this small way they had sought to place me at a disadvantage.

"You are no doubt thirsty after your drive," she said, her keen eyes seeming to search through mine into my mind.

"It was a very short one."

"It is a little early for tea, but on this occasion I think we will not wait."

"I am quite happy to wait."

She smiled at me, then turned to Simon. "Ring the bell, grandson." Simon immediately obeyed.

"We shall have much to say to each other," she went on, "and what more comfortable way of saying it than over a cup of tea?"

The parlormaid whom I had seen before appeared, and the old lady said: "Dawson, tea . . . please."

"Yes, madam."

The door was quietly shut.

"You will not wish to join us, Simon," she said. "We will excuse you."

I was not sure whether she used the word royally or whether she meant that we should both prefer him not to be with us; but I did know that I had passed the first small test and that she had unbent slightly towards me. My appearance and manners evidently did not disgust her.

Simon said: "Very well. I'll leave the two of you to become acquainted."

"And be ready to drive Mrs. Rockwell back to the Revels at five o'clock."

Simon surprised me by his acquiescence. He took her hand and kissed it and, although even then there was a certain mockery in his manner, I could see how she enjoyed this attention and that, although she tried to, she could not retain her autocratic manner with him.

We did not speak until the door closed on him; then she said: "I had hoped to see you when you were at the Revels previously. I was unable at that time to come to see you and I did not invite you because I felt certain that Gabriel would bring you to see me in due course. I am sure he would have done so had he lived. He was always conscious of his duty to the family."

"I am sure he would."

"I am glad that you are not one of those stupid modern girls who faint when any difficulty presents itself."

"How can you know these things on such a short acquaintance?" I asked, because I was determined that she should treat me as an equal. I had no intention of giving her the reverence she seemed to demand.

"My eyes are as sharp as they were at twenty. They have a great

deal more experience to help them along than they had then. Moreover Simon told me how admirably calm you were during that distressing time. I am sure you are not one of those foolish people who
say, We must not talk of this or that. Things exist whether we talk of
them or not; so why pretend they don't by never mentioning them?
Indeed, hiding the truth and making mysteries of straightforward
events is the way to keep them alive. Do you agree?"

"I think there may be occasions when that is true."

"I was pleased when I heard you had married Gabriel. He was always rather unstable. So many of the family are, I'm afraid. No back-
bone, that's the trouble."

I looked at her erect figure and I permitted myself a little joke.
"You evidently do not suffer from that complaint."

She seemed rather pleased. "What do you think of the Revels?" she
asked.

"I found the house fascinating."

"Ah. It is a wonderful place. There are not so many like it left in
England. That's why it is important that it should be in good hands.
My father was very capable. There have been Rockwells, you know,
who almost ruined the place. A house . . . an estate like that needs
constant care and attention if it is to remain in good repair. Matthew
could have been better. But a squire in his position should have dignity. There was always some woman. That's bad. As for Gabriel . . .
he was a pleasant creature but weak. That was why I was gratified
when I heard he had married a strong young woman."

The tea arrived and the parlormaid hovered. "Shall I pour,
madam?" she asked.

"No, no, Dawson. Leave us."

Dawson went away and she said to me: "Would you care to take
charge of the tea tray? I suffer from rheumatism and my joints are a
little stiff today."

I rose and went to the table on which the tray had been set. There
was a silver kettle over a spirit lamp, and the teapot, cream jug and
sugar bowl were all of shining silver. There were cucumber sandwiches, thin bread and butter, a seed cake and a variety of small cakes.

I had the feeling that I was being set yet another task to ascertain
if I could perform this important social activity with grace. Really,
I thought, she is an impossible old woman; and yet I liked her in spite
of herself and myself.

I knew that my color was heightened a little, but apart from that

I showed no sign of perturbation. I asked how she liked her tea and gave her the requisite amount of cream and sugar, carrying her cup over to her and setting it on the marble and gilt round table by her chair.

"Thank you," she said graciously.

Then I offered her the sandwiches and bread and butter, to which she helped herself liberally.

I kept my place behind the tea tray.

"I hope you will come to see me again," she said, and I knew that her feelings for me were similar to mine for her. She had been prepared to be critical but something in our personalities matched.

I vaguely wondered whether in about seventy years' time I should be just such an old lady.

She ate daintily and heartily and she talked as though there was so much to say that she feared she would never say half she wanted to. She encouraged me to talk too and I told her how Gabriel and I had met when we had rescued Friday.

"Then you heard who he was, and that must have been pleasant for you."

"Heard who he was?"

"That he was an extremely eligible young man, heir to a baronetcy, and that in due course the Revels would be his."

Here it was again—the suggestion that I had married Gabriel for money and position. My anger would not be controlled.

"Nothing of the sort," I said sharply. "Gabriel and I decided to be married before we knew a great deal about each other's worldly position."

"Then you surprise me," she said. "I thought you were a sensible young woman."

"I hope I am not a fool, but I never thought it was necessarily sensible to marry for money. Marriage to an incompatible person can be most unpleasant . . . even if that person is a rich one."

She laughed and I could see that she was enjoying our encounter. She had made up her mind that she liked me; what shocked me a little was that she would have liked me equally well if I had been a fortune hunter. She liked what she called my strength. How they admired that quality in this family! Gabriel had been looking for it and found it in me. Simon had presumed that I had married Gabriel for his money. I wondered whether he also would have thought no less of me for that. These people expected one to be shrewd and clever—

sensible, they called it. No matter how callous, as long as you were
not a fool, you were to be admired.

"So it was love," she said.

"Yes," I answered defiantly, "it was."

"Then why did he kill himself?"

"It is a mystery which has not been solved."

"Perhaps you will solve it."

I was surprised to hear myself say: "I hope so."

"You will if you are determined to."

"Do you think so? Surely there have been unsolved mysteries although many people had devoted their time and energy to the discovery of the truth."

"Perhaps they did not try enough. And now you are carrying the
heir. If your child is a boy, that will be the end of Ruth's hopes for
Luke." She sounded triumphant. "Luke," she went on, "will be another Matthew; he is very like his grandfather."

There was the briefest of silences and then I found myself telling
her how I had seen the schoolroom at the Revels with her initials in
the cupboard and scratched on the table, how Aunt Sarah had conducted me there and given me a glimpse of the old days.

She was interested and willing enough to talk of them.

"It's years since I have been up to the nurseries. Although I pay a
yearly visit to the Revels—at Christmas—I rarely go all over the house.
It's such an effort to go anywhere nowadays. I am the eldest of the
three of us, you know. I'm two years older than Matthew. I made
them all dance to my tune in those days."

"So Aunt Sarah implied."

"Sarah! She was always a scatterbrain. She would sit at the table
twirling a piece of hair round and round until she looked as though
she had been dragged through a hedge backwards . . . dreaming,
always dreaming. I believe she's becoming quite simple in lots of
ways."

"She's very alert in others."

"I know. She was always like that. I used to be at the house every
day in the first years of my marriage. My husband never got on with
my family. I think he was a little jealous of my feeling for them."

She smiled reminiscently and I could see that she was looking back
through the years, seeing herself as the willful, headstrong girl who
had always managed to have her own way.

"We met so few people," she said. "We were very isolated here in those days. That was before the railways came; we visited the county people and there was no other family into which I could marry but that of the Redvers. Sarah didn't marry at all . . . but perhaps she would not have done so whatever her opportunities. She was born to dream her life away."

"You missed the Revels very much after you left to marry," I said, replenishing her cup and handing her the cakes.

She nodded sadly. "Perhaps I should never have left it."

"It seems to mean so much to the people who've lived in it."

"It'll mean a great deal to you one day perhaps. If your child is a boy he will be brought up at the Revels, brought up to love and revere the house. That's tradition."

"I understand that."

"I am certain the child will be a boy. I shall pray for it." She spoke as though even the Deity must obey her commands, and I smiled. She saw the smile and she smiled with me.

"If it were a girl," she went on, "and Luke were to die . . ."

I interrupted in a startled way: "Why should he?"

"Some of the members of our family enjoy longevity; others die young. My brother's two sons were extremely delicate in health. If Gabriel had not died in the manner he did he could not have lived many more years. His brother died at an early age. I fancy I see signs of the same delicacy in Luke."

The words startled me; and as I looked across at her I thought I detected a gleam of hope in her eyes. I was imagining this. She had her back to the light. I was letting my thoughts run on.

Luke and my unborn child, if it is a boy, will stand between Simon and the Revels. By the way she spoke of the Revels and of Simon I knew they meant a good deal to her . . . perhaps more than anything else in her life.

If Simon were the master of the Revels, then she would return there to spend her last days.

I said quickly as though I feared she would read my thoughts: "And your grandson's father . . . your son . . . was he also delicate?"

"Indeed no. Peter, Simon's father, was killed while fighting for his Queen and country in the Crimea. Simon never knew him; and the shock killed his mother who never really recovered from his birth. She was a delicate creature." A faint scorn came into her voice. "It was not a marriage of my making. But my son had a will of his own.

. . . I would not have had him otherwise, although it led him into this disastrous marriage. They left me my grandson."

"That must have been a great consolation to you."

"A great consolation," she said more gently than I had heard her speak before.

I asked if she would have more tea; she declined and as we had both finished she said: "Pray ring for Dawson. I do not care to see used cups and plates."

When the tea things had been taken away she began to talk about Luke. She wanted to know my impressions of him; did I find him attractive, amusing?

I found this embarrassing, for I was not sure what I really thought of Luke.

"He is very young," I replied. "It is difficult to form an opinion of young people. They change so quickly. He has been pleasant to me."

"The doctor's beautiful daughter often visits the house, I believe."

"I have not seen her since my return. We have so few visitors now that we are a house of mourning."

"Of course. And you are wondering how I hear so much of what goes on at the Revels. Servants make excellent carriers of news. My gatekeeper's wife has a sister at the Revels."

"Yes," I said, "she is my maid, a very good girl."

"I am glad she gives satisfaction. I am pleased with Etty. I see a great deal of her. She is about to have her first child and I have always taken an interest in our people. I shall see that she has all that she needs for her confinement. We always send silver spoons to babies born on the Kelly Grange estate."

"That's a pleasant custom."

"Our people are loyal to us because they know they can trust us."

We were both surprised when Simon arrived to take me back to the Revels. The two hours or so I had spent with Hagar Redvers had been stimulating, and I had enjoyed them.

I think she had too, for when she gave me her hand she was even gracious. She said: "You will come and see me again." Then her eyes twinkled and she added, "I hope." And it was as though she recognized in me one who could not be commanded. I knew she liked me for it.

I said I would come again with pleasure and should look forward to the visit.

When Simon took me home we did not say very much; but I could see that he was rather pleased by the way things had gone.

During the next weeks I walked a little, rested a good deal, lying on my bed in the afternoons reading the novels of Mr. Dickens, Mrs. Henry Wood and the Brontë sisters.

I was becoming more and more absorbed in my child and this consoled me. Sometimes I would feel afresh the sorrow of Gabriel's death, and the fact that he would never know his child seemed doubly tragic. And each day, it appeared, there would be something to remind me poignantly of Friday. We had taken so many walks in the grounds about the house, and when I heard the distant bark of a dog, my heart would begin to beat fast with hope. I made myself believe that one day he would come back. Perhaps this was because I could not bear to believe that—as in the case of Gabriel—I should never see him again.

I tried to take an interest in the life of the neighborhood. I had tea with the vicarage family; I went to church and sat in the Rockwell pew with Ruth and Luke. I felt that I was settling in as I had not begun to do while Gabriel was with me.

Sometimes I would be taken to the nurseries by Sarah—she never seemed to tire of taking me there. I was introduced to the family cradle which was a beautiful piece of workmanship on rockers and was about two hundred years old. Sarah was making a blue padded coverlet for it, and her needlework was exquisite.

I visited Hagar once more and we seemed to grow even closer; I assured myself that I had found a good friend in her.

We did no entertaining at Kirkland Revels because of our being in mourning, but close friends of the family visited us now and then. Damaris came, and I was certain that Luke was in love with her, but I was not at all sure of her feelings for him. I wondered idly whether Damaris had any feelings. I had noticed that even with her father she seemed sometimes unresponsive, although she was docile enough. I wondered whether she had any real affection, even for him.

The doctor was often in and out of the house, to keep an eye on Sir Matthew and Sarah, he said; not forgetting Mrs. Rockwell, he would add, smiling at me.

He made out a little schedule for me. I was not to walk too far, I must give up riding; I must rest whenever I felt so inclined, and take hot milk before going to bed.

One day when I had gone for my morning walk, I was about a mile from the house when I heard the sound of carriage wheels behind me and turning saw the doctor's brougham.

He instructed his man to pull up beside me.

"You've tired yourself," he accused me.

"Indeed I have not. And I am nearly home."

"Please get in," he said. "I'm going to give you a lift back."

I obeyed, protesting that I was not in the least tired. In fact, he looked much more tired than I, and in my somewhat forthright manner I told him so.

"I've been up to Worstwhistle," he said. "That always tires me."

Worstwhistle! The mention of that place saddened me. I thought of those people with their poor clouded minds, shut away from the world. How good he was to give his services to such a place!

"You are very good to go there," I told him.

"My motives are selfish, Mrs. Rockwell," he answered. "These people interest me. Besides, they need me. It is a pleasant thing to be needed."

"That is so, but it is good of you all the same. I have heard from others how you comfort them, not only with your medical skill but with your kindness."

"Ha!" He laughed suddenly and his white teeth flashed in his brown face. "I have a great deal to be thankful for. I'll tell you a secret about myself. Forty years ago I was an orphan . . . a penniless orphan. Now it is a sad thing in this world to be an orphan, but to be a penniless orphan, my dear Mrs. Rockwell, that is indeed a tragedy."

"I can well believe it."

"I might have been a beggar . . . standing by the road shivering with cold, driven to frustration by hunger, but life was good to me after all. As I grew up it became the dream of my life to heal the sick. I had no hope of attaining my ambition. But I caught the notice of a rich man and he was good to me. He educated me, he helped me to realize my ambition. But for that rich man, what should I have been? Whenever I see a beggar by the roadside, or a criminal in his prison, I say to myself: There but for the grace of that rich man go I. Then I give myself to my patients. Do you understand me?"

"I did not know . . ." I began.

"And now you think a little less of me because I am not quite a gentleman, eh?"

I turned to him fiercely. "I think you are a very great gentleman," I said.

We had reached the Revels and he murmured: "Then will you do me a favor?"

"If it is in my power."

"Take great care of yourself . . . even greater care."

I was taking tea with Hagar Redvers, and she was talking—as she loved to—of her childhood and how she had ruled the nursery at the Revels, when suddenly that overcrowded room seemed to close in on me and I could no longer breathe. Something happened to me, and I was not quite sure what it was.

The next thing I remembered was that I was lying on the horsehair couch and smelling salts were being thrust beneath my nose.

"What . . . happened?" I asked.

"It's all right, my dear." That was Hagar's authoritative voice. "You fainted."

"Fainted! I . . . But . . ."

"Don't disturb yourself. I think it is a fairly common occurrence at this stage. Now lie still. I have sent for Jessie Dankwait. I have the utmost confidence in her."

I tried to rise, but those strong old hands sparkling with garnets and diamonds held me down.

"I think, my dear, you walked too far. This journey is becoming too much for you. You must be driven here next time."

She was sitting in the chair beside the sofa. She was saying: "I remember how I fainted when my son was on the way. It is such a horrible feeling, is it not? But it is surprising how, as the time progresses, one becomes accustomed to all the little inconveniences. Do you feel like some refreshment, my dear? I did wonder if a little brandy might be useful. But I think we should wait for Jessie Dankwait."

It could not have been much more than fifteen minutes later when Jessie Dankwait came into the room. I judged her to be in her middle forties; her face was rosy, her expression pleasant; her black bonnet, trimmed with jet beads which danced in rather a jolly fashion as she moved, was tied under her chin with black ribbons; on her gaberdine cloak jet also glistened. Beneath the cloak she wore a black dress and a very clean white starched apron.

I quickly discovered that she was the midwife who lived on the Kelly Grange estate, and as Hagar ruled over that estate like a queen over her kingdom, the midwife behaved as though she were a subject. I subsequently discovered that if any of the mothers were unable to pay her, Hagar paid for them. Jessie also acted as nurse, for she had received a certain amount of training in all branches of nursing.

She prodded me and questioned me and spoke knowledgeably about my condition. She came to the conclusion that everything was as it should be and that what I had experienced was natural enough considering the time of my pregnancy.

She thought that a cup of hot sweet tea was what I needed; and there was nothing to fear.

When she had left, Hagar ordered that a pot of tea should be made, and while I was drinking a cup of it she said: "You could not do better than engage Jessie when your time comes. I know of none so good in the neighborhood; that is why I employ her. She has more successful cases than any other midwife I have ever known. If I had been able to employ her for my daughter-in-law she would have been here today."

I said I thought it was an excellent idea, for I had been wondering what arrangements I should make.

"Then that's settled," said Hagar. "I shall tell Jessie to hold herself in readiness. It would be an excellent idea if you kept her at the Revels for a week or so beforehand. That is always wise."

It appeared that my affairs were being taken out of my hands, but I did not care. The change in my body seemed to be changing my character. I experienced a certain lassitude as I lay on that horsehair sofa listening to Hagar making plans for my future.

Jessie had not left the house, and when Hagar sent for her, before I left, to tell her that I had decided to use her services, she was delighted.

"Jessie will call on you regularly at the Revels," declared Hagar. "And you must take her advice. Now someone shall drive you back. And when you get there you should rest."

Simon was not at home, so one of the grooms drove me back. Ruth came out in some surprise when she saw how I had returned, and I hastily told her what had happened.

"You'd better go straight up and rest," she said. "I'll have dinner sent up to you."

So I went up and Mary-Jane came to me to make me comfortable; and I let her chatter on about her sister Etty who some months back had fainted in just the same way.

I looked forward to a leisurely evening, reading in bed.

Mary-Jane brought up my dinner and when I had eaten it she came back to tell me that Dr. Smith wanted to see me. She decorously but-

toned my bed jacket up to my neck and went out to say that I was
ready for the doctor.

He came into my room with Ruth, and they sat near the bed while
he asked questions about my faint.

"I understand it's nothing to worry about," I said. "Apparently it's
the normal occurrence at this stage. The midwife told me."

"Who?" asked the doctor.

"Jessie Dankwait. Mrs. Redvers has the utmost faith in her. I have
engaged her for the great occasion and she will be coming to see me
from time to time."

The doctor did not speak for a while. Then he said: "This woman
has a very good reputation in the neighborhood." He leaned towards
the bed smiling at me. "But I shall satisfy myself as to whether she is
practiced enough to take care of you," he added.

They did not stay long and after they had gone I lay back lux-
uriously. It was a pleasant feeling to know that all was being taken
care of.

It was two weeks later, when my peaceful existence was shattered,
and the horror and doubts began.

The day had been a glorious one. Although we were in mid-
September, the summer was still with us and only the early twilight
brought home the fact that the year was so advanced.

I had passed the day pleasantly. I had been along to the church
with Ruth, Luke and Damaris to take flowers to decorate it for the
harvest festival; they had not allowed me to do any of the decorating,
but had made me sit in one of the pews watching them at work.

I had sat back, rather drowsily content, listening to the hollow
sound of their voices as they talked together. Damaris, arranging
gold, red and mauve chrysanthemums on the altar, had looked like
a figure from the Old Testament, her grace and beauty never more
apparent. Luke was helping her—he was never far from her side—and
there was Ruth with bunches of grapes and vegetable marrows which
she was placing artistically on the sills below the stained-glass
windows.

It was an atmosphere of absolute peace—the last I was to know
for a long time.

We had tea at the vicarage and walked leisurely home afterwards.
When night came I had no premonition that change was near.

I went to bed early as was now my custom. The moon was nearly full and, since I would have the curtains drawn back, it flooded my room with soft light, competing with the candles.

I tried afterwards to recall that evening in detail, but I did not know at that stage that I should have taken particular note of it; so looking back it seemed like many other evenings.

Of one thing I was certain—that I did not draw the curtains on either side of my bed, because I had always insisted that the curtains should not be drawn. I had told Mary-Jane of this and she bore me out afterwards.

I blew out my candles and got into bed. I lay for some time looking at the windows; in an hour or so I knew that the lopsided moon would be looking straight in at me. It had awakened me last night when it had shone its light full on my face.

I slept. And . . . suddenly I was awake and in great fear, though for some seconds I did not know why. I was aware of a cold draught. I was lying on my back and my room was full of moonlight. But that was not all that was in my room. Someone was there . . . someone was standing at the foot of my bed watching me.

I think I called out, but I am not sure; I started up and then I felt as though all my limbs were frozen and for several seconds I was as one turned to stone. If ever I had known fear in my life I knew it then.

It was because of what I saw at the foot of my bed . . . something which moved yet was not of this world.

It was a figure in a black cloak and cowl—a monk; over the face was a mask such as those worn by torturers in the chambers of the Inquisition; there were slits in the mask for the eyes to look through, but it was not possible to see those eyes though I believed they watched me intently.

I had never before seen a ghost. I did not believe in ghosts. My practical Yorkshire soul rebelled against such fantasies. I had always said I should have to see to believe. Now I was seeing.

The figure moved as I looked. Then it was gone.

It could be no apparition, for I was not the sort of person to see apparitions. Someone had been in my room. I turned to follow the figure but I could see nothing but a dark wall before my eyes. So dazed was I, so shocked, that it was a second or so before I realized that the curtain on one side of my bed had been drawn so that the door and that part of the room which led to it were shut off from my view.

Still numb with shock and terror I could not move until suddenly

I thought I heard the sound of a door quietly closing. That brought me back to reality. Someone had come into my room and gone out by the door; ghosts, I had always heard, had no need to concern themselves with the opening and shutting of doors.

I stumbled out of bed, falling into the curtain which I hastily pushed aside. I hurried to the door, calling: "Who was that? Who was that?"

There was no sign of anyone in the corridor. I ran to the top of the stairs. The moonlight, falling through the windows there, threw shadows all about me. I felt suddenly alone with evil and I was terrified.

I began to shout: "Come quickly. There is someone in the house."

I heard a door open and shut; then Ruth's voice: "Catherine, is that you?"

"Yes, yes . . . come quickly. . . ."

It seemed a long time before she appeared; then she came down the stairs wrapping a long robe about her, holding a small lamp in her hand.

"What happened?" she cried.

"There was something in my room. It came and stood at the bottom of my bed."

"You have had a nightmare."

"I was awake, I tell you. I was awake. I woke up and saw it. It must have wakened me."

"My dear Catherine, you're shivering. You should get back to bed. In your state . . ."

"It came into my room. It may come again."

"My dear, it was only a bad dream."

I felt frustrated and angry with her. It was the beginning of frustration, and what could be more exasperating than the inability to convince people that you have seen something with your eyes and not with your imagination?

"It was not a dream," I said angrily. "Of one thing I am certain, it was not a dream. There was someone in my room. I did not imagine it."

Somewhere in the house a clock struck one, and almost immediately Luke appeared on the landing above us.

"What's the commotion?" he asked yawning.

"Catherine has been . . . upset."

"There was someone in my room."

"Burglars?"

"No, I don't think so. It was someone dressed as a monk."

"My dear," said Ruth gently, "you've been going to the Abbey and letting yourself get imaginative there. It's an eerie place. Don't go there again. It obviously upsets you."

"I keep telling you that there was actually someone in my room. This person had drawn the curtain about my bed so that I shouldn't see his departure."

"Drawn the curtain about your bed? I expect Mary-Jane did that."

"She did not. I have told her not to. No, the person who was playing this joke—if it was a joke—drew it."

I saw Ruth and Luke exchange glances, and I knew they were thinking that I was obsessed by the Abbey; clearly I was the victim of one of those vivid nightmares which hang about when one wakes and seem a part of reality.

"It was not a dream," I insisted fervently. "Someone came into my room. Perhaps it was meant to be a joke . . ."

I looked from Ruth to Luke; would either of them play such a stupid trick? Who else could have done it? Sir Matthew? Aunt Sarah? The apparition which had flitted across my room, quietly closing the door after it, must have been agile.

"You should go back to bed," said Ruth. "You should not let a nightmare disturb you."

Go back to bed. Try to sleep. Perhaps to be awakened by that figure at the bottom of my bed! It had merely stood there this time and looked at me. What would it do next? How could I sleep peacefully again in that room?

Luke yawned. Clearly he thought it strange that I should wake them because of a dream.

"Come along," said Ruth gently and, as she slipped her arm through mine, I remembered that I was in my nightdress and presented an unconventional sight to the pair of them.

Luke said: "Good night," and went back to his room, so that I was left alone with Ruth.

"My dear Catherine," she said as she drew me along the corridor, "you really are scared."

"It was . . . horrible. To think of being watched while I was asleep, like that."

"I've had one or two alarming nightmares myself. I know the impression they leave."

"But I keep telling you, I was not asleep."

She did not answer as she threw open the door of my room. The current of air disturbed the drawn bed curtain; and I remembered the draught I had felt, and I was certain then that someone had crept silently into my room, and drawn the curtain along one side of the bed before taking a stand there at the foot of it.

All human actions. Some person in this house had done this to me.

Why should that person wish to frighten me, knowing of my condition?

"You see," I said, "the curtain is drawn at the side of the bed. It was not like that when I went to sleep."

"Mary-Jane must have done it."

"Why should she come back after I had said good night to her, to draw a curtain which I had expressly asked should not be drawn?"

Ruth lifted her shoulders.

"Lie down," she said. "Why, you are cold. You should have put something on."

"There wasn't time. I didn't think of it in any case. I was after . . . whoever it was. I thought I might catch a glimpse of the way it went. But when I came out there was nothing . . . nothing. I wonder if . . . it's still here . . . watching . . . listening. . . ."

"Come, lie down. It can't be here because it was part of your dream."

"But I know when I am awake and when I'm asleep."

"I'm going to light your candles. You'll feel better then."

"The moon is so bright. I do not need candles."

"Perhaps it is better not to light them. I'm always afraid of fire."

She drew back the bed curtain and sat by the side of the bed.

"You will be cold," I said.

"I don't like to leave you while you are so disturbed," she replied.

I was ashamed to ask her to stay, and yet I felt afraid. But I was so convinced that what I had seen was no apparition that I was certain, if I locked my door on the inside, it could not come again to my room.

"I'm all right," I said. "I don't need company."

She rose smiling. "It is not like you to be afraid of dreams."

"Oh dear! Why can't you believe me? I *know* it was not a dream," I told her. "Someone is playing a trick on me."

"A dangerous trick . . . on a woman in your condition."

"It is someone who gives no thought to my danger."

She lifted her shoulders and the gesture was disbelieving.

"I am so sorry to have disturbed you like this," I said. "Please go back to your room."

"If you are sure . . ."

I got out of bed and reached for my dressing gown.

"Where are you going?" she asked.

"To lock the door when you have gone. If I lock that and the one which leads to the powder room, and the door of the powder room which opens onto the corridor, I shall feel safe."

"If you can only feel safe like that you must, but Catherine, who in this place would do such a thing? You must have been dreaming."

"So I could believe," I said, "but for the fact that I felt the draught from the door and heard it shut, and the apparition had had the fore-sight to draw that curtain on one side of my bed. I should think apparitions are rarely so practical."

I was losing a little of my fear. It was strange that a human enemy was much less alarming than a supernatural one.

I had not then begun to ask myself the all-important question: Why?

"Well, I will say good night," Ruth said. "If you are sure . . ."

"I am all right now."

"Good night, Catherine. If you should have any more . . . alarms, remember I am not very far away . . . only on the next floor. And Luke is near too."

"I'll remember."

When she had gone I locked the door after her and made sure the door of the powder room which opened onto the corridor was also locked on the inside.

I went back to bed, but not to sleep. I should not be able to sleep until daylight.

I turned the question over and over in my mind. Who had done this, and why? It was no ordinary practical joke. The person who had done this had meant to terrify me. I was not the sort of woman to be easily terrified, but the most strong-minded must be upset by seeing such a vision at the foot of their bed. And I was a woman, known to be pregnant.

I felt the menace then. Someone was plotting evil. It might be only indirectly aimed at me because of the precious burden I carried.

One prospective master of the Revels had died violently; was something being plotted against another?

That was the beginning of my period of terror.

5

I awoke soon after six o'clock the next morning, rose and unlocked my door; then I returned to bed and fell asleep to be awakened by Mary-Jane at my bedside with a breakfast tray.

"Mrs. Grantley said you should have a rest this morning," she told me.

I started out of a deep sleep remembering the horror of the previous night; I must have stared at Mary-Jane for she looked slightly alarmed. In those first moments of waking I had half expected her to turn into a black-clad apparition.

"Oh . . . thank you, Mary-Jane," I stammered.

She propped me up with pillows and helped me on with my bed jacket. Then she placed the tray on my knees.

"Is there anything else, madam?"

She was unlike herself, almost anxious to get out of the room. As she went I thought: Good heavens, has she heard already!

I sat up, sipping my tea. I could not eat. The whole thing had come back to me vividly in all its horror; I found that my eyes kept straying to the foot of my bed.

Realizing it was no use trying to eat, I put aside the breakfast tray and lay back thinking about last night, trying to assure myself that I had imagined it all. The draught . . . the bed curtain . . . Had I walked in my sleep? Had I opened the door? Had I myself drawn the bed curtain? "Gabriel," I murmured, "did *you* walk in your sleep?"

I was trembling, so I hastily pulled myself together.

There was a logical explanation of my horrific adventure. There was always a logical explanation, and I had to find it.

I got out of bed and rang for hot water. Mary-Jane brought it and set it in the powder room. I did not speak to her in my usual friendly way. My mind was too full of what had happened on the previous night and I did not want to talk about that with her . . . or anyone . . . just yet.

While I was finishing dressing there was a knock on my door and when I called, "Come in," Ruth entered. She said: "Good morning, Catherine," and looked at me anxiously. "How are you feeling this morning?"

"A little weary."

"Yes, you look it. It *was* a disturbed night."

"For you too, I'm afraid. I'm sorry I made such a fuss."

"It doesn't matter. You were really scared. I'm glad you did waken me . . . if it helped at all."

"Yes, it did help. I had to talk to somebody . . . real."

"The best thing we can do is to try to forget it. I know how that sort of thing can hang about though. I think Deverel Smith ought to give you something to make you sleep tonight. You'll feel all the better for a good night's sleep."

I was not going to argue with her any more, because I could see it was useless. She had made up her mind that I had been the victim of a nightmare, and nothing would change it.

I said: "Thanks so much for sending up my breakfast."

She grimaced. "I saw Mary-Jane taking the tray away. You didn't eat much of it."

"I had several cups of tea."

"You have to take care, remember. What do you plan to do this morning?"

"Perhaps a little walk."

"Well, I shouldn't go too far and—don't mind my saying this, Catherine—I should keep away from the Abbey for a while."

A faint smile curved her lips; it might have been apologetic. I was not sure, for Ruth only seemed to smile with her lips.

She left me and I went downstairs on my way out. I felt I wanted to get away from the house. I wished that I could ride out onto the moors, but I had given up riding and had curtailed my walking considerably.

As I came down to the hall Luke was coming in. He was in riding kit and looked surprisingly like Gabriel so that for a moment as he stood in shadow I could believe he was Gabriel. I gave a little gasp—my nerves had certainly been affected by what had happened and I seemed to be expecting to see strange things.

"Hello," he said. "Seen any more hobgoblins?"

He grinned and his careless unconcern gave me a twinge of alarm. I tried to speak lightly. "Once was enough."

"A hooded monk!" he murmured. "Poor Catherine, you were in a state!"

"I'm sorry I disturbed you."

"Don't be sorry. Any time you need assistance, call me. I've never been attracted to monks anyway. All that fasting, hairshirts, celibacy and so on . . . Seems to be so unnecessary. I like good food, fine linen and beautiful women. There's nothing of the monk about me. So if you want any help in tackling them, I'm your man."

He was mocking me, and I had come to the conclusion that the best way to treat the affair was lightly. My own opinions would not change, but it was no use trying to force them on others.

He and his mother were persisting in the belief that I had experienced a particularly terrifying nightmare. I would not seek to change that opinion. But nevertheless I was going to find out who in this house had played such a cruel trick on me.

"Thank you," I said, trying to speak as lightly as he had. "I'll remember that."

"It's a pleasant morning," he said. "A pity you can't ride. There's just that nip of autumn in the air to make riding a pleasure. However, perhaps before long. . . ."

"I'll manage without," I told him; and as I passed him his smile was enigmatic and I had a feeling that he was picturing me as I looked in my dishabille the night before. I remembered then that Hagar Redvers had said he was like his grandfather, and Sir Matthew had an eye for women.

I passed out into the open air. It was wonderful what fresh air could do. My fear evaporated and as I walked among the beds of chrysanthemums and Michaelmas daisies I felt capable of tackling any menace that might present itself.

If you believe that was a human being playing a trick, I told myself, all you have to do is search your room and the powder room before retiring and lock doors and windows. Then if you are disturbed by apparitions you will know that they are of the supernatural class.

This was a test of my belief. It was, I reminded myself, all very well to be brave on a fresh bright morning like this, but how should I feel when darkness fell?

I was determined to test myself, to prove that I really did believe that some human being had played that trick on me.

I returned to the house for luncheon which I took with Ruth and

Luke. Luke made a reference to my "nightmare" and I made no con-
tradiction of the term. That lunch was very like others; I fancied Ruth
seemed relieved. She said I looked better for my walk, and it was true
that I did eat well, for I found I was hungry after having had no
breakfast.

When I rose from the luncheon table William came into the dining
room with a message from Sir Matthew. He would like to see me if I
could spare the time to visit him.

I said I would go at once if he was ready.

"I will take you to his room, madam," William told me.

He led me up the staircase to a room on the first floor which was
not far from my own. I was beginning to learn where the family had
their apartments. They lived mainly in the south wing: Sir Matthew
on the first floor where I now had my room, Ruth and Luke on the
second; and the third of course was where I had lived with Gabriel
during the short time we had been together in the house. Sarah was
the only member of the family who occupied rooms other than in the
south wing. She clung to the east wing where the nurseries were. The
rest of the house was not being used at this time, but I was told that
in the past Sir Matthew had entertained lavishly and that the Revels
had often been filled with guests.

The kitchens, bakehouses, and sculleries were on the ground floor
and an extension of the south wing. The servants' sleeping quarters
were on the top floor of the west wing. I had not seen them but Mary-
Jane had told me this. So few people in such a large house!

I found Sir Matthew sitting up in bed, a woollen bed jacket buttoned up to his neck and a nightcap on his head. His eyes twinkled as
I came towards him.

"Bring a chair for Mrs. Gabriel, William," he said.

I thanked William and sat down.

"I hear you had a disturbed night, my dear," he said. "Nightmare,
Ruth tells me."

"It's over now," I said.

"Frightening things, nightmares. And you ran out of your room on
your bare feet." He shook his head.

William was hovering in the next room which I presumed was a
dressing room. The door was open and he would hear all that was
said. I had a vision of the servants' discussing the night's disturbance,
and I wished to change the subject.

"And how are you today?"

"All the better for seeing you, my dear. But I'm a sad subject. I'm old and the body gets worn out in time. Now you are young, and we cannot have you upset . . ."

"I shall not be scared in future," I said quickly. "It was the first time anything like it had happened . . ."

"You have to take care now, Catherine, my dear."

"Oh yes, I'm taking care."

"I heard nothing of all this."

"I'm so pleased. I should hate to think I had disturbed you too."

"I don't sleep well but when I do it's like the sleep of the dead. You'd have to shout somewhat loudly to awaken me. I'm glad I've seen you, my dear. I wanted to satisfy myself that you were your bright and beautiful self again." He smiled jauntily. "It was only for that reason that I asked you to come and see me in this state. What do you think of me, eh . . . poor old fellow in a nightcap!"

"It's quite becoming."

"Catherine, you are a flatterer. Well, my dear, remember you are a very important member of the family now."

"I do remember," I said. "I shall do nothing that would be harmful to the child."

"I like your outspoken ways, my dear. God bless you; and thank you for coming and saying a few kind words to an old man."

He took my hand and kissed it, and as I went out I was still aware of William, hovering in the dressing room.

The whole house knows, I thought; and I wondered why Aunt Sarah had not been to see me. I should have thought she would have wanted to talk about the affair.

I went to my room but I could not settle there, and I thought of the servants' talking together; and it occurred to me that the story would soon reach the ears of Hagar and Simon Redvers. I felt disturbed at the idea of their hearing a version other than my own. I cared very much for the good opinion of Hagar and I believed that she would be very scornful of anything fanciful.

I decided then that I would go and see her and tell her exactly what had happened, before her opinions were colored by other people's views.

I set out and walked over to Kelly Grange; it was three o'clock when I arrived.

Dawson took me into a small room on the ground floor and said she would tell Mrs. Rockwell-Redvers that I was there.

"If she is resting," I said, "please do not disturb her. I can wait awhile."

"I will inquire, madam," Dawson replied.

In a few minutes she returned with the message that Mrs. Rockwell-Redvers would see me at once.

She was sitting in her high-backed chair as she had been on the occasion when I had first seen her. I took her hand and kissed it as I had seen Simon do—that was a concession to our friendship. I was no longer afraid that she would treat me with haughtiness. We now accepted each other as equals, and that meant that we could be quite natural together.

"It is good of you to call," she said. "Did you walk?"

"It is such a short distance really."

"You don't look as well as you did when I last saw you."

"I did not sleep well."

"That is bad. Have you seen Jessie Dankwait?"

"This has nothing to do with Jessie Dankwait. I wanted to tell you about it before you heard it from another quarter. I wanted you to hear my version."

"You are overexcited," she said coolly.

"Perhaps. But I am calmer than I have been since it happened."

"I want very much to hear about it. Please tell me."

So I told her what had occurred, omitting nothing.

She listened. Then she nodded almost judicially.

"It is quite clear," she said, "that someone in the house is trying to alarm you."

"It seems such a foolish thing to do."

"I would not call a thing foolish if there is a reasonable motive behind it."

"But what motive?"

"To scare you. Perhaps to ruin your hopes of producing a child."

"This seems a strange way to go about that. And who . . . ?"

"It may be the beginning of a series of alarms. I think we must be on our guard against that."

There was a tap on the door. "Come in," she called and Simon entered.

"Dawson told me that Mrs. Catherine was here," he said. "Have you any objection to my joining you?"

"I have none," said his grandmother. "Have you, Catherine?"

"But . . . no."

"You don't sound very sure," he said, smiling at me.

"It is because we were discussing something which Catherine came here to tell me. I have no idea whether she would wish you to hear it."

I looked at him—and I thought I had never seen anyone so vital, so much a part of the present time. He radiated practical common sense.

"I have no objection to his hearing what has happened."

"Then we'll tell him," said Hagar and proceeded to do so. It was a considerable comfort that she told him the story as I had told it to her. Never once did she say, "Catherine thinks she saw," or "Catherine believed it was," but always, Catherine saw and it was. How grateful I was for that.

He listened intently.

"What do you think of it?" Hagar asked when she had finished.

"Someone in the house is playing tricks," he said.

"Exactly," cried Hagar. "And why so?"

"I imagine it could concern the heir who will in due course make his appearance."

Hagar gave me a triumphant look.

"It was a terrifying experience for poor Catherine," she said.

"Why did you not make an attempt to catch the trickster?" asked Simon.

"I did," I retorted indignantly. "But by the time I had recovered myself he had gone."

"You are calling it 'he.' You have some reason to believe the creature is of the masculine gender?"

"I don't know. But one must call it something. *He* comes more naturally then *she*. He was very quick; he must have been out of the door and along the corridor in a very short time, and then . . ."

"And then where did he go?"

"I don't know. If he had gone downstairs I must have seen him. He could never have run down the stairs and across the hall in time. I can't imagine how he went along the corridor so swiftly."

"He must have gone into one of the rooms there. Did you look?"

"No."

"You should have done."

"Ruth appeared then."

"And Luke came later," said Hagar significantly.

"Did Luke appear to have been rushing about?"

"You suspect Luke?" I asked.

"I merely wonder. It must have been someone in the house, I suppose. If the idea was to frighten you, it must have been either Ruth, Luke, Matthew or Sarah. Did you see them all?"

"Not Matthew, nor Sarah."

"Ah!"

"I cannot imagine either of them running about the house in the night dressed up as a monk."

Simon leaned towards me. He said: "The Rockwell family are all a little crazy about their old traditions." He smiled at Hagar. "Everyone," he added. "I wouldn't trust any one of them where the old Revels is concerned, and that's a fact. They're living in the past half the time. Who could help it in that old fortress? It's not a house. It's a mausoleum. Anyone who lives there for any length of time is likely to get strange ideas."

"And you think I have!"

"Not you. You're not a Rockwell simply because you married one. You're a forthright Yorkshire woman who'll blow a blast of common sense into the stuffy old place. You know what happens to the dead when they are exposed to fresh air, don't you? They molder and crumble away."

"I'm glad you don't think I imagined all this, because that is what they are all trying to pretend I did. They call it a nightmare."

"Naturally the trickster would want that put about."

"I shall be prepared for him next time."

"He won't play the same game twice. You can be sure of that."

"He won't get an opportunity to. I intend to lock my doors tonight."

"But he may try something else," warned Simon.

"I'm ready for tea," said Hagar. "Ring for Dawson, and the three of us will have it together. Then, Simon, you must drive Catherine back to the Revels. She walked one way, and here and back is too far."

The tea was brought and once again I presided over the tea cups.

I was feeling almost normal now; the comfort I drew from these two astonished and delighted me. They believed in me; they refused to treat me as an hysterical subject; and that was wonderful.

I wanted that teatime hour to go on and on.

Hagar said as she stirred her tea: "I remember once Matthew played a trick on me. Strangely enough he came into *my* bedroom. Really, it must have been something like your affair. I had my curtains drawn about the bed. It was midwinter, I remember. . . . Christmas time. The snow was deep outside and the east wind was driving a blizzard. We had a few people in the house . . . those who had arrived before the bad weather started. We thought they would have to stay with us well beyond the Christmas holidays unless there was a thaw. We children had been allowed to watch the ball from the minstrels' gallery. It was a wonderful sight . . . the dresses and the decorations. Well, that wasn't the point. We children had had too much plum pudding I daresay, because we grew rather quarrelsome . . . at least Matthew and I did. Poor Sarah never joined in our quarrels.

"To get to the point, I had been discussing our ancestors and Matthew was wishing that he could wear those wonderful plumed hats and lace collars as they did in the days of the Cavaliers. I said: 'Like Sir John! Don't say you want to be like him in the least little bit.' 'But I do want to be exactly like Sir John,' Matthew said. 'I hate Sir John,' I cried. 'I *like* Sir John,' he answered. Then he twisted my arm and I made his nose bleed. I shouted that Sir John was a coward."

She laughed and her eyes sparkled at the memory. "You see, Catherine, Sir John was the master of Kirkland Revels at the time of the Civil War. Marston Moor had gone to Cromwell and Fairfax, and Prince Rupert was on the run. Sir John was naturally a Royalist and he went on declaring he'd hold the Revels against Cromwell or die in the attempt. Never should the Revels pass out of the Rockwells' hands. But when the Parliamentarians came into Kirkland Moorside, he disappeared . . . he and everyone in the house. Just imagine the soldiers coming into the Revels. They would have hanged him on one of his own oaks if they had found him. But he just disappeared. It's been one of the mysteries of our house . . . how he and his household managed to disappear at the moment the Roundheads entered Kirkland Moorside. They took away all the valuables with them too. They were brought back after the Restoration. But I told Matthew that John was a coward because he did not stay and fight but walked out and calmly handed over the Revels to the enemy. Matthew didn't agree with me. Anything would have done to quarrel about on that day. Sir John happened to be the cause."

She stirred her tea thoughtfully and the haughtiness left her face as she looked back into the past.

Then she went on: "And so Matthew decided to play a practical joke with me as his victim. I was awakened to see the curtains of my bed divided, and there was a face drawn into a hideous scowl under a plumed hat. A voice hissed: 'So you are the one who dared call me a coward! You will regret that, Hagar Rockwell. I am Sir John and I've come to haunt you!' I was startled out of my sleep and for a few seconds I really did think my careless words had brought our ancestor from the tomb. Then I recognized Matthew's voice and saw his hand clutching a candle. I leaped out of bed and grabbed the hat. I rammed it down on his head, boxed his ears, and threw him out of my room."

She laughed again; then she looked at me apologetically. "It reminded me, although it was really so different."

"Where did he find the plumed hat?" I asked.

"There are lots of clothes put away in chests in the house. It was probably right out of period. I remember we were both put on bread and water and confined to our rooms for a day for disturbing our governess."

"The difference is that you caught your intruder," said Simon. "I wish we could discover who this monk really is."

"At least," I put in, "I shall be on my guard for the future."

Simon changed the subject and I found myself talking of the affairs of the neighborhood: the home farm which was attached to the Grange and which he managed, and the smaller homesteads on the estate of which he would one day be the landlord. It was clear that he and Hagar felt deeply about the Kelly Grange estate, but in a different way from that worship of a house which I felt obtained at the Revels. I had never heard the Rockwells discuss their tenants in the same way, and I was sure that Sir Matthew would not greatly care whether a man had been hurt when ploughing or that his wife was expecting a child again.

Hagar might look back to the traditions of the past but she had her keen eyes on the present. She might long to be mistress of the Revels and for Simon to be its master, but that did not mean she was indifferent to the Kelly Grange estate. Far from it. I believed that she would have liked to unite the two.

As for Simon he was so much the practical man; a house would never mean more to him than the stones of which it was built; and tradition in his opinion, I was sure, should be made to serve man, not man tradition.

There was so much about him that angered me, for I could never forget his hinting that I was a fortune hunter, but on that day I needed his clear cold common sense, and I was grateful for it.

So those two gave me the strength and courage I badly needed. I knew that when I was alone in my room that night I should remember them and their belief in me, and it would help me to believe in myself.

Simon drove me back at five o'clock and, as I heard him drive off and turned to go into the house in which the first shadows of evening were beginning to fall, I felt my courage begin to ebb.

But I kept thinking of those two and as I mounted the stairs to my room I did not once look over my shoulder to see if I was being followed, although I wanted to.

Matthew, Luke and Ruth seemed to watch me rather furtively through dinner; as for Sarah, she had made no mention of the affair, which surprised me. I managed to appear quite normal.

After dinner Dr. Smith and Damaris called to take wine with us. I was sure that Ruth had sent for him, telling him what had happened, for when Damaris and Luke were whispering together, Ruth drew Sir Matthew aside—Aunt Sarah had already retired—and the doctor said to me: "I hear there was a little trouble last night."

"It was nothing," I said quickly.

"Ah, you have recovered from it," he said. "Mrs. Grantley thought she ought to tell me. I have made her promise, you know, to keep an eye on you."

"There was no need to tell you this."

"A nightmare, was it? That was what Mrs. Grantley called it."

"If it had been merely a nightmare I should not have left my room and awakened others. In my opinion it was not a nightmare."

He glanced at the rest of the company and whispered: "Could you tell me all about it?"

So once more that day I told the story.

He listened gravely, but he made no comment.

"You may not sleep very well tonight," he said.

"I think I shall."

"Ah, you are a young lady of such sound good sense."

"I propose to lock my doors so that there is no possibility of the joker's coming into my room. Then I shall feel perfectly safe."

"Wouldn't you like a sleeping draught?"

"It will not be necessary."

"Take it in case. You don't want two bad nights running. I've got it here with me."

"It's unnecessary."

"There's no harm in having it at hand. Put it by your bed. Then if you can't sleep . . . take it and in ten minutes you'll be in a deep and restful sleep."

I took the small bottle and slipped it into the pocket of my gown. "Thank you," I said.

"You needn't fear," he told me with a smile. "You won't become an addict after one dose, believe me. And I want you to have good nights . . . plenty of rest and good plain food. So don't think you're being brave by refusing to take the draught. Think of the rest and relaxation you need . . . for the little one."

"You are very attentive, Dr. Smith."

"I am very anxious to look after you."

So when I retired that night I put the sleeping draught by my bed as I had promised. Then I searched my room and locked the doors. I went to bed; but I did not sleep as readily as I had believed I should. I would doze and start out of my sleep, my gaze going immediately to the foot of my bed.

I was by no means an hysterical subject, but I had received a violent shock and even the calmest of people cannot expect to recover immediately.

One of the clocks in the house was striking midnight when I took Dr. Smith's draught. Almost immediately I sank into a deep and restful sleep.

Within a few days I had completely recovered from my shock, but I was still watchful. Nothing else of a similar nature had happened, but each night I locked my doors and was now sleeping normally without those distressing sudden awakenings to stare about the room, looking for an apparition.

The household had ceased to refer to the incident, and I guessed that in the servants' hall they had decided that it was one of the queer things which happen to women who are expecting a child.

But I was no less determined to discover who had been disguised as the monk and, as I brooded on it one morning, I remembered that Hagar had said there had been clothes of all kinds in various chests about the house. What if in one of the chests there was a monk's robe? If I could find such a thing I should be on my way to solving the mystery.

There was one person who might be helpful in this respect. That was Sarah—and I decided to go along and see her.

It was after luncheon, at which she did not appear, when I made my way to her apartments in the east wing.

I knocked at the door of her tapestry room, and I was pleased when she called to me to come in.

She was delighted that I should come to see her without being asked.

"Ah," she cried, creeping around me and standing with her back to the door as she had the first time I had come here, "You've come to see my tapestry."

"And *you*," I answered.

That pleased her. "It's coming along nicely," she said, leading the way to the window seat on which was the blue satin coverlet she was making for the cradle. "Nearly finished," she said, spreading it out for me to see.

"It's exquisite."

"I was afraid," she said.

"Afraid?"

"If you'd died it would have been such a waste of time."

I looked astonished, and she said: "You were in your bare feet. You might have caught your death."

"So you heard about it?" I said.

"I've used such a lot of my blue silks."

"What did you think about . . . my fright?"

"All that work would have been in vain."

"Who told you about it?"

"But it would have done for some other baby. There are always babies." Her eyes widened and she went on: "Perhaps Luke's. I wonder if Luke will have *good* babies?"

"Please don't talk about my child as though it will never be born," I said sharply.

She recoiled as though I had struck her.

"It made you angry," she said. "People are angry when they are frightened."

"I'm not frightened."

"Are you angry?"

"When you talk like that about my baby."

"Then you're frightened, because angry people are really frightened people."

I changed the subject. "The coverlet is lovely. My baby will like it."

She smiled, well pleased.

"I went to see your sister a few days ago. She told me about a Christmas time when Matthew dressed up."

She put her hand to her mouth and began to laugh. "They quarreled so," she said. "She made his nose bleed. It went all over his jacket. Our governess was cross. They had nothing but bread and water for a whole day. He'd dressed up, you see . . . to frighten her. . . ." She looked at me, her brows puckered; I could see that she was struck by the similarity of the incidents. "What are you going to do, Hagar? What are you going to do about . . . the monk?"

I did not remind her that I was Catherine. Instead I said: "I want to see if I can find the clothes."

"I know where the hat is," she said. "I was there when he found it."

"Do you know where the monk's robe is?"

She turned to me, startled. "Monk's robe? I never saw it. There is no monk's robe. Matthew found the hat and he said he was going to frighten her when she was asleep. It was a hat with such a lovely feather. It's still in the chest."

"Where is the chest?"

"You know, Hagar. In that little room near the schoolroom."

"Let us go and look at it."

"Are you going to dress up and frighten Matthew?"

"I'm not going to dress up. I merely want to see the clothes."

"All right," she said. "Come on."

So she led the way. We went through the schoolroom and past the nurseries till we came to a door at the end of a corridor. She threw this open. There was a smell of age as though the place had not been ventilated for years. I saw several large chests, some pictures stacked against the walls, and odd pieces of furniture.

"Mother changed the Revels when she came here," mused Sarah. "She said we were overcrowded with furniture. She put some here . . . and some in other places. . . . It's been here ever since."

"Let us look at the clothes."

I saw that there was a film of dust on everything, and I looked intently about me, for if anyone had been at these chests recently would they not have left some mark in the dust?

I saw an imprint on the top of a chest which was Sarah's, and she was now ruefully looking at her hands.

"The dust," she said. "No one's been in here for a very long time. Perhaps not since we were children."

It was not easy to lift the lid, as the thing was not only heavy but stiff; but we managed between us.

I looked down at the garments which were there. Gowns, shoes, cloaks, and there was the hat itself on which Sarah seized with a cry of triumph.

She put it on her head and she looked as though she had stepped right out of the picture gallery.

"Hagar must have had a fright," I said.

"Hagar wouldn't be frightened long." She was looking at me intently. "Some people are not frightened for long. For a while they are and then . . . they stop being frightened. You are like that, Hagar."

I was suddenly conscious of the stuffiness of the attic, of the strangeness of the woman who stood before me, whose childlike blue eyes could be so vague and yet so penetrating.

She bent over the chest and brought out a silk pelisse which she wrapped around her. The hat was still on her head.

"Now," she said, "I feel I am not myself. I am someone else . . . someone who lived in this house long long ago. When you wear other people's clothes perhaps you become like them. This is a man's hat though and a woman's pelisse." She began to laugh. "I wonder, if I put on the monk's robe, whether I should feel like a monk."

"Aunt Sarah," I said, "where *is* the monk's robe?"

She paused as though thinking deeply and for a moment I thought I was on the road to discovery. Then she said: "It is on the monk who came to your bedroom, Catherine. That's where the monk's robe is."

I began taking clothes from the chest, and as I could not find the robe I gave my attention to the smaller trunks and ransacked them. When I could not find what I sought I felt deflated. I turned to Sarah who was watching me earnestly.

"There are other chests in the house," she said.

"Where?"

She shook her head. "I hardly ever leave my part of the house."

I felt the faintness coming over me again; the room was so airless, so confined; it smelt of dust and age.

What did Sarah know? I asked myself.

Did she know who had come to my room in the guise of a monk? I wondered if it had been Sarah herself.

As this feeling became stronger I wanted to get away, back to my own room. I wondered what would happen to me if I fainted in this room among all these musty relics of the past, as I had in Hagar's house.

"I must go now," I said. "It has been interesting."

She held out her hand to me as though I were an acquaintance who had made a formal call.

"Do come again," she said.

Gabriel and Friday were constantly in my thoughts. I was still hoping that one day Friday would come back to me. I simply could not bear to think that he was dead. But there was one matter which surprised me; although I remembered so vividly the occasion of my meeting with Gabriel, I had to concentrate to remember exactly what he looked like. I reproached myself for this because in some ways it seemed disloyal; and yet, deep in my secret thoughts, I knew that although we had been husband and wife, Gabriel and I had been almost strangers in some respects. Each day some revealing action had betrayed to me the fact that I had a great deal to learn about him. I told myself that this was due to an innate reticence in his nature. But was this so? I had been fond of Gabriel; I had missed him deeply; but what did I miss? Was it a friend rather than a lover?

Now I carried Gabriel's child and I believed that when I held my baby in my arms I should be happy. Already I loved my child and the force of my emotion was teaching me that the feeling I had had for Gabriel was shallow compared with this new love. I longed for the spring as I never had before because, with the coming of spring, my baby would be born. But there were many dark days between me and that happy time.

The weather had set in damp and, even when the rain ceased, the mist was with us. It crept into the house like a gray ghost, and shut out the view from the windows. I liked to walk whenever possible, and I did not mind the rain, for it was not cold yet and was that gentle damp which came from the south, which put a soft bloom on the skin. I felt very well, only impatient of the dragging of time.

I was delighted when I noticed for the first time the lines of green in the brown fields on the Kelly Grange land. The young wheat was pushing through the earth: the promise of a new year and a reminder that spring was on its way. My baby was due to be born in March and this was November. Four more months to wait.

I had been over to Kelly Grange to see Hagar, and Simon had driven me back. We no longer talked of the monk incident, but I had not ceased to be watchful; and there were occasions when I awoke in the night startled from some vague dream, and hastily lighted a candle to make sure that I was alone in my room.

My feelings towards Simon were undergoing a change and this was the result of my friendship with his grandmother. Hagar always welcomed me and if she did not say how pleased she was to see me —she was after all a Yorkshire woman and therefore not given to demonstrations of affection—I was certainly made aware of her pleasure in my company. And when I was with her the conversation invariably turned to Simon. I was reminded again and again of his many virtues. I believed I understood him; he was blunt even to the extent of tactlessness; there was a hardness in his nature which I imagined no one but his grandmother had ever penetrated; he liked undertaking difficult tasks, which most people would find impossible, and proving that they weren't—all part of the arrogance, of course, but admirable in its way. He was not uninterested in women. Hagar hinted at certain entanglements. Not that he had suggested marriage with any of these women. Hagar saw nothing immoral in this: a liaison would not have been nearly as shocking to her as a *mésalliance*.

"He has far too much sense for that!" she said. "When he marries he'll marry the right woman. He'll see to that."

"Let us hope," I retorted, "that she whom he considers right will be able to apply the same adjective to him."

Hagar looked startled. I think it astonished her that anyone should not see this grandson of hers as she did. Which showed, I told myself at the time, that even the most sensible people had their weaknesses. Hagar's was undoubtedly her grandson. I wondered what his was. Or if he had any at all.

Still, I should always be grateful to him for believing my version of what I saw in my bedroom that night, and I was less cool with him than I had been before that happened.

I said good-by to him and went straight up to my room.

It was late afternoon and in half an hour or so the darkness would descend upon us. There were shadows on the stairs and in my room, and as I opened the door I felt that horrible sense of evil which I had experienced when I opened my eyes and saw the monk.

This was perhaps a slight matter to arouse my feelings, but it was reminiscent: the curtains were drawn about my bed.

I walked straight to them and drew them back. I was half expecting to see the monk there, but of course there was nothing.

I looked hastily round the room and went into the powder closet. There was no one there.

I rang the bell and very soon Mary-Jane appeared.

"Why did you pull the curtains about my bed?" I demanded.

Mary-Jane stared at the bed. "But . . . madam . . . I didn't. . . ."

"Who else would have done that?"

"But, madam, the curtains are *not* drawn about your bed."

"What are you suggesting? That I imagined they were? I have just drawn them back."

I looked at her fiercely and she recoiled from me.

"I . . . I did nowt to 'em. You've always said that you didn't want them drawn. . . ."

"Who else would have been here?" I asked.

"No one else, madam. I always do your room myself as Mrs. Grantley said I should."

"You must have drawn them," I said. "How otherwise could they have been drawn?"

She backed away from me. "But I didn't, madam. I didn't touch them."

"You've forgotten. You must have forgotten."

"No, madam, I'm sure I didn't."

"You did," I answered unreasonably. "You may go now."

She went, her face stricken. The relationship between us had always before been so pleasant, and it was unlike me to behave as I had done.

When she had gone I stood staring at the door and Sarah's words came back to me. "You're angry because you're frightened."

Yes, that was it. The sight of the drawn curtains had frightened me. Why? What was there so strange about drawn curtains?

The answer to that was simple. It was because I had been reminded of that other terrifying occasion.

After all, anyone might have drawn the curtains . . . to shake out the dust, say . . . and then forgotten them and left them drawn. Why could not Mary-Jane have admitted to that?

Simply because that had not been the case. Mary-Jane had not drawn the curtains. She would have remembered if she had, because I had always insisted that I would not have them drawn about the bed while I slept.

I was trembling slightly. I was thinking of it all again, that sudden waking in the night . . . that awful apparition and then turning to pursue, only to be faced by a wall of blue silk. It had reminded me, that was all, and it had frightened me. But I was already asking myself whether it was possible that I was not forgotten, that the weeks of peace were now over and new terrors were being devised for me.

I had been angry because I was afraid; but I had no right to turn that anger against Mary-Jane.

I felt very contrite and went at once to the bell. Mary-Jane came immediately in answer to my summons, but her bright smile was missing and she did not meet my eye.

"Mary-Jane," I said, "I'm sorry."

She looked at me in surprise.

"I had no right to say what I did. If you had drawn the curtains you would have said so. I'm afraid I was overwrought."

She looked expectant and still bewildered. Then she said: "Oh . . . madam, it's of no account."

"It is, Mary-Jane," I insisted. "It was unjust, and I hate injustice. Go and bring the candles. It's growing dark."

"Yes, madam." She went out of that room happier than when she had left it a few minutes before.

By the time she came back with the candles I decided to be frank with her. I was anxious that she should not think that I was the sort of woman who vented her anger on other people when she was suffering from some personal irritation. I wanted her to know the reason.

"Put them over the fireplace, and on the dressing table. That's much brighter. The room looks different already. Mary-Jane . . . when I saw those bed curtains drawn I was reminded of that occasion . . ."

"I remember, madam."

"And I thought someone was playing another trick. So I wanted it to have been you who drew them. That would have been such a comforting explanation."

"But it wasn't, madam. I couldn't say it was if it wasn't."

"Of course you couldn't. So I'm left wondering who did it . . . and why."

"Anyone could have come in, madam. You don't lock the doors during the day."

"No, anybody could have done it. But . . . perhaps it's not important. Perhaps I'm too sensitive. It may be due to my condition."

"Our Etty isn't quite like she used to be, madam."

"I believe women are often so."

"Yes. She used to like to hear Jim sing. He's got quite a voice, Jim has. But now she can't abide it; she can't bear what she calls noise of any sort."

"Well, that's how we are, Mary-Jane. It's as well to be prepared for our strangeness. I've a dress here which I thought might do for you. I can't get into it any more."

I brought out a dark green gaberdine dress trimmed with red and green tartan, and Mary-Jane's eyes glistened at the sight of it.

"Why, madam, it's grand. And it's sure to fit."

"Then take it, Mary-Jane. I'd like you to have it."

"Oh, thank you, madam."

She was a gentle creature. I believe she was as pleased that the pleasantness of our relationship had been restored as she was to have the dress.

When she had gone I felt that some of her pleasure remained behind her. I caught a glimpse of my reflection in the looking glass. I looked young, and my green eyes were brilliant. Candlelight is always so flattering.

But even as I looked I found I was peering beyond my own reflection; I was trying to probe the shadows in the room. I was expecting some shape to materialize behind me.

Fear had come back.

That night I slept badly. I kept waking to stare about my bed. I kept fancying that I heard the swish of silk. But I was mistaken. The curtains remained as I had left them and I saw no more apparitions in my room.

But who had drawn the curtains? I did not want to ask, for fear of attracting suspicious glances again. But I was on the alert.

It was only a few days later when it was discovered that the warming pan was missing from my room.

I had not noticed that it was gone, so could not say exactly how long it had been absent from its place on the wall over the oak chest in my bedroom.

I was sitting up in bed while Mary-Jane brought my breakfast tray to me. I had taken to having breakfast in bed on Dr. Smith's orders, and I must say that I was ready enough to indulge myself in this way, because, on account of the disturbed nights I was having, I almost invariably felt delicate in the mornings.

"Why Mary-Jane," I said, my eyes straying to the wall, "what have you done with the warming pan?"

Mary-Jane set down my tray and looked round. Her astonishment was obvious.

"Oh, madam," she said, "it's gone."

"Did it fall or something?"

"That I couldn't say, madam. I didn't take it away." She went over to the wall. "The hook's still there, any road."

"Then I wonder who . . . I'll ask Mrs. Grantley. She might know what has happened to it. I rather liked it there. It was so bright and shining."

I ate my breakfast without giving much thought to the warming pan. At that stage I did not realize that it had any connection with the strange things which were happening to me.

It was that afternoon before I again thought of it. I was having tea with Ruth and she was talking about Christmas in the old days and how different it was now—particularly this year when we were living so quietly on account of Gabriel's death.

"It was rather fun," she told me. "We used to take a wagon out to bring the yule log home; and there was the holly to gather too. We usually had several people staying in the house at Christmas. This time it can't possibly be more than family. I suppose Aunt Hagar will come over from Kelly Grange with Simon. They generally do, and stay two nights. She's almost certain to manage that journey."

I felt rather pleased at the prospect of Christmas, and wondered when I could go into Harrogate, Keighley or Ripon to buy some presents. It seemed incredible that it was only last Christmas when I was in Dijon. Rather lonely those Christmases had been because most of my companions had gone home to their families and there were usually no more than four or five of us who remained at the school. But we had made the most of the festivities and those Christmases had been enjoyable.

"I must find out if Aunt Hagar will be able to make the journey. I must tell them to air her bed thoroughly; last time she declared we were putting her into damp sheets."

That reminded me. "By the way," I said, "what has happened to the warming pan which was in my room?"

She looked puzzled.

"It's no longer there," I explained. "Mary-Jane doesn't know what has become of it."

"Warming pan in your room? Oh . . . has it gone?"

"So you didn't know. I thought perhaps you'd given orders for someone to remove it."

She shook her head. "It must have been one of the servants," she said. "I'll find out. You may be needing it when the weather turns, and we can't expect this mildness to continue long now."

"Thank you," I answered. "I'm thinking of going into Harrogate or Ripon soon. I have some shopping to do."

She raised her eyebrows and studied my figure speculatively. "Do you think you should go . . . now that the time is getting on? I mean . . . some of us could shop for you, you know."

I shook my head. "Oh, no. I feel so well and I want to go."

There was a look of resignation on her face as she said: "Well, it's up to you. We might all go together. I want to go, and Luke was saying something about taking Damaris in to do some Christmas shopping."

"Do let us. I should enjoy that."

Next day I met her on the stairs, when I was on the point of going out for a short walk because the rain had ceased for a while and the sun was shining.

"Going for a walk?" she asked. "It's pleasant out. Quite warm. By the way, I cannot discover what happened to your warming pan."

"Well, that's strange."

"I expect someone moved it and forgot." She gave a light laugh and looked at me somewhat intently, I thought. But I went out and it was such a lovely morning that I immediately forgot all about the missing warming pan. There were still a few flowers left in the hedgerows such as woundwort and shepherd's-purse, and although I did not go to the moor I thought I saw in the distance a spray of gorse, golden in the pale sunshine.

Remembering instructions I curtailed my walk and as I turned back to the house, I glanced towards the ruins. It seemed quite a long time since I had been to the Abbey. I knew I could never go there now without remembering the monk, so I stayed away, which showed of course that my protestations of bravery were partly false.

I stood under an oak tree and found myself studying the patterns on the bark. I remembered my father telling me that the ancient Britons used to think that marks on the trunk of the oak were the outward signs of the supernatural being who inhabited the tree. I traced the pattern with my finger. It was easy to understand how such fancies had grown. It was so easy to harbor fancies.

As I stood there I heard a sudden mocking cry above me, and looked up startled, expecting something terrifying. It was only a green woodpecker.

I hurried into the house.

When I went to the dining room that evening for dinner I found Matthew, Sarah and Luke there; but Ruth was absent.

When I entered they were asking where she was.

"Not like her to be late," said Sir Matthew.

"Ruth has a great deal to do," Sarah put in. "And she was talking about Christmas and wondering which rooms Hagar and Simon would want if they came for a short holiday."

"Hagar will have the room which was once hers," said Matthew. "Simon will have the one he has always had. So why should she be concerned?"

"I think she's a little worried about Hagar. You know what Hagar is. She'll have her old nose into every corner and be telling us that the place is not kept as it was when Father was alive."

"Hagar's an interfering busybody and always was," growled Matthew. "If she doesn't like what she sees here, then she can do the other thing. We can manage very well without her opinions and advice."

Ruth came in then, looking slightly flushed.

"We've been wondering what had become of you," Matthew told her.

"Of all the ridiculous things . . ." she began. She looked round the company helplessly. "I went into . . . Gabriel's old room and noticed something under the coverlet there. What do you think it was?"

I stared at her and felt the color rushing to my cheeks, and I was fighting hard to control my feelings, because I knew.

"The warming pan from your room!" She was looking straight at me, quizzically and intent. "Whoever could have put it there?"

"How extraordinary!" I heard myself stammer.

"Well, we've found it. That's where it was all the time." She turned to the others. "Catherine had missed the warming pan from her room. She thought I'd told one of the servants to remove it. Who on earth could have put it into the bed there?"

"We ought to find out," I said sharply.

"I asked the servants. They quite clearly knew nothing about it."

"Someone must have put it there." I heard my voice rise unnaturally high.

Ruth shrugged her shoulders.

"But we must find out," I insisted. "It's someone playing these tricks. Don't you see . . . it's the same sort of thing as the curtains being drawn."

"Curtains?"

I was annoyed with myself because the drawing of the bed curtains had been a matter known only to the one who had done it, and Mary-Jane and myself. Now I should have to explain. I did so briefly.

"Who drew the curtains?" screeched Sarah. "Who put the warming pan in Gabriel's bed? And it was your bed too, wasn't it, Catherine? Yours and Gabriel's."

"I wish I knew!" I cried vehemently.

"Someone must have been rather absent-minded," said Luke lightly.

"I don't think it was absent-mindedness," I retorted.

"But, Catherine," put in Ruth patiently, "why should anyone want to pull your bed curtains about your bed or remove the warming pan?"

"That's what *I* should like to know."

"Let's forget all about it," said Matthew. "That which was lost is found."

"But why . . . *why* . . ." I insisted.

"You are getting excited, my dear," whispered Ruth.

"I want to know the explanation of these strange things which are happening in my room."

"The duckling is getting cold," said Sir Matthew. He came to me and slipped his arm through mine. "Never mind about the warming pan, my dear. We shall know why it was moved . . . all in good time."

"Yes," said Luke, "all in good time." And he kept his eyes on my face as he spoke, and I could see the speculation there.

"We'd better start," said Ruth, and as they sat down at the table I had no alternative but to do the same; but my appetite had deserted me. I kept asking myself what the purpose was behind these strange happenings which seemed in some way to be directed towards me.

I was going to find out. I must find out.

Before the month was out we were invited to the vicarage to discuss the last-minute plans for the imminent "Bring and Buy" sale.

"Mrs. Cartwright always gets the wind in her tail at such times," said Luke. "This is nothing to the June garden fête or her hideous pageants."

"Mrs. Cartwright is an energetic lady," said Ruth, "possessing all the qualities to make her an excellent wife for the vicar."

"Does she expect me to go?" I asked.

"Of course she does. She'd be hurt if you didn't. You will come? It's only a short walk, but if you like we can drive there."

"I feel perfectly fit to walk," I said quickly.

"Then we'll go along. It's an excellent opportunity for you to meet some of our neighbors. Now that we're in mourning, the vicarage rather than the Revels has become the center of our village. In the past, meetings were held here."

We set out about ten-thirty, and in a quarter of an hour had arrived at the vicarage, a pleasant gray stone house close to the church. We joined one or two people going in the same direction and Ruth introduced me. I was studied with a certain amount of curiosity because they all knew that I was the wife whom Gabriel had married somewhat hastily and whom he had left pregnant after two weeks of marriage.

They were summing me up, which I accepted as normal in the circumstances. I expected there were some of them who believed that shortcomings in myself may have been the reason for Gabriel's death.

Mrs. Cartwright, whom I had of course already met, was a large, somewhat florid woman with a powerful personality. She assembled us all in her drawing room, which seemed small but only because I was accustomed to the rooms at the Revels, and here morning coffee with biscuits was being served by a maid.

I was conducted to the window from which I could see the churchyard. I could just make out the Rockwell vault with the wrought ironwork above it, and my thoughts immediately went to Gabriel.

When all the guests were present Mrs. Cartwright addressed us in her booming voice and told us of the need for speed. The sale must be in time to give people opportunities of buying their Christmas presents. "So please ransack your attics, and any little *objet d'art* will be appreciated. Perhaps it is something which you no longer value. That does not mean that no one else will. Please try to bring in your offerings before the day. It does give us time to decide how to price them. And on the day . . . do come and buy. Remember it is for the good of the church, and the roof does need attention. As you all know, there's deathwatch beetle up there in the rafters. I know you will help. But the need is immediate, ladies. Has anyone any suggestions?"

There were some, and Mrs. Cartwright considered them and asked for counter opinions. It was all very businesslike and I admired our vicar's wife for her energy.

When the business of the meeting had been settled she came and sat in the window with me and told me how glad she was to see me there.

"It is wonderful to see you looking so well and to know that there is to be an addition to the family. I know that Sir Matthew is delighted . . . absolutely delighted. It is a comfort to him in the circumstances. . . ." She was one of those women who carry the whole of a conversation for the sheer joy of talking, and a better talker than a listener, I discovered. "Such a great deal of work to be done. The people here are so good . . . so helpful . . . but between ourselves they are rather slow in taking action . . . if you know what I mean. One has to prod . . . prod . . . to get anything done. This sale of work will not produce half the profit unless it takes place well before Christmas. I do hope you will be able to bring us a little something . . . and you will come and buy, won't you? Some little thing . . . just anything . . . More than one, of course, if you have it. Anything . . . but the more valuable the better. Forgive me for begging so persistently."

I said it was in a good cause and I would see what I could find. "I have a brooch of turquoises and pearls . . . very small."

"Ideal! How generous of you. And tomorrow . . . could we have it then? I'll send someone for it."

"It's a little old-fashioned."

"No matter. It will be wonderful. I am so pleased that you have come. You are going to be such a help to us . . . particularly when . . . Well, at the moment of course you are feeling less energetic than you will later. I can talk of these matters with feeling. I have six of my own. Ah yes, it is hard to believe, is it not? And the youngest is nineteen. He's going into the church. I'm glad one of them is. I was beginning to be afraid . . . As I was saying, you'll be so helpful later, I know . . . with the pageant. I do want a pageant in the ruins this summer."

"Have you had one before?"

"Five years ago was the last. Of course the weather was tragic. Rain . . . rain, rain. That was July. I think we might choose June this year. July *is* a wet month really."

"What sort of a pageant was it?"

"Historical. It must be historical . . . with such a setting. The costumes were excellent."

"How do you find the costumes?"

"We were lent some from the Revels and we made others. We were helped considerably from the Revels with the Cavaliers, but we made our own Roundheads. They were easy to do."

"Yes, I suppose they would be. So you started with the Civil War, did you?"

"Good heavens, no! We went back to before the Dissolution. It was the only thing to do with that wonderful setting all ready for our use. It was most effective. People said that on that day it was as though the Abbey was no longer a ruin."

I tried to keep the note of excitement out of my voice. "So some of the players were dressed as monks."

"Indeed yes. Many of them. They all played many parts . . . you know. A monk in one scene was a gay Cavalier in another. It was necessary, you know. We haven't enough players. The men are so difficult and shy! There was many a female monk on that day, I do assure you."

"I suppose their costumes were easy to make."

"The simplest really. Just a black robe and a cowl . . . so easy to make it really effective, and against the gray ruins. I really think that part was the most successful."

"It must have been. After all, there was the Abbey to help."

"How wonderful that you should be so interested. I'm certainly going to try a pageant this year. But June . . . mind you. July is definitely a wet month."

Ruth was trying to catch my eye, and I rose. I felt I had made an important discovery and I was very pleased that I had decided to come to the vicarage this morning.

"It's time we went," said Ruth, "if we're not to be late for luncheon."

We said good-by to Mrs. Cartwright and started for home.

I found it difficult to make conversation. I kept saying to myself: Somebody who played the part of a monk in the pageant five years ago had a monk's costume which still exists today. The person who came into my bedroom used it.

How could I find out who had played a monk in the pageant five years ago? Who, in our household, that is to say. It could only be Ruth, I guessed. Luke would have been too young. But would he? Five years ago he would have been twelve years old. He was probably tall for his age. Why should he not have played the part of a monk? Sir Matthew and Aunt Sarah would have been too old. That left Ruth and Luke.

I said: "Mrs. Cartwright was talking to me about the pageant. Did you play a part in it?"

"You don't know Mrs. Cartwright very well if you think she would let any of us escape."

"What part did you play?"

"The King's wife . . . Queen Henrietta Maria."

"Just that part and no other?"

"It was an important part."

"I only asked because Mrs. Cartwright said that some people played several parts since she was short of players."

"Those would be the people who had small parts."

"What about Luke?"

"He was well to the fore. He was in and out of everything. . . ."

Luke! I thought; and I remembered that it had been some time before he had appeared on that night; he had plenty of time to take off the robe and put on a dressing gown. He must have been very quick getting up to the second floor, but he was young and active.

And the bed curtains and the warming pan? Why not? He was the one who would have had every opportunity. My doubt was becoming almost a certainty. Luke was trying to terrify me; he was trying to kill my child before it was born. Obviously Luke was the one who had most to gain from the death of my child.

"Are you feeling all right?" It was Ruth at my side.

"Oh yes . . . thanks. . . ."

"Were you whispering to yourself?"

"Oh no. I was thinking of Mrs. Cartwright. She's very talkative, is she not?"

"She certainly is."

The house was now in view and we were both looking towards it. My eyes went, as they always did, to that south parapet from which Gabriel had fallen. There was something different about it. I stared and Ruth was staring too.

"What is it?" she said, and she quickened her pace.

There was something dark on the parapet; from this distance it looked as though someone was leaning over it.

"Gabriel!" I think I must have said it aloud because Ruth at my elbow said: "Nonsense! It can't be. But what . . . But who?"

I began to run; Ruth was beside me restraining me and I could hear my breath coming in great gasps.

"Something's there," I panted. "What . . . is it . . . ? It looks . . . limp. . . ."

Now I saw that whoever was there was wearing a cloak and the hood of the cloak and part of the cloak itself were hanging over the parapet. It was impossible to see the rest.

"She'll fall. Who is it? What does it mean?" cried Ruth as she ran ahead of me into the house. She could go so much faster than I; I found it difficult to get my breath but I hurried after her as quickly as I could. Luke appeared in the corridor. He looked at his mother and then turned to stare at me, laboring up behind.

"What on earth's happened?" he asked.

"There's someone on the parapet," I cried. "Gabriel's parapet."

"But who . . . ?"

He had started up the stairs ahead of me and I went after him as fast as I could.

Ruth appeared on the stairs and there was a grim smile about her lips. She was holding something in her hand which I recognized as a blue cloak which belonged to me—a long winter cloak designed to shut out the winds; there was a hood attached to it.

"It's . . . mine," I gasped.

"Why did you hang it over the parapet like that?" she demanded almost roughly.

"I . . . but I did no such thing."

She and Luke exchanged glances.

Then she murmured: "It was made to look exactly like someone leaning over . . . about to fall. It gave me quite a shock when I saw it. It was such a silly thing to do."

"Then who did it?" I cried. "Who is doing all these silly cruel things!"

They were both looking at me as though they found me very odd, as though certain doubts they had had concerning me were being confirmed.

I had to find out the meaning of these strange happenings. I was becoming nervous, continuously watching for the next. They were such stupid tricks—except of course the appearance in my bedroom of the monk. If they had intended to alarm me they could not have chosen anything more calculated to do so. But these minor irritations . . . What did they portend?

Luke and Ruth seemed to have made up their minds that I was eccentric—but perhaps that was too kind a word. I was aware of them, watching me on every occasion. It was unnerving.

I did think of going to see the Redvers and telling them everything, but I was growing so distrustful of everyone that I was not even sure of Hagar. As for Simon, he had taken my view of the monk incident, but what would he think of the bed curtains, warming pan and cloak?

There was something sinister behind this and I had to find out what it was. I wanted to do so by myself because a distrust which was stirring in me was directed against every person who was connected with the Revels.

The very next day I set out to call on Mrs. Cartwright. What she had to say about the pageant the day before had seemed important and I wondered whether I could glean more from her.

Besides the turquoise brooch I found an enamel box which I had had for years and had no particular use for, so I took this along as well.

I was fortunate to find her in. She was effusive in her welcome and expressed great pleasure in the brooch and box.

"Ah, Mrs. Rockwell, this is kind of you. And to save me the trouble of sending! I can see you are going to be a great help to us. Such a comfort. I am sure these lovely things of yours will fetch a good price. And if you would like a preview I'll be only too delighted to show it to you." She looked at me slyly as though she thought this was my reason for coming.

I hesitated. I had no wish to arouse suspicions and I felt that since these strange happenings were taking place it was very necessary for me to have a reason for everything I did.

"Well," I began. She interrupted conspiratorially: "But of course. And why not? You deserve it. It's an excellent way of doing one's Christmas shopping, particularly when it is not quite so easy to get about. I think people who help us *should* have special privileges. . . . Have a look around, and then perhaps you will drink a cup of coffee with me?"

I said there was nothing I should like better; so she took me into a small room where the articles were set out and I selected a scarf pin, a snuff box and a Chinese vase. She was delighted with me not only as the bringer but as a buyer, and I felt that had put her in a good mood for confidences.

As soon as we were drinking coffee together in her drawing room I turned the conversation to pageants. That was easy. It was a subject very near to her heart.

"And do you really propose to put on a pageant this summer?"

"I shall do my utmost."

"It must be very interesting."

"It is indeed, and *you* must have a prominent part. I always thought that members of our leading family should. Don't you agree?"

"But yes," I said. "Have they always been amenable? I mean do they always take part in these affairs?"

"Oh yes, they have always been what I should call a *dutiful* family."

"I'd like to hear about the pageant. I suppose Mrs. Grantley and Luke would take parts."

"They did last time."

"Yes, Mrs. Grantley was telling me. She was the wife of Charles I."

"Yes, we did a big Civil War scene. That was because the Revels was actually occupied by the Parliamentarians. It's wonderful luck that they didn't destroy the place . . . the vandals! But then all the valuables had been hidden away."

"That must have been exciting. Where were they hidden?"

"Now my dear Mrs. Rockwell, that's something your family might know more about than I do. It is a mystery though, I believe."

"And you did that scene in the pageant?"

"Not exactly . . . we just had the advance of the Roundheads, you know, and the occupation. Then we had the restoration of the family with the restoration of the King . . . linking up, you see, Rockwell history and England's history."

"And you showed the Abbey before the Dissolution. That must have been very interesting."

"Indeed it was, and I propose to do that again. I mean it is essential. And of course it gives everyone an opportunity to play a small part."

"It must have been most impressive to see all those black-robed figures about the place."

"It was indeed."

"Luke was only a boy then—too young, I suppose, to play much of a part."

"Oh no . . . not at all. He was most enthusiastic. He was one of our best monks. He was almost as tall as a man then. The Rockwells are a tall family, as you know."

"You have an excellent memory, Mrs. Cartwright. I do believe you remember the parts which everyone played."

She laughed. "Among our immediate neighborhood, of course. But this pageant was quite a big thing and we had people from all around playing parts; and of course that was good because it brought in the spectators."

"How many monks did you use?"

"A great number. Almost everyone had to be pressed into service. I even tried to get Dr. Smith."

"Did you succeed?"

"No. It was his day for going to . . . that institution, and then of course he said he had to be on duty in case he was called somewhere."

"And his daughter?"

"She had a part of course. She was the little Charles. She looked wonderful in velvet breeches with her long hair. She was too young for it to seem immodest, and the 'When did you last see your father?' scene was most affecting."

"She couldn't play a monk?"

"Indeed not. But I shall never forget her Prince Charles. Everyone was splendid. Even Mr. Redvers—and no one could say acting was in his line."

"Oh, what part did he play?"

"He was merely a monk, but he did join in."

"How . . . interesting."

"Will you have more coffee?"

"Thank you, no. That was delicious. But I should be going back now."

"It *was* so good of you to come, and I *do* hope the purchases will be satisfactory."

We parted with mutual thanks and as I walked home I felt bemused.

I was sure I had solved the mystery of the costume. Some person had used a pageant costume in which to frighten me.

Luke had had one at some time. Did he still possess it? Simon had had one too. Yet he had not mentioned this when I had told him of my experience.

At first I decided that I would discuss the matter of the costumes with Hagar and then I hesitated, because if I did so, Simon would hear of it; and I was not sure that I wanted Simon to know that I had discovered so much.

It seemed ridiculous to suspect Simon, for how could he possibly have been in the house at the time? And yet I had to remind myself that he was next in succession to Luke.

It was alarming to feel that I could trust no one, but that was exactly how I did feel.

So when I called to see Hagar the next day I said nothing of the cloak incident, although I longed to discuss it with someone. Instead I tried to keep the conversation on everyday matters and I asked Hagar if there was any Christmas shopping I could do for her. I told her that I hoped to go into one of the towns with Ruth and perhaps Luke, and if I did so I should be happy to execute any of her commissions.

She pondered this and eventually made a list of things which she would like me to get for her; and while we were discussing this, Simon came in.

"If you'd like to go to Knaresborough," he said, "I can take you. I have to drive in on business."

I hesitated. I did not really believe he would have tried to frighten me, and yet I reminded myself he had not liked me in the beginning; it was only because of my friendship with his grandmother that we were brought together. I was unaccountably depressed because I felt it was only reasonable not to place him outside suspicion. If he could really be trying to harm someone in my position he must be the exact opposite of the man I had been sure he was. Still, I was determined not to trust him.

My hesitation amused him. It had not occurred to him that I suspected him of villainy, only that I feared to offend the proprieties.

He said with a grin: "Ruth or Luke might like to come with us. If they'll come, perhaps you would deign to."

"That would be very pleasant," I replied.

And it was eventually arranged that when Simon went to Knaresborough he should take Luke, Damaris and myself with him.

The day was warm for early December. We left soon after nine in the morning and planned to be back by dark, which was of course soon after four.

As we sat together in the carriage, Luke and Simon appeared to be in high spirits; and I found myself catching them; Damaris was quiet, as usual.

It occurred to me that whenever I was away from the house I recaptured my old common sense. I ceased to believe that there was anything for me to fear. At least, I could assure myself, there was nothing with which I could not cope. I could believe, as I listened to Luke's bright conversation, that he had played these tricks on me to tease me. As for the first, he now probably realized he had gone too far, and that was why he was amusing himself with things like warming pans. He always regarded me in a slightly sardonic way. How foolish I had been to be afraid. I had merely been the victim of youthful high spirits.

That was my mood as we drove into Knaresborough.

I knew the town slightly from the past and it had always delighted me. I thought it was one of the most interesting and charming old towns in the West Riding.

We drove to an inn where we had some light refreshment and afterwards separated, Simon to do the business which had brought him here, Luke, Damaris and I to shop, having arranged to meet in two hours' time at the inn.

Very soon I had lost Luke and Damaris who, I presumed, had wandered off while I was in a shop because they wanted to be alone together.

I made the purchases Hagar had commissioned and a few for myself and then, as I had almost an hour to spare, I decided that I would explore the town, something I had never before had an opportunity to do.

It was very pleasant to be there on that bright December afternoon. There were few people about and as I looked at the gleaming river Nidd and those steep streets of houses with their red roofs, at the ruined castle with its fine old keep, I felt invigorated, and I wondered how I could such a short time ago have been so frightened.

As I made my way to the river I heard a voice behind me calling "Mrs. Catherine," and turning I saw Simon coming towards me.

"Hello, have you finished your shopping?"

"Yes."

He took his watch from his pocket. "Almost an hour before our rendezvous. What do you propose to do?"

"I was going to wander along the riverbank."

"Let's do it together."

As he took my parcels and walked beside me, two things struck me—one was the strength which radiated from him, the other was the loneliness of the riverbank.

"I know what you want to do," he said. "You want to try your luck at the well."

"What well?"

"Haven't you heard of the famous well? Haven't you ever visited Knaresborough before?"

"Once or twice with my father. We did not visit the well."

He clicked his tongue mockingly. "Mrs. Catherine, your education has been neglected."

"Tell me about the well."

"Let's find it, shall we? If you hold your hand in the water, then wish and let your hand dry, you will get your wish."

"I am sure you do not believe such legends."

"There's a great deal you don't know about me, Mrs. Catherine; although of course that's something else you haven't realized."

"I am sure you are the most practical person and never wish for that which can't reasonably be yours."

"You once told me that I was an arrogant man. Therefore you doubtless think I regard myself as omnipotent. In that case I might wish for anything and believe I have a chance of getting it."

"Even so you would realize that you had to work for what you wanted."

"That might be so."

"Then why bother to wish, when work would suffice?"

"Mrs. Catherine, you are in the wrong mood for the Dripping Well. Let us for once cast out common sense. Let us be gullible for once."

"I should like to see the well."

"And wish?"

"Yes. I should like to wish."

"And will you tell me if it comes true?"

"Yes."

"But don't tell me what you have wished, until it comes true. That is one of those conditions. It has to be a secret between you and the powers of darkness . . . or light. I'm not sure which it is in this case. There's the well, and there is Mother Shipton's Cave. Did your father tell you the story of Old Mother Shipton?"

"He never told me stories. He talked to me very little."

"Then it looks as though I must explain. Old Mother Shipton was a witch and she lived here . . . oh, about four hundred years ago. She was a love child, the result of union between a village girl and a stranger who persuaded her that he was a spirit possessed of supernatural powers. Before the child was born he deserted her, and little Ursula grew up to be a wise woman. She married a man named Shipton and so became 'Old Mother Shipton.' "

"What an interesting story. I've often wondered who Old Mother Shipton was."

"Some of her prophecies came true. It is said that she foretold the fall of Wolsey, the defeat of the Armada and the effect the Civil War would have on the West Riding. I used to remember some of her prophecies; there's a rhyme about them.

" *'Around the world thoughts shall fly*

In the twinkling of an eye. . . .' I used to know the whole thing and chant it to my grandmother's cook until she chased me out of the kitchen. I made it sound like an evil prophecy intended for her alone. I remember:

" *'Under water men shall walk*

Shall ride, shall sleep, and talk;

In the air men shall be seen . . .' And it ends:

" *'The world then to an end shall come*

In Nineteen hundred and Ninety-one.' "

"We have some years left to us then?" I said, and we were laughing together.

Now we had reached the Dripping Well.

"It's a magic well," he said. "It's known also as the Petrifying Well.

Anything which is dropped in this well will eventually become petrified."

"But why?"

"It has nothing to do with Mother Shipton, although I don't doubt some people would like to say it has. There's magnesian limestone in the water. It's actually in the soil and gets into the water which drips through and down into the well. You must let the water drip onto your hands and wish. Will you go first or shall I?"

"You first."

He leaned over the well and I watched the water, which was seeping through the sides of the well, drip onto his hand.

He turned to me holding out a wet hand.

"I am wishing," he said. "If I leave this water to dry I cannot fail to get my wish. Now it's your turn."

He was standing close to me as I took off my glove and leaned over the well.

I was conscious of the silence all about us. I was alone in this spot and only Simon Redvers knew I was here. I leaned forward and the cold water—I was sure it was the coldest water I had ever known—dripped onto my hand.

He was immediately behind me and there came to me then a moment of panic. In my mind's eye I saw him not as he had been a few seconds before, but wrapped in a monk's robe.

Not Simon, I was saying to myself. It must not be Simon. And so vehement was my thought that I forgot any other wish than that.

I could feel the warmth of his body, so close was he, and I held my breath. I was certain then that something was about to happen to me.

Then I swung round. He stepped back a pace. He had been standing very near to me. Why? I asked myself.

"Don't forget," he said. "It's got to dry. I can guess what you wished."

"Can you?"

"Not a difficult task. You whispered to yourself: 'I wish for a boy.'"

"It has turned cold."

"That was the water. It is exceptionally cold. That has something to do with the lime, I think."

He was staring beyond me and I was conscious of a certain excitement in him. At that moment a man appeared close by. I had not noticed his approach, but perhaps Simon had.

"Ah, trying t'well," said the man pleasantly.

"Who could pass by without doing so?" answered Simon.

"Folks come from far and wide to test t'well, and to see Mother Shipton's Cave."

"It's very interesting," I said.

"Oh, ay. Happen so."

Simon was gathering up my parcels. "You must make sure the water has dried on your hand," he told me; and I held it out before me as we walked along.

He took my arm in a possessive manner and drew me away from the well into those steep streets which led up to the castle.

Luke and Damaris were waiting at the inn for us and we had a quick cup of tea and then drove home.

It was dusk when we reached Kirkland Moorside. Simon dropped Damaris at the doctor's house and then drove Luke and myself on to the Revels.

I felt dejected when I entered my room. It was because of these new suspicions which had come to me. I was fighting them, but they would not be dismissed. Why had I felt frightened at the side of the well? What had Simon been thinking as he stood beside me? Had he been planning something which the casual arrival of a stranger had prevented his carrying out?

I really was astonished at myself. I might pretend to scorn the powers of the Dripping Well, but I had made my wish involuntarily and I fervently hoped it would come true.

Please let it not be Simon.

Why should I care whether it was Luke or Simon?

But I did care. It was then that I began to suspect the nature of my feelings for this man. I had no tenderness for him, but I found that I felt more alive in his company than I did in that of any other person. I might be angry with him—I so often was—but being angry with him was more exciting than being pleasant with anyone else. I cherished his opinion of my good sense and I was happy because he admired good sense more than any other quality.

Each time I saw him my feelings towards him underwent a change, and I understood now that I was more and more under the spell of his personality.

It was since he had loomed so large in my life that I had begun to understand what my feelings for Gabriel had been. I knew that I had loved Gabriel without being in love with him. I had married Gabriel because I had sensed a need in him for protection, and I had wanted to give it; it had seemed so reasonable to marry him when I could give him comfort and he could provide me with an escape from a home which was beginning to affect me more than ever with its melancholy. That was why I had found it difficult to remember exactly what he looked like; that was why, although I had lost him, I could still look forward to the future with hopeful expectation. Simon and the child had helped to do that for me.

It had been a cry from the heart when I had wished at the well: Please, not Simon.

I had now become aware of a change in the behavior of everyone towards me. I intercepted exchanged glances; even Sir Matthew seemed what I can only call watchful.

I was to discover the meaning of this through Sarah, and the discovery was more alarming than anything which had gone before.

I went to her apartments one day and found her stitching at the christening robe.

"I'm glad you've come," she greeted me. "You used to be interested in my tapestry."

"I still am," I assured her. "I think it's lovely. What have you been doing lately?"

She looked at me archly. "You would really like to see?"

"Of course."

She giggled, put aside the christening robe and standing up, took my hand. Then she paused and her face puckered. "I'm keeping it a secret," she whispered. Then she added: "Until it's finished."

"Then I mustn't pry. When will it be finished?"

I thought she was going to burst into tears as she said: "How can I finish it when I don't know! I thought you would help me. You said he didn't kill himself. You said . . ."

I waited tensely for her to go on but her mind had wandered. "There was a tear in the christening robe," she said quietly.

"Was there? But tell me about the tapestry."

"I didn't want to show it to anyone until it was finished. It was Luke . . ."

"Luke?" I cried, my heart beating faster.

"Such a lively baby. He cried when he was at the font, and he tore the robe. All that time it hasn't been mended. But why should it be, until there's a new baby waiting for it?"

"You'll mend it beautifully, I'm sure," I told her, and she brightened.

"It's *you!*" she murmured. "I don't know where to put you. That's why . . ."

"You don't know where to put me," I repeated, puzzled.

"I've got Gabriel . . . and the dog. He was a dear little dog. Friday! It was a queer sort of name."

"Aunt Sarah," I demanded, "what do you know about Friday?"

"Poor Friday. Such a good little dog. Such a *faithful* dog. I suppose that was why . . . Oh dear, I wonder if your baby will be good at the christening. But Rockwell babies are never good babies. I shall wash the robe myself."

"What were you saying about Friday, Aunt Sarah? Please tell me."

She looked at me with a certain concern. "He was your dog," she said. "You should know. But I shan't allow anyone to touch it. It's very difficult to iron. It has to be gophered in places. I did it for Luke's christening. I did it for Gabriel's."

"Aunt Sarah," I said impulsively, "show me the tapestry you're working on."

A light of mischief came into her eyes. "But it isn't finished, and I didn't want to show it to anyone . . . until it is."

"Why not? I saw you working on one, before you'd finished it."

"That was different. Then I knew . . ."

"You knew?"

She nodded. "I don't know where to put *you,* you see."

"But I'm here."

She put her head on one side so that she looked like a bright-eyed bird. "Today . . . tomorrow . . . next week, perhaps. After that where will you be?"

I was determined to see the picture. "Please," I wheedled, "do show me."

She was delighted by my interest which she knew was genuine. "Well, perhaps you," she said. "No one else."

"I'll not tell anyone," I promised.

"All right." She was like an eager child. "Come on."

She went to the cupboard and brought out a canvas, and held the picture close to her body so that I couldn't see it.

"Do let me see," I pleaded.

Then she reversed it, still holding it against her. Depicted on the canvas was the south façade of the house; and lying on the stones in front of it was Gabriel's body. It was so vivid, so real, that I felt a sudden nausea as I looked at it. I stared, for there was something else. Lying beside Gabriel was my dog Friday, his little body stiff as it could only be in death. It was horrible.

I must have given a startled gasp, for Sarah chuckled. My horror was the best compliment I could have given her.

I stammered: "It looks so . . . real."

"Oh, it's real enough . . . in a way," she said dreamily. "I saw him lying there, and that was how he looked. I went down before they could take him away, and saw him."

"Gabriel . . ." I heard myself murmur, for the sight of the tapestry had brought back so many tender memories, and I could picture him more clearly than I had since the first days of my bereavement.

"I said to myself," Aunt Sarah continued, "that must be my next picture . . . and it was."

"And Friday?" I cried. "You saw him . . . too?"

She seemed as though she were trying to remember.

"Did you, Aunt Sarah?" I persisted.

"He was a faithful dog," she said. "He died for his faithfulness."

"Did you see him, dead . . . as you saw Gabriel?"

Again that puckered look came into her face. "It's there on the picture," she said at length.

"But he's lying there beside Gabriel. It wasn't like that."

"Wasn't it?" she asked. "They took him away, didn't they?"

"Who took him away?"

She looked at me questioningly. "Who did?" It was as though she were pleading with me to give her the answer.

"You know, don't you, Aunt Sarah?"

"Oh yes, I know," she answered blithely.

"Then please . . . please tell me. It's very important."

"But you know too."

"How I wish I did! You must tell me, Aunt Sarah. You see, it would help me."

"I can't remember."

"But you remember so much. You must remember something so important."

Her face brightened. "I know, Catherine. It was the monk."

She looked so innocent that I knew she would have helped if she could. I could not understand how much she had discovered. I was sure that she lived in two worlds—that of reality and that of the imagination; and that the two became intermingled so that she could not be sure which was which. People in this house underrated her; they spoke their secrets before her, not understanding that she had a mind like a jackdaw, which seized on bright and glittering pieces of information and stored them away.

I turned my attention to the canvas and, now that the shock of seeing Gabriel and Friday lying dead was less acute, I noticed that the work had taken up only one side of the picture. The rest was blank.

She read my thoughts immediately, which was a reminder that her speculations—if speculations they were—were those of a woman who could be astute.

"That's for you," she said; and in that moment she was like a seer from whom the future, of which the rest of us were utterly ignorant, was only separated by a semitransparent veil.

As I did not speak she came close to me and gripped my arm; I could feel her hot fingers burning through my sleeve.

"I can't finish," she said peevishly. "I don't know where to put *you* . . . that's why." She turned the canvas round so that I could not see the picture and hugged it to herself. "You don't know. I don't know. But the monk knows . . ." She sighed. "Oh dear, we shall have to wait. Such a nuisance. I can't start another until I finish this one."

She went to the cupboard and put the canvas away. Then she came back to peer into my face.

"You don't look well," she said. "Come and sit down. You'll be all right, won't you? Poor Claire! She died, you know. Having Gabriel killed her, you might say."

I was trying to shake off the effects of seeing that picture, and I said absently: "But she had a weak heart. I'm strong and healthy."

She put her head on one side and looked quizzically at me.

"Perhaps it's why we're friends . . ." she began.

"What is, Aunt Sarah?"

"We *are* friends. I felt it from the first. As soon as you came I said, 'I like Catherine. She understands me.' Now I suppose they say that's why . . ."

"Aunt Sarah, do tell me what you mean. Why should you and I understand each other better than other people in the house?"

"They always said I am in my second childhood."

A wild fear came into my mind. "And what do they say about me?"

She was silent for a while, then she said: "I've always liked the minstrels' gallery."

I felt impatient in my eagerness to discover what was going on in her muddled mind; then I saw that she *was* telling me and that the minstrels' gallery was connected with her discovery.

"You were in the minstrels' gallery," I said quickly, "and you over-heard someone talking."

She nodded, her eyes wide, and she glanced over her shoulder as though she expected to find someone behind her.

"You heard something about me?"

She nodded; then shook her head. "I don't think we're going to have many Christmas decorations this year. It's all because of Gabriel. Perhaps there'll be a bit of holly."

I felt frustrated but I knew that I must not frighten her. She had heard something which she was afraid to repeat because she knew she should not, and if she thought I was trying to find out she would be on her guard against telling me. I had to wheedle it out of her in some way, because I was sure that it was imperative that I should know.

I forced myself to be calm and said: "Never mind. Next Christmas . . ."

"But who knows what'll have happened to us by next Christmas . . . to me . . . *to you . . .* ?"

"I may well be here, Aunt Sarah, and my baby with me. If it's a boy they'll want it brought up here, won't they?"

"They might take him away from you. They might put you . . ."

I pretended not to have noticed that. I said: "I should not want to be separated from my child, Aunt Sarah. Nobody could do that."

"They could . . . if the doctor said so."

I lifted the christening robe and pretended to examine it, but to my horror my hands had begun to shake and I was afraid she would notice this.

"Did the doctor say so?" I asked.

"Oh yes. He was telling Ruth. He thought it might be necessary . . . if you got worse . . . and it might be a good idea before the baby was born."

"You were in the minstrels' gallery."

"They were in the hall. They didn't see me."

"Did the doctor say I was ill?"

"He said: 'Mentally disturbed.' He said something about its being a common thing to have hallucinations . . . and to do strange things and then think other people did them. He said it was a form of per-secution mania, or something like that."

"I see. And he said I had this?"

Her lips trembled. "Oh, Catherine," she whispered, "I've liked your being here. I don't want you to go away. I don't want you to go to Worstwhistle."

The words sounded like the tolling of a funeral bell, my own funeral. If I were not very careful they would bury me alive.

I could no longer remain in that room. I said: "Aunt Sarah, I'm supposed to be resting. You will excuse me if I go now?"

I did not wait for her to answer. I stooped and kissed her cheek. Then I walked sedately to the door and, when I had closed it, ran to my own room, shut the door and stood leaning against it. I felt like an animal who sees the bars of a cage closing about him. I had to escape before I was completely shut in. But how?

I very quickly made up my mind as to what I would do. I would go and see Dr. Smith and ask him what he meant by talking of me in such a way to Ruth. I might have to betray the fact that Sarah had overheard them, but I should do my utmost to keep her out of this. Yet it was too important a matter to consider such a trifle.

They were saying "She is mad." The words beat in my brain like the notes of a jungle drum. They were saying that I had hallucinations, that I had imagined I had seen a vision in my room; and then I had begun to do strange things—silly unreasoning things, and imagined that someone else did them.

They had convinced Dr. Smith of this—and I had to prove to him that he and they were wrong.

I put on my blue cloak—the one which had been hung over the parapet—for it was the warmest of garments and the wind had turned very cold. But I was quite unaware of the weather as I made my way to the doctor's house.

I knew where it was because we had dropped Damaris there on our way back from Knaresborough. I myself had never been there before. I supposed that at some time the Rockwells had visited the Smiths and that in view of Mrs. Smith's illness, such visits had not taken place while I was at the Revels.

The house was set in grounds of about an acre. It was a tall, narrow house and the Venetian blinds at the windows reminded me of Glen House. There were fir trees in the front garden which had grown rather tall and straggly; they darkened the house considerably.

There was a brass plate on the door announcing that this was the doctor's house, and when I rang the bell the door was opened by a gray-haired maid in a very well starched cap and apron.

"Good afternoon," I said. "Is the doctor at home?"

"Please come in," answered the maid. "I'm afraid he is not at home at the moment. Perhaps I can give him a message."

I thought that her face was like a mask, and remembered that I had thought the same of Damaris. But I was so overwrought that everything seemed strange on that afternoon. I felt I was not the same person who had awakened that morning. It was not that I believed I was anything but sane, but the evil seed had been sown in my mind, and I defy any woman to hear such an opinion of herself with equanimity.

The hall seemed dark; there was a plant on the table and beside it a brass tray in which several cards lay. There was a writing pad and pencil on the table. The maid took this and said: "Could I have your name, please?"

"I am Mrs. Rockwell."

"Oh!" The maid looked startled. "You wished the doctor to come to you?"

"No, I want to see him here."

"It may be an hour before he is here, I'm afraid."

"I will wait for him."

She bowed her head and opened a door, disclosing an impersonal room which I supposed was a waiting room.

Then I thought that I was, after all, more than a patient. The doctor had been a friend to me. I knew his daughter well.

I said: "Is Miss Smith at home?"

"She also is out, madam."

"Then perhaps I could see Mrs. Smith."

The maid looked somewhat taken aback, then she said: "I will tell Mrs. Smith you are here."

She went away and in a few minutes returned with the information that Mrs. Smith would be pleased to see me. Would I follow her?

I did so and we went up a flight of stairs to a small room. The blinds were drawn and there was a fire burning in a small grate. Near the fire was a sofa on which lay a woman. She was very pale and thin, but I knew at once that she was Damaris's mother, for the remains of great beauty were there. She was covered with a Paisley shawl and the hand which lay on that shawl looked too frail to belong to a living human being.

"Mrs. Rockwell of Kirkland Revels," she said as I came in. "How good of you to come to see me."

I took her hand but relinquished it as soon as I could; it was cold and clammy.

"As a matter of fact," I said, "I came to see the doctor. As he is not in I thought I would ask if you could see me."

"I'm glad you did."

"How are you today?"

"Always the same, thank you. That is . . . as you see me now. . . . I can only walk about this room and then only on my good days. The stairs are beyond me."

I remembered that Ruth had said she was a hypochondriac and a great trial to the doctor. But that was real suffering I saw on her face and I believed that she was more interested in me than in herself.

"I have heard you are going to have a child," she said.

"I suppose the doctor has told you."

"Oh . . . no. He does not talk about his patients. My daughter told me."

"I have seen a great deal of her. She is so often at the Revels."

The woman's face softened. "Oh yes. Damaris is very fond of everyone at the Revels."

"And they of her. She is very charming."

"There is only one fault that can be found with her. She should have been a boy."

"Oh, do you think so? I hope for a boy but I shan't really mind if my child is a girl."

"No, I didn't mind—one doesn't oneself."

I was talking desperately to keep my mind off my own plight, and I suppose I was not really thinking much about her or her affairs, but I said: "So it was the doctor who cared."

"Most ambitious men want sons. They want to see themselves reproduced. It's a tragedy when they are disappointed. Please tell me, is anything wrong?"

"Why do you ask?"

"I thought you looked as though it might be so."

"I . . . I want to consult the doctor."

"Of course. You came here to do that, didn't you? I'm sure he won't be long."

Let him come soon, I was praying. I must speak to him. I must make him understand.

"Do you want to see him so very urgently?" she asked.

"Yes . . . I did."

"It's on your own account, of course."

"Yes."

"I remember when I was having my children, I was continually anxious."

"I didn't know you had more than one, Mrs. Smith."

"There is only Damaris living. I have made many attempts to have a son. Unfortunately I did not succeed. I bore two stillborn daughters and there were others whom I lost in the early stages of pregnancy. My last, born four years ago . . . born dead . . . was a boy. That was a very bitter blow."

Although I could not see her face clearly because her back was to the light, I was aware of the change in her expression as she said: "It was the doctor's wish that we should have a boy. For the last four years . . . since the birth of the boy, I have never been well."

I was in a hypersensitive state. Worried as I was about my own problem, I was aware that she too had a problem of her own. I felt a bond between us which I could not fully understand and which I felt she saw clearly but was uncertain of my ability to see. It was a strange feeling. I was already beginning to ask myself whether my imagination was betraying me. But as soon as such a thought came into my head I dismissed it.

I was myself—practical, feet on the ground. Nobody, I told myself fiercely—perhaps too fiercely—is going to tell me that I'm going out of my mind.

She spread her hands on the Paisley shawl with an air of resignation.

"One thing," she said with a little laugh, "there could be no more attempts."

Conversation between us flagged; I was wishing that I had remained in that impersonal waiting room for the doctor's return.

She tried again. "I was very upset when I heard of your tragedy."

"Thank you."

"Gabriel was a charming person. It is hard to believe . . ."

"It is impossible to believe . . . what they said of him," I heard myself reply vehemently.

"Ah! I am glad you do not believe it. I wonder you don't go back to your family . . . to have your child."

I was puzzled, for I noticed that there was a little color in her cheeks and I could see that the thin white hands were trembling. She was excited about something and I fancied she was wondering whether to confide in me. But I was watching myself, and I thought desperately: Am I always going to watch myself from now on?

"My child—if a boy—will be the heir of the Revels," I said slowly. "It's a tradition that they should be born in the house."

She lay back and closed her eyes. She looked so ill that I thought she had fainted, and I rose to look for the bell, but just at that moment Damaris came in.

"Mother!" she cried, and her face looked different because the masklike quality had left it. She looked younger, a lovely vital girl. I knew in that moment that she was very fond of the invalid. Her face changed as her gaze fell on me. "But Mrs. Rockwell! What . . . ? How . . . ?"

"I called on the doctor," I said, "and as I had to wait I thought I'd make use of the opportunity to see your mother."

"Oh, but . . ."

"Why, have I done something I shouldn't? I'm sorry. Are you not allowed to receive visitors?"

"It is the state of her health," said Damaris. "My father is very careful of her."

"He is afraid they will overexcite her . . . or what?"

"Yes, that is it. She has to be kept quiet." Damaris went to her mother and laid a hand on her brow.

"I'm all right, my darling," said Mrs. Smith.

"Your head's hot, Mother."

"Would you like me to go?" I asked.

"Please no," said Mrs. Smith quickly, but Damaris was looking doubtful. "Sit down, Damaris," she went on, and turning to me: "My daughter is overanxious on my behalf."

"And I expect the doctor is," I said.

"Oh yes . . . yes!" Damaris put in.

"I know he must be because he is so kind to all his patients. I hear his praises sung wherever I go."

Mrs. Smith lay back, her eyes closed, and Damaris said: "Yes, yes. It is so. They rely on him."

"I hope he will soon be back," I said.

"I am sure he would have hurried back if he had known you would be waiting for him."

Damaris sat down near her mother and began to talk. I had never heard her talk so much before. She talked of our trip to Knaresborough and the Christmas holiday; she talked of the "Bring and Buy" sale and other church activities.

It was thus that the doctor found us.

I heard his footsteps on the stairs and then the door was flung open. He was smiling but it was a different kind of smile from that which I usually saw on his face, and I knew that he was more disturbed than I had ever seen him before.

"Mrs. Rockwell," he cried. "Why, this is a surprise."

"I decided to make the acquaintance of Mrs. Smith while I was waiting."

He took my hand and held it firmly in his for a few seconds. I had a notion that he was seeking to control himself. Then he went to his wife's sofa and laid a hand on her brow.

"You are far too excited, my dear," he said. "Has she been exciting herself?"

He was looking at Damaris and I could not see his face clearly.

"No, Father." Damaris's voice sounded faint as though she were a little girl and not very sure of herself.

He had turned to me. "Forgive me, Mrs. Rockwell. I was concerned on two counts. On yours and that of my wife. You have come to see me. You have something to tell me?"

"Yes," I said, "I want to speak to you. I think it is important."

"Very well," he said. "You will come to my consulting room. Shall we go now?"

"Yes, please," I said; and I rose and went to Mrs. Smith's couch.

I took the cold and clammy hand in mine and I wondered about her as I said good-by. She had changed with the coming of her husband, but I was not sure in what way, for it was as though a shutter had been drawn over her expression. I believed he was going to scold her for exciting herself. She had the air of a child who had disobeyed.

Her welfare is his greatest concern, I thought; which is natural. He who is so kind to his patients would be especially so to her.

I said good-by to Damaris and the doctor led the way down to his consulting room.

As he shut the door and gave me a chair at the side of the roll-top desk and took his own chair, I felt my spirits rise a little. He looked so benign that I could not believe he would do anything but help me.

"Now," he said, "what is the trouble?"

"Strange things have been happening to me," I burst out. "You know about them."

"Yes," he admitted. "Some you yourself have told me. I have heard of the rest through other sources."

"You know then that I saw a monk in my bedroom."

"I know that you thought you saw that."

"So you don't believe me."

He lifted a hand. "Let us say at this stage that I know you saw it
—if that comforts you."

"I don't want comfort, Dr. Smith. I want people to accept what I
tell them as truth."

"That is not always easy," he said, "but remember I am here to
help you."

"Then," I said, "there were the incidents of the bed curtains, the
warming pan and the cloak over the parapet."

"That cloak you are wearing," he said.

"So you know even that."

"I had to be told. I am, you know, looking after your health."

"And you believe that I have fancied all these things—that they did
not really happen outside my imagination."

He did not speak for a moment and I insisted: "Do you? Do you?"

He lifted a hand. "Let us review this with calm. We need calm,
Mrs. Rockwell. You need it more than you need anything else."

"I am calm. What I need is people who believe in me."

"Mrs. Rockwell, I am a doctor and I have had experience of many
strange cases. I know I can talk to you frankly and intelligently."

"So you do not think I am mad?"

"Do not use such a word. There is no need to."

"I am not afraid of words . . . any more than I am afraid of people who dress up as monks and play tricks on me."

He was silent for a few seconds, then he said: "You are going
through a difficult time. Your body is undergoing changes. Sometimes when this happens the personalities of women change. You
have heard that they have odd fancies for things to which they previously have been indifferent . . . ?"

"This is no odd fancy!" I cried. "I think I should tell you immediately that I am here because I know you have been discussing
what you call my case with Mrs. Grantley and that you have both
decided that I am . . . mentally unbalanced."

"You overheard this!" he said; and I could see that he was taken
aback.

I had no intention of betraying Aunt Sarah, so I said: "I know
that you have been discussing this together. You don't deny it."

"No," he said slowly, "that would be foolish of me, wouldn't it?"

"So you and she have decided that I am crazy."

"Nothing of the sort. Mrs. Rockwell, you are very excited. Now before your pregnancy you were not easily excited, were you? That is one change we see."

"What are you planning to do with me . . . to send me to Worstwhistle?"

He stared at me, but he could not disguise the fact that the thought had been in his mind.

I was stricken with fury . . . and panic. I stood up but he was immediately beside me. He laid his hands on my shoulders and gently forced me back into my seat.

"You have misunderstood," he said, resuming his seat and speaking very gently. "This is a painful matter to me. I am very fond of the family at the Revels and their tragedies affect me deeply. Please believe that there is no question of your going to Worstwhistle . . . at this stage."

I took him up at once. "Then at what stage?"

"Please, please, be calm. Very good work is done at . . . that place. You know I am a regular visitor there. You have been overwrought for some weeks. You could not hide this from me."

"I have been overwrought because someone is trying to make me appear hysterical. And how dare you talk to me of that place! You must be mad yourself."

"I only want to help you."

"Then find out who is doing these things. Find out who had monks' robes at the pageant. We might discover who still has one."

"You are still thinking of that unfortunate incident."

"Of course I think of it. It was the beginning."

"Mrs. Rockwell . . . Catherine . . . I want to be your friend. You can't doubt that, can you?"

I looked into those dark brown eyes and I thought they were very soft and gentle.

"I became interested in you from the moment Gabriel brought you to the Revels," he went on. "And when your father came to the funeral I saw how matters stood between you. That touched me deeply. It made you seem so . . . vulnerable. But I am being too candid."

"I want to hear what you have to say," I insisted. "I want nothing held back."

"Catherine, I wish you would trust me. More than anything I want to help you through this difficult time. Damaris is not much younger than you, and when I have seen you together I have often wished that you, too, were my daughter. One of my dearest wishes was to be the father of a large family. But you are growing impatient with me. Let me say briefly that I have always felt towards you as I would towards a daughter, and I have hoped that you would confide in me, that I might be able to help you."

"The best way in which you could do that would be to find out who it was who dressed up as a monk and came to my bedroom. If you could find that person, I should be in no need of help."

He looked at me sadly and shook his head.

"What are you suggesting?" I demanded.

"Only that I want you to confide your troubles in me . . . as you would to your own father." He hesitated and, shrugging his shoulders, added: "As you might have done to a father who was closer to you than your own. I would gladly protect you."

"So you think someone is threatening me?"

"Something is. It may be heredity. It may be . . ."

"I don't understand you."

"Perhaps I have said too much."

"No one is saying quite enough. If I knew everything that was in the minds of these people about me, I should be able to show you all that you have misjudged me when you think me . . . unbalanced."

"But you believe now that I want to help you. You do, I hope, look on me as a friend as well as a doctor?"

I saw the anxiety in his eyes and I was deeply moved. He had noticed my father's indifference to me and in some way I had betrayed how that had hurt me. He had called me vulnerable. I had not thought of myself in that way before, but I was beginning to realize that it was exactly what I was. I had longed for the affection which had been denied me; Uncle Dick had given it to me, but he was not here with me at this most important crisis in my life. Dr. Smith was offering his sympathy and with it that particular brand of paternal devotion for which I had longed.

"You are very kind," I said.

A look of pleasure touched his features. He leaned forward and patted my hand.

Then he was suddenly very serious. "Catherine," he said, as though he were considering very carefully what he was saying, "a short time ago you told me that you wanted me to be absolutely frank. I have convinced you, haven't I, that I have your welfare at heart? I want you to know too that I owe a great debt to the Rockwell family.

I am going to tell you something which is not generally known, because I want you to understand my deep devotion to the family of which you are now a member. You may remember I told you that I began my life as an unwanted child, a poor orphan, and that it was a rich man who gave me my opportunity to do the work I longed to do. That man was a Rockwell—Sir Matthew in fact. So you see I can never forget the debt of gratitude I owe to the family and to Sir Matthew in particular."

"I see," I murmured.

"He wants his grandson to be born strong and healthy. I long to make that possible. My dear Catherine, you must place yourself in my hands. You must take great care of yourself. You must let me take care of you. And there is one fact of which I believe you are ignorant; and I am now turning over in my mind whether or not I should tell you this."

"You must tell me. You must."

"Oh Catherine, it may be when you have heard it, that you will wish I had not spoken. I am asking myself at this moment—as I have so many times—whether it is wiser to tell you or not."

"Please tell me. I don't want to be left in the dark."

"Are you strong enough to hear this, Catherine?"

"Of course I'm strong enough. The only thing I can't bear is lies . . . and secrets. I am going to find out who it is who is doing this to me."

"I am going to help you, Catherine."

"Then tell me what this is."

Still he hesitated. Then he said: "You must realize that if I tell you, I do so because I want you to understand the need for you to listen to my advice."

"I will listen to your advice . . . only tell me."

Still he paused and it was as though he were seeking the right words.

Then suddenly they came rushing out. "Catherine, you know that I have for some years made a habit of visiting Worstwhistle."

"Yes, yes."

"And you know what Worstwhistle is."

"Yes, of course I know."

"I am in a very trusted position there and I have access to the records of patients. As a medical man . . ."

"Naturally," I interrupted.

"A close relative of yours is in that institution, Catherine. I do not think you know of this . . . in fact I am sure you do not. Your mother has been a patient at Worstwhistle for the last seventeen years."

I stared at him; I felt as though the walls of the room were about to collapse upon me; there was a rushing in my ears. It seemed to me that this room with its roll-top desk, this man with the gentle eyes, were dissolving and in their place was a house made dark, not because the Venetian blinds were always drawn, but because there was always there an atmosphere of brooding tragedy. I heard a voice crying in the night: "Cathy . . . come back to me, Cathy." And I saw him, my tragic father, going off regularly each month and coming back dispirited, sad, melancholic.

"Yes," went on the doctor, "I fear it is so. I am told that your father is devoted to his wife, that he pays regular visits to the institution. Sometimes, Catherine, she knows who he is. Sometimes she does not know him. She has a doll which at times she knows to be a doll; and at others she thinks it is her child . . . you, Catherine. At Worstwhistle all that can be done for her is done . . . but she will never leave the place. Catherine, you see what I mean? Sometimes the seed is passed on. Catherine, do not look . . . so stricken. I am telling you that we can care for you . . . that we can help you. That's what I want to do. I am only telling you this so you will put yourself in my hands. Believe me, Catherine."

I found that I had buried my face in my hands and that I was praying. I was crying: "Oh God, let me have dreamed this. Let this not be true."

He had risen and was standing by my chair; his arm was about my shoulders.

"We'll fight it, Catherine," he said. "We'll fight it together."

Perhaps the word "fight" helped me. It was a lifelong habit of mine to fight for what I wanted. I kept thinking of that vision I had had. The curtain had been pulled about my bed. Who had pulled it? There had been a draught from the door. I would not accept this theory that I was the victim of delusions.

He sensed the change in my mood. "That's the spirit, Catherine," he said. "You don't believe me, do you?"

My voice sounded firm as I said: "I know someone is determined to harm me and my child."

"And do you believe that I would be so cruel as to concoct this story about your mother?"

I did not answer. There were my father's absences from home to be explained. How could he have known of these? And yet . . . I had always been led to believe that she had died.

Suppose it were true that my mother was in that place—it was not true that my mind was tainted. I had always been calm and self-possessed. There had never been any signs of hysteria. Even now when I had been subjected to this terror, I believed that I had been as calm as anyone could hope to be in the circumstances.

I was as certain as I ever had been that whatever had happened to my mother, I had not inherited her insanity.

"Oh, Catherine," he said, "you delight me. You are strong. I have every hope that we shall fight this. Believe me, it is true that your mother, Catherine Corder, has been in Worstwhistle for the last seventeen years. You accept that, don't you, because you know that I would not tell you this unless I had made absolutely sure. But what you won't accept is that you have inherited one small part of her insanity. That's going to help us. We'll fight this."

I faced him and said in a firm voice: "Nothing will convince me that I have imagined these things which have happened to me since I came to the Revels."

He nodded. "Well then, my dear," he said, "the thing for us to do is to find out who is behind this. Have you any suspicions?"

"I have discovered that several people possessed a monk's robe five years ago at the time of the pageant. Luke had one, Simon Redvers had one. And both of them are in line to inherit the Revels."

He nodded. "If anyone has been deliberately seeking to harm you . . ." he murmured.

"They have," I answered vehemently. "They have."

"Catherine," he said, "you are exhausted by your emotions. I should like you to go home and rest."

I was aware how weary I was, and I said: "I should like to be at home. I should like to be in my room . . . alone to rest and think of all this."

"I would drive you back but I have another patient to see."

"I don't want them to know that I've been to see you. I want to walk home and go in . . . just as though nothing unusual has happened."

"And you want to say nothing of all this?"

"At present yes. I want to think."

"You are very brave, Catherine."

"I wish I were wiser."

"You are wise too, I think. I am going to ask you to do me a favor; will you?"

"What is it?"

"Will you allow Damaris to walk back with you?"

"That is not necessary."

"You said you would take my advice, and this news of your mother has been a great shock to you. Please, Catherine, do as I say."

"Very well. If Damaris has no objection."

"Of course she will have none. She will be delighted. Wait here and I will go and fetch her. I am going to give you a little brandy first. Please don't protest. It will do you good."

He went to a cabinet and brought out two glasses. He half filled one and gave it to me. The other he filled for himself.

He lifted the glass and smiled at me over it.

"Catherine," he said, "you will come through all this. Trust me. Tell me anything you discover which you think is important. You know how much I want to help."

"Thank you. But I can't drink all this."

"Never mind. You have had a little. It will help to revive you. Now I am going to find Damaris."

He went and I was not sure how long I remained alone. I kept going over it in my mind: my father's leaving Glen House and not returning until the following day. He must have stayed a night near the institution . . . perhaps after seeing her he had to compose himself before returning home. So this was the reason for that house of gloom; this was why I had always felt the need to escape from it. He should have warned me; he should have prepared me. But perhaps it was better that I had not known. Perhaps it would have been better if I never had known.

Damaris came into the room with her father. She was wearing a heavy coat with fur at the collar, and her hands were thrust into a muff. I thought she looked sullen and reluctant to accompany me, so I began to protest that I was in no need of companionship.

But the doctor said determinedly: "Damaris would like a walk." He smiled at me as though everything were normal and he had not almost shattered my belief in myself by his revelations.

"Are you ready?" asked Damaris.

"Yes, I am ready."

The doctor shook my hand gravely. He said I should take a sedative tonight as I was sleeping badly, implying to Damaris, I thought, that this was the reason for my coming. I took the bottle he gave me and thrust it into the inside pocket of my cloak; and Damaris and I set out together.

"How cold it is!" she said. "We shall have snow before morning if this continues."

The wind had whipped the color to her cheeks and she looked beautiful in her little hat which was trimmed with the same fur as her muff.

"Let's go through the copse," she said. "It's a little longer but we shall escape the wind."

I was walking as though in my sleep. I did not notice where we went. I could only go over and over in my mind what the doctor had told me, and the more I thought of it the more likely it seemed.

We stopped in the shelter of some trees for a while, for Damaris said she had a stone in her boot which was hurting her. She sat on a fallen tree trunk and removed the boot shaking it and then putting it on again. She grew red trying to do the buttons up.

Then we went on, but the boot was still hurting her and she sat down on the grass while the operation was repeated.

"It's a tiny piece of flint," she said. "This must be it." And she lifted her hand to throw it away. "It's amazing that such a little thing could cause such discomfort. Oh dear, these wretched buttons."

"Let me help."

"No, I can do them myself." She struggled for a little while, then she looked up to say: "I'm glad you met my mother. She was really very pleased to see you."

"Your father seems very anxious about her."

"He is. He's anxious about all his patients."

"And she is, of course, a very special patient," I added.

"We have to watch her or she will overtax her strength."

I thought of Ruth's words. She was a hypochondriac and it was because of the doctor's life with her that he threw himself so whole-heartedly into his work.

But my mind was filled by one thought only as I stood there among the trees.

Was it true? I did not ask that question about my mother be-cause everything fitted so well. I knew that must be true. What did I mean then? I had asked the question involuntarily: Am I like my mother? In doing so I had admitted my doubts.

Standing there in the woods on that December day I felt that I had come as near to despair as I had in my whole life. But I had not touched the very bottom yet. That was imminent but at that moment I believed that nothing worse could happen to me.

Damaris had buttoned her boots; she had thrust her hands into her muff and we were off again.

I was surprised when I found that we had come out of the trees on the far side of the Abbey, and that it was necessary to walk through the ruins to the Revels.

"I know," said Damaris, "that this is a favorite spot of yours."

"It was," I amended. "It is some time since I have been here."

I realized now that the afternoon was fading and that in an hour or so it would be dark.

I said: "Luke must take you home."

"Perhaps," she answered.

It seemed darker in the ruins. It was naturally so because of the shadows cast by those piles of stones. We had passed the fishponds and were in the heart of the Abbey when I saw the monk. He was passing through what was left of the arcade; silently and swiftly he went; and he was exactly as he had been at the foot of my bed.

I cried out: "Damaris! There! Look!"

The figure paused at the sound of my voice, and turning, beckoned. Then he turned away and went on. Now the figure had disappeared behind one of the buttresses which held up what was left of the arcade; now it was visible again as it moved into the space between one buttress and the next.

I watched it, fascinated, horrified, yet unable to move.

I cried out: "Quick! We must catch him."

Damaris clung to my arm holding me back.

"But there is no time to waste," I cried. "We'll lose him. We know he's somewhere in the Abbey. We've got to find him. He shan't get away this time."

Damaris said: "Please, Catherine . . . I'm frightened."

"So am I. But we've got to find him." I went stumbling towards the arcade, but she was dragging me back.

"Come home," she cried. "Come home at once."

I turned to face her. "You've seen it," I cried triumphantly. "So now you can tell them. You've seen it!"

"We must go on to the Revels," she said. "We must go at once."

"But . . ." I realized that we could not catch him because he could move so much faster than we could. But that was not so important.

Someone else had seen him, and I was exultant. Relief following so fast on panic was almost unendurable. Only now could I admit how shaken I had been, how frightened.

But there was no need to fear. I was vindicated. Someone else had seen.

She was dragging me through the ruins and the house was in sight.

"Oh Damaris," I said, "how thankful I am that it happened then . . . that you saw."

She turned her beautiful, blank face towards me and her words made me feel as though I had suddenly been plunged into icy water.

"What did you see, Catherine?"

"Damaris . . . what do you mean?"

"You were very excited. You could see something, couldn't you?"

"But do you mean to say you didn't!"

"There wasn't anything there, Catherine. There was nothing."

I turned on her. I was choking with rage and anguish. I believe I took her arm and shook her.

"You're lying," I cried. "You're pretending."

She shook her head as though she was going to burst into tears.

"No, Catherine, no. I wish I had . . . How I wish I could have seen . . . if it meant so much to you."

"You saw it," I said. "I know you saw it."

"I didn't see anything, Catherine. There wasn't anything."

I said coldly: "So you are involved in this, are you?"

"What, Catherine, what?" she asked piteously.

"Why did you take me to the Abbey? Because you knew it would be there. So that you could say that you saw nothing. So that you could tell them I am mad!"

I was losing control, because I was thoroughly frightened. I had admitted my fear when I thought there was no longer reason to be afraid; and that was my undoing.

She was clutching at my arm but I threw her off.

"I don't need your help," I said. "I don't want your help. Go away. At least I've proved that you are his accomplice."

I stumbled on. I could not move very fast. It was as though the child within me protested.

I entered the house; it seemed quiet and repelling. I went to my room and lay on my bed, and I stayed there until darkness came. Mary-Jane came to ask if I wished to have dinner sent up to me; but I said I was not hungry, only very tired.

I sent her away and I locked the doors.

That was my darkest hour.

Then I took a dose of the doctor's sedative and soon I fell into merciful sleep.

6

There is some special quality which develops in a woman who is to have a child; already the fierce instinct is with her. She will protect that child with all the power of which she is capable and, as her determination to do so increases, so it seems does that power.

I awoke next morning refreshed after the unbroken sleep which the doctor's sedative had given me. The events of the previous day came rushing back to my mind and even then I felt as though I were at the entrance of a dark tunnel it would be disastrous for me to enter, but into which I might be swept by the bitter blast of ill fortune.

But the child was there, reminding me of its existence. Where I went there must the child go; what happened to me must have its effect on the child. I was going to fight this thing which was threatening to destroy me—not only for myself but for the sake of one who was more precious to me.

When Mary-Jane came in with my breakfast she did not see that anything was different, and I felt that was my first triumph. I had been terrified that I should be unable to hide the fear which had almost prostrated me on the previous day.

"It's a grand morning, madam," she said.

"Is it, Mary-Jane?"

"A bit of a wind still, but any road t'sun's shining."

"I'm glad."

I half closed my eyes and she went out. I found it difficult to eat, but I managed a little. The sun sent a feeble ray onto the bed and it cheered me; I thought it was symbolic. The sun is always there, I reminded myself, only the clouds get in between. There's always a way of dealing with every problem, only ignorance gets in the way.

I wanted to think very clearly. I knew in my heart that what I had seen had been with my eyes, not with my imagination. Inscrutable as it seemed, there was an explanation somewhere.

Damaris was clearly involved in the plot against me; and what more reasonable than that she should be, for if Luke wished to frighten me into giving birth to a stillborn child, and Damaris was to be his wife, it was surely reasonable enough to suppose that she would work with him.

But was it possible that these two young people could plot so diabolical a murder, for murder it would be even though the child had not come into the world.

I tried to review the situation clearly and work out what must be done. The first thing that occurred to me was that I might go back to my father's house. I rejected that idea almost as soon as it came. I should have to give a reason. I should have to say, "Someone at the Revels is trying to drive me to the brink of madness. Therefore I am running away." I felt that it would be an admission of my fear and if, for one moment, I accepted the view that I was suffering from hallucinations, I had taken the first steps on that road along which someone here was trying to force me.

I did not think at this time I could endure the solemnity, the morbid atmosphere of my father's house.

I had made my decision: I could never know peace of mind again until I had solved this mystery. It was therefore not something from which I could run away. I was going to intensify my search for my persecutor. I owed it to myself—and to my child.

I must now make a practical plan, and I decided that I would go to Hagar and take her into my confidence. I should have preferred to act alone, but that was impossible because my first step, I had decided, must be to go to Worstwhistle and confirm Dr. Smith's words.

I could not ask anyone at the Revels to drive me there; so I must go to Hagar.

When I had bathed and dressed, I set out immediately for Kelly Grange.

It was about half past ten when I arrived, and I went straight to Hagar and told her what the doctor had told me.

She listened gravely and when I had finished she said: "Simon shall take you to that place immediately. I think with you that should be the first step."

She rang for Dawson and told her to send Simon to us at once. Remembering my suspicions of Simon I was a little anxious, but I realized that I had to get to Worstwhistle even if it did mean taking

a chance; and as soon as he entered the room my suspicions vanished, and I was ashamed that I had ever entertained them. That was
the effect he was beginning to have on me.

Hagar told him what had happened. He look astonished and then
he said: "Well, we'd better get over to Worstwhistle right away."

"I will send someone over to the Revels to tell them that you are
taking luncheon with me," said Hagar; and I was glad she had thought
of that because I should have aroused their curiosity if I had not
returned.

Fifteen minutes later Simon was driving the trap, with me sitting
beside him, along the road to Worstwhistle. We did not speak much
during that journey; and I was grateful to him for falling in with my
mood. I could think of nothing but the interview before me which
was going to mean so much to me. I kept remembering my father's
absences from home and the sadness which always seemed to sur-
round him; and I could not help believing that there was truth in
what the doctor had told me.

It was about midday when we came to Worstwhistle—a gray stone
building which to my mind resembled nothing so much as a prison.
It *was* a prison, I told myself—stone walls within which the afflicted
lived out their clouded lives. Was it possible that my own mother
was among those sad inhabitants, and that there was a plot afoot to
make me a prisoner here?

I was determined that should never be.

Surrounding the building was a high wall and when we drew up at
the heavy wrought-iron gates, a porter came out of the lodge and
asked our business.

Simon told him authoritatively that he wished to see the superintendent of the establishment.

"You have an appointment with him, sir?"

"It's of the utmost importance," Simon replied and threw the man
a coin.

Whether it was the money or Simon's manner, I was not sure, but
the gates were opened to us and we drove along a gravel drive to the
main building.

A man in livery emerged as we approached and Simon dismounted
and helped me down.

"Who'll hold the horse?" he asked.

The porter shouted and a boy appeared. He held the horse while
we, with the man in livery, went towards the porch.

"Will you tell the superintendent that we wish to see him immediately on a matter of great urgency?"

Again I was grateful for that authoritative arrogance which resulted in immediate obedience.

We were led through the porch into a stone-flagged hall in which a fire was burning; but it was not enough to warm the place, and I felt the chill. But perhaps it was a spiritual rather than a physical chill.

I was shivering. Simon must have noticed this, for he took my arm and I found comfort in that gesture.

"Please to sit in here, sir," said the porter; and he opened a door on our right to disclose a high-ceilinged room with whitewashed walls, a heavy table, and a few chairs. "Your name, sir?"

"This is Mrs. Rockwell of Kirkland Revels, and I am Mr. Redvers."

"You say you had an appointment, sir?"

"I did not say so."

"It's usual to make one, sir."

"We are pressed for time and, as I said, the matter is urgent. Pray go and tell the superintendent that we are here."

The porter retired, and when he had gone Simon smiled at me.

"Anyone would think we were trying to see the Queen." Then his face softened into a tenderness which I had never seen him give to anyone before except perhaps Hagar. "Cheer up," he said, "even if it's true, it's not the end of the world, you know."

"I'm glad you came with me." I hadn't meant to say that but the words slipped out.

He took my hand and pressed it firmly. It was a gesture which meant that we were not foolish, hysterical people and should be able to take the calm view.

I walked away from him because I did not trust my emotions. I went to the window and looked out, and I thought of the people who were held captive here. This was their little world. They looked out on the gardens and the moor beyond—if they were allowed to look out of windows—and this was all they knew of life. Some had been here for years . . . seventeen years. But perhaps they were kept shut away. Perhaps they did not even see the gardens and the moor.

It seemed that we waited a very long time before the porter returned. Then he said: "Come this way, will you please."

As we followed him up a flight of stairs, and along a corridor, I caught a glimpse of barred windows and shivered. So like a prison, I thought.

Then the porter rapped on a door, on which the word SUPERINTENDENT had been painted. A voice said "Come in"; and Simon, taking my arm, drew me into the room with him. The whitewashed walls were bare; the oil cloth polished to danger point; and it was a cold and cheerless room; at a desk sat a man with a tired gray face and a resentful look in his eyes, because, I presumed, we had dared invade his privacy without an appointment.

"Pray sit down," he said, when the porter had left us. "Am I to understand that your business is urgent?"

"It is of the utmost urgency to us," said Simon.

I spoke then. "It is good of you to see us. I am Mrs. Rockwell, but before my marriage I was Catherine Corder."

"Oh." The gleam of understanding which came into his face was a blow which shattered my hopes.

I said: "You have a patient here of that name?"

"Yes, that is so."

I looked at Simon, and try as I might I could not speak because my tongue had become parched, my throat constricted.

"The point is," went on Simon, "Mrs. Rockwell has only very recently heard that a Catherine Corder may be here. She has reason to believe that this may be her mother. She has always been under the impression that her mother died when she was very young. Naturally she wishes to know whether the Catherine Corder in this establishment is her mother."

"The information we have about our patients is confidential, as you will appreciate."

"We do appreciate that," said Simon. "But in the case of very close relatives would you not be prepared to give the information which was asked?"

"It would first be necessary to prove the relationship."

I burst out: "Before my marriage my name was Catherine Corder. My father is Mervyn Corder of Glen House, Glengreen near Harrogate. Please tell me whether the patient you have here, who bears the same name as myself, is my mother."

The superintendent hesitated; then he said: "I can tell you nothing except that we have a patient here of that name. It is not such an unusual name. Surely your father would supply the information you are seeking from me?"

I looked at Simon who said: "I should have thought that such a close relation had a right to know."

"As I said, the relationship would first have to be proved. I do not think I could betray the trust placed in me by my patient's relations."

"Tell me," I cried wildly, "does her husband come to visit her regularly each month?"

"Many of our patients' relatives visit them regularly."

He surveyed us coldly and I could see that he was adamant. Simon was exasperated, but he could not move the superintendent.

"Could I see . . . ?" I began.

But the superintendent held up his hand in horror. "Certainly not," he said sharply. "That would be quite impossible."

Simon looked at me helplessly. "There's only one thing to do," he said. "You must write to your father."

"I think you are right in that," said the superintendent rising to imply that he had given us enough of his time. "Our patient has been placed here by her husband, but if he gives you permission to see her we should raise no objection, providing of course that she is well enough to receive you when you come. That is all the help I can give you."

He pulled the bell and the porter reappeared. We were led out to the waiting trap.

I felt frustrated as we drove away. Simon did not speak until he had put about a mile between us and the institution. Then he pulled up. We were in a lane over which the trees would make an arch of green in the summer; now we could see the blue-gray sky between the black branches, and the clouds being chased across it by the keen wind.

I did not feel the wind; nor, I imagine, did Simon.

He turned to me and slid his arm behind me, although not touching me.

"You're depressed by all this," he said.

"Do you wonder?"

"It wasn't altogether illuminating, was it?"

"Illuminating enough. They have a Catherine Corder there. He did tell us that."

"She may not be connected with you."

"I think it is too much of a coincidence if she should not be. I haven't told you, have I, that my father used to disappear at regular intervals? We did not know where he went. I used to think that he went visiting some—woman . . ." I laughed harshly. "I know now that he went to Worstwhistle."

"Can you be so sure?"

"Something tells me it is so. Dr. Smith, remember, has seen her records and he has told me that she is my mother."

Simon was silent for a few seconds and then he said: "It's not like you, Catherine, to despair."

I noticed that he had dropped the Mrs. and I believed that that was a sign of the change in our relationship.

"Would you not feel like despair if all this were happening to you?"

"The best way to fight something that frightens you is to go right up to it and look it in the face."

"I am doing that."

"Well, what is the worst that could happen?"

"That another Catherine Corder should be taken to that place. That her child should be born there."

"We'll not let it happen. Nobody could do that, could they?"

"Could they not? If the doctor was convinced that it was the best place for me?"

"It's all such nonsense. I never knew anyone so sane. You're as sane as I am."

I turned to him and said vehemently: "I am, Simon, I *am*."

He took my hands and, to my astonishment—for I had not until this moment thought him capable of such a gesture towards me— he kissed them, and I could feel the fervor of those kisses through my gloves.

Then he pressed my hand so tightly that I winced at the pain of his grip.

"I'm with you in this," he said.

I knew a moment of great happiness. I felt the strength of him flowing into my body, and I was grateful, so grateful that I wondered whether such gratitude must be love.

"Do you mean it?"

"Heart and soul," he answered. "Nobody shall take you where you don't want to go."

"The way things have been going alarms me, Simon. I'm looking this right in the face, as you said. And I am frightened. I thought I should fight it better by pretending not to be afraid, but pretense isn't going to help, is it? Ever since I saw the monk the first time, life has changed for me. I've been like a different person . . . a frightened person. I now know that all the time I've been wondering what is going to happen next. It has made me nervous . . . different, Simon, different."

"Anyone would feel so. There's nothing strange about that."

"You don't believe in ghosts, Simon, do you? If people say they see a ghost, you think they're lying or that they've imagined they saw something."

"I don't think that about you."

"Then you can only think that inside the monk's robe was a real person."

"Yes, I think that."

"Then I must tell you all the truth. Nothing must be held back." And I told him of the apparition I had seen in the Abbey when Damaris was with me, and how she had declared there had been nothing there. "I think that was the worst moment of all because then I began to doubt myself."

"We must assume that Damaris knows what's going on; she must be a party to the plot."

"I am sure Luke wants to marry her, but does she want to marry Luke?"

"Perhaps she wants to marry the Revels," said Simon; "and she couldn't do that, could she, unless the place was Luke's."

"You're helping me . . . you're helping a lot."

"It's what I want to do more than anything."

"How can I thank you!"

His arm was round me now; he drew me to him and kissed me lightly on the cheek. I could feel his cold face pressed against mine for a few seconds and the warmth which enveloped me surprised me.

"It is strange that I should look to you for comfort."

"Not at all strange. We're two of a kind."

"Oh yes, you admire my common sense. You thought it was very clever of me to marry Gabriel . . . for his possessions."

"So you remember that."

"It is not the sort of thing one is likely to forget. I suppose you would not blame whoever it is who wants to drive me mad . . . if they succeed."

"I'd wring his neck if I could find him."

"Then your attitude has changed."

"Not in the least. I didn't admire you for, as I thought, marrying

Gabriel for what he could give you. I admired you for your sharp wits and your courage . . . which I knew were there."

"I am not being very courageous now."

"You are going to be."

"I must be, it seems, if I am to retain your good opinion."

He was pleased by the lightness which had crept into our conversation; as for myself I was surprised that, with the burden of suspicion which was lying heavily upon me, I could indulge in it; but it did me good—that much I knew.

"Yes," he repeated, "you are going to be. And I am here to help you."

"Thank you, Simon."

He looked at me intently for a few seconds and I read in his looks the knowledge which he wished me to share. He and I were about to embark on a new relationship; it was an exciting one; it would be one of stimulation to us both, of fierce disagreements and splendid accord. We were two of a kind. He had recognized that, as I did now. I knew what he was telling me, and I wanted to listen so much.

I went on: "There have been times when I did not know whom I could trust."

"You will trust me," he said.

"It sounds like a command." I smiled. "It often does when you make a statement."

"That is a command."

"And you think you have a right to command me?"

"Yes . . . in view of . . . everything, I do."

I did not want to move from this spot. I felt as though I had found a peaceful place in which to rest and be happy. Behind me lay that grim institution with its dark secrets; ahead of me the Revels and, somewhere not far distant, was my father's house. But here I was suspended between threats of disaster, and here I wanted to stay.

I believed in that moment that I was in love with Simon Redvers and he with me. It was a strange conclusion to arrive at at such a time in a cold country lane.

It did not seem strange to me that these strong emotions I felt were for Simon Redvers. In some way he reminded me of Gabriel; he was Gabriel without his weakness. When I was with Simon I understood what had made me hurry into that marriage with Gabriel. I had loved him in a way, for there are many kinds of love. Pity is love, I thought;

the need to protect is love. But there was a deep and passionate love of which I knew nothing; I knew though, that to love completely one must know every phase of loving, and that was the real adventure: to widen one's emotions, to discover their depth as the years passed.

But I was a long way from such an adventure. There was so much to be lived through first. I had to be delivered of a child and of my fear. And at this moment I could not peer very far into the mist which hid the future.

But Simon was with me, and such a thought, even at this time, could set my senses singing.

"Very well," I said, "I am ready to listen to your commands."

"Ready then. The first thing we're going to do is drive to an inn a mile along this road. There we are going to eat."

"I couldn't eat."

"You have forgotten that you suggested I should command."

"But the thought of food revolts me."

"There is a quiet little room just off the inn parlor where the host serves his special guests. I am always a special guest. His specialty is a pudding made with steak and mushrooms. It has to be tasted to be believed. We'll have a claret which he will bring from his cellar especially for us. I defy you to resist when you smell the aroma of mine host's specialty."

"I will come with you and watch you enjoy it."

He took my hand again, brought it halfway to his lips, then pressed it and smiled at me.

It was strange that I could be almost happy as we bowled along that road with the wind in our faces and the wintry sun trying to smile at us; but I was.

I even ate a little of the special pudding; and the claret warmed me.

Simon was practical as he always would be.

"Your next step," he said, "is to write to your father. You must ask him for the truth. But mind you, whatever the truth, we are not going to be downhearted."

"But suppose that is really my mother in that place?"

"Well, suppose it is."

"Let's look at it clearly, Simon. My mother in that place . . . and myself, according to some, seeing visions, doing strange things."

"We don't believe in the visions, do we?" he said gently.

"I don't. And how can I thank you and your grandmother for supporting me in this?"

"You don't have to thank us for having an opinion, Catherine. If we could only catch the monk in the act, that is all we should need to prove our case. It's my opinion that he's found some place in which to hide himself. We must try to discover it. Next week the Christmas festivities will begin, and my grandmother and I will spend two nights in the house. That may give us a chance to discover something."

"I wish it were this week."

"It will soon come."

"And if they try anything in the meantime . . . ?"

He was silent for a few seconds, then he said: "If you should see the monk again, tell no one. I believe he wants you to talk of what you've seen, but do not give him that satisfaction. Continue to lock your doors at night so that you can't be startled from your sleep. You haven't been, have you, since you began to lock them? I think that's significant. In the meantime you will hear from your father—and you are not going to be distressed, whatever he has to tell you. I never did believe that we relied on our ancestors for what we are. We are in command of our own fates."

"I'll remember that, Simon."

"Yes, do remember it. What we are and what we become is in our own hands. Think of it like this: What is the population of England today? Some ten times what it was a few hundred years ago. Has it struck you that if we could trace our ancestors back far enough we must all be related in some way with each other? In all our families there have very likely been rogues and saints, madmen and geniuses. No, Catherine, each of us is an individual with his—or her—own life in his hands."

"You are philosophical," I said. "I had never thought that. I had thought you practical in the extreme, excelling in good, straightforward common sense, but without imagination and therefore without sympathy."

"That's the mask I wear. We all wear them, don't we? I'm tough; I'm shrewd; I'm a blunt man who doesn't mince his words. That's the outward me. Not a very attractive personality, you'll agree, as you did on our first meeting. Brash, determined that no one shall get the better of him—therefore he's going to start trying to get the better of everyone else. That's part of me . . . I don't deny it. I'm all of that.

But perhaps I'm something else besides. A man's made up of many parts. . . ." He looked at me slyly. "And a woman is probably more complex still."

"Please go on," I said. "You're doing so much for me."

"All right. When you go back to the Revels how are you going to feel?"

"I don't know, except that it won't be so good as I feel here."

"No," he said. "You're going to be afraid. You're going to hurry up the stairs, turning to see if you are being pursued; you're going to throw open the door of your room, and you're going to look anxiously about you to see if he's there. Then you're going to lock him out, but you won't lock out your fear completely, because it's there in your mind and with the darkness your fear will grow stronger."

"You are right of course."

He leaned across the table and took my hand.

"Catherine, there is nothing to fear. There is never anything to fear. Fear is like a cage which prevents our escaping, but *we* make the bars of the cage ourselves. We see them as strong iron bars . . . unbreakable. They are not so, Catherine. We ourselves have the power to take those bars in our hands and break them. They can be strong; they can be flimsy; for we ourselves have made them what they are."

"You are telling me *I* have nothing to fear!"

"Nothing has really harmed you, has it? You have only been frightened."

"How can I know that it never will?"

"The motive, at least, is becoming clear to us. This person—or persons—is seeking to unnerve you. Your life is not in danger. If you were to die violently, following Gabriel, suspicions would certainly be aroused. No, it is the child who is threatened. This person's motive is to reduce you to such a state of fear that your chances of producing a healthy child are endangered. In view of Gabriel's death, it has to appear natural."

"And Gabriel's death . . ." I began.

"I am beginning to think that was the first act in the drama."

"And Friday?" I murmured, remembering then the night before Gabriel's death, when Friday had behaved strangely and insisted on going into the corridor. I told Simon of this. "There was someone there. Waiting. But for Friday it might have been that night. And then Friday disappeared."

He put his hand over mine. "We don't know how it happened," he said. "Let us concern ourselves with what lies ahead of us; we can only conjecture what happened in the past. If we can discover the identity of our monk, if we can catch him in his robe, then we can demand an explanation; and I have no doubt that we shall learn what part he played in Gabriel's death."

"We must find him, Simon."

"We must. But if you see him again, ignore him. Do not try to tackle him. Heaven knows what he might do. If there's anything in our conjectures about Gabriel, remember we may be dealing with a murderer. You must do as I say, Catherine."

"I will, Simon."

"And remember," he added, "you are not alone. We're fighting this . . . together."

We left the inn and he drove me back to the Revels. I was pleased because, although my visit to Worstwhistle had not given me the satisfaction for which I had hoped, I no longer felt alone, and that was a wonderful comfort.

I wrote to my father and I believed that I should have the truth from him in a few days' time, because he would understand my need to know quickly; and when I had posted the letter I felt strengthened. Nothing unusual happened the next day, and during the following morning Dr. Smith came to the house.

He wanted to see me alone, and Ruth left us in the winter parlor together.

He looked at me almost tenderly as he came to the chair in which I was sitting. He laid his hand on the arm of the chair and said gently: "So you paid a visit to Worstwhistle."

"I wanted to be sure," I explained.

"Of course you did. And you satisfied yourself that I had been speaking the truth?"

"They would tell me nothing."

He nodded. "The superintendent acted in the only way possible. Naturally he must respect the privacy of his patients and their relations. But you did discover that there was a patient of that name in the institution."

"Yes."

"Catherine, believe me. I am telling you the truth when I say I know that patient to be your mother. Your father, Mervyn Corder, visits her regularly each month. No doubt he thought he was wise in keeping this from you."

"If the patient in Worstwhistle is my mother, no doubt he did."

"I am glad to see you calmer, Catherine. If you had asked me, I would have taken you to Worstwhistle. You would have seen then that I could have done so much more for you than Simon Redvers could possibly do."

I was almost on the point of telling him that I had written to my father, but I did not do so. Simon had said that the two of us would solve the mystery together, and I wanted to keep this our secret matter.

Besides, there was little I hoped for from anything my father could tell me. It seemed obvious that the Catherine Corder who was in Worstwhistle must be my mother.

"Perhaps later," the doctor was saying, "I will take you to the place and you might see her."

"Would that serve any useful purpose since I have never known her?"

"But you would like to see your own mother?"

"I doubt if she would know me."

"She has her lucid moments. There are times when she is vaguely aware of what has happened to her."

I shivered. I was not going to tell him that I had a horror of entering that place; that I had a strange premonition that if I crossed that threshold again, I might become a prisoner there. If I told him that, he would listen with sympathy, but he would be telling himself that it was part of my overwrought condition which made me imagine that, as I imagined that I saw "visions."

I could not be so frank with him as I was with Simon. This was a further indication of my feelings for the latter. I told myself that I could trust no one—not even Dr. Smith—for I knew that he was ready to believe I was in an unbalanced state. But it wasn't true that I trusted no one. I trusted Simon.

Christmas was three days away. The servants had decorated the hall with branches of holly, and there was mistletoe too. I had heard some of the female servants giggling with the men as this was fixed up in the most appropriate places. I had seen the dignified William seize Mary-Jane and give her a resounding kiss under the pearly berries. Mary-Jane responded good-humoredly; it was all part of the fun of Christmas.

Then I received the letter. I was in the garden when I saw the postman coming towards the house. I had been looking out for him because I did not believe my father would keep me long in suspense.

And I was right. There was his handwriting on the envelope. With wildly beating heart I hurried to my bedroom, and took the precaution of locking the doors before I opened the letter.

My dear Catherine, I read.

I was startled and shocked to receive your letter. I understand your feelings and, before you read any farther, I want to assure you that the Catherine Corder who is now in Worstwhistle is not your mother, although she is my wife.

I had meant, of course, to tell you the truth on your marriage, but I did not feel I could do so without consulting my brother, who is deeply concerned in this.

My wife and I were devoted to each other, and two years after our marriage we had a child—a daughter named Catherine. But this was not you. My wife adored our daughter and could scarcely bear the child out of her sight. She spent the greater part of her time in the nursery supervising everything concerned with her. We had a nurse of course. She came to us with good recommendations, and she was affectionate, fond of children and efficient—when she was not under the influence of gin.

One day when my wife and I had been visiting friends, there was mist on the moor and we lost our way. We were two hours later than we had expected to be, and when we returned the damage had been done. The nurse, taking advantage of our absence, had become intoxicated; and while she was in this state she had decided to bathe the baby. She put our child into a bath of scalding water. There was only one consolation—death must have been almost instantaneous.

My dear Catherine, you who are about to become a mother will understand the grief which overtook my wife. She blamed herself for leaving the child in the nurse's care. I shared her grief, but hers did not grow less as time passed. She continued to mourn the child and I began to be alarmed when she gave way to accusations against herself. She would pace through the house wildly sobbing, wildly laughing. I did not know then what this tragedy had done to her.

I used to tell her that we would have more children. But I could see that the need to pacify her was urgent. And then your Uncle Dick had this idea.

I know how fond you are of your Uncle Dick. He has always been so good to you. That is natural, Catherine, when the relationship between you is known. He is your father, Catherine.

It is difficult to explain this to you. I wish he were here so that he could do it himself. He was not a bachelor as he was thought to be. His wife—your mother—was French. He met her when he was in port for a spell at Marseilles. She came from Provence and they were married within a few weeks of their first meeting. They were ideally suited and deeply regretted your father's long absences. I believe he had almost decided to give up the sea when you were about to be born. Strangely enough tragedy hit us both in the same year. Your mother died when you were born; and that was not more than two months after we had lost our child.

Your father brought you to us because he wanted a settled home for you, and he and I believed at the time that having a child to care for would help to comfort my wife. You even had the same name. We had called our child Catherine after my wife, and your father—because you were coming to us—had decided that you should be Catherine too. . . .

I stopped for a few seconds. I was seeing it all so clearly; events were fitting together neatly to make the picture.

I was exultant because that which I had feared was not true after all.

Then projecting myself into the past I seemed to remember her, the wild-eyed woman who held me tightly, so tightly that I cried out in protest. I thought of the man whom I had known as my father, living through those weary years, never forgetting the happiness he had shared with the woman in Worstwhistle, dreaming that he was back in those days of anguish, calling for her to return . . . not as she was now, but as she had been.

I was filled with pity for him, for her; and I wished that I had been more tolerant of that gloomy house with its drawn blinds and the sunlight shut out.

I picked up the letter.

Dick thought that you would feel more secure with us than you could be with him. It was no life for a child, he said, with a father who was constantly away from home, particularly one who had no mother. He could not leave the sea now that your mother was dead; he told me that he missed her more when he was ashore than when he was at sea, which was natural enough.

So we let you believe that you were my daughter, although I often said to him that you would have been happier to know you were his. You know how devoted to your interests he always was. He was determined that you should receive part of your education in your mother's country and that was why you were sent to Dijon. But we wanted everyone to think of you as my child because I was sure in the beginning that your aunt would come to think of you as her own more readily that way.

If only it had worked! For a while we thought it would. But the shock had been too much for her to bear and it was necessary to send her away. When she had left we moved to Glen House. It seemed better to cut ourselves off from old associations, and there we were not far from her place of asylum. . . .

How I wished I had known! Perhaps then I should have been able to do something to comfort him.

But the past was over and I was happy on that December morning because I was delivered of my fears.

Now I would set to work to discover who in this house was my enemy; and I would go to it with such a will that I could not fail.

My baby would be born in the early spring and I would never for a minute be parted from my child. Uncle Dick—no, my father, but I should never be able to call him that; he would always be Uncle Dick to me—Uncle Dick would come home.

I would watch over my child, and Simon would be there, and our relationship would develop as such relationships should, gradually budding, flowering, bearing fruit.

Yes, I was happy on that day.

It seemed as though the Fates had determined to be kind to me, for another incident took place on the very next day which could not fail to raise my spirits further.

During the previous day I had hugged the news to myself. I had had my meals in my own room because, although I wanted to flourish the letter under the noses of Ruth, Luke, Sir Matthew and Aunt Sarah, I had decided that for a while I was going to keep this news to myself. Nothing could have strengthened me more. My fear had gone. I was certain that if I awakened to find the monk at the foot of my bed I should be quite calm. But I was determined to discover who the monk was, and I would do this because I was no longer hampered by terrible doubts.

Caution, I said to myself. For the time being no one must know. Simon? I asked myself. Should I tell Simon and Hagar?

The wind was bitingly cold and I decided that if it snowed I might do myself some harm, so I stayed indoors. I did think of sending a letter to them. But how could I be sure, absolutely sure, that it would not be intercepted?

The news could wait. In the meantime I would plan what I was going to do next.

It was after luncheon when Mary-Jane came to me in a state of excitement.

"It's our Etty, madam," she said. "Her time's come. . . . Two days before Christmas. We hadn't thought it would be till the New Year."

"You want to go and see her, don't you, Mary-Jane?"

"Oh well, madam . . . me dad's just sent word. Me mother's gone over there."

"Look, Mary-Jane, you go along and see how she's getting on. You may be able to help."

"Thank you, madam."

"There's a terrible wind blowing."

"Oh, I won't mind that, madam."

"Just a moment," I said. And I went to my wardrobe and brought out my heaviest cloak. It was the blue one which had been hung across the parapet. I put it about Mary-Jane and pulled the hood right over her head. "This will keep out the wind," I said. "It buttons right up, you see . . . and the cold can't penetrate."

"That's good of you, madam."

"I don't want you catching cold, Mary-Jane."

"Oh madam . . . thank you." Her gratitude was indeed sincere. She went on rather shyly: "I'm . . . so pleased, madam, because you've seemed so much better this last day or so."

I laughed as I finished buttoning the cloak.

"I am better. So much better," I told her. "Go on now . . . and don't worry about getting back. Stay for the night if they want you."

It was about dusk when she returned. She came straight up to my room and I saw at once that she was deeply disturbed.

"Etty . . ." I began.

She shook her head. "The baby was born before I got there, madam. A lovely girl. Our Etty's all right."

"What's wrong, then?"

"It was when I was coming home. I came round by the Abbey. And I saw it, madam. It gave me a turn. You see, it was nearly dark . . ."

"You saw . . . what?" I cried.

"*It,* madam. The monk. It looked at me and it beckoned."

"Oh, Mary-Jane, how wonderful! What did you do? What *did* you do?"

"I stood for a second or two staring. I didn't seem as if I could move. I was struck all of a heap. Then . . . I ran. It didn't follow me. I thought it was going to."

I put my arms about her and hugged her. "Oh Mary-Jane, I only needed this."

She looked at me in some astonishment, and I stood back to gaze at her.

She was about my height and the cloak was all-enveloping. She had been mistaken for me, because she was wearing my cloak, the well-known cloak which had been put over the parapet.

She was loyal; there was a bond between us; I knew that she looked upon me as the kindest mistress she had ever had. Ruth was too cold to win affection; Aunt Sarah too strange. Mary-Jane had enjoyed working for me because the relationship between us was warmer than that which usually existed between a maid and her mistress. I decided then that I would take Mary-Jane into my confidence to some extent.

"Mary-Jane," I said, "what did you think it was? A ghost?"

"Well, madam, I don't rightly believe in such things."

"Nor do I. I believe that what is inside that monk's robe is no ghost."

"But how did it get into your bedroom, madam?"

"That's what I'm going to find out."

"And did it pull the curtains and take the warming pan away?"

"I believe it did. Mary-Jane, for the time being will you please say nothing to anyone of what you have seen. Our monk thinks that it was I who was hurrying home through the Abbey ruins at dusk. He has no idea that it was you. I want to keep him in ignorance . . . for awhile. Will you do this?"

"I always want to do as you say, madam."

Christmas morning dawned bright and frosty. I lay in bed happily reading my letters and greetings. There was one from the man whom

I still thought of as my father. He sent me Christmas greetings and hoped that his previous letter had not upset me. A letter from my real father had arrived on the previous day and in this he told me that he hoped to be home in the spring.

That longed-for spring! Then I should have my child. What else? But I did not want to look beyond that. That was enough.

As I lay in bed my thoughts went back—indeed they were never far away—to the desire to discover the identity of the person who was trying to harm my child, and I went over the various monk incidents in detail, for those were the ones in which I was sure I should find the clue to the identity of my persecutor.

The monk had appeared in my room, sped along the corridor when I hurried after him, and then disappeared. The more I thought of this, the more excited I became. Was there some secret hiding place in the gallery? The monk had been seen not only in the house but in the Abbey ruins. What if there was some connecting passage between the Abbey and the house? What if two people played the role of monk? What if Luke and Damaris had both worn the robe —Damaris, on the first night I had seen it, thus enabling Luke to appear in his dressing gown on the second floor; Luke, when I was with Damaris in the ruins?

I remembered the old plan of the Abbey which I had seen when I first came to the Revels. It was somewhere in the library. If I could find some indication on that plan where a connecting passage could possibly be, I might have begun to solve the problem. I did possess two vital clues. There was the arcade in the ruins where the monk had been seen on two occasions—by Damaris and me and by Mary-Jane. I would study the plan very closely at that spot. And there was the minstrels' gallery in the house.

I was so excited, I could scarcely wait to dress.

Why should I?

I slipped on a robe and hurried down to the library. I had little difficulty in finding the plan. It was in a leather binding with a few details about the Abbey; the parchment roll on which these were written was yellow with age.

As I took the roll and tucked it under my arm I heard a movement behind me and, turning sharply, I saw Luke standing in the door-way.

He was looking at me with that alertness which I had noticed in people's faces recently and which had once filled me with alarm but now had no power to hurt me.

"Why, if it isn't Catherine! Happy Christmas, Catherine . . . and a fruitful New Year."

"Thank you, Luke."

He was standing in the doorway barring my way. I felt embarrassed, not only because of what I was carrying but because I had only a robe over my nightdress.

"What's wrong, Catherine?" he asked.

"But nothing."

"You look as though you're afraid I'm going to gobble you right up."

"Then my looks are deceptive."

"So you really feel quite benevolent towards me on this Christmas morning?"

"Shouldn't one feel so towards the whole world on this of all mornings?"

"You're taking the words out of old Cartwright's mouth. We shall have to go and hear him preaching his Christmas sermon." He yawned. "I always feel I'd like to time him by stop watch. I heard of someone's doing that the other day. Some local bigwig. It's a fact. He'd go to church, set his watch . . . ten minutes' sermon and no more . . . when the ten minutes were up he'd snap his fingers and that sermon had to stop—and it did, for the parson had his living to think of." His eyes narrowed and he went on: "I'm thinking of doing it myself one day, when . . ."

I looked at him sharply. I knew very well what he meant: when he was in command.

I felt uneasy even though the library was full of daylight.

"Well, what are you reading?" His firm fingers were on the leather case.

"Oh, it's just something I've seen in the library. I wanted to have another look."

He had taken the roll, in spite of my efforts to retain it, for I had to let it go; I could not indulge in a tug o'war here in the library for no apparent reason at all.

"The old Abbey again!" he murmured. "Do you know, Catherine, you've got an obsession for abbeys . . . monks . . . and such like."

"Haven't you?" I asked.

"I? Why should I? I was born here. We take all that for granted. It's the people who are new to the place who think it's all so marvelous."

He put the roll under my arm.

"Why, Catherine," he went on, "we're standing under the mistletoe."

Then he put his arms round me and kissed me quickly on the lips.

"Merry Christmas, Catherine, and a happy New Year!"

Then he stood aside and bowed ironically. I went past him with as much dignity as I could, and started up the stairs. He stood at the library door watching me.

I wished that he had not seen what I had been carrying. I wondered how much of my thoughts he had read. Luke bothered me. I didn't understand him; and I had the feeling that he was the one who resented my presence here more than any . . . he and Ruth together. If it were Ruth and Luke, I thought, it would be easier for them than anyone; and the fact that Damaris had lied as she did could mean that she had done so for Luke.

When I reached my room I got into bed again and studied the plan.

It was headed Kirkland Abbey with the date 1520, and as I looked at it, it was as though the place came alive under my eyes, as though walls were built up where they had decayed, as though roofs were miraculously replaced. There it was—a series of buildings which housed a community, sufficient unto itself, which had no need of outside resources, since it was completely self-supporting. It was so easy to picture it all. I realized that I had learned the topography of the Abbey fairly well. It was not that I had visited the place so much but my impressions had been so vivid. The central Norman tower was an excellent landmark. I traced it with my finger. The north and south transept, the sanctuary, the gallery, the chapter house, the monks' dorter. And the arcade, with its buttresses, where I had seen the monk, was that which led to the dining hall, to the bakehouses and malthouse. Then my eyes fell on the words: "Entrance to the cellars."

As there were cellars beneath the Abbey, there would almost certainly be tunnels connecting them with other underground chambers. Such a labyrinth was a feature of abbeys of the period. I knew this because I had read accounts of our well-known abbeys such as Fountains, Kirkstall and Rievaulx. I noticed with rising excitement that the cellars were on that side of the Abbey which was nearest to the Revels.

I was so intent that I did not hear a knock on my door, and Ruth had come in before I realized she was there.

She stood at the end of my bed in the spot where the monk had stood.

"Merry Christmas," she said.

"Thank you, and the same to you."

"You seem absorbed."

"Oh . . . yes." Her eyes were on the roll and I guessed she recognized it.

"How are you feeling?"

"Much, much better."

"That's good news. Are you going to get up? Our guests will be arriving very soon."

"Yes," I said, "I shall get up now."

She nodded; and her eyes went once more to the plan. I fancied she looked a little anxious.

By the time the family was ready to go to church, Simon and Hagar had still not arrived.

"They are usually here before this," said Ruth. "Perhaps something has happened to delay them. However, we shall go to church. We must be in our pew on Christmas morning."

Matthew and Sarah came down to the hall dressed for church. This was indeed a rare thing and I realized that I had very seldom seen either of them dressed for going out. The carriage would take them to the church and bring them back, and it was one of those traditions that their pew should be occupied on Christmas Day.

There was something which I was longing to do, and that was go to the Abbey and look for those cellars; and I wanted to do it when no one could follow me there. If only I could make some excuse for not going to church, I could be sure that for about two hours there would be no one to surprise me.

I should have liked to go to church with them and to take my place in the pew, for I was beginning to feel a fondness for the old traditions and a need of the peace which the Christmas service would give me. But I had a more imperative need—the protection of my child; and I decided to practice a little deception.

When they were stepping into the carriage I stood very still for a moment, putting my hands to my body.

Ruth said sharply: "What's wrong?"

"It's nothing, but I really don't think I shall go with you. The doctor said I should be very careful indeed not to overtax myself."

"I'll stay behind with you," Ruth told me. "You should go to bed at once."

"No," I insisted. "Mary-Jane will help me. She is very good and understands perfectly."

"But I feel I should stay behind," said Ruth.

"Then if you feel that, I must come with you, for I am certainly not going to allow you to miss the Christmas service."

She hesitated. Then she said: "Well, if you insist . . . What are you going to do?"

"Go to my room. . . . I do want to feel well for the rest of the day."

She nodded. Then she said to the groom: "Go and bring Mary-Jane to me . . . and quickly, or we shall be late for church."

Mary-Jane came hurrying out.

"Mrs. Rockwell doesn't feel well enough to accompany us to church," she said. "Take her to her room and look after her."

"Yes, madam," said Mary-Jane.

Ruth, satisfied, got into the carriage and in a few seconds they were driving away, while Mary-Jane and I went up to my room.

When we were there I said: "We're going out, Mary-Jane."

"But madam . . ."

I knew I had to take Mary-Jane into my confidence to a greater extent. When the monk had appeared before her he had brought her into this mystery, and the fact that she had come straight to me and told me what she had seen, and had kept her promise to tell no one else, proved her to be an ally.

"I feel quite well," I said. "I should have liked to join the church party, but there is something else I have to do. We are going to the Abbey."

I made her wrap herself in the blue cloak, and I myself wore another of dark brown.

Then we set out for the Abbey.

I was anxious that we should lose no time, for I did not know how long our explorations would last and it was necessary that we should be back in the house before the church party returned.

"I have been looking at a plan of the Abbey," I told Mary-Jane. "I have it with me here. When we have seen the monk in the ruins he has been near one spot and that is close by the entrance to the cellars. Let us go there immediately."

"If we see the monk, what shall we do?" she asked.

"I don't think we shall this morning."

"I'd like to give him a piece of my mind. Gave me a turn, he did, even though *I'm* not expecting."

"I should hope not," I said; and we laughed together, rather nervously I thought, because Mary-Jane realized as well as I did that we were not concerned with a mere practical joker and that there was a sinister implication behind all that had happened. "What we have to do," I told her, "is find out if there is some means of getting from the Abbey ruins into the house. We must remember that a long time ago certain valuables remained hidden for some years and probably members of the family too. You see, Mary-Jane, everything points to the fact that there is a secret entrance."

Mary-Jane nodded. "It wouldn't surprise me, madam. Why, this house is full of odd nooks and crannies. Happen it's there somewhere if we could find it."

When we reached the ruins I felt slightly breathless—with excitement and exertion—and Mary-Jane slowed us down a little. "You've got to remember how it is with you, madam."

I did remember. I was determined to take the utmost care of myself. I thought then, there was never a child in need of as much care as this one; the danger which threatens it makes it so.

We went along the arcade from buttress to buttress as I had seen the monk do; and we came to what I knew to be the bakehouse and malthouse. Now we had reached the remains of a spiral staircase which I was sure must lead to the cellars. Having studied my plan so well, I knew that we had been working back towards the house, and this was a part of the ruins which was very likely the nearest to the Revels.

Warily I descended the stairs ahead of Mary-Jane and at the bottom of them we came to two passages both leading in the direction of the house. These had evidently been tunnels, and I felt disappointed when I saw them because they, like the nave and transepts, had only the sky for their roofs.

However we each walked along one of these, that half-wall dividing us, and when we had gone about fifty yards they merged into one and we were in what could easily have been a dwelling place. There were several large chambers, the remains of brick walls showing us where they had been divided. I suspected that this was the place where the valuables had been hidden at the time of the Civil War.

In that case there must be some connecting link with the house. We had to find it.

We crossed these chambers and that seemed like the end of the ruins. I could see the Revels now, very close, and I knew that the part of it which contained the minstrels' gallery was immediately opposite us. I was excited yet exasperated, for it appeared that we could go no farther.

Mary-Jane looked at me helplessly as though to ask what next. But I glanced at my watch and saw that if we did not return to the house we should not be back by the time the church party returned.

"We'll have to go," I said, "but we'll come again."

Mary-Jane in her disappointment kicked at several large stones which were propped against a crumbling wall. There was a hollow sound but the significance of this did not occur to me until later, because my mind was on the conjectures which might arise if it were discovered that I had feigned indisposition in order to visit the ruins.

"Another time," I went on. "Perhaps tomorrow. But we must go now."

It was fortunate that we returned to the house when we did, for I had been in my room no more than a few minutes when Mary-Jane came to tell me that Dr. Smith was below and asking for me.

I went down to him at once.

"Catherine," he said, taking my hand in his and looking searchingly into my face, "how are you?"

"I am well, thank you," I answered.

"I was disturbed when I saw you were not at church with the others."

"Oh, I thought it would do me more good not to go today."

"I see. You merely felt you needed a rest. I was there with my daughter—and took the first opportunity of slipping out."

"But you would have known if I had been taken ill. Someone would have come for you."

"It's true I thought it must mean only some slight indisposition. Nevertheless I wanted to see you for myself."

"How attentive you are!"

"But of course I am."

"Yet I am not really your patient, you know. Jessie Dankwait is coming to the Revels in due course."

"I shall insist on being at hand."

"Come into the winter parlor," I said. "There is a good fire there."

We went into the parlor which looked charming, for holly decorated the walls, and the scarlet berries were particularly big and plentiful that year.

"Wasn't that your maid I saw when I arrived?" asked the doctor as we seated ourselves by the fire. "I believe she has a sister who has just had a baby."

"That is so. Mary-Jane was so very excited on the day the child was born. She went to see her, and whom else do you think she saw?"

He was smiling as though he were very pleased to see me in such good spirits.

"You'll be surprised," I went on, "when I tell you that Mary-Jane saw the monk."

"She saw . . . the monk!"

"Yes. I had made her wear one of my cloaks, and she came home by way of the ruins. The monk was there and went through the same performance, beckoning her."

I heard his deep intake of breath. "Indeed!"

"I have told no one, but you must know, of course, because you suspected that I might be losing my mind, and I do want you to know that I am as balanced as I ever was. And there is something else even more wonderful."

"I am eager to hear it."

"I have heard from my old home." I told him what my father had told me. He relaxed visibly. Then he leaned forward and grasped my hand warmly in his.

"Oh Catherine," he said fervently, "this is indeed wonderful news. Nothing could have pleased me better."

"You can imagine how I feel."

"I certainly can."

"And now that Mary-Jane has seen the monk . . . well, everything is changed since that dreadful day when you told me . . ."

"I have been so anxious ever since. I could not make up my mind whether I had been right to tell you or whether I should have held my peace."

"I think you were right to tell me. It is better to have these matters brought into the open. You see, I have now been able to clear up all doubts."

He was suddenly very grave. "But, Catherine, you were saying that Mary-Jane saw the apparition. What does this mean?"

"That someone is threatening the life of my child. I must discover the identity of that person. At least I know of one who is involved."

I stopped and he said quickly: "You know of one who is involved?"
Still I hesitated, for it was not easy to tell him that I suspected his daughter.

But he was insistent and I blurted out: "I'm sorry, but I have to tell you that Damaris is involved in this."

He stared at me in horror.

"She was with me when we returned to the house," I went on. "You will remember that you insisted she should accompany me. We saw the monk—and she pretended not to see him."

"Damaris!" he whispered, as though to himself.

"There was no doubt that she saw, and yet she denied doing so. She must know who this person is who is trying to unnerve me. When she denied that she saw him, I knew at once that she was an accomplice."

"It can't be true! Why . . . why?"

"I wish I knew. But at least I have made some discoveries in the last few days. The trouble is that it is so difficult to trust anyone."

"That is a reproach and I believe I deserve it. You must believe me, Catherine, when I tell you that I suffered torment when I discovered there was a Catherine Corder in Worstwhistle, and her connection with you. I told the Rockwells—Sir Matthew and Ruth—because I considered it my duty to do so. I only wanted you to go there for a few days for observation. I had made no suggestion that you should go . . . in the ordinary way. I was thinking of what was best for you."

"It was such a blow when I heard my name mentioned in connection with the place."

"I know. But . . . this is becoming a nightmare. Damaris . . . my own daughter . . . to have played a part in it. There must be some mistake. Have you told anyone of this?"

"No, not yet."

"I think I understand your reasoning. The less you say of these matters, the easier it will be to catch your enemy. But I am glad you have told me."

There was a knock on the door and William entered.

"Mrs. Rockwell-Redvers and Mr. Redvers have arrived, madam."

So the doctor and I went downstairs together to welcome Hagar and Simon to the Revels.

That afternoon Simon and I had an opportunity to talk together. The wind was still blowing from the north but the snow had held off. The older members of the family were in their rooms resting. I did not know where Ruth and Luke were. Ruth had said that as I felt too unwell for church that morning I ought to rest before tea. I said I would do this, but I was restless in my room and I came out after ten minutes and went along to the winter parlor, where Simon was sitting thoughtfully by the fire.

He rose delightedly when I entered the room.

"You've been looking radiant since we arrived," he told me. "The change is remarkable. I'm sure something good has happened. You've discovered something?"

I felt myself flush with pleasure. Simon's compliments would always be genuine. That was his way—so I knew that I did look radiant.

I told him about the letter and Mary-Jane's adventure; and how we had gone on a tour of exploration that morning.

I was thrilled to see the way he received the news of my parentage. His face creased into a smile and then he began to laugh.

"There couldn't be better news for you, could there, Catherine?" he said. "As for me . . ." He leaned towards me and looked into my face. "If you came from a line of raving lunatics I should still say you are the sanest woman I've ever met."

I laughed with him. I was very happy there in the winter parlor . . . the two of us sitting by the fire; and I thought: If I were not a widow, this might be considered a little improper.

"You told the doctor?" he said. "You were with him when we arrived."

"Yes, I told him. Like you, he was delighted."

Simon nodded.

"And about Mary-Jane?"

"Yes, I told him that too. But, Simon, I have decided not to tell anyone else . . . except your grandmother of course. I want no one else to know just yet."

"That's wise," he said. "We don't want to put our monk on his guard, do we? How I wish he would appear at this moment; I should like to come face to face with him. I wonder if there's a chance of his putting in an appearance tonight."

"Perhaps there are too many people in the house. However, let us hope he does."

"I'd catch him, I'll guarantee."

"I believe you would."

Simon looked down at his hands and I noticed afresh how strong they were. I guessed he was thinking of what he would do to the monk if he caught him.

"I have a map of the Abbey," I said. "I've been trying to find another way into the house."

"Any luck?"

"None at all. I took Mary-Jane down to the ruins while the others were at church this morning."

"I thought you were supposed to be resting."

"I didn't say so. I merely said I wished to stay at home. The rest was presumed."

"The deceit of a woman!" he mocked me; and I was so happy in this friendship between us. "Now tell me," he went on; "what have you discovered?"

"Nothing for certain, but I believe it possible that some connecting passage exists."

"Why are you so sure?"

"Because of the way in which the monk appeared both in the house and in the Abbey ruins. He would have to keep his costume somewhere. Then he disappeared so neatly on the first night I saw him. I believe he has an accomplice."

"Damaris," he said.

I nodded. "Who might play the monk on certain occasions."

"It's possible."

"I have a suspicion that the way into this hiding place is in the minstrels' gallery."

"Why?"

"Because that's the only place into which he could have disappeared on that first night."

"Good God!" he cried. "That's true."

"I feel certain that there is some way out of the house in the gallery there."

"Could there be . . . and the household know nothing about it?"

"Why not? The Roundheads lived here for some years and they didn't find it."

"What are we waiting for?" asked Simon.

He rose and together we made our way to the minstrels' gallery. The gallery had always seemed an uncanny place because it was so dark. There was no window up there, and the only light came from the hall. Heavy curtains hung on either side of the balcony. In the past the idea must have been for the musicians who played there to be heard and sometimes not seen.

On this afternoon it was dismal and eerie.

It was not large. It would hold an orchestra of ten men perhaps, but they would have been somewhat cramped. The back wall was hung with tapestry which clearly had not been moved for years. Simon went round tapping the walls, but he could only do so through the tapestry, which was not very helpful.

At one spot he found that the tapestry could be pulled aside, and my excitement was great when behind this we discovered a door. I held the tapestry back while he opened it, but it was only an empty cupboard which smelled damp and musty.

"He could have hidden in this cupboard until the hue and cry was over," said Simon, closing the door.

"But he came from the second floor."

"You mean Luke?"

"Well . . . I was thinking of Luke," I answered, letting the tapestry fall into place.

"H'm," murmured Simon.

There was a sudden movement behind us; we had had our backs to the door which led into the gallery, and we turned like two guilty people.

"Hello," said Luke. "I thought the ghosts of the minstrels had returned to haunt us when I heard voices in here."

I fervently wished then that I could have seen his face.

"This gallery's not used enough," said Simon. "It reeks of age."

"It could scarcely accommodate a modern orchestra. At the last ball we gave we had the players on the dais in the hall."

"So much more effective to have them in the gallery," I heard myself say.

"Yes, playing the harpsichord or the sackbut or psaltery . . . or whatever they did play in the dim and distant past." Luke's voice sounded mocking. I thought: This morning he found me in the library. This afternoon it is the minstrels' gallery.

We all came out onto the stairs and Luke returned with us to the winter parlor.

There we sat by the fire idly talking together, but I felt that there was a wariness among us of which each was conscious.

Dinner that evening was to be served in the hall, for even though we were still in mourning Christmas was Christmas, and for centuries Christmas dinner had been eaten there.

The long refectory table had been dressed with taste. At intervals candles burned in candlesticks of pewter, shining a light on the gleaming cutlery and glass on the table, and sprigs of holly were strewn on the huge lace tablecloth. It would have seemed impossible not to be festive at such a table. Candles burned in their sconces on the walls and I had never seen the hall so brightly lighted. As I came down the stairs I thought: This was how it must have looked a hundred years ago.

I was wearing a loose tea gown of mole-colored velvet with wide hanging sleeves which fell back from the elbows, and ruffles of lime-green lace at the neck. I had sent to Harrogate for it, and I felt I could not have had anything more suitable for my condition and this occasion.

It was the custom, Ruth had told me, to exchange gifts at the dinner table and I saw that brightly colored packages were piled up at various places on the table. I saw that our names had been written on pieces of parchment and set in the places we were to take. We were fairly widely spaced at such a large table, for there were only seven of us to dine, although after dinner several people would call on us, as Sir Matthew had said, to take wine. I knew that among these people would be Dr. Smith and Damaris, and Mr. and Mrs. Cartwright and some members of their family.

Ruth was already there talking to William who was busy at the wagon with two of the maids.

"Ah," she said as I came down, "are you feeling better?"

"I am feeling very well, thank you."

"I'm so glad. It would have been unfortunate if you had not felt well tonight. But if you should feel tired before everyone leaves, you must slip away. I'll make your excuses for you."

"Thank you, Ruth."

She pressed my hand; it was the first time I had felt any warmth from her. The Christmas feeling, I told myself.

Hagar was the next to arrive. I watched her sweep down the staircase, and although she had to walk with the aid of a stick she made a magnificent entrance. She was dressed in a velvet gown of heliotrope, a shade which was becoming to her white hair, and a style which had been fashionable twenty years before. I had never seen anyone with as much dignity as Hagar; I felt that everyone must be a little in awe of her, and I was glad that she and I had become such friends.

She was wearing an emerald necklace, earrings and a ring in which was a huge square-cut stone.

She put her cool cheek against mine and said: "Well, Catherine, it is pleasant to have you here with us. Is Simon down yet?" She shook her head in affectionate exasperation. "I am sure he is dressing under protest."

"Simon never did like what he calls dressing up for an occasion," said Ruth. "I remember he once said that no occasion was worth all the trouble."

"He has his opinions about such matters," agreed Hagar. "And here's Matthew. Matthew, how are you?"

Sir Matthew was coming down the stairs and I saw Aunt Sarah behind him.

Sarah was looking excited; she had put on a gown with rather extreme *décolletage*. It was of blue satin decorated with ribbons and lace and it had the effect of making her appear very young—but perhaps that was the excitement one sensed in her.

Her eyes went to the table. "Oh, the presents!" she cried. "Always the most fascinating part, don't you think, Hagar?"

"You never will grow up, Sarah," said Hagar.

But Sarah had turned to me: "You like the presents, don't you, Catherine. You and I have a lot in common, haven't we?" She turned to Hagar. "We decided that we had when . . . when . . ."

Simon came down the stairs then. It was the first time I had seen him dressed for the evening, and I thought that if he was not handsome he looked very distinguished.

"Ha!" cried Hagar. "So you have succumbed to custom then, grandson."

He took her hand and kissed it, and I watched the contented smile at her lips.

"There are times," he said, "when there is no alternative but to succumb."

We were standing together in that candlelit hall when suddenly we heard the sounds of a violin coming from the minstrels' gallery.

There was immediate silence and everyone was looking up. The gallery was in darkness but the violin went on playing, and the tune it played was one I knew well as "The Light of Other Days."

Hagar was the first to speak. "Who is it?" she demanded.

No one answered and the wail of the violin filled the hall.

Then Simon said: "I'll investigate."

But as he moved towards the staircase a figure appeared at the balcony. It was Luke, his long fair hair falling about his pale face.

"I thought it was appropriate to serenade you all on such an occasion," he called.

He began to sing in a very pleasant tenor voice and to accompany himself with the violin.

When I remember all
The friends, so linked together,
I've seen around me fall
Like leaves in wintry weather;
I feel like one,
Who treads alone
Some banquet hall deserted,
Whose lights are fled
Whose garlands dead,
And all but he departed!

When he had finished, he bowed, laid down his violin and shortly afterwards was running down the stairs to join us.

"Very effective!" murmured Simon dryly.

"You're like your grandfather," put in Hagar. "Fond of admiration."

"Now Hagar," protested Sir Matthew with a laugh, "you were always hard on me."

"I have often said," Ruth put in affectionately, "that Luke should sing more and practice more with the violin."

We sat down at the table and while William and the maids began to serve us, we looked at our presents. Sarah squealed with delight as a child might have done; the rest of us opened our gifts decorously and murmured conventional thanks to each other.

There was one present beside my place which held a certain significance. This bore the inscription "A Happy Christmas from Hagar and Simon Rockwell-Redvers," in Hagar's bold handwriting. I wondered why they had given me a joint present and my heart sank a little because I imagined that Simon had had nothing for me and that Hagar had probably added his name to hers to hide this fact. But when I opened the box I stared in amazement, for it contained a ring. I knew that it was a valuable one and that it was not new. It was some family heirloom, I guessed—a ruby set in a circle of diamonds. I lifted it out of the case and looked from Simon to Hagar. Simon was watching me intently; Hagar was giving me the special smile which usually she reserved for Simon only.

"But this is too . . . too . . ." I stammered.

I was aware that the attention of all at the table was on me and the ring.

"It has been in the family for generations," said Simon. "The Redvers family, that is."

"But it's so beautiful."

"Oh, we did have some possessions, you know," said Simon. "The Rockwells didn't have everything."

"I didn't mean . . ."

"We know what you mean, my dear," said Hagar. "Simon is teasing. Slip it on your finger. I want to see if it fits."

It was too small for the middle finger of my right hand on which I tried it first, but it fitted perfectly on the third finger.

"It looks becoming, does it not?" Hagar asked, glaring round at the rest of the company as though daring them to contradict her.

"It is such a beautiful ring," Ruth murmured.

"The Redvers seal of approbation, Catherine," added Luke.

"How can I thank you?" I said, looking at Hagar, for I could not look at Simon then. I knew that there was a significance about this and that everyone at the table was aware of it, although I was not . . . entirely. But I did know it was a very valuable present and that in giving it to me Simon and Hagar were proclaiming their affection for me; perhaps they meant to tell the person who was persecuting me that he had not only to deal with me but them also.

"By wearing it," Simon answered.

"It's a talisman," cried Luke. "Do you know, Catherine, while you wear that ring nothing can harm you. It's the old family tradition. There's a curse on it . . . no, sorry, a blessing. The genie of the ring will protect you from the powers of evil."

"Then it's doubly precious," I said lightly. "Since it not only preserves me from evil but is so decorative. I am so grateful to you for giving me such a lovely present."

"Puts the rest of our little gifts to shame, doesn't it," sighed Luke. "But always remember, Catherine, it is the spirit of the gift that counts."

"It is a good thing to remember," Hagar's voice boomed authoritatively.

Because I was afraid that I might betray the emotion this gift aroused in me, I decided to say no more before the others but to thank both Hagar and Simon privately; so I hastily turned to my soup which William had served, and by the time the turkey, with its chestnut stuffing, was being eaten I was conscious of a quiet peaceful pleasure.

The Christmas pudding was brought in—magnificent with its wreath of holly round the base and the sprig stuck jauntily into the top. William poured the brandy over it and Sir Matthew at the head of the table set it alight.

"Last Christmas," said Sarah, "it was very different. The house was full of guests. Gabriel was sitting where you are sitting now, Catherine."

"Don't let's talk of sad things," said Matthew. "Remember this is the first day of Christmas."

"Christmas is a time for remembering," protested Sarah. "It's the time when you recall the departed."

"Is it?" said Ruth.

"Of course it is," cried Sarah. "Do you remember, Hagar, that Christmas when we joined the party for the first time?"

"I remember," said Hagar.

Sarah had leaned her elbows on the table; she was staring at the flaming pudding.

"Last night," she said, in a hollow voice, "I lay in bed thinking of all the Christmases of my life. The first one I remembered was when I was three. I woke up in the night and heard the music and I was frightened. I cried, and Hagar scolded me."

"The first of many a scolding from Aunt Hagar, I'm certain," said Luke.

"Someone had to take charge of the family," Hagar answered serenely. "It might not have done you much harm, Luke, to have encountered a little more discipline."

Sarah was going on dreamily: "Right through them all I went until I reached last Christmas. Do you remember how we drank the toasts afterwards? There was a special one to Gabriel after his escape."

There was a silence of some seconds which I broke by asking: "What escape was that?"

"Gabriel's," said Sarah. "He might have been killed." She put her hand to her lips. "Just think if he had . . . he would never have met Catherine. You wouldn't be here with us today, Catherine, if he had died. You wouldn't be going to . . ."

"Gabriel never told me about this accident," I said.

"It was hardly worth mentioning," said Ruth sharply. "One of the walls in the ruins collapsed; he was close by and there was a slight injury to his foot. It was nothing much . . . a matter of bruises."

"But," cried Sarah, her blue eyes flashing almost angrily, I thought, because Ruth was trying to make light of something which she thought important, "just by chance he saw what was about to happen. He was able to escape in time. If he hadn't seen it . . . he would have been killed."

"Let's talk of something cheerful," said Luke. "It didn't happen. So that's that."

"If it had," murmured Sarah, "there wouldn't have been any need to . . ."

"William," said Ruth, "Mr. Redvers's glass is empty."

I was thinking of Gabriel, of the fear he had seemed to have of his home; I remembered the cloud which had appeared during our honeymoon when he had discovered the coastal ruins which must have reminded him of Kirkland Abbey. Was the falling of the wall really an accident? Did Gabriel know that someone in the Revels was trying to kill him? Was that the explanation of his fear? Was that why he had married me—so that there would be two of us to fight against the evil which threatened? Had that evil caught up with Gabriel? If so, it meant that someone wanted his inheritance. That person must have been horrified when, after murdering Gabriel—and I had come to the conclusion now that Gabriel had been murdered—he found that there was another who might step into Gabriel's shoes: my child.

It was all so clear; and there in the candlelit hall, while we were formally served with Christmas pudding, I realized as I never had before the certainty that the person who had murdered Gabriel was now determined that my child should never be born, in case it should be a boy.

There was one way of making absolutely sure that I did not produce a son—and that was by killing me.

There had been no attempt on my life. No, as Simon had said, that would have been too suspicious in view of Gabriel's sudden and violent death. I began to see a pattern forming. I was in danger—acute danger—but I was no longer terrified as I had been. It was not danger which could frighten me so much as the fear that my mind was tainted and that I was imagining all the uncanny occurrences. How strange it was that this actual danger was far more tolerable than something which I might have conjured up in a distorted imagination.

I found myself looking at Luke. With his long fair hair falling about his pale face I thought he looked like a cross between an angel and a satyr. He reminded me of the figures which were carved on the stonework. There was a satanic gleam in his eyes as they met mine. It was almost as though he read my thoughts and was amused by them.

We drank toasts in champagne. My turn came and they all stood, their glasses lifted. I believed that one of those people who were drinking my health might at that very moment be planning to kill me, but it must not be a violent death—it would have to appear a natural one.

The meal over, the table was quickly cleared by the servants, and we were ready to receive our guests. There were more people than I had expected. Dr. Smith and Damaris were the first arrivals and I wondered what was happening to the doctor's wife and what she thought of being left alone on Christmas Day.

I asked Damaris and she said that her mother was resting. It was long past her time for retiring to bed and the doctor would not allow Christmas or anything else to interfere with her routine.

The Cartwrights came with several members of their family including married sons and daughters and their families. That was the extent of the guests, and like Sarah I began to wonder about other Christmases—only I thought of Christmases in the future, not the past.

There was no dancing and the guests were conducted to a drawing room on the first floor; even the conversation was quiet. Everyone was remembering Gabriel on that day, because it was due to his death that the traditional entertaining had not taken place.

I found an opportunity of thanking Hagar for the ring. She smiled and said: "We wanted you to have it . . . both of us."

"It is very valuable. I must also thank Simon for it."

"Here he is."

Simon was standing beside us, and I turned to him. "I was thanking your grandmother for this magnificent ring."

He took my hand and studied the ring. "It looks better on her hand than it did in its case," he remarked to his grandmother.

She nodded and he continued to hold my hand for a few seconds, his head on one side, regarding the ring with a smile of satisfaction about his lips.

Ruth joined us.

"Catherine," she said, "if you want to slip away to your room, I should do so. You mustn't tire yourself. That's the very thing we wish to avoid."

I did feel then so moved by new emotions that I wanted to go to my room, for there was a great deal I had to think about. Moreover I knew that I should be resting.

"I think I will," I said.

"We shall be here tomorrow," Hagar reminded me. "We might go for a drive tomorrow morning—the three of us—unless you would like to come, Ruth?"

"I daresay people will be calling all the morning," said Ruth. "You know how it is on Boxing Day."

"Well, we shall see," said Hagar. "Good night, my dear. I am sure you are wise to retire. It must have been a long day for you."

I kissed her hand, and she drew me to her and kissed my cheek. Then I gave my hand to Simon. To my astonishment he bent down swiftly and kissed it. I could feel his kiss, hard and warm on my skin. I flushed faintly and hoped Ruth did not notice this.

"Slip away, Catherine," said Ruth. "I'll make your excuses to everybody. They'll understand."

So I slipped away, but when I was in my room I knew I could not sleep. I was too excited.

I lighted the candles and lay down on my bed. I turned the ring round and round on my finger. I believed that it was a ring which the Redvers treasured and that it had been given to me because they wished to imply that they wanted me to be one of them.

I had been lying thus when the monk had come to my room and the strangeness had begun. I kept going over everything that had happened, right from the first, and I was conscious of an urgency. Time was short. Already I was easily tired and forced to leave the party before it was over. This mystery should be solved . . . and quickly solved.

If I could find that way into the house . . . if I could find the monk's robe . . .

We had not really examined the minstrels' gallery thoroughly. We had found the cupboard, but we had not looked behind the tapestries on the walls. How long, I wondered, was it since that tapestry had been taken down?

I rose from my bed—I had not undressed—for I was filled with a great desire to have another look at the gallery.

I went along the corridor. I could hear the sound of voices and they were coming from the drawing room on this floor; quietly I descended the first flight of stairs to the minstrels' gallery. I opened the door and went in.

The only light came from the numerous wall candles in the hall.

So it was dark and gloomy in the gallery and I told myself that I had been foolish to hope to discover anything in this poor light.

I leaned over the balcony looking down on the hall, of which I had a good view apart from that section immediately below.

And as I stood there the door opened and a shape loomed on the threshold. For a moment I thought it was the monk and, in spite of my belief that I wanted to see him, a shudder of fear ran through me.

But this was no monk. It was a man in ordinary evening dress and when he whispered: "Why . . . Catherine!" I recognized the voice of Dr. Smith.

He went on speaking very quietly. "What are you doing here?"

"I couldn't sleep."

He came into the gallery and we stood side by side near the balcony.

He put his fingers to his lips. "There is someone down there," he whispered.

I was surprised that he should consider that a matter for secrecy as there were so many guests in the house, and was about to say so when he seized my arm and drew me closer to the balcony.

Then I heard the voices.

"Damaris! We're alone at last." The sound of that voice gave me a pain which was almost physical. It was not only the words but the tone in which they were spoken, which was so significant. For it was both tender and passionate, and only rarely had I heard that timbre in the voice. It was Simon who was speaking.

Then Damaris: "I am afraid. My father would not be pleased."

"In these matters, Damaris, we do not please our fathers but ourselves. . . ."

"But tonight he is here. Perhaps he is watching us now."

Simon laughed and at that moment they moved towards the center of the hall. He had his arm about her.

I turned away, not wanting to look. I was afraid they might be aware of us. My humiliation would have been complete if Simon knew that I had looked on at his flirtation with Damaris.

As I walked towards the door of the gallery, the doctor was still beside me; and together we went up the stairs to the first floor. He seemed preoccupied, scarcely aware of me, and I had no doubt that he was very worried about his daughter.

"I shall forbid her to see that . . . philanderer!" he said.

I did not answer; I had clasped my hands together and touched the ring which but a short time ago had seemed to have such significance.

"Perhaps it would be useless to forbid her," I suggested.

"She would have to obey me," he retorted; and I saw the veins, prominent at his temples. I had never known him so agitated before and that seemed to mark the depth of his affection for her. I warmed to him because such parental concern was exactly what I had so sadly missed during the absences of my real father.

"He is overbearing," I said, and my own voice was very angry. "I believe he would always find a way of getting what he wanted."

"I am sorry," said the doctor. "I am forgetting you. You should be resting. I thought you had retired to do that. What made you come to the gallery?"

"I couldn't sleep. I was too excited, I suppose."

"At least," he said, "this is a warning to us both."

"What made *you* come to the gallery?" I asked suddenly.

"I knew they were down there together."

"I see. And you would frown on a match between them?"

"A match! He would not offer her marriage. The old lady has other plans for him. He'll marry *her* choice and it won't be my daughter. Besides . . . she is for Luke."

"Is she? She did not seem to think so tonight."

"Luke is devoted to her. If only they were older they would be married by now. It would be a tragedy if she were ruined by this . . ."

"You do not think very highly of his honor."

"His honor! You have not been here long enough to know his reputation in the neighborhood. But I am keeping you and it grows late. I shall be taking Damaris home immediately. Good night, Catherine."

He took my hand. It was the one on which was the Redvers ring.

I went to my room. I was so upset that I forgot to lock my doors that night. But there were no midnight visitors, and I was alone with my emotions.

That night I learned the true nature of these emotions, and I blamed myself for allowing them to become so strong, disguised as they were by the semblance of dislike. I had been angry with him because I thought he did not esteem me enough. I had been hurt because I wanted that esteem.

That night I learned that hatred grows out of the strength of one's own emotions; and that when a woman comes close to hating a man she should be watchful, for it means that her feelings are deeply engaged.

He is a cheat, I told myself, as I tried to shut out the echo of his voice talking to Damaris. He is a philanderer who amuses himself with any female who is handy. I happened to be at hand. What a fool I am. And how we hate those who make us aware of our own folly. Hate and love. There are times when the two can run side by side.

7

I did not sleep well that night and it must have been nearly morning when I was awakened by Mary-Jane. It was dark and she was carrying a lighted candle.

"Mary-Jane!" I said. "What is the time?"

"It's six o'clock, madam."

"But why . . . ?"

"I wanted to tell you yesterday, but with all the Christmas preparations I didn't get a chance. I only found it yesterday. It was while we were getting the hall ready."

I sat up in bed and cried: "Mary-Jane, you have found the way out of the house?"

"I think so, madam. It is in the gallery . . . in the cupboard. There are two floorboards there with a gap between them, enough to get your fingers in. I thought there was something not usual about them so I put fingers down and gripped one of the boards. It lifted up easy. Then I saw the great black space below, so I got a candle and looked down. There are some stairs leading down. That's all, madam. William was calling me then, so I let the board fall back and didn't say anything . . . thinking I'd come straight to you to tell you. But then I had to go to the kitchens and help and I couldn't get another chance, but I've been thinking about it all night."

"We must look into this at once," I said.

"I thought you'd want to."

"There's no one up yet?"

"Only the servants, madam, and they're not in this wing. They'll be coming to do the hall in half an hour's time though."

"Well, we must move quickly," I said; "we're going to have a look at those stairs now."

"Shouldn't you dress yourself first, madam?"

"No, I can't wait," I said. "I'll put on my cloak over my night-gown."

So together Mary-Jane and I left my bedroom and quietly made our way to the minstrels' gallery. I was afraid all the time that Luke would suddenly appear, but Mary-Jane was with me, and it would be difficult for him to do me any harm.

I was excited, for this was the proof I needed. The only person in this house whom I could trust was Mary-Jane, and we were together in this.

The house was very quiet, and for that reason even my slippered tread seemed noisy. But we reached the gallery and no one appeared.

Mary-Jane very gently shut the door, and I held the candle while she opened the cupboard and showed me the floorboards. She knelt and lifted one of these up and, as she had explained, it came up easily; evidently it had been cunningly made to act as a trap door.

I leaned over the aperture, holding the candle. I could see the flight of steps which she had told me about. I longed to go down there, but it would be necessary to take a short leap onto the top step and I dared not trust myself to do that.

But Mary-Jane was lithe and slim. I turned to her.

"You get through," I said. "And I'll hand you the candle. Just look round and tell me what you see down there."

She had turned a little pale, but she was the sort who would despise what she would call the gormless; and after that second's hesitation she lowered herself through the aperture and when she was standing on the steps I handed her the candle.

She said: "It seems like a big room down there. It's very cold."

"Just have a quick look round," I ordered. "Then we'll try to find the way in from the Abbey side."

There was silence for a while. I peered down. I could see her gingerly descending the stairs, and sharply I warned her to be careful.

"Oh, ay," she assured me. "I'm safe on me feet, madam."

I heard her voice again when she had descended the steps. "I can see a light in the distance. That must be the way out. I'll just have a quick look."

My heart was beating madly. I wanted to be down there with her, but I dared not risk slipping on those stone steps. I glanced over my shoulder. I could not rid myself of the feeling that someone was watching us. But there was no one there; there was no sound at all in that silent house.

I heard a sudden call from Mary-Jane. "I've found something, madam."

"I can't see you now," I called. "Where are you?"

Her voice sounded faint. "The candle nearly went out, madam."

"Come back now, Mary-Jane. Bring what you've found if you can carry it."

"But, madam . . ."

"Come back," I said authoritatively.

Then I saw the candle again and breathed more freely.

Mary-Jane appeared on the steps; she was holding the candle in one hand and something under her arm. She handed a bundle up to me and I knew at once that it was the monk's robe. I took the candle from her and in a second or so Mary-Jane had scrambled through the aperture and was safe in the gallery.

"I was alarmed when you disappeared from sight," I said.

"I wasn't all that brave meself, madam, down there. Gave me the shivers."

"Why, you are cold, Mary-Jane."

"It's cold down there, madam. I found the robe though."

"Let's go along to my room. We don't want anyone to find us here."

We let down the floorboard of the cupboard and satisfied ourselves that it showed no signs of having been disturbed; and taking the robe with us we went back to my room.

When we were there Mary-Jane put the robe about her and I shuddered.

"Take it off," I said. "We must guard this. If anyone dares say that I've seen visions because my mind is disturbed, we can prove that it was not visions I saw."

"Shouldn't we tell someone? Shouldn't we show them the robe?"

The day before I should have said, "Yes. We will tell Mr. Redvers." But I could no longer say that. I no longer trusted Simon, and if I could not trust Simon I trusted nobody.

"We will say nothing of this for the moment, Mary-Jane," I said. "We have the evidence here. I will put it in my wardrobe and the door shall be locked so that no one can steal it."

"And then, madam?"

I looked at the clock over the fireplace and saw that it was seven o'clock.

"You will be missed if you stay here much longer. I will go back to bed. You will bring my breakfast in the ordinary way. I shall want very little to eat. Bring my hot water earlier. I want to think what I ought to do next."

"Yes, madam," she said.

And she left me.

Ruth came to my room to see how I was.

"You look exhausted," she said. "Yesterday was too much for you."

"I do feel tired," I admitted.

"I should stay in your room all day. I'll keep them away. Then perhaps you'll feel well enough to join us this evening. There will only be the family; and Simon and Hagar will be leaving early tomorrow morning. The carriage always comes for them sharp at nine-thirty on the day after Boxing Day."

"Yes. I should like to rest awhile," I said.

All that day I lay on my bed and thought about the events which had led up to my discovery of the robe. I went over everything, beginning with my meeting with Gabriel and Friday. Gabriel knew there had been an attempt on his life in the ruins, and he was afraid. He had hoped that I would be able to help him to fight whatever threatened him. Then there was the night before he died, when Friday had heard someone in the corridor. It would have been that night when Gabriel met his death but for Friday. Friday had obviously been killed so that he could not again give the warning. Sarah knew this and she conveyed it on her tapestry. How much more did she know? So Gabriel had died and I had been of little interest to the murderer until it was disclosed that I was to have a child. The idea to make me seem mad must have come when Dr. Smith thought it his duty to tell the family that there was a Catherine Corder in Worstwhistle.

What a diabolical mind was behind that plot! I did not believe the idea was to send me to Worstwhistle, but to build up a case of insanity against me and then possibly stage my suicide before the child was born.

Why was I thinking of the plot in the past tense? It still existed. And when my would-be murderer discovered that his robe was missing, what would he do? Perhaps he would think there was need for prompt action.

I was undecided. Perhaps I should go back to Glen House. But how could I do this in secret? If I announced my intention I could expect immediate action. I was certain that I should not be allowed to leave this house.

I thought of them . . . Luke and Simon. I tried not to think of Simon. It was Luke, I told myself. It must be Luke. And Damaris was helping him.

Damaris! But had I not learned something last night of the relationship between Damaris and *Simon!*

My thoughts went round and round like a mouse in a cage. I had the robe; I should have been triumphant if I could have shared my knowledge with Simon.

But what could I ever share with Simon now?

I was wishing again, as I had wished when I let the water from the Knaresborough well trickle on my hands: "Not Simon. Oh please, not Simon!"

I joined the family at dinner. Simon was attentive and appeared anxious on my behalf and, although I had told myself that I would give no sign of my changed feelings towards him, I could not help a coolness creeping into my manner.

He was next to me at dinner, which we took in the hall as we had on the previous night.

"I am disappointed," he told me, "that I've had no opportunity of being with you today. I had planned that we should take a drive together . . . you, my grandmother and myself."

"Would not the weather have been too cold for her?"

"Perhaps, but she would not admit it. She too was disappointed."

"You should have made up a party with the others."

"You know that would not have been the same thing at all."

"Perhaps Damaris would have accompanied you."

He laughed, and lowered his voice. "I have something to tell you about that."

I looked at him interrogatively.

"Because," he added, "you obviously noticed. It is often necessary to go by devious ways to reach a certain goal."

"You are talking in riddles."

"Which is not inappropriate. We have a riddle to solve."

I turned away because I fancied Luke was trying to listen to our conversation; but fortunately Aunt Sarah was talking loudly about Christmases of the past, and although she was repeating what she had said yesterday she seemed determined that no one should miss a word.

After dinner we retired to the first-floor drawing room, and there were no other visitors that night. I talked to Sir Matthew and would not leave his side, although I could see that Simon was growing exasperated with me.

I left the company early and had not been in my room more than five minutes when there was a knock on the door.

"Come in," I called, and Sarah entered.

She smiled at me conspiratorially and whispered as though to excuse the intrusion: "Well, you were interested. That's why . . ."

"What do you mean?" I asked.

"I've started to fill it in."

My thoughts immediately went to the half-finished piece of tapestry which she had shown me when I was last in her room. She was watching me and her face seemed suddenly full of knowledge.

"Can I see it?"

"Of course. That's why I came. Will you come back with me?"

I rose eagerly and when we were in the corridor she put her fingers to her lips. "Don't want anyone to hear us," she said. "They're still in the first-floor drawing room. It's early yet . . . for a Boxing night. All very well for you to retire early. That's on account of your condition. But the others . . ."

We mounted the stairs and went through to her wing. It was very silent in this part of the house and I shivered—whether with cold or apprehension, I was not sure.

She led the way to her tapestry room, and she was now as excited as a child with a new toy which she wants to show off. She lighted several candles from the one she was carrying; then setting that one down she ran to the cupboard. She took out the canvas and held it in front of her as she had on another occasion. I could not see very clearly although it was obvious that the blank side had now been filled in with something. I picked up a candle and held it close to the canvas. Then I saw the outline of a drawing.

I looked closer. On one side were the dead bodies of Gabriel and Friday, and on the other a faint pencil drawing. This was of another building, and the effect was that of looking through barred windows into a room which was like a prison cell. In that cell was the faint outline of a woman who held something in her arms. I felt a thrill of horror as I realized this was meant to be a baby.

I looked into Sarah's face. Illumined as it was by the light of the candles all shadows and lines seemed to be eliminated; she was rejuvenated—more than that; she seemed not quite human. I longed to know what secrets, what motives lay behind those calm eyes.

"I suppose that figure is myself," I said.

She nodded. "You saw the baby, did you? You see, the baby is born."

"But we seem to be in a sort of prison."

"I think it would feel like being in prison."

"Aunt Sarah, what would feel like being in prison?"

"There," she said. "That place."

I understood. "That's all cleared up," I explained. "It was all a mistake. The doctor made a mistake. There is no need to think of that any more."

"But it's here," she insisted. "It's here in the picture."

"That's because you don't know all that's happened."

She shook her head almost petulantly, and my apprehension increased. I knew she moved quietly about the house, listening from secret places; and then quietly in this room she recorded the family's history. The history of the Rockwells was the most important thing in her life. That was why she spent hours over her exquisite tapestry. Here in this room she was supreme, a sort of goddess looking on at the follies of her creatures; elsewhere she was of no account—merely poor Sarah who was a little simple.

I was foolish to allow myself to be upset by the vague ideas which circulated in her wandering mind.

"In a prison," she murmured, "there has to be a jailer. I can see him. He's all in black, but he has his back to me and his hood makes it impossible to recognize him."

"The monk!" I spoke lightly, for I could think of that creature without fear now.

She came up to me and looked into my face. "The monk is very near you, Catherine," she said. "The monk is waiting for you, waiting to catch you. You should not think the monk is not near . . . and coming nearer."

"You know who it is!" I accused her.

"It's a lovely night," she answered. "The stars are wonderful. There is frost in the air, and, Catherine, the view is beautiful from the balcony."

I drew away from her.

"You're right," I said. "It is cold here. I think I should go back to my room."

"Wait awhile, Catherine."

"I think I should go."

I went to the door but she had caught my robe and was clinging to it. I had begun to shiver again, but this time not with cold.

"The candle," she said. "You'll need one. Take mine."

Still holding my robe she drew me into the room. She picked up one of the lighted candles and thrust it into my hand. I grasped it and, disengaging myself, hurried along the corridor half expecting her to pursue me.

I was breathless when I reached the sanctuary of my room and my apprehension remained with me. I could not dismiss Sarah's ramblings from my mind because I was certain that there was some meaning hidden within them.

How uncertain I was on that night! I longed to confide in someone. When I was with Simon I could not help trusting him and I doubted my ability to resist him; I believed that if I told him what I had discovered and he gave me a plausible explanation, I should be only too glad to meet him halfway. Readily would I believe any story he could tell me if only it would exonerate him from the murder of Gabriel and from the attempted murder of me and my child.

I believed that night that I dared not listen to Simon. I had to remain aloof. For the first time I could not trust my own good sense. I was at the mercy of my feelings for this man. It was humiliating, and yet in a way it was exhilarating, because love must always be like that. And I learned that night, if I had not known it before, that I was in love with Simon.

The next day Simon and Hagar left Kirkland Revels. I said goodby warmly to Hagar, coolly to Simon. He was aware of my changed attitude and it seemed to amuse him. I thought: Can he really be as cynical as that?

When they had left I went to my room. I wanted to be quiet and formulate some plan. I knew that I must act quickly, because it might be that already the robe had been missed.

The only person in whom I could confide was Mary-Jane; and what could she do to help me? Still, at such a time it was a comfort to confide in anybody. I thought of going to Sir Matthew, showing him what I had discovered, and asking him to make up a party to explore the passage between the house and the Abbey. Ruth? Could I tell Ruth? I was not sure of Ruth, and it would not have surprised me to learn that she—although not the prime mover in the plot against me—was not unaware of what was going on. Sarah? What sense could one hope to get from Sarah? And Luke . . . I still clung to my belief that Luke was my real enemy.

I could not make up my mind.

I was in my room trying to come to some decision when I noticed an envelope lying on the floor by the door. I hurried to it and picked it up. There was nothing written on it. I opened the door, hoping to find someone hurrying away, but there was no one there; the letter might have been quietly pushed under my door some minutes before I had noticed it.

I shut my door and slit the envelope. There was a single sheet of paper inside; and on it was written in a shaky handwriting:

Go back to your old home without delay. You are in imminent danger.

I stared at it. I did not know the handwriting and I wondered whether the shakiness was a method of disguising it, for the letter was unsigned and there was no address on the paper.

Who had pushed that letter under my door? And what did it mean? Was it yet another trick?

But there was something tangible about a piece of paper. No one could say I had imagined this.

I went to my window and looked out. Then my heart began to hammer wildly because I saw someone hurrying away from the house and I recognized her—Damaris!

I was certain that it was she who had come quietly into the house and left that note under my door. Why had she done this?

I suspected Damaris of working against me. How could I do otherwise when she had been with me and had seen the monk, and then had declared she had not?

I looked back at the paper. I would not let myself believe that she was working with Simon in this. And yet the position was desperate. I must look at the facts; I must face the truth. I had seen them together on Christmas night, and what had been implied by their words shocked me deeply. But I couldn't believe this of Simon. My common sense might try to insist that I did, but my ridiculous feminine emotions refused to be convinced.

Someone had sent Damaris to put that note under my door. Was it Luke? He could have done it himself. Dr. Smith? I looked again at the handwriting and because I had seen his I decided that those words could not in any circumstances have been written by him.

Then I remembered that occasion when I had called at his house. I thought of the sick woman, the wife who was such a disappointment to him that he threw himself so wholeheartedly into his work. The shaky handwriting might be that of a sick woman, a woman who was in some stress.

I put the paper into my pocket, wrapped myself in my heavy cloak and left my room. I paused on the stairs by the minstrels' gallery; then I opened the door and looked inside, because I thought that someone might be hiding there.

There was no one.

I went down through the hall and out of the house.

There was a bitterly cold wind blowing but I was impervious to the weather. I hurried away from the house, looking back only once to see if I was being followed. I could see no one, but I felt that from every window eyes might be watching me.

I went on until I came to the doctor's house. It seemed more gloomy than it had on that other occasion. The Venetian blinds were all drawn and the wind whistled through the firs.   •

I rang the bell and the maid let me in.

"The doctor is not at home, Mrs. Rockwell," she said.

"I have come to see Mrs. Smith."

She looked surprised. "I will tell her you are here."

"Please tell her that I am very eager to see her on a matter of importance."

The maid went away almost reluctantly, while I wondered what I should do if Mrs. Smith refused to see me. I might ask for Damaris. I would insist on knowing whether it was she who had brought the note, why she had denied seeing the monk, what part she had played and was playing in this plot against me. I was determined to know the truth without delay.

In a few moments the maid returned.

"Mrs. Smith will see you," she said; and I followed her up the stairs to the room which I had visited once before.

I was astonished to see Damaris with her mother. She was standing by Mrs. Smith's chair, and it seemed as though she were clinging to her mother for protection. Mrs. Smith looked even more emaciated than when I had last seen her; her eyes were enormous and they seemed to burn with some deep purpose.

She said in a quiet voice: "Good morning, Mrs. Rockwell. It was good of you to call."

I went forward and took the hand she extended; and then the door shut on the maid and we three were alone.

"Why did you come here?" she asked quickly. "This is the last place you should come to."

I took the sheet of paper from my pocket and held it out to her.

"Have you shown this to anyone else?" she asked.

"To no one."

"Why . . . do you come here?"

"Because I believe you wrote that and sent it to me. I saw Damaris leaving the house."

There was silence.

Then I cried: "You did write it, didn't you?"

Damaris put her arm about her mother. "You must not be disturbed," she said. She looked at me almost defiantly. "You are making her ill."

I answered: "I think she can help me to find out who has been trying to make *me* ill."

"You must not fret, my darling," said Mrs. Smith to Damaris. "She has come here, and it was very unwise of her. But she is here now and I must do what I can."

"You already have . . ."

"If she would only take my advice!"

"What is your advice?" I demanded.

"Go away from here. Do not delay a moment. Return at once to your father's house today. If you do not . . . it will be too late."

"How do you know?"

"There is a great deal I know," she said wearily.

"Will you tell me this: Did you write that note?"

She nodded. "Because I know that you must get away if you wish to give birth to a child that will live."

"How can I know that I can trust you?"

"What could I possibly gain by warning you?"

"Don't you see that I'm in the dark?"

"Yes, I do. You are headstrong. You will not take my advice and go. You want to solve mysteries. You are too bold, Mrs. Rockwell."

"Tell me what you know," I said. "You owe that to me."

"Mother," gasped Damaris, and the mask dropped from her lovely face. I knew that she was terrified.

I took the thin, clammy hand. "You must tell me, Mrs. Smith," I said. "You know you must tell me."

"Unless I tell you everything you will never believe me. You will never understand."

"Then tell me everything."

"It is a long story. . . . It goes back many years."

"I am in no hurry."

"You are wrong. You should be in a great hurry."

"I shall not leave until you tell me."

"And if I can convince you that your child is in danger, that you are in danger, will you go to your father's house today?"

"If I think that necessary, I will."

"Mother," said Damaris, "you must not. . . You dare not."

"You are afraid still, Damaris?"

"So are you, Mother. We both are. . . as we always have been."

"Yes," said Mrs. Smith, "I am afraid. But I am thinking of the child . . . and of her. We cannot stand by and see that happen to her . . . can we, Damaris? We must not think of ourselves . . . We must think only of her now."

I was beside myself with impatience. "You must tell me," I said. "Come now."

Still she hesitated, then bracing herself as for a mighty effort she began:

"I married against my family's wishes. You may think my story has nothing to do with this. I am merely trying to tell you how I happen to know . . ."

"Yes, yes," I cried.

She plucked at the blanket which was wrapped about her knees.

"I had a small fortune of my own. As you know, when a woman marries, her fortune becomes her husband's. He needed the fortune . . . so he married me. I had a great opinion of him. He was the dedicated doctor and I wanted to work with him. I wanted to help him . . . his patients loved him so. He was so self-sacrificing. But you see there were two doctors. There was the doctor who went among his friends and patients . . . such a charming man, so solicitous of others. And there was the doctor at home. They were two different men. He liked to play his part but we couldn't expect him to act all the time, could we, Damaris?"

Damaris murmured: "You must not . . . oh, you must not. When he hears . . ."

"You see," went on Mrs. Smith, "he believed himself to be not quite mortal like the rest of us. He had done brilliantly at his work and from such humble beginnings. I admired that . . . at the start. But he soon tired of playing the part for me. That happened before Damaris was born. He was very angry that she was not a boy. He wanted a son, to be exactly like himself—which in his eyes meant perfect. Damaris quickly learned to understand him. Do you remember, Damaris, how you would be playing, somewhere happily forgetful . . . because children do forget and when they are happy for an hour they believe thay have always been so. Then we heard his step in the hall; and you would come to me and cower beside me, remembering."

"He ill-treated you?" I asked.

"Not physically. That is not his way. But he hated me. Why should he do otherwise? He had wanted my money and when that was his, and after many attempts I had failed to give him a son, I was of little use to him. Those dreary years of sadness and terror . . . I cannot think how I have lived through them."

"So it is Dr. Smith who has tried to destroy me. Why . . . why?"

"I will tell you that too. I met his foster mother. She lives not far from here in a little cottage on the moors. He was brought to her when he was a baby. He was born to a gypsy girl who had forsaken her people for a while to work in the kitchens at the Revels. She was married to a gypsy named Smith; but when her child was born she did not want him and she deserted him. Sir Matthew took an interest in the girl. I do not know whether he was ever her lover, but that was what Deverel always believed. He believed that he was the son of Sir Matthew. Do you begin to understand now?"

"I begin to see some light," I said.

"And when Sir Matthew had him educated and trained as a doctor he was certain of this. He married me, and our daughter was called Damaris because the Rockwells had always chosen names from the Bible for their children. But it was a son he wanted. He wanted to see a son of his in the Revels. And so . . ."

She turned to Damaris, who was crying quietly.

"I must tell her this," she soothed. "It is the only way. I should have told her before. But you know how we have always feared his anger."

"Please go on," I pleaded.

"After several miscarriages I was warned that I ought to have no more children . . . but he wanted a son. I tried again. There was no son. The child was born dead and I . . . well, I have been an invalid ever since. Imagine how he hates me! I cannot even give him a son. I think that he would have rid himself of me if it had not been for Damaris." She put out a hand and stroked her daughter's hair. "You see, he does not know how far she would betray him if he attempted to destroy me." She turned to Damaris. "You see, my darling, in some ways we have him in our power." Then to me: "It was four years ago that I did my best to bear him a son. Before that I was not strong but I was able to take my part in the life of the neighborhood. I played a part in the pageant . . . only one of the monks, it was true. I still had my robe though . . . until a few months ago."

I caught my breath and said: "So it is yours, that robe?"

"Yes, it was mine. I had kept it. I am a little sentimental about such things. It was a reminder to me of the days when I was not an invalid."

"Damaris helped him," I said accusingly. "She swore that she had seen nothing."

"I had to," whispered Damaris, with a sob in her voice. "He told me what I had to do. We always obeyed him. We dared do nothing else. I was to take you to the ruins . . . not too quickly . . . to give him time to get there before us. And then, when he appeared, I was to pretend I saw nothing. There is a way from the ruins into the house. He discovered it when he was a boy. So he appeared to you in the house as well."

Now that I had the vital facts, events began to fall into place. I saw how he had everything fitted so neatly. I was filled with a wild exultation, and the reason was that the wish I had made at the Knaresborough well had come true. It was not Simon.

"Why . . . why?" I demanded.

"He was determined to live in the Revels one day. As the poor boy, he had watched the guests come and go. He had seen the picnics in summer, the skating parties in the winter; he had looked through the windows at the balls. He was obsessed by the Revels because he believed that he was Sir Matthew's son and therefore belonged there. He was determined to get there one day, and he saw that the way to do so was through Damaris. She was to marry Luke."

"But how could he be sure of that?"

"My daughter has a rare beauty. I do not think Luke is unaware of it. They were thrown together always. It may have been that he would have found some way of insisting on that marriage. He discovered the secrets in people's lives and used them when he found it expedient to do so. He would have discovered some things perhaps which Sir Matthew would not want made known . . . or perhaps Mrs. Grantley. The marriage would have taken place. He was not unduly concerned about Gabriel. Gabriel was delicate; he himself diagnosed that weak heart—the same complaint of which his mother had died.

Perhaps Gabriel's heart was sound; perhaps he was preparing the way to Gabriel's end. . . . I do not know everything. But when Gabriel married you he became a menace. He feared what actually did happen—that you might have a child. He was determined that Gabriel must die, and you at that time were of little interest to him. So Gabriel . . . died."

"It is not difficult to imagine how," I said grimly. And I pictured it. Did he lure Gabriel onto the balcony, or did Gabriel go there as he had made a habit of doing? There was no Friday on that night to warn him of a sinister presence. And then as he stood there, a stealthy movement from behind, a hand over his mouth and his body lifted and sent hurtling over the balcony.

Suicide? It seemed a reasonable verdict.

She said: "We are wasting time. Believe me, there is nothing more I can do for you. I have helped you all I can. Go at once to your old home. There you will be safe."

"You know that he plans something?"

"We know that. He is angry. He does not take us into his confidence, but there are certain things we cannot help knowing. Something has happened to anger him."

I knew what that was. He had discovered that the robe had been removed. He was planning some immediate action against me. I thought of his coming into the minstrels' gallery on Christmas night, and I wondered what would have happened to me then if Simon and Damaris had not been in the hall.

I caught their nervous excitement. I knew I had to act promptly. I could not see how he could harm me now, because I had so much evidence against him, but I did not doubt that he was diabolically clever.

"Go at once," pleaded his wife. "Do not wait for anything. He may return here at any moment. If he found you . . . if he knew what we had told you . . ."

"Yes," I agreed. "I will go at once. How can I thank you for telling me this? I know what it must have meant to you."

"Don't waste time in thanking us. Please go, and he *must* not see you leave this house."

So I went, and when I came through the fir trees to the gate I was trying to make up my mind what I should do.

I was not going to Glen House. I was going to Kelly Grange. But first I would return to the Revels because I was determined that I would take the monk's robe with me. I was not going to allow anyone in future to believe that I had suffered from hallucinations.

As I walked back to the Revels, I was in a state of great excitement. I was certain that the account I had heard was a true one. How could I doubt that sick woman? Her fear had been genuine. Besides, now that I knew who my enemy was it was easy to understand how he had been in a position to act as he did. I thought back to the very beginning . . . the occasion when Friday had warned us of an intruder and had insisted on being taken out to the corridor; the next day when he had been missing and I had gone to look for him and lost my way and been brought home by Simon, Deverel Smith had been present on our return. He could have heard Gabriel say that he was going to order some milk for me. He might have seen the maid bringing it up, and have explained to her that I was upset about the loss of my dog and he would slip a sedative into my milk. Such a possibility had not entered my mind; on that tragic morning none of us thought of anything but Gabriel's death. But this could have been the reason why I slept so quickly and so deeply.

Then how easy it was for him to slip in and out of the house; to pull the curtains about my bed, to remove the warming pan, and to put my cloak over the balcony.

He could come by the secret entry and if he were seen, on the stairs, in the hall, he would always have a plausible answer. He had been worried about Sir Matthew . . . Sarah . . . and latterly myself, and had dropped in to assure himself that all was well.

And Simon? I had to face the truth. I believed that Damaris regarded her father's determination to marry her to Luke with repulsion; and what I had originally thought was an affection between her and Luke was merely Damaris's desire to please a father whom she feared, and Luke's natural interest in an attractive girl—and with one as beautiful as Damaris that interest would naturally be intensified. But with Simon . . . it would be different; and I did not believe that any woman could be completely indifferent to the virile charm of Simon Redvers. Even I—down-to-earth and sensible person that I believed myself to be—could not.

I must not think of Simon. But Hagar was my friend. I could rely on her. So I was going to the Revels; I was going to take the monk's robe from my wardrobe and go with it to Kelly Grange. I would tell

Mary-Jane to pack some of my things, and she could bring them over in the carriage later. I should walk because I was not going to let anyone but Mary-Jane know that I was leaving.

Those were my plans as I entered the Revels.

I rang my bell, and Mary-Jane came to my room.

"Mary-Jane," I said, "I am going at once to Kelly Grange. Pack some things that I shall need. I will send for you and them. But I propose to go on immediately."

"Yes, madam," said Mary-Jane, her eyes wide with surprise.

"Something has happened," I told her. "I cannot stop to explain now. But I am going to leave this house at once."

As I spoke I heard the sound of carriage wheels, and I went to the window.

I saw Dr. Smith alight and, because I no longer saw him as the benevolent doctor, I felt myself tremble.

"I should be gone," I said. "I must leave at once."

I hurried out of the room, leaving a bewildered Mary-Jane staring after me; I went along the corridor, down the first flight of stairs; then I heard the doctor's voice; he was talking to Ruth.

"Is she at home?"

"Yes, I saw her come in only a few minutes ago."

"That is fortunate. I will go and get her now."

"What if she . . . ?"

"She will know nothing until I have her safely there."

My heart began to hammer uncertainly. He was already striding across the hall. I slipped into the minstrels' gallery quickly, thinking that I might hide myself there while he went to my room. Then I should run out of the house and to Kelly Grange.

Ruth had remained in the hall and I wondered how I should get past her. Would she tell the doctor that I had run out of the house? If so, how long would it take him to catch up with me?

I quietly shut the door of the gallery and I immediately thought of the cupboard. If I could escape by way of the secret tunnel they would not catch me.

But even as I, my body bent so that I should not be seen from the balcony, went towards the cupboard, the door of the gallery opened and he was standing there.

"Oh . . . hello, Catherine." He was smiling the benign smile which had deluded me in the past.

I could say nothing for the moment; my voice had lost itself in my constricted throat.

"I came to call on you, and I saw you come in here as I started up the stairs."

"Good morning," I said and I felt that my voice sounded calmer than I had thought possible.

He stepped into the gallery and shut the door. When I glanced over the balcony I could see Ruth standing below.

"It's a fine morning," he went on. "I wanted you to come for a little drive with me."

"Thank you. I was just going out for a walk."

"But you have just come in."

"Nevertheless I am just going out again."

He lifted a finger and there was something so sinister in that playful gesture that I felt a shudder run down my spine.

"You are doing too much walking, and you know I don't allow that."

"I am perfectly healthy," I answered. "Jessie Dankwait is pleased with me."

"The country midwife!" he said contemptuously. "A drive will do you good."

"Thank you, but I do not wish to go."

He came towards me and took my wrist; he held it tenderly yet firmly.

"I am going to insist today, because you are looking a little pale."

"No, Dr. Smith," I said. "I do not wish to go for a drive."

"But, my dear Catherine" (his face was close to mine and his gentle, suave manner seemed more horrible than violence), "you are coming with me."

I tried to walk past him, but he caught and held me firmly. He took the robe from me and threw it on the floor.

"Give that to me and let me go at once," I said.

"My dear, you must allow me to know what is good for you."

I was filled with sudden panic. I called: "Ruth! Ruth! Help me."

I saw her start up the stairs, and I thanked God that she was at hand.

She opened the door of the minstrels' gallery; he was still holding me in a grip so firm that I could not extricate myself.

"I am afraid," he said to her, "that she is going to give us a little trouble."

"Catherine," said Ruth, "you must obey the doctor. He knows what's best for you."

"He knows what is best! Look at this robe. He is the one who has been playing those tricks on me."

"I fear," said the doctor, "that it is more advanced than I believed. I am afraid we are going to have trouble. It is a mistake to delay too long in these matters. It has happened before in my experience."

"What diabolical plan have you in mind now?" I demanded.

"It is the persecution mania," murmured the doctor to Ruth. "Believing that they are alone against the whole world." He turned to me. "Catherine, my very dear Catherine, you must trust me. Have I not always been your friend?"

I burst out laughing and it was laughter which alarmed me. I was truly frightened now, because I began to see what he planned to do with me, and that Ruth either believed him or pretended to, and I was alone with them . . . and friendless. I knew the truth, but I had been a fool. I had told no one of my discovery. I could still do that. . . . But whom could I tell . . . these two whose plan was to destroy me? For Ruth, if not his accomplice, was no friend to me.

"Look," I said, "I know too much. It was you, Dr. Smith, who decided that my child should never be born. You killed Gabriel and you were determined to kill anyone who stood between Luke's inheriting the Revels. . . ."

"You see," he said sadly, "how far advanced it is."

"I found the robe, and I know too that you believe you belong here. I know it all. Do not think that you can deceive me any more."

He had seized me firmly in his arms. I smelt a whiff of what might have been chloroform as something was pressed over my mouth. I felt as though everything was slipping away from me and I heard his voice, very faint as though it were a long way off.

"I hoped to avoid this. It is the only way when they are obstreperous. . . ."

Then I slipped away . . . into darkness.

I have heard it said that the mind is more powerful than the body. I believe that to be so. My mind commanded my body to reject the chloroform even as it was pressed over my mouth. This was not possible of course; that would have been asking too much, but as it began to affect my body my brain continued to struggle against it. I must not sink into unconsciousness. I knew that if I did I should wake up a prisoner, and that all the evidence which I had acquired would be destroyed and my protests called the aberrations of the mentally sick.

So even as my body succumbed, my mind fought on.

So it was that I was half conscious of being in that jolting carriage with the evil doctor beside me. And I summoned all my will power to fight the terrible drowsiness which was lulling me into a sense of utter forgetfulness.

I realized he was taking me to Worstwhistle.

We were alone in his brougham and the driver could not hear what was said. The swaying of the vehicle was helpful; the clop-clop of the horse's hoofs seemed to be saying: "Doom is at hand. Fight it. Fight it with all your might. There is still time. But once you enter that grim gray building . . . it will not be so easy to come out."

I would not enter. I would never let anyone be able to tell my child that once its mother had been an inmate of Worstwhistle.

"You should not struggle, Catherine," said the doctor gently.

I tried to speak but the effect of the drug was claiming me.

"Close your eyes," he murmured. "Do you doubt that I will look after you? There is nothing for you to fear. I shall come and see you every day. I shall be there when your child is born. . . ."

My mind said: "You are a devil. . . ." But the words did not come.

I was frightened because of this terrible drowsiness which was seeping over me, and which would not let me fight for my future and that of my child.

Subconsciously I knew that this had been his plan all along, to get me to Worstwhistle before my child was born, to attend to me there and to make sure, if my child was a boy, that he did not live.

If I gave birth to a daughter or a stillborn child, then I should be of no more interest to him, because I should no longer menace Luke's accession to the Revels and the marriage with Damaris.

But, fight as I would, I could only remain in this half-conscious state. And I reserved my strength for the moment when the carriage wheels should stop and he would call strong men to help him bring another reluctant victim to that grim prison.

The carriage had drawn up.

We had arrived. I felt sick and dizzy, and only half conscious.

"Why, my dear Catherine," he said, and he put his arm about me; and once more I felt his gentle touch to be more hurtful than a blow. "You are unwell. Never mind. This is the end of the journey. Now you shall know peace. No more fancies . . . no more visions. Here you shall be cared for."

"Listen . . ." I began, and I seemed to drawl the words. "I . . . am not going in there."

He was smiling. "Leave this to me, my dear," he whispered.

There was the sound of running footsteps and a man took his stand on one side of me; I felt him take my arm.

I heard their voices.

"She knows where she's going, this one . . ."

Then the doctor's voice: "They have their lucid moments. Sometimes it's a pity."

I tried to scream but I could not; my legs were buckling under me. I was being dragged forward.

I saw the great iron door swing open. I saw the porch with the name over it—the name which must have struck terror into a thousand hearts and minds.

"No . . ." I sobbed.

But they were so many; and I was so weak against them.

I heard the sudden clatter of a horse's hoofs. Then the doctor said sharply: "Quickly! Get the patient inside."

And there was a note of fear in his voice to replace that gentle assurance which had been there before.

Then my whole being seemed to come alive again, and I realized that what seemed to make the blood run hot in my veins was hope.

A voice I knew well, a voice I loved was shouting: "What the devil's all this!"

And there he was—the man whom I had failed to dismiss from my thoughts although I had tried—striding towards me; and I knew that he came like a knight of old, and that he had come to save me from my enemies.

"Simon," I sobbed; and as I fell forward I felt his arms about me.

I ceased to fight the lassitude then; I accepted the darkness.

I was no longer alone. Simon had come to stand beside me and fight my battle for me.

8

So I did not enter Worstwhistle on that terrible day. Simon was there to prevent that. Mary-Jane had left the house with all speed while I was struggling in the minstrels' gallery, and had gone to Kelly Grange to tell what was happening, for she had overheard what the doctor had said about taking me away, and she knew enough to guess where.

Simon had gone straight there and, although I was not able to see how he fought for my freedom, I knew it had happened.

He had faced Deverel Smith and had accused him on the spot of the murder of Gabriel. He had threatened the superintendent with the loss of his post if he dared take me in merely on Dr. Smith's word. I could imagine the power of him as he fought that battle for my freedom and the life of my child.

Of course he won. Simon must always win. He was invincible when he determined on what he would have. I have grown to learn that, and I would not have it otherwise.

I often wonder what Deverel Smith had thought as he stood there knowing that his elaborate scheme had been foiled at the very last moment. Because, if once he had had me accepted in Worstwhistle as a patient whom he certified as of unsound mind, it would not have been easy to prove that I had not suffered from insanity, even if only temporarily.

But Simon had come.

He took me to Kelly Grange where Hagar was waiting for me, and I stayed there until my child was born. That happened prematurely, which was not to be wondered at, but my Gabriel soon picked up and became a strong little boy. We doted on him—Hagar and I; and I think Simon did too, but he had determined to make a man of the boy and he rarely showed the softer side of his feelings. I did not mind, because I wanted Gabriel to be the kind of boy who would appreciate being treated as a man rather than a baby. I wanted my son to be strong.

But there were other happenings before the birth of Gabriel.

I often think of Deverel Smith, of his belief in himself, and I am sure he saw himself as godlike, powerful beyond other men, of stronger intellect, of greater cunning. He had not believed that he could be defeated. He bore a grudge against life which he had determined to satisfy. He believed that he was the son of Sir Matthew and that no one should stand between him and his inheritance. If Gabriel was the legitimate son, he would reason, he was himself the elder son; and so he eliminated Gabriel.

We never learned exactly how that happened; and whether Gabriel was lured onto the balcony or went there of his own accord and was surprised there will remain a mystery; but he killed Gabriel to make the way open for Luke, and when Luke had married Damaris he would have come to live at the Revels. In his subtle, sinister way, he would have been master of the Revels because he would have made himself aware of some weakness in the people who lived about him and used a subtle blackmail in order to dominate them.

That was his delight—to dominate. Ruth told me, much later, that he had discovered an indiscretion of hers. She had indulged in a love affair after the death of her husband which could have created a distressing scandal if it had become common knowledge. It was not that he had said: "If you do not support me I shall tell of this matter which you are so anxious to keep secret." But he had intimated that he was aware of it and in exchange for his silence he expected her support and an outward show of friendship. Subtly he had forced her to his side, and she had always made a show of welcoming him to the Revels and extolling his virtues whenever she had an opportunity.

Perhaps Deverel Smith had also held some sway over Sir Matthew. In any case he had no doubts about the support of both Sir Matthew and Ruth for a marriage between Luke and Damaris.

I have often wondered what would have happened in that household but for Simon. I should have been out of the way—I do not care to think even now of what my future would have been. But there at the Revels, I imagined him the master . . . holding his gentle but evil sway over them all.

But it was not to be so; and how could he endure to see all that he had schemed for lost . . . because of one strong man?

How he must have hated Simon; but Simon could return hate with hate. *He* would have no mercy and Deverel Smith knew it. When he stood facing Simon at the portals of Worstwhistle he must have realized that at last he faced an adversary stronger than himself.

So he died—as he had lived—dramatically. When Simon demanded a carriage to take me back to Kelly Grange—for he had galloped to Worstwhistle on one of his fastest horses—and when it was brought for him and he had lifted me in and prepared to leave for Kelly Grange, Deverel Smith had already gone back to the Revels.

He went to the house and right to the top of the east wing, to that balcony which was the only one in the house from which a Rockwell had not fallen to his death. He threw himself over in a last defiant gesture, as though by so doing he proved to the world what he had always sought to prove to himself: he was of that family, and Kirkland Revels meant to him all that it ever could to any member of the family who had been born there and lived his life within its walls.

There is little else to say. Mrs. Smith—whose health improved after her husband's death—went away with Damaris. I heard later that Damaris made a brilliant marriage in London. Luke went up to Oxford and there collected several bad debts and became involved in some trouble with a young woman. That was all part of growing up, said Sir Matthew, who had done it all before him. Ruth had changed too. Her manner to me grew warmer and, though we should never be great friends, she was contrite because of her readiness to play the doctor's game, even though she was ignorant of his wickedest motives. Sarah remained—as she always had been—my good friend. Gleefully she told me she had completed the picture. I was there, with Gabriel and Friday, but I was in my own room at Kirkland Revels, not in a cell. She had wanted to warn me because she had known I was in imminent danger, but she had not realized that the monk and the doctor were one and the same, and this had baffled her. How happy she was now that the danger was past; she was as eager for the birth of my child as I was.

It was a wonderful day when Gabriel was born and it was known that he would live and that I should recover from my ordeal, which was a little more severe than it would have been but for the upsets of the preceding months. I remember lying with my child in my arms, experiencing that wonderful feeling of lassitude which I suppose is one of the most enviable feelings a woman can have. People had been coming to see me; and then, suddenly, there was Simon.

He had already told me that he had begun to suspect the doctor; and it was he who, after Deverel Smith's death, discovered the way into the secret chamber from the Abbey side. Mary-Jane and I had come near to finding it on that Christmas morning. Had we removed the stones which, in her exasperation, Mary-Jane had kicked, we should have disclosed the flight of steps leading down to the chamber in which she found the robe. We eventually learned that the passage connecting the house with the Abbey vaults had been constructed when the house was built. Considering the emergencies which could so easily arise, the proximity to the house of such an excellent hiding place would have seemed too important to be overlooked.

It was some years later, when exploring the tunnels, I discovered a secret recess hidden by a pile of stones and, removing these, came on Friday's grave. I guessed then that Deverel Smith had poisoned him and buried him in this spot. There was nothing left but his bones.

Simon had come to the conclusion that the doctor's motive was to prevent my bearing a living child, so that Luke should inherit, and marry Damaris.

"For that reason," he had explained, "I paid attention to her. I knew she was not as interested in young Luke as she pretended to be, and I wanted to see the effect on her father if someone else began paying court to her."

"It sounds as good a reason as the other," I told him.

"What other?" he wanted to know.

"That she happens to be one of the most attractive women either of us can ever have seen."

He grinned at that and seemed pleased; and now that I know him well I understand that it was my jealousy that pleased him far more than Damaris's charms.

And when he stood looking at my son I saw the regret in his face, and I said: "What is it, Simon?"

Then he looked straight at me and said: "He's a grand chap, but there's one thing wrong with him."

"What's that, Simon?"

"He ought to be mine," said Simon.

That was a proposal of marriage, and it was for this reason that as I lay there with the child I experienced the happiest moment of my life which I had known up to that time.

All that spring and summer we made our plans. Because my son Gabriel would one day be master of Kirkland Revels he should be brought up between the Revels and Kelly Grange, and this would mean that to some extent the two estates would be as one.

Uncle Dick came home and it was wonderful to accept the close relationship between us. He gave me away when, the following Christmas, I married Simon. And as we came down the aisle together I thought: And that is the end of the beginning.

Then I wondered what the future would hold for us and if in the years ahead we should weather the storms which must surely beset two such personalities as ours. Life perhaps would not always be calm between us. We were both headstrong, and neither of us meek.

But as we came out into the Christmas sunshine, my spirits were lifted. I knew there was nothing to fear, for there was love between us, and it is love which casts out fear.